Chris Brookmyre was a journalist before becoming a full-time novelist with the publication of his award-winning debut *Quite Ugly One Morning*, which established him as one of Britain's leading crime writers. His 2016 novel *Black Widow* won both the McIlvanney Prize and the Theakston Old Peculier Crime Novel of the Year award. Brookmyre's novels have sold more than two million copies in the UK alone.

CHRIS BROOKMYRE

THE CUT

ABACUS

First published in Great Britain in 2021 by Little, Brown
This paperback edition published by Abacus in 2022

1 3 5 7 9 10 8 6 4 2

A CIP catalogue record for this book
is available from the British Library.

ISBN 978-0-3491-4384-2

Typeset in Caslon by Palimpsest Book Production Limited, Falkirk, Stirlingshire
Printed and bound in Great Britain by Clays Ltd, Elcograf S.p.A.

Papers used by Abacus are from well-managed forests
and other responsible sources.

MIX
Paper from
responsible sources
FSC® C104740

Abacus
An imprint of
Little, Brown Book Group
Carmelite House
50 Victoria Embankment
London EC4Y 0DZ

An Hachette UK Company
www.hachette.co.uk

www.littlebrown.co.uk

For Gabriel Robertson

The tragedy of old age is not that one is old, but that one is young.

Oscar Wilde

Prologue

Jerry crouched alongside Millicent's bed and checked again for a pulse. There was nothing. He tried the neck, tried the wrist, tried the neck again. There was no doubt, much as he wished to deny it. He recognised that unseeing, glassy-eyed stare, and he knew what it meant. There was no point in even trying CPR. This was a done deal, and this time it had been no heart attack, no incidental consequence of a passive act. This was murder.

Once again, he had witnessed how quickly the world as he understood it could change. It had been less than a minute since he opened the front door.

He had crept in quietly, keen not to disturb Millicent and listening out for any hint that she might still be awake. He had left the lights off, aware that even the glow around the doorframe might be enough if she wasn't quite asleep yet. He could smell the toast that she must have had for supper.

He was walking in his stocking soles to stay silent, which was why he so clearly heard the thump. He had flipped the nearest switch and pulled open the door to Millicent's bedroom, light from the hall spilling in to illuminate a scene that knocked the breath from him.

PART ONE

PART ONE

Pebbles

Millicent Spark's life ended on the twenty-third of January, 1994.

That was the way she saw it, anyway. She didn't physically die that day, but everything thereafter was merely a prelude to interment, a succession of holding areas before final admission to the grave.

The world she once inhabited had been thousands of miles across, spanning a multiplicity of cities, time zones and cultures, all of it promising wider realms beyond which she hoped to reach one day. Then it had all been reduced to a succession of tiny boxes and confined spaces, all in preparation for that tiniest box in that most confined space of all.

The rain was a swirling smir as she walked down Great Western Road; walking along it, but somehow not upon it. As always, it was like she was traversing a memory or an echo of a place, even ones she had never visited. This version of it did not feel real; or maybe the harsher truth was that it was real, but she was not.

Undeniably, the rain was real, and worsening. This would have consequences for her mission. Vivian had set her a task: she had asked Millicent to go and purchase something for her from John Lewis, in town. She had also instructed her to buy herself a cup of coffee and a cake. This latter Millicent had immediately filed under 'optional', as in, 'not happening', on the grounds that Viv would never know. But that was before Viv had given her something called a loyalty card, which had to be stamped as evidence that she had achieved her goal.

Millicent knew what she was about. Asking her to fetch a pebble from the seabed merely to get her into the water.

'You just need to take it in small steps,' Vivian kept saying. Viv saw a world that she assumed Millicent would be eager to explore and make the most of, if she could only get over her reluctance. All Millicent saw was a world in which she did not belong. The one in which she did belong had ended decades ago. This one held nothing but fear and danger, a place she did not recognise or know how to navigate.

She did not feel she could even affect it, interact with it. At best she could drift through this realm like a wraith. A ghost. She remembered that movie from a better time: Patrick Swayze unable to open a door, reluctant to accept the alternative of passing through it. Millicent could relate. She had problems with doors these days too.

There was another prescribed element to this morning's exercise, which was that she had to use automated transport, specifically the Underground. She was not allowed to walk. Millicent liked to walk. It was simplest. It was one way in which she could comfortably experience the freedom of the wider world around her. She could do so without being noticed by anyone, without having to negotiate any new technology. Without making herself conspicuous.

Viv said she wanted Millicent to bring back her tickets as proof. More pebbles.

Tickets could be plausibly lost. So could loyalty cards. Then it was a matter of whether Viv wanted to call her a liar to her face.

That would just leave the purchase. She could manage that much. She would walk the whole way, she had thought: down Great Western Road, across to Woodlands Road and then along Sauchiehall Street to the Buchanan Galleries. But she had reckoned without the Glasgow weather. As she crossed Otago Street, it changed from a swirling smir to a torrential downpour, and she knew that if she tried to walk all the way to town in this, she would be as drenched as had she jumped into the river. She dashed for shelter instinctively, and despite her unease, she propelled herself towards Kelvinbridge Underground station.

She had actually missed the rain. That was one of the weirdest things about her time away. For more than two decades she had seldom felt more than a few drops of it. She had seldom felt much

6

sunshine either. Weather had become something that happened on the other side of walls and windows, in that fading world she was no longer connected to.

She hurried beneath the canopy that descended from Great Western Road to the station below, the rain hammering upon the brown Perspex in angry squalls. As she stepped onto the escalator, the sensation of movement and the feel of the rubber handrail exhumed an anxiety that went all the way back to childhood.

Auntie Phyllis had taken her into town as a treat. They were going shopping and then for something called high tea. Millicent recalled her excitement at the scale and grandeur of the department store, a wonder of colours, textures and lovely smells. It was the first time she had ever seen a moving staircase. She had been transfixed, leaning over to watch the strange illusion of the metal stairs seemingly collapsing and compressing themselves into nothing as they disappeared into the grate at the bottom.

'Millie, for goodness' sake. Stand away from there. What if your hair gets caught in the mechanism and you get dragged down?'

The machine had been instantly transformed before her eyes from a mechanical wonder to a diabolical threat, but she had not merely envisaged an agonising incident of her hair being yanked from her scalp. Rather, she saw her entire body being ground head-first between the metal teeth, like she was being pulled through the big mincer at the Cooperative butcher counter. A fear of escalators had stayed with her through childhood.

She watched the maw of the ticketing hall nearing and widening below. The sight brought on a precipitous panic at being conveyed inexorably downwards, as though into hell. She turned and attempted to ascend, but couldn't climb fast enough to reverse her progress, merely staying at roughly the same point, like treading water.

She saw two young boys gliding down towards her, wondering briefly why they weren't in uniform. Then she remembered that her estimation of young people's ages was still undergoing a recalibration. Anybody under thirty looked to her like they ought to be in school. They could be twenty, she realised. Teenagers, at least.

'Sake,' one of them said with a laugh. He was wearing a blue baseball cap from which rainwater was dripping. 'Whit ye daein' ya maddy?'

'Let me past,' she urged, a burn in her thighs as she tried to up the pace of her climb.

'You'll knacker yoursel',' said the other. He had a rash of rather angry red acne, one particularly pressured red lump looking almost pulsatile in its lividity.

'If you're wanting back up, you should just let it take you down and then swap over to the other stair.'

She stopped trying to climb, gripping the rail as the escalator continued to take her down backwards. What he had said made sense.

She turned around gingerly but swiftly, concerned to be facing the right way at the crucial point when she would have to step off. It was a remnant of her childhood phobia that she considered the moment of alighting still fraught with peril. She exited with a skip that must have looked considerably jauntier than it felt, its purpose being to give her feet maximum clearance from the metal teeth.

The two boys had stopped to observe the end of her descent. She could read a mixture of concern and amusement in their faces. She wondered which had caused them to wait.

'Are you all right, but?' the one in the cap asked. 'Have you had a funny turn?'

'Do you want us to call somebody?' asked his spotty pal.

It was perhaps the thought of Viv being asked to ride out to the rescue that prompted a reflex response.

'Don't bloody patronise me.'

'Hey, there's no need to be rude. Just trying to help.'

'No, you're quite right, and I should reciprocate by helping you, perhaps by recommending something to cover up your acne. The first thing that leaps to mind is a bucket.'

The words were out before Millicent was aware of speaking them, hearing them like they were being said by someone else. That was how it always felt when she inhabited this persona and donned its mask.

There was a bulging look of shock in his eyes, but instead of anger or hurt, it gave way to an eruption of laughter. His companion looked tickled too, though only after a moment's hesitation to see how his mate was taking it. In their laughter there was no anger, no malice, but no absolution either.

She heard their voices echo as they walked away into the ticket hall.

'Aw man, she pure ripped you. A bucket, man.'

'Never mind cream for ma plooks. It's something for this burn I need.'

'Mad auld bat.'

With those words, she saw herself through their youthful eyes, and it was worse than any insult they might have thrown back. She was a crazy old lady, bamboozled by a moving staircase and lashing out at those trying to help her.

Belonging

To be fair, Jerry was surprised that it had taken quite this long for one of the braying posh boys to accuse the weirdo from Dreghorn of being a thief.

From the moment he first rocked up at the halls of residence, he had felt like he didn't belong, and little that had happened since had disabused him of this notion. It would have been reassuring to learn that everybody felt the same way, being new to uni, new to living away, new to the city, but he felt like he was an absolute beginner surrounded by veterans. Which would have made some sense had they all been second- or third-year students, but so many of his fellow freshers seemed so much more comfortable in their new environment. It was like they had all been on an induction course. Maybe it was a final-year option at posh schools.

He had come back from his morning lecture and was walking through the common area when he detected an energy change in the room. He didn't need to believe in a sixth sense or any of that pish to know that his presence was the thing that changed it. He immediately felt scrutinised. Had to be that prick Danby. Who the hell had that for a first name? Him and his mates acted like they owned the place, probably because they knew that given enough time, they probably would. Or Daddy would, at least, but when he signed it over to them, they'd tell themselves they had earned it. Born three-nothing up and convinced they'd scored a hat trick.

Danby had been talking to the warden when Jerry walked in. He suspected that wasn't good.

'There he is,' he heard Danby say, before calling out: 'Hey, you, Rob Zombie, I want a word.'

Jerry had spent years growing his hair into dreads like Chris Barnes, Rob Flynn or indeed Rob Zombie, but he doubted Danby would have recognised any of them. The guy had called him that purely because of what it said on the T-shirt he was wearing.

Jerry just kept walking to his room, where he slung his backpack and his battle jacket on the bed and closed the door. Less than ten seconds later, there was an insistent hammering on it. Even the cadence screamed entitlement.

Part of him wanted to let the fucker stand there, just lock the door and stick on his headphones, but he knew he would only be postponing a problem.

Jerry opened his door, and there, of course, was Danby, with his two wingmen hovering behind, and that lassie Philippa, who was always staring at him like he was a sideshow freak.

More significantly, he was also in the company of the warden, pulling up the rear. She had an uncomfortable expression. She didn't want to be there but knew she had to.

'What do you want?' Jerry asked.

'I think you know.'

This skinny hipster fud wanted his avocado smashed.

'Mate, given that you rarely condescend to speak to me, I'm at a loss here. Help me out.'

'My phone's gone missing. Toby says he saw you with one that looks remarkably similar to mine.'

Yeah, there it was. Boy was calling him a thief, right to his coupon. Jerry looked to the warden to confirm she was taking in the significance of what just happened. She wore a neutral expression, like she was just here as an observer, but the lack of a greater response spoke volumes, far as he was concerned.

'In the interests of social harmony between the classes, I'll limit my response to saying I think Toby should get his eyes tested. Cannae see you slumming it with my three-year-old generic Synergis handset.'

'I didn't see you with an old Synergis,' said Toby. 'I saw you yesterday with a new Galaxy Nine.'

At this point the warden decided to arbitrate.

'Look, let's not turn this into something it doesn't have to be,' she said, looking appealingly toward Jerry. 'Maybe it was a prank, maybe it was a misunderstanding, whatever. But if you have Dan's phone, just hand it back and we can leave it at that. Is that fair?'

She looked to Danby for his assent, which he gave with a grudging nod. He would be wanting to take this as far as he could, and Jerry guessed getting his missing phone back would be less of a result than getting the rough-spoken metalhead oik emptied from the halls.

'So just to be clear, your phone goes missing, and your first thought is to come banging on my door accusing me of stealing it? I'm trying to work out which prejudice drove you harder, that I sound like I'm from the wrong socio-economic background, or as we call it, Ayrshire, or whether you noticed I'm a bit brown and that put me at the head of the queue as a likely suspect.'

Danby's face flushed with outrage, just like Jerry knew it would.

'Don't you dare try and insinuate this is about race.'

'Not nice being accused of something horrible, is it, mate?'

Danby turned to the warden.

'Philippa saw him the other day coming out of that dodgy electronics place on Dumbarton Road, Fonezone. Everybody knows it's full of hooky gear. The owner pays cash and asks no questions.'

'I'm confused. Toby saw me with your phone yesterday, but Philippa saw me selling it in Fonezone. Is it Shröedinger's handset?'

'I saw the guy behind the counter give you money,' Philippa mumbled uncomfortably, looking at her shoes.

'That's not how the transaction normally goes in a shop,' Danby added with a note of triumph.

Jerry could tell from the warden's expression that this had landed. He did remember seeing Philippa on Dumbarton Road. It was too late to deny that he had been in the shop, or even that she had seen what she thought.

He felt a flush of shame and hated them all for witnessing it.

'I was selling my ancient iPod because I was skint. Not everybody's daddy sets them up a trust fund,' he added.

Philippa tutted. Danby spluttered scornfully.

Maybe she didn't have a trust fund, and maybe Danby didn't either, but Jerry was damn sure that whatever their fathers gave them, it was more than his. The only thing Daddy had given Jerry Kelly was pigmentation.

Yer maw shagged a sailor.

That's what they used to say in school. He had heard it a hundred times before he was old enough to even understand why and how it was intended to be hurtful. Half the kids saying it probably didn't understand at that age either. Some of them probably didn't even know they were being racist.

By the time he was old enough to grasp what it meant, he was also mature enough to grasp that it represented an entirely unfair and inaccurate depiction of the depths of his parents' relationship. As far as he was aware, they hadn't actually conversed long enough for her to ascertain what he did for a living.

He never knew who his father was, and he barely knew his mother either. She had dumped him with his granny and run off several times before he was two years old. Whenever she came back, she always swore to her mother it would never happen again. Eventually she made good on her vow inasmuch as she only ran away once more. She took an overdose in a squat in Manchester.

His granny was helping him out with the rent for the halls. That was how he liked to think of it. He was supplementing that with what he got doing late shifts at a fast-food place. When he applied to uni, Jerry had looked into his options and worked out it would be cheaper to get a season ticket for the train. His gran had insisted it was important that he got away.

'Find your place somewhere better than this, son,' she had said.

It had sounded good when she said it. But now anyone could see his place wasn't here. And one of those people was him.

Doors had opened all along the corridor, people leaning out of their rooms in response to the raised voices. Danby glanced backwards, taking in the scene. It was no longer merely a stand-off, but one with an audience.

'If you've nothing to hide, why not open your door and let us take a look. Because I'd put down a hundred to one that my Galaxy's in there.'

Danby had a glint in his eye as he said this, sweeping his hand

13

around to indicate everybody who was now looking: a wee flourish to indicate that he thought this was a masterstroke.

Folk like Danby weren't plagued by questions about their place in this world. Wherever they went, they knew they had a right to be there. From the moment Jerry turned up, they were just waiting for him to become a problem. Or were hoping he'd become a problem so that they would have a pretext for getting rid of him.

The warden took a step forward, putting herself between Danby and Jerry's door.

'Just to be clear,' she told Jerry, covering herself first and foremost. 'You do not need to submit to any search, and he has no right to demand one.'

Then she addressed Danby.

'Are you going to ask everybody else to open their doors, and are they to remain under suspicion if they don't?'

Danby folded his arms, saying nothing, but the unspoken answers were, in order:

No.

But Jerry will.

Meaning this was still a win for Danby, and he knew that.

Jerry had heard it said there were two types of rich people: smart people who knew they'd got lucky, and lucky people who thought they were smart. The Achilles heel of entitled British posh boys was that their assumed superiority meant they always overestimated their own intelligence and underestimated that of their opponents.

'No, it's fine,' Jerry told the warden. He stepped aside and beckoned Danby forth.

'On you go, if that's what you really want. But bear in mind that there's no going back from it.'

Danby looked wary, wondering what he was missing. It was Jerry's turn to draw attention to their audience.

'If you do search my room, everybody here will find out unequivocally that I'm a thief . . . or you're a cunt.'

Jerry let it hang.

The boy wouldn't have made a card player. There was a quivering twitch to his bottom lip as he realised his mistake and the consequences of it. He'd claimed he'd lay a hundred to one, but Jerry was the guy who had named the stakes.

'The warden's right. I don't have the right to search your room. But believe me, I'll be keeping an eye out for that phone, and if I see you with anything like it, I'll be going to the police.'

'You do that, mate. And don't forget to check Fonezone an' all.'

Jerry waited for them to walk away before he shut the door, just to drive the point home. He watched them all depart, then closed it softly.

He let out a long sigh. He had derived some satisfaction from the sight of Danby and his retinue walking away, defeated, but it felt like a Pyrrhic victory. He had come out of it on top, but it hadn't been a pleasant experience for anybody.

To his surprise, he actually felt bad for Danby. Probably because he *had* stolen his phone.

Sliding Doors

As Millicent shuffled towards the ticket machines, she saw a man hastening from the escalators, rainwater cascading off a recently folded umbrella. She hung back, letting him pass. She anticipated that she would need some time at this and didn't want anyone asking her if she wanted help. As she waited, she took out a piece of paper bearing Vivian's instructions.

'Why don't you just come along with me?' Millicent had asked as Vivian wrote it all down. 'It's you that's wanting this stuff.'

'Of course I could get it myself, but the whole point is for you to venture out there on your own. It's going to be arduous the first time, we both know that. It will be arduous the second time too, but it will get easier the more you do it, and your future self will thank you for not shying away just because it's hard.'

Like Millicent didn't know what it was to endure hardship.

Vivian was a seventy-five-year-old woman who lived in a realm of boundless opportunities, indefatigable in her optimism, seemingly waking every morning with a smile on her face and a fresh and exciting plan for her day. She radiated enthusiasm and imbued any room she walked into with a sense of well-being that made you want to smash her face in with an axe. Millicent pictured her slumped on the settee, the blade embedded from forehead to cheekbone, bisecting one eye. She saw vividly how she would achieve it, every intricate step. She could almost feel the syringe, imagine the blood spurt. The memories never left, no matter how she tried to banish them.

It was an unworthy thought. Vivian was so patient, so generous, so kind. She really didn't deserve having Millicent in her life, an unwarranted burden. It was another reason things would be better if she wasn't around much longer.

She stepped forward and examined the screen. To her relief, she could instantly see what Viv told her to look for: Concession single. Why concession? she wondered. What was being conceded? Then she remembered. She qualified: OAP, albeit without the P part. She had missed a bit on the superannuation.

The Underground was a circle; two circles in fact, inner and outer. Perhaps she could just go round and round for a while, then come back and tell Vivian the shop never had the thing she wanted. But she knew what Vivian was like. If she came back without reporting success, she would only make her do it again tomorrow.

Millicent knew what it was to be facing something inescapable. Submitting to someone else's will was all but second nature, a place of comfort and security. It was her own will that presented all the problems.

She took her ticket and followed the sign for the platforms, her progress stopped by the barriers. She couldn't see a guard, so she remained in place, waiting with a patience ingrained over decades.

She heard a door open and saw a man in a yellow over-vest emerge from the ticket office, heading in her direction.

'Problem with the ticket?' he asked.

Millicent was unsure how to reply, then it dawned on her that the answer was no. There was no problem with the ticket, or with the machine. The problem was with her. It had been a year now, but she still caught herself waiting outside doors, until it belatedly struck her that she did not need permission to open them.

That was what Vivian didn't understand; what nobody seemed to understand. Just because the doors to the world had been unlocked, that didn't mean Millicent was capable of walking through them. When you have not known it for so long, freedom could be a terrifying thing.

She stopped at the head of the staircase and took some slow breaths before descending. Reassured by the quiet, she walked down to find the Outer Circle platform deserted but for a man and a toddler, the man holding his daughter's hand while he thumbed inevitably at his phone. Everybody seemed to be transfixed by these tiny portals into places they would rather be, heedless of what was before them in the here and now. She knew what that felt like, but she also knew why this world wasn't enough.

She thought of how long she had ached to be out here in the very place this man and so many like him were shunning. That was until she got here and found that it wasn't the place she remembered. The world she had left behind was long since gone, and couldn't be contacted again with any device.

She heard a rumble from along the tunnel.

'Come on, Toots.'

Gripping her father's hand, the little girl approached the train with mild trepidation, perhaps afraid that when the doors slid open, they might close again on her.

Millicent coaxed herself to step through them without anyone else's prompting. Before she could do so, the calm of the platform became a riotous cacophony, an overwhelming mass of noise and colour and movement as the train disgorged dozens of passengers: schoolkids in bright uniforms, screeching and shouting over each other as they bustled forth.

Millicent clutched herself, paralysed. She wanted to close her eyes as they swarmed around her, but to do so was to place herself back in an amalgam of dining halls, corridors, public areas. Too many voices, too many bodies; aggression, suspicion, grudges and hatreds in the air. Keenly honed instincts sensing weakness and vulnerability; counter instincts hardening her carapace.

'The noise of you,' she heard herself say. 'Like seagulls on a tip.'

Yes, that would shame them all into a meek silence. She'd probably get a written apology too.

Stupid cow.

Mad old bat.

Mythology

Jerry remained staring at the door, unable to clear the sight of Danby and his pals from his head. He had got away with it, but that felt incidental. What was troubling him was that he didn't know why he had stolen the guy's phone. When you didn't understand your own reasons for doing stuff, it was a very bad sign.

He poured himself a glass of water while he booted up his laptop. He urgently needed distraction, to get his head somewhere else. He remembered that on the walk back from his last lecture he had got an alert informing him that *Complete and Utter Cult* had dropped their latest episode, a special edition on lost and abandoned movies.

The description mentioned Frankenheimer's *Island of Dr Moreau* and Gilliam's *Don Quixote*. This was perfect. Grand visions and hubristic folly: there was nothing like someone else's failings to make you feel better. But when he opened his browser and went to the channel, what he saw felt like a cold knife in the guts. The image they had chosen to illustrate the episode was the poster from *Mancipium*.

That poster.

The very mention of *Mancipium* had once meant something irresistibly enticing, but now he felt haunted by it. Enslaved, one might even say. There was a time when his favourite YouTubers talking about it would have been the most exciting thing in the world. But one night everything had changed, and he didn't live in that world anymore.

Jerry's gran used to run a video shop, back when that was a thing. She had started off renting pirated VHS and Betamax tapes from her house. She circulated lists so customers could phone up, then she'd drive around delivering the rentals and picking up returns. By the time Jerry came along, she had long since gone legit with a shop on the parade, between the chippy and a tanning salon.

Jerry spent most of his pre-school years in the back shop, unless one of his gran's friends could take him for a while. He was serving customers by the time he was ten, and by the time he was thirteen – before streaming finally killed the place off – he had regularly been left to mind the store of an evening while his gran worked shifts at Tesco.

His gran was his legal guardian, effectively his single parent, but the way he saw it, he hadn't been raised by her alone. He was raised by his gran and her movie catalogue, surrounded by tapes and DVDs all his life. He didn't just mean the shop, either. Gran seldom threw anything out. The house was full of old tapes that were no longer fit for rental, as well as barely watchable nth-generation pirate copies dating back to the business's illegal dial-a-video origins.

There wasn't a lot of Truffaut or Ingmar Bergman in there. It was a collection curated by the tastes of what folk were wanting to rent in Ayrshire through the Eighties, Nineties and early 2000s. Aside from a selection of cartoons for the kids, of which he knew every frame by the time he was four, it was predominantly a blend of Hollywood hits and exploitation movies, with the ratio heavily favouring the latter. In any given year, there weren't that many blockbusters, which was why the store's bread and butter was what were known as straight-to-video titles, and of those, the genre that always guaranteed a steady return was horror.

Long before anybody had coined the term 'fuck budget', Gran had decided there was only a finite number of things she could afford to be arsed about. These included, at a basic level, putting food on the table and making sure Jerry was dressed in clean clothes. At a higher tier of importance was ensuring he was doing well in school and not getting in bother with the teachers. The allegedly damaging effects of whatever films he happened to be watching at a tender age did not weigh heavily on her mind.

Jerry first watched *Zombie Flesh Eaters* when he was nine. It didn't warp or traumatise him for life, but it did mean there was no going back to *Star Wars* or *Harry Potter* after that. It was like when he first heard proper metal. Everything else seemed tame by comparison.

He worked his way through every horror film on the shelves, and not only was it a buzz, but it changed how he thought about films. He rewound and watched the gory bits over and over until he could see how they had achieved the effect. Then he started to notice other elements that contributed to the experience: the shot juxtapositions that fooled the eye, the framing techniques that generated suspense. It was his contention that you could learn more about composition and editing from watching horror than from the entire works of any acclaimed arthouse auteur.

Horror wasn't merely a genre, though: it was a culture. It had its history, its apocrypha, its mythology. The televangelist Billy Graham claiming the very celluloid of *The Exorcist* was possessed. The rumours that *Cannibal Holocaust* showed actual footage of murder. Separate planes carrying *The Omen*'s cast and producer both being struck by lightning, before a plane used for aerial filming crashed and killed everybody on board.

And then there was *Mancipium*.

There was a sense of the legendary about it. Its very name, among other things, literally meant thrall, and to hear it unexpectedly brought up in conversation was something of a shibboleth, like movie-geek freemasonry.

Jerry had first found reference to it when he was thirteen, in an old copy of *Starburst* magazine that had been sitting in a cupboard since the late Nineties. The main article had been about supposedly cursed films, and focused particularly on *The Exorcist*, but there had been a sidebar on this apparently notorious movie Jerry had never heard of. This, he learned, was because it had never been released, reputedly because the film was so disturbing that its producers themselves had suppressed it once they saw what they had created.

In words that had burned themselves into Jerry's excited young brain, the magazine described *Mancipium* as '*a film about the seductive nature of evil that could itself, they feared, seduce people into evil deeds.*' As a budding devotee of the genre, this had seemed mind-blowing: a movie so horrifying that it didn't even get as far as being banned. Its own creators, realising they had spawned a monster, smothered it before its evil could be unleashed.

The article went so far as to suggest that the producers not only burned the negative, but did so in the presence of a priest. However, just like in any classic horror movie, it appeared they had not entirely succeeded at containing the danger, hence its inclusion in an article about movie curses.

In common with *The Exorcist*, it was stated that bad things subsequently happened to many of the people involved in making it. Its director, Alessandro Salerno, killed himself; its star, Paulo Nietti, went missing; and its producer, Lucio Sabatini, fell from his yacht and drowned. But worse, in the case of *Mancipium*, it was claimed that bad things subsequently happened to people who merely *saw* it.

> The rumours surrounding the film are believed to have inspired last year's Japanese horror hit *Ringu,* in which anyone who watches a cursed videotape dies within a week.

Jerry must have read and reread that article a dozen times, illustrated only with a tiny thumbnail of the poster: the same image he was to have his fateful encounter with on that disastrous night last year. When the poster had caught his eye, he had felt a rush of excitement at discovering a fellow initiant. In other circumstances he'd have been impatient to meet him. As it was, he wished he could erase the man's image from his mind.

If he was being positive, he would say that night was the reason he was here today, the motivation to turn his life around. Problem was, that wasn't quite working out too well right now either. Danby had been unsuccessful in trying to brand him a thief, but the damage done in the last few minutes was irreparable. Jerry didn't see how he could continue to stay in this place. The atmosphere was poisonous, and it was only going to get worse.

That season ticket for the train was starting to look like it would have been the better option. Two voices were arguing against it, though. The first was his gran's, warning him that moving away wouldn't be easy but assuring him it would be worth it.

'It will be the making of you,' she had insisted.

The second voice was his own, echoing the warning he'd given Danby just a moment ago. Of all people, Jerry Kelly knew what it was to have done something you couldn't go back from.

Experience

Millicent inched forward in the queue, relieved to find herself in a situation that made sense: waiting in line. This was going to be the easiest part of her morning's quest. All she had to do was order coffee and cake. Then the child behind the counter asked what she wanted.

Coffee and cake. Just coffee and cake. How hard was that?

As she opened her mouth to speak, she caught sight of the boards on display behind the counter: five columns of options, not one of them simply 'coffee'. It wasn't merely that she hadn't heard of half of them; there were just too many. She was paralysed.

She felt a tap on her shoulder.

'You're next,' said a slight man accompanied by a large dog.

Millicent's mouth remained open but she still didn't know what to say.

'Is it a latte, maybe? A cappuccino?' asked the girl. Then: 'Do you need a wee minute?' her voice suddenly cloying, talking like Millicent was a child.

The little man with the big dog tutted and sighed.

Millicent's instinct told her just to leave, but she needed her proof for Vivian.

'Maybe I can serve this gentleman while you're deciding?' the girl suggested.

That would probably have been okay, but the problem was, he made a move. He didn't wait for her assent, he simply stepped across her. 'I just want a flat white to go,' he said, speaking like she wasn't there.

She had to stand her ground.

Millicent threw an arm up to block his path, turning to confront him.

'Where do you think you're going?'

'I'm in a bit of a hurry,' he explained.

'Allow me to explain to you the concept of hierarchy,' she replied. 'At its most basic, it derives from who was here first, and we call this "a queue".'

'It's just to give you a wee minute to make up your mind,' the girl offered.

'No, he can wait his turn like he's supposed to, and not act like I don't exist.'

'There's no need for that attitude,' the man said.

'And there's no need for you hassling me either. How urgent is this coffee you're needing? Is it defibrillator coffee? And what are you doing with a dog twice the size of you? How does that work? Do *you* hump *its* leg?'

At that point she felt another hand on her shoulder. This time it was another member of staff, a woman wearing a stern expression.

'I'm afraid I'm going to have to ask you to leave. We don't tolerate this kind of anti-social conduct towards our customers or our staff.'

Millicent felt the shop melt around her.

'But I need to get my card stamped,' she said feebly, her voice failing.

'If you don't leave, I'll have no hesitation in calling the police. It's company policy to prosecute.'

At the very mention of the police, she felt the blood drain from her face, a familiar hollow forming in her gut. She knew the consequences. She shuffled towards the door, the manager opening it for her.

'And never mind stamped: your card's marked,' the woman told her. 'Don't come back.'

Millicent kept her head down as she hurried through the Buchanan Galleries, avoiding eye contact as a matter of long-ingrained habit. It was that bit harder with so many reflective surfaces, but fortunately the only sideways glance she caught was her own.

She had accepted that she would never again see the woman she had once been but could never get used to the sight of the one she had become. She appeared taller than she felt, for one thing. Her perception of herself had become of someone shrunken and small. But what troubled her most was that her face looked so hollow and fearful. She didn't know why she should find it surprising. She had spent a quarter of a century afraid. She looked forward to the day when that fear would finally end.

Half in love with easeful death.

Sometimes it felt like death was the only thing she did not fear. Death would be a deliverance, a corporeal manifestation of her spiritual state. Millicent's fears were not rooted in the worry that she might die. The thing she was truly afraid of was how long she might still live: what miseries and torments might yet be inflicted upon her before the final mercy.

She took some reassurance from the fact that it was John Lewis Vivian had asked her to visit, wondering whether that had factored in her choice. Viv had astutely noted that she found it comforting to encounter things that hadn't been erased in her absence. But the corollary of seeking solace in institutions that still endured was the awareness of their rarity.

Millicent wasn't from Glasgow, and had only visited the city a few times before she went away. This particular John Lewis store hadn't been here back then, though she did remember the area, because it had been intimidatingly insalubrious. Its principal land-mark in her mind was a creepily decrepit hotel, one that survived now only in a movie called *The Big Man*. It was adapted from a book by William McIlvanney and would be referred to by most as a Liam Neeson movie, but to Millicent it was first and foremost a Jenny Shircore film: lots of facial injuries, with a rich variety of bruising, swelling and scars.

The entrance to the store presented no doors to open. She was able to stroll, head down, from the mall to the shop floor, finding herself immediately in the department she needed to visit.

She approached the counter tentatively, fumbling for the piece of paper on which Vivian had written what she wanted. She could see two pretty and immaculately presented young women behind the displays. There was no avoiding eye contact at this point.

'Can I help you?' asked the nearer one. Her name badge identified her as Maya. She wore a wide smile as she made her greeting, though something in her tone indicated that she suspected Millicent was in the wrong place, or at least somewhere to which she was thoroughly unaccustomed.

Millicent read from the scrap of paper.

'I need a facial multi-palette and vanity case.'

The girl conferred with her colleague.

'I think that's the Rimmel one,' she suggested.

The other girl nodded. She crouched behind the counter and produced a large brushed-aluminium box, flipping it open to reveal several hinged tiers accommodating a wide selection of colours and tones.

It was only now that she was seeing the size of it that she deduced Vivian's true intentions. Despite what she had said, and the money Vivian had given her, it wasn't for herself at all.

She recalled a conversation from a few weeks ago, Vivian saying that Millicent ought to volunteer to help out at a nearby retirement home.

'It would give you a sense of perspective on what old age really looks like.'

Vivian was very big on recalibrating the scale of such matters in her own favour.

'The ladies there have someone who comes in and does their hair. Tom said you used to be good with make-up. Perhaps you could give them a wee bit of pampering.'

Millicent had responded with a noncommittal mumble, instantly purging the notion from her mind, but evidently Vivian had not forgotten. Millicent felt horribly trapped.

'This is the display one,' Maya added. 'Kayley, can you go and get a boxed one from stock?'

Millicent wanted to tell her not to bother. It would make no difference, as she had no intention of using the thing, but Kayley was already on her way.

'She might be a wee minute,' Maya said. 'The stockroom is away in the back.'

'That's no problem,' Millicent replied. She had to keep reminding herself that everybody expected things instantly now, and a few moments' delay was an intolerable inconvenience that could only be ameliorated by resort to one's mobile phone.

Maya's perfectly symmetrical eyebrows raised by way of overture to a suggestion. Closer inspection revealed that they comprised precisely no hair, but were in fact drawn on.

'See while we're waiting, do you want to try a couple of things?'

Millicent's instinct was to refuse, to be left alone and not inconvenience anyone. This girl surely had better things to do.

'I don't have much money. I'm just picking this set up for a friend.'

Maya smiled again.

'It's free, no obligation to purchase anything. Just a wee bit of fun. Come on, I'm quiet the now.'

Maya beckoned her behind the counter, where she had a seat waiting. Millicent complied. Acquiescence was usually a safe place to hide.

As Maya brushed the first bit of foundation upon her, she felt a welling of emotions and an early inkling that she wanted to cry. She was practised at staunching the process long before it reached her tear ducts: suppressing emotions and putting on a mask behind which nobody could see how afraid, how sad, how hopeless she was feeling. When people detected those things, it was an advertisement of vulnerability, an invitation to attack and exploit.

The threat of the police at the coffee shop had shaken her, but hadn't precipitated anything like this. That was because she was used to fending off threat. She was less used to kindness.

'Just going to use a wee bit of foundation here, and then we'll try a few lippies and see what suits your tone. I've got Bobbi Brown, Tom Ford, Charlotte Tilbury.'

The names meant nothing to her. Their mention prompted thoughts of a few that did. Tom Savini. Rob Bottin. Jenny Shircore.

Maya caught her eye in the mirror, reading her baffled look.

Her smile was now solicitously apologetic.

'Do you have much experience with make-up?' she asked, wrinkling her nose in anticipation of the expected answer.

Millicent considered the question, all the things she could say, the stories she could tell. All buried too deep. All too painful to exhume.

The response came easily. There was safety and comfort to be found there. In the truth there was only pain.

'Not much, no.'

The rain was reduced to a spotty drizzle as she made her way home. No: made her way back. Not home. It was Vivian's home. It was Carla's home. It was where Millicent stayed. Another temporary box, another holding area.

She drifted through the Glasgow streets, disconnected from her surroundings. She was at Charing Cross, halfway to the West End before she even remembered she was supposed to be taking the Underground.

So what? She had her ticket from earlier. She had the purchase she had been sent for. That was plenty. Small steps, Viv.

The vanity case weighed on her mind as it did her arm, and not just because she had been sent to purchase it under false pretences.

Maya's words kept playing in her head.

Do you have much experience with make-up?

She tried not to think about the answer she did not give. It hurt too much. Other people talked about bittersweet memories. She didn't know what that felt like. All she knew with regard to the past was pain, fear, loss and regret.

The word that best connoted with 'sweet' in her mind was 'release'.

I can't get no sweet release.

It was from a song one of her fellow inmates used to sing. Millicent had never heard the original, didn't know who it was by or even what it was called, but she knew what it meant. That was explicit in the next line.

Let me rest in peace.

As she crossed the expressway, her eyes were drawn to a ragged offering of flowers and plastic wreaths tied to the railings. They'd been there for a couple of weeks, the flowers now little more than stalks gripping a last few wilted petals.

They'd put her on suicide watch when she was first sentenced. Took her belt and laces, kept eyes on her twenty-four/seven.

There was nobody watching these days, though.

She wasn't quite ready, but she knew she very soon would be. She had to put a few things in order first. She had to choose her time, choose her location. She didn't want to cause any great fuss or inconvenience for anyone, least of all Vivian. She didn't deserve that. She had been nothing but kind, if in a wrong-headed, misguided, patronising and counter-effective way.

They could finally put her in that littlest box, in that narrowest space, her final credit etched in stone.

Millicent Spark.
Make-up artist.
Murderer.
Born 25 April, 1947

They'd get the date of death wrong. They'd be out by a quarter of a century.

Innocence

Jerry was on his way back from the coffee shop down the street when he noticed that the social space was relatively quiet: only a few folk sitting around, and crucially none of them was Danby or any of that lot. He had a cup of hot chocolate and a scone, which he was planning to take upstairs to his room, but he decided instead to have a seat on one of the curved sofas.

The irony of the term 'social space' weighed heavily on him. He had been living here several weeks now and was barely on speaking terms with anybody. He had made some friends on his courses and been to a couple of meetings of the metal society, but here at the halls was where he tended to be most inclined to retreat into himself. He felt like the people living the closest to him were also the people he least wanted to open up to. He wasn't sure why, but there was a weird vulnerability about it. Maybe everybody felt a bit of that when they left home, but it had to be worse when you knew there was no home to go back to anymore.

As he sipped his hot chocolate, he tuned in to the conversation around him. They were talking about what got them interested in their course, what had made them choose Glasgow Uni in particular. If the topic was 'how you ended up here', Jerry had a hell of a story. He just couldn't imagine the circumstances under which he would be prepared to share it with another human being.

He could remember every detail of it, though. Every detail.

They got in through a wee window at the back, taking them right into a sitting room. It was a hot summer evening in a city where nobody had air conditioning. These big older buildings all had sash and case windows with H-shaped brackets on the inside that the owners maybe thought were a security measure, stopping the frame travelling up past a few inches when you opened them for ventilation. They were actually for washing the windows: you hung the frame on the hinge and swung it out from the casement. All it took was a crowbar and the hinges popped away from the wood.

It was Jerry's turn to keep the edgy. His job was to get to the front and look out for the owners coming home, or in a tenement like this one, for anybody at all coming into the close. They rotated the duties in case the look-out was seen, same as they took turns ringing the doorbells to make sure nobody was home. They had a cover story in case somebody answered, saying they were looking for 'Bob Miller', who lived at a similar-sounding address. If you were in fourteen Greenleaf Road you said you were looking for fourteen Greenleaf Gardens or whatever.

There were three of them: Rossco, Keansy and Jerry. They had come up from Dreghorn in Rossco's brother's van. As always, he had lent them it in exchange for a cut, plus full deniability.

They were operating on the principle of 'don't shit where you eat'; or more literally, don't tan houses in your own neighbourhood, because everything gets more complicated. Plus there was the fact that the houses in their own neighbourhood seldom had much in them worth stealing. The West End was a different story, though.

Rossco's strategy was to hit older folk, as they generally couldn't be arsed with the technology and hassle of alarm systems, especially if they'd been living in the same place since nineteen canteen. The rule of thumb was only to take cash and jewellery, targeting stuff the owners might plausibly have mislaid. It confused the timeline for reporting it to the polis if they didn't notice for a few days. To that end, they also tried not to make a mess. If there was time, they would even repair the H-brackets before they left. An exception could be made for something that might be immediately conspicuous by its absence, but only if it was worth the added risk.

It felt frustrating to walk past high-end electronics gear and know it was out of bounds, but nobody wanted to risk lugging a big widescreen telly out of a close. Jerry had suggested they could get away with it if they all wore matching overalls or polo shirts. It was all about the optics, looking like you're meant to be there. You could walk out with anything from anywhere if you gave the impression you were going about your job.

Rossco said it was too much hassle, but Jerry suspected that his principal objection was that it hadn't been his idea. Rossco always had to be in charge, and he didn't take well to any hint of dissent or challenge. He was hard as fuck yet weirdly insecure, which made for a highly volatile combination.

Jerry was supposed to be heading through to the front of the house, but he was held up by his surroundings. He always got a buzz from being where he wasn't supposed to, and sometimes he was really struck by the décor. They were usually old people's houses, but they never looked much like his gran's place. He would find himself wondering: did they have taste because they had money, or did they have money because they had taste?

However, what had arrested him about this gaffe was nothing to do with opulence or aesthetics. The walls were bedecked with framed movie one-sheets, and not the usual stuff, either. A lot of people put up posters to make it look like they were cineastes, but it was always the same films: *Some Like It Hot*, *Pulp Fiction*, *Titanic*, *Gone With the Wind*. Maybe *The Shining* if they wanted to seem a bit darker. Made him wonder if they sold a multi-pack at Ikea. This was different. This was hardcore. *The Last House on the Left*, *The Burning*, *Suspiria*, *Zombie Flesh Eaters*. This was somebody properly into their horror, into their quality trash. This was the home of someone he could relate to.

His eye was drawn to smaller images about the place, framed photographs on the mantelpiece and sideboard. Two older guys, side by side, smiling. Photographs of them as younger guys. Photographs of them separately, photographs of them together. This was their place. This was their stuff.

Fuck.

The way Jerry saw it, if you weren't fussed enough to put the requisite effort into protecting your gear, then you could obviously afford to lose it. Sometimes he even justified his theft on the intellectual grounds that he deserved to have something more than its owner did if he was smarter at thieving than they were at security. It was bollocks. If he didn't know it was wrong, he wouldn't feel bad about it.

And the main thing he felt bad about was his gran.

His gran had brought him up, on her own, and though she never said as much, he knew she was driven by a need to do a better job with him than she'd managed with her daughter. She had raised him from the age of two, and she'd done it while still working full time.

And now she was dying.

Pancreatic cancer. Inoperable. Untreatable. Metastatic. All the words you never wanted to hear. It was like something out of a daft joke, the doctor giving her only a few months to live, except there was no punchline. Just a punch to the gut. All those years she had been all he had, and suddenly he was given notice that he wouldn't have her much longer.

At a time like that, people become closer, don't they? They realise what they mean to each other and put aside what obstacles lie between them. Problem was, Jerry already knew what she meant to him, and part of him was angry with her because she was going to leave. He was looking for obstacles to put between them, because he wanted to distance himself now so that it hurt less when it came.

There had been a kind of silent stand-off between them. She knew who he was running about with, and the dogs in the street knew what they were involved in. Sometimes she would talk about it in abstract, tacitly asserting what she knew without forcing him to acknowledge the truth of it, because then he wouldn't have to lie to her face. She would talk about how clever he was, what he was capable of at school, how far he might go if he screwed the nut.

'It would destroy me to see you chuck it all away, son.'

But she was already destroyed. That was what made it all seem futile.

Like every parent before her, she had worried about him 'running with the wrong crowd'. And like every parent before her, she had forgotten what it was like to be that age. Sometimes it's the only crowd. When you're a teenager in a small town, you've got to carve out a place for yourself, and you don't always get to be picky.

There were people you might call your pals even though you didn't particularly like them, and they didn't much like you. You just hung about together because there was nobody else. And in the case of bampots like Rossco, because it was better to be in with them than having them on your case.

You've got to fit in. Got to go along to get along. Got to be morally flexible. Plus, it was nice to have a bit of money. But above all, there was the buzz. When they hit a place, the excitement cleared his head like a drug, and he didn't care about anything other than getting out clean. That night more than ever he had needed some of that.

He looked at the bookcase opposite the window through which he had just broken in.

The shelves below bore dozens of old VHS tapes, from German Krimi through Italian Gialli to the Eighties golden age of exploitation horror. *Der Frosch mit der Maske*, *Black Gloves and White Lace*, *Blood Ceremony*, *Don't Go in the Woods*, *Happy Birthday to Me*, *Cannibal Holocaust*, *I Spit on Your Grave*, *SS Experiment Camp*, *Nightmares in a Damaged Brain*. This guy had the lot.

Then Jerry saw the thing that stopped him dead. Sitting on a low shelf, there was a poster of *Mancipium*. It had been mounted on a box frame, under glass. Jerry was slack-jawed. Despite its legend, it was a film with almost no memorabilia, and consequently no iconography: only stories, and a few grainy production stills that sometimes came up on Google Images (and spookily, sometimes they didn't). Yet here was a full-colour poster, listing the major cast and crew credits.

His heartbeat racing and his brain in a spin, Jerry scanned the spines of the handwritten cassette sleeves, thinking what if, what if, what if. But no. That would have been serious *Da Vinci Code* shit, finding an actual copy. The poster was headfuck enough.

Jerry lifted the frame gently, examining the poster more closely. The colours were still vivid, indicating it had been looked after, kept out of the sun.

He felt a less-than-playful thump to his shoulder, causing him to almost lose his grip on the thing.

'Whit ye daein' wi' that?' Rossco demanded.

Rossco had his phone in his hand. What was he up to? Checking Twitter in the middle of a job?

'Put it back. Too bulky. Remember the rules.'

'It's worth more than anything else in here,' he replied. This was probably not true, but it was certainly worth more to Jerry. Unfortunately, now Rossco knew that.

'Give us it here, then.'

He should have kept his mouth shut. The same thing had happened a few weeks ago, when Jerry found an original VHS copy of *Star Wars*, predating all George Lucas's retrospective self-vandalism. It was currently on a shelf in Rossco's house.

Jerry hesitated and Rossco sensed his reluctance. His eyes flashed with a warning about the pecking order here.

'You'll need me to move it,' Jerry said as he handed it over.

'We'll see.'

Rossco was putting it in his backpack when they heard the front door open, the three of them looking back and forth between them as it closed again. It dawned on everybody simultaneously that the person who was meant to be keeping the edgy was right there in the room. Rossco gave Jerry a glare that said he'd be getting leathered later, but for now there was no time to waste. They were standing in a flat with only one outside door. They'd have to bail the way they'd come in, through the window.

Rossco was first out, barging past Keansy to make his escape. Pecking order again. Jerry knew he would have to go last because it had been his fuck-up.

Keansy was halfway out the window when the bloke came through the door. It was one of the old boys from the photographs.

He and Jerry stood there, each rendered motionless as they regarded each other with mutual fear. That was the freeze-frame image that would remain etched in Jerry's mind for ever after. The thing he could never go back from. The last moment before innocence ended.

Reflections

Lucio switched on his bedside lamp and checked the time. It was twelve fifteen. Neither of the girls draped across his bed even twitched at the light coming on. Crazy little whores were sleeping the sleep of the just: as in, just had a shitload of cocktails, coke and cock way past any sixteen-year-old's bedtime. Lucio envied them their oblivion. The yacht was rocking gently, enough to cause one of the empty champagne bottles on the carpet to roll half a turn in each direction, but the motion had been no help in lulling him.

It was after midnight: that meant it was now Thursday. It was May 13th, 1993, the first day of the Cannes Film Festival. The day they were supposed to announce.

There was coke on the edge of his palm from where he had brushed it on the nightstand. He could feel it on the back of his throat, the burn like a twisted echo of the one he felt when it hit his sinuses. He told himself it was acid reflux from combining it with champagne, but more likely he had overdone it, too eager to get his head somewhere else.

He surveyed the scene before him: the master suite on his private yacht, moored here for the duration of the festival. Two aspiring teenage 'actresses' sprawled naked on the king-size bed, exhausted from the threesome they had just enjoyed.

He thought of a story Alfie Bertrand told him, about the famous footballer George Best. He had won the European Cup with Manchester United, back when it meant something, before this new Champions League bullshit they had brought in. A few years later the guy had ended up playing for Hibernian in Edinburgh. One night he was walking back to his hotel room, a former Miss World on one arm and a bottle of champagne in the other, when he was accosted by a porter who said: 'Georgie, where did it all go wrong?'

Everyone at the table had found Alfie's story real funny. They had been finance types: investors and sales agents. Lucio had laughed too, but inside he saw the tragedy beneath the punchline. It had all gone wrong, because once upon a time this guy was the best in the world, an artist doing what he loved, what he was born to do. Back then the girls and the champagne were merely the trappings of success. Now they were all he had left.

Lucio stood up and looked at himself in the full-length wardrobe mirror that ran along one wall. He was forty-two and starting to look it: pot-bellied where he used to have a washboard, grey flecks showing at the roots of hair that was years since being a luxuriant mane. Where had he gone, the young dude who used to gaze back at him? That was how age ambushed you: it chipped away with incremental change you barely noticed, then something jolted the picture so that its true extent revealed itself.

Lucio didn't need to ask where it all went wrong. The man in the mirror had looked different only two hours ago. The whole picture had looked different two hours ago.

How do you respond when all your plans have crashed and burned? When you have dozens of guests still celebrating the thing that they don't yet know ain't gonna happen?

In Lucio's case, the answer was that he did four lines before downing a bottle and a half of Krug and fucking two girls whose combined age would still be ten years less than his own. But now his dick was limp, the girls were asleep, his throat burned and the man he saw in the mirror still had all his problems waiting for him.

Where did it all go wrong, Georgie?

As he stared at his reflection, he thought of all the better times he had watched himself on this bed, enjoying those trappings of success. And in that moment he had an idea.

Lucio's poppa always said, if you want to be happy, you need to want the work more than the reward. And if you want to work, you need to be prepared to get your hands dirty.

It had all gone wrong before, plenty of times. Never this badly, but resilience was not a matter of scale. It was a matter of belief. He had always bounced back. That was why he was Lucky Lucio. *L'uomo che fa accadere.*

The man who makes it happen.

Accommodation (i)

'Well, I think the camera work here is really reminiscent of Godard's *Weekend*,' said Felicity, sitting with one leg tucked under herself like she was combining this tutorial with a yoga session. Jerry knew from a brief conversation that she was the same age as him, eighteen, but came across like she was about twenty-five.

He didn't know how they did it: hold forth in front of peers or strangers with absolute conviction and seemingly no self-consciousness, even when they were talking utter shite.

That was how it always started, too: 'Well, I think . . .'

First term, he heard a bloke do that in a lecture. Not even a tutorial, a fucking lecture. Interrupted the woman who was paid to actually know what she was talking about in order to say, 'Well, I think . . .' followed by a massive mouth-jobbie.

Did they teach this stuff at public school? That the second you opened your gub, the room would become rapt with attention, everybody on tenterhooks waiting for the next precious word that dripped from your lips, and whatever pish you spewed would be instantly transmuted into the wisdom of Solomon by virtue of your better breeding?

They all had that same whiny accent too. The one they all thought wasn't an accent. That was why they felt it was their right to make you repeat yourself, just to underline that there was something lacking in your diction. Because clearly there was nothing lacking or divergent in theirs, even when they were recycling the spare 'r's they had left over from their pronunciation of words like floor and door by talking about draw-ring a picture.

And the worst of it was, it worked. They sounded like they knew what they were talking about, because they spoke in the same accent as the folk reading the news or narrating documentaries. Whereas what came out of his mouth sounded like exactly what it was: the half-formed ramblings of a no-mark from Dreghorn.

He had heard about impostor syndrome: the feeling that you've no right to be there, it's not for you, and you're going to get found out. He wondered, was it an actual syndrome if you really were an impostor? There should be fucking ID checks and quarantine in the West End to stop folk like him just breezing in. Giving Scotland a showing up in front of all these nice respectable middle-class kiddies from Melton Middle and Crumpetshire.

They were analysing the way directors conveyed information and emotion in non-textual ways. This was meat and drink to Jerry, especially after this morning's politics lecture, which had been on the Leveson Inquiry. They had been shown a video of that horrible old bastard Roger Wincott's appearance before the committee, being challenged about his newspapers' use of phone-hacking. They could have shown the same clip in here too, given they were discussing subliminal techniques in conveying information.

Wincott was playing the doddery old man who couldn't be expected to know what was going on across every inch of his media empire. He had been accompanied by his ice-queen daughter too. Pure theatre: a frail old man needing one of his children there for support. Not that the inquiry had left any doubt Julia Fleet had been neck-deep in it all, but it helped to present themselves as a family pulling together, rather than a many-tentacled monster.

'There's definitely a French New Wave aesthetic about it,' Felicity went on. 'There was this amazing Godard retrospective at the South Bank that I went to during the summer.'

Weird flex but okay, Jerry thought. What she just said was of course fuck-all to do with anything, and the only New Wave John Carney was thinking about when he shot this film was Duran Duran. Felicity just wanted everybody to know she went to art movies at the South Bank, knew who Jean Luc Godard was, and was worthier of Karima's time and attention than anybody else present.

Karima Saeed, the tutor, nodded patiently. From her expression

Jerry could tell she knew Felicity was miles out, but she also had to be encouraging.

'Yes, but what can we say here about the shift between this scene and the one immediately before it. What has been used to escalate the tension and generate a rising sense of menace?'

The image was freeze-framed on the screen, Ferdia Walsh-Peelo as young Connor running down a corridor pursued by Don Wycherley's menacing Brother Baxter.

Felicity suggested it was the colours that had been chosen for the scene. 'The walls look deliberately washed-out to create an unsettling sense of claustrophobia and fear,' she said.

Jerry seriously doubted this. It was a shot from inside a school, and it looked a lot like the colour scheme where he was educated. Maybe Felicity was right, though. Everything at Dreghorn Academy had seemed intended to unsettle the poor bastards going through it.

Karima wore a strained expression, like she appreciated Felicity's stab at this but it wasn't what she was looking for.

It had to be hard for the tutor. The answer was fucking obvious but she was trying to get them there without spelling it out. A part of Jerry wanted to say it, wanted the pat on the head and the gold star. A bigger part wouldn't let him speak, afraid he'd fumble it, or that it would just sound wrong coming out of his mouth.

'It's the rapid editing,' suggested Philippa, the same one who had seen him in Fonezone and decided that meant he had stolen Danby's Galaxy. 'It creates a sense of the kinetic and makes the viewer disoriented.'

Philippa's powers of observation in combination with deductive reasoning remained consistent. She hadn't seen what she thought, either on the screen or on Dumbarton Road, though in the case of the latter she hadn't been wrong in her conclusions.

Jerry rolled his eyes then instantly wished he hadn't, because Karima saw him. He should have known Karima would be looking his way. She was always bloody looking his way, beckoning a contribution or gauging his response.

'What do you reckon to it, Jerry?'

'Don't know,' he mumbled.

'You looked like you disagreed with the last contribution.'

'No, I just maybe thought Felicity's suggestion about the colour scheme was more on the money.'

He felt a certain shame in saying this, and it was doubled by Karima's expression, the disappointment in her face. She knew he was lying, though if she knew why, she was doing better than him.

The tutorial broke up and he quietly put his notes in his bag while the others kept on chatting to Karima. One of them started wanging on about the framing in Whit Stillman's *Love & Friendship*, a film that looked like it had been hurriedly shot in instalments at a National Trust property whenever one of the guides was having a fag break.

He was on his way to the door when Karima called him back.

'Jerry, can you hang on a minute? I'd like a word.'

He kept his head down as the others filed past. He clocked a few eyes on his T-shirt, a Machine Head one today. Metal tees worked like an invisibility cloak: people had a cursory glance and then knew not to pay you any further attention. Philippa seemed to hover longer than anyone else, but he kept his eyes to the carpet. He couldn't take any more insinuations from her, especially as they were probably true.

Philippa let the door close gently, leaving him with Karima, who wrinkled her brow as an overture to what she had to say.

'Is everything okay, Jerry?'

'Sure,' he replied, making eye contact as long as he could tolerate, which was about three photons' worth.

'I just wondered if there was a reason you didn't say anything during the class. The purpose of these tutorials is to generate discussion, get the ideas flowing.'

'I wasn't the only one who didn't say much,' he countered, aware the usual few had hogged the conch.

'I wouldn't have an issue if you were simply the only person who said nothing. My problem is that you were the only one who had something to say but didn't say it. Why did you roll your eyes?' she added, before he could issue a denial.

'I shouldn't have done that. It was rude. I'd had a bit of a dis-agreement with Philippa earlier and I was still salty about it.'

'That might be true, but it's not why you did it. She said the director used rapid editing to create a sense of danger. Why did you disagree?'

He didn't answer. He knew that often enough if you let the silence grow, someone else would fill it, accepting your *omertà* as a show of penitence. Karima wasn't looking for that, though. Every time he looked up, she was still staring back.

He sighed. Surrender. Surrender.

'Because it was fuck-all to do with editing. There was only one edit: static two-shot to a Steadicam. The move to the Steadicam created a natural sense of motion, and because it's following the boy down the corridor, it tells you something physical is about to happen. He's being followed and therefore you know he's about to get attacked.'

Karima was nodding, but she still looked bemused.

'This is what exasperates me. You grasp this kind of thing intui-tively. That was clear from your first essay. But your work since has been getting weaker and weaker. It's like you're refusing to engage. Your last assignment fell well below standard, and the latest one is overdue.'

He responded promptly to that, happy to have a reason that would plausibly cover it.

'I'm spending a lot of my evenings working to help meet my rent. The number of shifts has gone up lately, and I can't say no to them or I'll end up with no shifts at all. It's hard to fit everything in.'

'I'm not questioning that there can be financial hardships and demands on your time, but to me that doesn't explain everything that's going on here. You're a bright boy. I'm starting to wonder if you're self-sabotaging. Are you trying to get yourself thrown out?'

'Why would I do that?'

'Lots of reasons. I've seen it before. People struggling to fit in, having doubts about their future, missing friends or family back home.'

Jerry felt heat in his cheeks.

'There are people you can talk to if you're struggling. I don't want to lose you. I think you've got something to say. I just can't work out why you won't say it.'

When he finally exited the tutorial room, he spotted that Philippa was still hanging about. She wasn't with anyone either. Shite.

He started walking at pace, head down. As he passed her, she fell into step alongside him. She was wearing a Savage Earth Heart tee, because of course she'd be into that indie-folky pish.

'Jerry, I want to clear the air,' she said, in that breathy voice of hers. He just kept walking.

'I *was* outside Fonezone that day. I didn't lie about seeing you. But I just want to say—'

'You've *just said* plenty,' he interrupted.

'I know, and I'm sorry. Look, can we talk properly? Maybe grab a coffee?'

What, so that you can feel better about yourself? he wanted to retort, but his own phony self-righteousness made him gag. Yes, she hadn't seen what she thought – he really had been flogging an old iPod for a few quid – so she had no right to jump to that conclusion, but it was still the right conclusion.

He couldn't bring himself to say anything, as he was feeling too churned up. He was angry, but mainly it was her trying to be nice that he couldn't handle.

Jerry kept walking and she let him go. He needed space. His head was a jumble of conflicting emotions. He kept coming back to the words 'self-sabotage'. When Karima suggested it, he hadn't felt any strong urge to contradict. And he wasn't only thinking about his deteriorating coursework and the essay he hadn't written.

He thought also of Philippa, of Danby, and the toxic situation at the halls. Stealing phones and skipping classes. Self-sabotage. Was that what was going on here? Why would he self-sabotage?

Maybe because he was out of his depth and afraid he couldn't handle it.

Gran had lived long enough for him to get his exam results, back in early August. He had never seen her so happy. He had screwed the nut, hit the books, determined to get into uni and give himself the chance she wanted for him.

He had promised her he would make a success of this. Make a success of himself. He had told her so many lies in recent years, broken so many promises: he couldn't break this one. But if it was out of his hands, if he was booted out, that would be different. That wouldn't be a betrayal. He'd given it his best shot but he'd come up short. What could you do?

Except that he hadn't given it his best shot. That was what Karima had clocked. He owed his gran that much. He owed himself that much.

That said, it wasn't easy trying to write an essay when you'd been working until one in the morning five or six nights of the week. Gran had left him what little she had, which he had budgeted carefully to spread throughout his degree, but without the shifts, he'd struggle for rent.

He thought once again about how much cheaper it was back in Dreghorn, how he could get a place there and maybe take the train. But down that route he saw how easy it would be to not take the train, just get a job and forget about the uni thing. That made him think how his gran hadn't merely wanted him to come here because of where it might take him, but where it would take him away from.

Jerry was cutting through the John McIntyre building when he passed a noticeboard papered with the usual flyers for meetings, club nights and student societies. Amidst the collage his eye was caught by one boasting 'cheap student living in Hyndland', above a picture of a big sandstone house.

He stopped and looked again, checking he had read right. The rent quoted was about a third of what he was paying in the halls, offering a room twice the size in a very upmarket neighbourhood.

Jerry immediately had two questions. One, what was the catch; and two, who the hell advertised digs IRL, on a noticeboard, and quoting a landline.

The answer to both was the same: old people.

He scanned the accompanying text. The deal was you got cheap accommodation somewhere tasty, but obviously no late-night mad wans, and you had to make yourself available to help out and spend social time with the three old women you were sharing with. Something about breaking down barriers between the generations and helping them keep a young perspective.

The dog-eared flyer looked like it had been up there a while. The room was probably already gone, but he figured it was worth a phone call. Jerry had lived with one old woman all his life. If there was a possibility of moving out of the halls, it was worth a pop.

He reached into his jacket, fished out Danby's Galaxy Nine and dialled the number.

A Social Call

Millicent was packing a case. In the year since her release, she had not accumulated a great deal of clothing or other personal items, but she felt bad about making it someone else's responsibility to deal with them.

Her bedroom already looked like she was moving out, mainly because it had always looked like she'd just moved in. The walls were bare, her pictures remaining in a stack leaning against one wall. Her brother Alastair had kept them all the time she was inside, but she had never been able to bring herself to put them up. The memories they evoked were just too painful. They were mementoes of a time she did not wish to remember, of people she once knew but would never see again. Principal among those people were Alastair and herself.

Alastair was the only one who had stayed close throughout everything. The one person who had truly loved her, unconditionally. And my, hadn't she thrown up some conditions.

Most of the people she considered her friends had dropped her as soon as the story broke, appalled at what she had done. It was hard to blame them. When you wake up covered in blood, a knife on the floor, your head full of pills and vodka, lying in bed alongside the body of your boyfriend who's been stabbed to death, in a fifth-floor flat that's locked from the inside, it's kind of hard to say: 'It's not what it looks like.'

Nonetheless, there were a few who got in touch to say they still cared about her, regardless of what she'd done, but time and distance saw them fade too. The number of visitors quickly trickled away, then the letters stopped coming. Again, she didn't blame them. She said so little during the visits anyway, and she never wrote back. It was as though she was cauterising the wound rather than letting it fester.

Alastair wouldn't be dissuaded, though. No amount of silence put him off. Sometimes he would fill the time by talking about what was going on in his life, throwing her this lifeline to the outside world so that she knew she could still grab it if she felt the need. Sometimes he would simply be there, instinctively knowing that was enough.

He had taken her in after her release. She didn't know how she would have survived otherwise. There were programmes to prepare you for life on the outside: you got moved to a proper house inside the prison walls where you lived like a normal person, cooking and cleaning and going on escorted trips to the shops. She got none of that because her release came suddenly. Her sentence management had always been all over the place, so it was fitting that the end of it should be a shambles too.

Alastair had lost his husband, Tom, only a few months before she got out. At that point, all they had was each other.

When she first came to live with him, that was the only time she thought things might be okay. She was scared and confused by the world she found herself in, but she was with someone she trusted. Someone patient, who had seen first-hand all she had gone through, and who assured her that in time she might find her feet.

'Give it a year,' he had told her. 'The picture will look clearer after that.'

They'd be like one of those strange retired couples, he used to say. People might even think they were married rather than brother and sister.

Then he had died too.

She recalled the reading of Alastair's will, the sense of numbness and unreality as she sat in the solicitor's draughty office.

'He's left you everything,' the solicitor said. Malcolm Gates was his name, a lanky and physically awkward man with a surprisingly soothing manner.

49

He's left you everything. In truth she had been left with nothing. Nothing that mattered. Her lifeline was gone, the last thing connecting her to this world. She had no one left who knew who she used to be, and nobody to miss her if she went too.

Tom's sister Vivian offered her a room at her place, which she shared with her friend Carla. Vivian had been close to Alastair, or at least close enough to Tom to know what it was like to lose your brother. Millicent accepted because she didn't know what else to do.

Alastair had left her the flat, but she was scared to live alone. She wasn't sure she could look after herself. Twenty-four years of not having to cook a meal, organise a budget, run a household, and she'd never been much good at those things back in the day anyway.

Vivian had even helped her let out Alastair's flat because she wasn't ready to sell it.

'It will be a regular income for you,' she had told her. 'You won't need to worry about money.'

Millicent had distantly grasped that this was important, but only in abstract. She hadn't needed to worry about money in decades. She didn't know what anything cost. She couldn't even think of anything she wanted to own.

Give it a year and the picture will be clearer.

She had decided to apply her brother's advice to life with Vivian and Carla. A full year had now passed, and Alastair had been right. The picture was clear.

She had called this morning and made an appointment with Malcolm Gates, in order to make her own will. She felt better already, calmer because she now had a sense of resolution. She was no longer afraid, adrift and purposeless in a world that made no sense; no longer overwhelmed by facing a thousand confusing choices when she had no compass for making everyday decisions. She still found it hard to walk through a bloody door without someone telling her she had permission.

She had seen so many lawyers in her life, and none of them had ever been able to give her what she was hoping for. But Malcolm Gates would. When he formalised her wishes and confirmed her affairs were in order, he would be giving her permission to walk through one last door.

She looked at the make-up kit and vanity case Vivian had made her buy. It was still sitting in a John Lewis bag on the floor since Vivian 'surprised' her by telling her it was actually a gift. She decided she ought to leave it somewhere obvious, next to the receipt, and was placing it on top of her chest of drawers when she heard the doorbell.

She looked at her watch and sighed as she remembered the appointment. Normally she would ignore the doorbell as any callers were usually looking for Vivian or Carla, and accordingly she would leave them to answer. However, she knew who this was and was self-conscious about either of her housemates having any dealings with her. Ideally, she would visit when neither of them was home, but as Viv and Carla effectively constituted one of the woman's tick-boxes, that was unlikely ever to happen.

'It's for me,' she told Carla rather tersely, spotting her emerge inquisitively from the kitchen where she and Viv already had a visitor.

She hurried to the front door and opened it to her social worker, Anne, here on her regular parole-mandated home visit.

'Hello, Millicent,' she said, in the kind of cheery sing-song voice that made Millicent want to put a plastic bag over Anne's head and secure it tightly with a zip-tie. Preferably a transparent bag so that she could see the look on her face as she suffocated. 'And how are we today?' she went on in her breathily infantilising tone.

'Fine,' Millicent replied flatly, showing her through to her bedroom where they wouldn't be seen, though the silly cow would insist on having a moment with the others before she could get rid of her.

'Are you going somewhere?' Anne asked, indicating the suitcase.

Millicent felt momentarily insecure at the notion her intentions might be apparent.

'No, I'm just organising some things. Planning a clear-out.'

'It's just that you need to inform me and receive my prior permission if you intend to travel outside the United Kingdom, the Channel Islands or the Isle of Man.'

Millicent could picture the exact phrasing written down

somewhere, to the letter. She had dealt with people like Anne for decades: a rulebook with shoes. All that had changed on the outside was that sometimes the clipboards had become iPads.

'I know. I'm not going anywhere.'

This wasn't strictly true. She remembered Viv mooting the idea of them going out for dinner to a hotel one night this week, but the furthest they would be going was Knightswood.

She thought of a time when she used to travel, the months at a time she would be out of the country on a job. All these places she would never see again. She felt a twinge of regret at that, but it was like the movies she couldn't bear to watch, the pictures she couldn't bring herself to put up. Nostalgia was a temptation with a hidden sting, and she feared the pain of what she'd lost would be overwhelming.

'Okay, then,' Anne said, glancing at her tablet. 'Let's just run through a few things.'

Anne spoke as though this had just occurred to her. As though it wasn't exactly the same routine every time. They plodded through the prescribed list of questions regarding her conduct, her home environment, how she was spending her days. The assessment was officially of Millicent's welfare, but every tick on Anne's list was for her own satisfaction and peace of mind. Boxes had to be ticked or she couldn't move on to the next page, then the next client.

'Okay, now just in case you are planning a wee trip within the UK, I need you to acknowledge that you are required to provide me with details – such as make, model, colour and registration – of any vehicle you own, hire for more than a short journey or have regular use of, prior to any journey taking place.'

No I bloody don't, she wanted to say, but it was simpler just to nod acknowledgment, because it didn't matter. They had been over this before. There had been a clerical error that erroneously appended this condition to her records. It wasn't applicable because she didn't have a driving licence, as she'd explained to Anne's predecessor, Josie. Josie had confirmed this and remembered it from then on. Anne probably remembered too, but was worried in case the condition had been added legitimately since.

Her first priority, always, was covering her own ample arse.

Millicent could see Anne being what they sometimes referred to in the business as a glory kill. She wasn't someone who would die at the start for a shock to set the tone, or someone you cared about whose death upped the stakes. Rather, she was someone the audience would have limited sympathy with, so there was a perverse sense of pleasure in seeing the ingenuity or spectacle of how the murderer despatched her.

Anne moved on to asking about whether she was having any 'emerging issues' with alcohol and drugs, as these were cited as having been a factor in Millicent's crime. Anne had no need to know about the stockpiles of diazepam and codeine she had been prescribed for, respectively, non-existent muscle spasms and the resultant non-existent back pain. But that wasn't the kind of emerging issue Anne was interested in. There wasn't a box for imminent suicide.

Millicent answered no, with an undisguised tone of impatience. The fact that she had no addiction issues at the time of her offence, and had no record of it throughout a quarter century of incarceration, meant that it was self-evidently ridiculous to suggest she might have suddenly developed a problem now. Josie had grasped this right away and exercised her discretion by only asking the first time. Josie looked at the whole picture, looked at the person, and made her judgment according to that.

Anne, by contrast, insisted on going through the motions at every visit. This was because Anne was just a tubby half-wit. Millicent knew she wasn't supposed to 'body shame', but it was hard to be regularly subject to an exercise in passive-aggressive moral judgment from someone who didn't have the personal fortitude to occasionally say no to a chocolate biscuit.

It was an unacknowledged element of her sentence that she should forever be subject to morons. That was what they should tell kids as a deterrent to ending up on the wrong side of the law: it wasn't just the deprivation of liberty you risked, but the deprivation of dignity. Part of your punishment was that you would permanently be answerable to people for whom the 'not to be taken internally' warnings were written on jars of Vicks Vaporub, in case they spread it on their bloody toast.

There was no deliverance from it after your release either. She had gone to sleep drunk one night in 1994 and woken up in the early hours, into a hellish new world where she would spend the rest of her adult life beneath a tyranny of delegated authority. This world of social workers like Anne, prison guards, police officers; and always floating above it all, playing a game that entailed no personal consequences, were lawyers, lawyers, lawyers.

She could still picture the first one she had to deal with, though she didn't even remember his name. He was the duty solicitor at the police station that night. He looked about fifteen and seemed almost as nervous as she was. She had first met him in the interview room where she had been dumped. She was disoriented, nauseous, hung over, maybe even still drunk and out of it on whatever she had taken throughout the evening.

There was this weird smell in her nostrils too. It turned out to be coming from her hair, which was matted with Markus's blood. She hadn't seen it, or she'd have rinsed it out. She had taken off the T-shirt she wore to bed before the police arrived. That counted against her at the trial, for reasons she still didn't quite follow.

There were tapes and transcripts, which she had pored over at various times down the years, but she had very little memory of it actually happening. Only a few fragments had stuck. One was of listening to her own 999 call.

'I need police. An ambulance. I don't know. Police. I think it's too late for . . . He's dead. I . . . somebody killed him. I just woke up and he's in the bed. You need to get here. I don't know what's happened.'

It was only as she heard her own voice on the tape and wondered why they were playing it that she began to understand what was happening. This quicksand feeling, sinking ever deeper into the realisation of how serious her predicament was. And then somewhere in the midst of it all, there came the dawning awareness that she would never see Markus again.

Markus.

Looking back, if she was being honest with herself, everything didn't change when she woke up in the early hours of that terrible morning. It had changed the first time she laid eyes on him, inside the Petit Carlton bar in Cannes. The first time she felt the spark ignite between them. The first time they kissed. The first time they made love. The first time they argued.

The first time she hit him.

Impressions

Jerry had no idea how old Vivian Montgomerie was, but he was sure that whatever the actual number, she probably looked young for it. She had wiry grey hair with silvery highlights, sculpted to her head in a way that made him think of Roman laurels, and was dressed in a patterned blouse and a pair of loose trousers made of a rich and soft material. He got the impression she was someone who had always been stylish and thus wasn't dressing to look younger; she was just somebody who knew what clothes worked on her and had the money to buy them.

They were seated in a large kitchen, around one of those island affairs in the middle with pots and pans hanging above it from a frame. He was sure it was perfectly safe but it looked distractingly precarious to have so much metal suspended above their heads. The closest thing to that in his gran's house had been the pulley for the washing.

The décor was all very trendy, little of it suggesting old people lived here, with the exception of a folded-up wheelchair in the hall. It clearly didn't belong to either of the women in the kitchen, so it had to be the other one, whom he hadn't yet seen. He wondered just how infirm she was, and what level of help they would be expecting from him.

Vivian was seated directly opposite, her housemate Carla to his left. Carla looked an earth-mother hippy type, with frizzy hair and a port wine birthmark on her cheek. In contrast to Vivian's effortless sartorial elegance, he suspected she might have made her own clothes, the environmental benefits of self-sufficiency and preservation of resources trumping aesthetic considerations.

Not that he was in any position to judge. Determined to make a good impression, he thought he had best wear something other than his usual garb of jeans and a metal T-shirt. That was until a search through his wardrobe confirmed that he didn't own anything other than jeans and metal T-shirts. He had some vague notion that there might be an actual shirt with an actual collar and actual sleeves in there somewhere, but he realised he had been thinking of one his gran bought him for wearing to a wedding. When he was ten. Consequently, the only concession he was able to make to being presentable was choosing the one with the least offensive and intimidating artwork. Turned out to be Darkthrone, the name reassuringly illegible.

Vivian had told him on the phone that the room they were offering was still free and invited him to have a look around whenever suited. She sounded almost amused when he said he could pop round that same afternoon, which made him fear he was coming on too eager. Nonetheless, she had said she was at home, so there was no time like the present.

He kind of expected her to take one swatch at him on the doorstep and tell him the room had just been let, yet here he was, drinking a mug of tea and listening to her lay out the proposed arrangement in detail.

Neither she nor Carla had baulked at the mere prospect of him living here, so he was wondering what the catch was. The place was gorgeous. Why were they so struggling for takers that they were willing to consider him?

'Now, we wouldn't expect you to be at our beck and call, or to be spending every evening together, but it's important you realise that the social element is at the very heart of this,' Vivian said. 'The prospect of living with three old women is not for everybody, so you shouldn't embark upon this just because it sounds like cheap digs. You would need to be committed to the idea, and open to the prospect of having your own perspective and some of your precon-ceptions changed. You need to think very clearly about what you'd be getting into.'

Jerry sipped his tea and nodded. He only had one card to play here, so there was no point fannying about.

'I really don't,' he said, which made Vivian straighten on her stool.

'I was raised by my late grandmother,' he clarified. 'I've lived with an older woman my whole life, so whatever these preconceptions are, I probably don't have them.'

'Well, that's refreshing to hear,' Vivian replied. 'But bear in mind, it's different when it's family. This is three strangers.'

This made Jerry wonder about the absence of the third one. He knew she was home, as he'd overheard a discussion about her having a visitor. It just seemed weird that she hadn't stuck her head around the door. Maybe she would only run the rule over him if he passed the initial interview. Or maybe she was bedridden, he thought, remembering the wheelchair.

'Believe me,' he said, 'if you'd seen the folk I'm sharing with at the moment, you'd understand why I regard this as a major step up in quality.'

Vivian smiled indulgently. She seemed friendly, but there was a seriousness beneath it that said, *don't try to fuck me about.*

'I was a lecturer here for thirty years. I know what students are like. Flatmates can fall out, but they can make up too. Especially when they find they're missing out on the social scene.'

'I don't have flatmates as such. I'm in halls, and there's nothing I'm worried about missing out on. The reason I called was that I don't feel like I fit in there. I could do with concentrating on my studies anyway.'

He could tell this was the right line. Vivian seemed satisfied by his response, if still a little wary. He wondered if they'd had others who didn't work out, bailing after a week or whatever.

'Just as long as you're clear that we can't be having parties or late-night comings and goings,' said Carla.

'I do have to work late shifts sometimes,' he admitted, suddenly fearing his chances were in the balance. 'At the Phonecia on Gibson Street. Is that going to be a problem?'

He had calculated that if he got this room, the drop in rent would mean he could cut back on his hours, and despite what he'd told Karima, he knew Aldo at the takeaway would be fine with this as long as he was still free to work the busy Friday and Saturday nights.

The Catch 22 was, if he couldn't work then, he couldn't afford to live here.

'As long as it's just you that's coming home, it won't be an issue,' Vivian told him.

'The Phonecia,' said Carla, curious, 'is that a vegetarian place?'

'No. I mean, they do falafel and a few other veggie options, but there's meat.'

'Are you a vegetarian?' she asked, in a cheery way that suggested she'd be delighted if he said yes, while leaving him in no doubt that any other answer would be the wrong one.

'Eh, no,' he answered, wondering if this was the moment it all fell through. No point in lying, though. It might be worse if he got found out later. 'Is that a deal-breaker?'

'Not at all,' she replied, though her smile was now shot through with disappointment. 'It just has ramifications for the menu.'

'I'm happy to go along with whatever's on offer,' Jerry assured them both. 'And I'll cook veggie for everybody if that keeps things simpler.'

'That's very obliging, but we won't be making any unnecessary stipulations,' said Vivian. 'If you decide you want to stay here, we will endeavour to make sure it works for everybody. We don't want to put any obstacles in the way.'

'Oh, I definitely want to stay. As long as you're happy to have me.'

They both smiled.

It was starting to look good, but Jerry was aware they still hadn't addressed the main thing that he thought would count against him.

'To be honest, it doesn't say so on the flyer, but reading between the lines I kind of thought you might be looking for a girl.'

There was a pause, Vivian and Carla glancing at each other.

'I admit I envisaged it being a young woman,' Vivian said. 'And certainly I assumed it would more likely be young women who responded, but we haven't had any takers so far.'

'That's lucky for me,' he replied. 'Surprising too. I'd have thought somebody would have piled in right away. How long has the ad been up?'

Vivian and Carla shared another look. Something passed unspoken.

'It's been a while,' Vivian replied. 'Not everybody is as relaxed as you about the prospect of living with three old ladies.'

Now Carla was looking at Vivian, but Vivian wasn't meeting her eye.

'I mean, we've had some interest,' Vivian went on, 'but nobody who followed it up.'

Carla sighed.

'Oh, for God's sake, Viv. Full disclosure. He's going to meet her at some point anyway.'

Carla turned to Jerry.

'It's not the prospect of living with three old women. It's one in particular. They didn't follow up because they met Millicent, our other housemate.'

'Is she the one in the wheelchair?' he asked, wondering if his predecessors had baulked at nursing duties.

'She's not in a wheelchair,' Vivian said, puzzled. Then something occurred to her. 'Oh, you mean the one in the hall. No, that's left over from when I broke my ankle skiing.'

This came as a relief, though clearly the third housemate was a problem for other reasons.

'Anyway, Carla is making an unfair extrapolation,' Vivian said, not sounding like she quite believed herself.

'Oh, come on. We had two perfectly eager girls come and look at the place. On each occasion she was horribly rude to them and they both decided they didn't fancy laying themselves open to that on a daily basis.'

Vivian conceded the point with a regretful smile.

'I would admit Millicent can be a bit of a handful. And I've just realised how it must look that she's not here right now, but it's not that we've kept her out of the picture deliberately. It just so happened she's got her . . . a visit this afternoon.'

'Rude?' Jerry asked, thinking of the level of interpersonal etiquette he was used to from the likes of Rossco.

'She can be a little brusque, but she always apologises later.'

'That's true,' added Carla. 'She always apologises, then she often says something worse shortly after that.'

'She's had a difficult life,' Vivian said quietly. It had the ring of an excuse that she knew was wearing thin.

There was little question that Jerry had just found the catch, the reason this berth was still open. He wondered how horrible this Millicent woman would need to be before the halls looked a better prospect. Could she be worse than putting up with Danby?

'It's only right that you appreciate this arrangement won't be without its challenges,' Vivian said, which was less than reassuring. 'The fact is, my thinking in offering this room was that I don't want us to become insular old women. I want us to expose ourselves to a different, younger perspective. And I thought, in particular, that Millicent might benefit from that. She is someone who, for reasons outwith her control, has become a little closed off to the idea of new possibilities.'

This set off alarms.

'Just to be clear,' Jerry said. 'Would one of those be the possibility that folk can be a colour other than white?'

Carla failed to stifle a laugh.

'No. She's not without her peccadilloes, but that's not one of them. Millicent doesn't need racism in order to be offensive.'

'Carla,' Vivian chided.

'To be fair, she's been in a better frame of mind the past day or so,' Carla conceded. 'She seems more settled somehow, less anxious. So maybe she . . .'

Carla cut herself off as they all heard a door close out in the hall, followed by approaching footsteps on the parquet floor.

'Drumroll,' Carla whispered, a fraction before the kitchen door opened.

A tall and thin woman entered, dressed in a black polo neck and black jeans. Jerry thought of his gran saying there was an upper age limit for jeans. She had never specified what it was, but Millicent looked well past it. He got an Eighties or Nineties vibe about her look, giving the impression she was dressing the same way she had done for decades.

She was slightly bowed in her posture, and together with all that black, he initially thought she looked like the Slenderman's mum.

Then he noticed how she shrank against the wall, like she was self-conscious about her height. Or maybe trying to present the smallest possible target.

There was something hunted and timid about her, which was hard to square with the descriptions he had just heard. But he'd heard similar things said about him when he was a kid. When you were the only brown face in the playground, you learned ways to minimise your profile. You also learned what to do when that didn't work. The words 'dangerous when cornered' popped into his head. Forewarned is forearmed.

She was accompanied by a chubby woman with a council ID pinned to her badged blue polo shirt, visible beneath an unzipped matching bodywarmer. Jerry clocked her for a social worker, and could have done it without the logos. He had seen a few in his time. He remembered them coming round the house when he was wee, Gran getting uptight, tidying and cleaning. Gran telling lies about the hours she worked at the video store. Telling him not to mention how he went there with her 'in case they take you away'. That was the scariest thing in the world, and though nothing like it ever came to pass, the sight of a social worker still provoked an instinctive anxiety.

'Jerry, this is Millicent and . . . Anne,' said Vivian. Her reluctance to give any further context confirmed his impression, but it also made him curious. Millicent didn't look like the kind of old lady who needed a social worker. She didn't appear to be infirm, though not all disabilities were visible, as the posters said.

She's had a difficult life.

What did that mean? His first thought was domestic abuse. That might explain a lot.

Anne was regarding him with undisguised curiosity, like she was afraid he was about to be a problem. It was a look he was used to. Millicent by contrast gave him a quick glance then looked away like he was of limited relevance. Not a promising start.

'Anne just needs to take a nosey around,' Millicent stated in a weary tone of strained patience. She clearly wanted Anne to GTF as soon as. He wondered if he'd be next.

'This is Jerry, Millicent,' said Vivian. 'He is interested in coming to stay with us.'

Anne's expression of concern deepened. Vivian appeared to notice and offered an explanation.

'I read about similar arrangements whereby people like ourselves offer cheap accommodation to students, and they in return spend some social time and help out with us. It's so that we don't become isolated from the emerging generations, nor them from us.'

Vivian spoke with the sort of warmth and enthusiasm that he imagined she had used to sell the idea to her housemates. Jerry assumed it worked better on them than it did on Anne.

'I will need to look into this,' she said. 'If there's a change of domestic circumstances, there might—'

'You don't have to look into anything,' Millicent interrupted. 'It would only be an issue if he was a criminal.' She looked directly at Jerry.

'Are you a criminal?'

Jerry was startled by the directness of the question, not least because it sounded like a genuine inquiry rather than a rhetorical one. He became conscious that he was taking just a wee bit too long to answer, concerned about what they might infer from that. He knew the longer it went on, the better his eventual response would need to sound. Ironically, the truth came to his rescue.

'Well, I havenae been caught yet, so not officially.'

Vivian and Carla laughed. Anne retained her expression of worried gormlessness.

'So, as you can see, everything is just exactly as it all was the last time,' Millicent said with laboured emphasis.

'But it won't be if there is a change to the make-up of the household,' Anne countered. 'I'll need to look into it.'

'You do that,' said Millicent. 'Anne's just looking out for all our welfare with a bit of due diligence,' she told the room. 'I mean, it wouldn't do for her to knowingly let people share a house with someone who might murder them in their beds.'

There was a look of dismay on Anne's face, disproportionate to Millicent's remark.

'I don't think that's appropriate,' said Carla.

'Oh, lighten up, Carla, it was just a joke.'

One Jerry didn't get. Was she saying he looked like a killer? Good thing he never wore the Mortician T-shirt.

Millicent addressed him again, nodding to her housemate.

'Has she asked if you're a vegetarian yet?'

Jerry decided it would be wise not to respond. He was getting a glimpse of the politics he would be stepping into. He was also getting a glimpse of the cornered creature baring her claws.

She glanced at his chest. He sensed disapproval.

'What does that even say?'

'Darkthrone.'

'Which is what? A horror film?'

'A band.'

She wrinkled her nose.

Millicent went to the door and held it open, an unmistakable gesture towards her visitor.

'Anne and I are just going to go back through and finish up. Anne's still got a few more boxes to tick, haven't you, dear?'

Vivian and Carla bade Anne a polite goodbye. Jerry wasn't sure how it would be appropriate to respond and so said nothing.

'You're seriously planning to live here?' Millicent asked him. 'Now that you've met all of us, I mean?'

'I think so.'

She nodded, like she was weighing something up. He wondered if they each had a veto and she was about to bring hers down on him.

'Vivian will be happy,' she said, which sounded ostensibly positive until he decoded the unspoken implication. 'There were a couple of inquiries before, both girls. Delicate types. Neither of them seemed to have much of a sense of humour. I'm assuming you are more robust about such matters.'

Jerry decided the best response was to meet her head-on.

'I guess we'll find out. Maybe you and me can talk some more once you're done with your parole officer.'

The mood in the room changed instantly. It was an utter

record-scratch moment. If somebody had been pouring tea, they'd have overflowed the mug. What the fuck had he just said?

It was Anne who broke the silence, mainly because she didn't seem to be tuned to the same energy as everyone else.

'We don't actually have parole officers in Scotland. We have mandated social work visits.'

She hadn't finished saying this before he put it together.

A difficult life.

. . . she's got her . . . a visit this afternoon.

All the awkwardness. A matter everybody had to tiptoe delicately around, and he had just tramped it through the carpet.

Anne *was* her parole officer.

He glanced around this showroom kitchen, the heart of this beautiful house where he would not now be living. He had utterly Hibsed it.

Vivian was looking towards Millicent. Jerry sensed the veto hammer was coming down here and now.

'Oh, *you* can stay,' Millicent said, a wee smirk on her chops. 'You must stay.'

History

'Is there anything you guys want to tell me?' Jerry asked, once the door was closed and he estimated Millicent to be beyond earshot. 'Anything it might be helpful for me to know?'

Vivian looked a wee bit flushed. Carla, meanwhile, had an air of vindication about her. She'd obviously gotten over being exposed by the vegetarianism question, and Jerry hoped it had put him in credit that he had taken the fifth.

'Millicent was released from prison a little over a year ago,' Vivian said. 'When she first got out, she went to live with her brother, Alastair, but he died shortly after. He was married to my late brother, Tom. When Alastair died, Millicent had nobody. She was unused to looking after herself. We took her in.'

'It was the decent thing to do,' Carla said. Jerry wondered if she was still trying to convince herself it was the right thing to do, as it had clearly been Vivian's idea. But either way, Carla had gone along with it, so props to her.

'What was she in for?'

Carla bit her bottom lip.

'It's not regarded as polite or appropriate to talk about that,' Vivian said. 'I don't just mean among us, but apparently that's the case inside too.'

'Nobody likes to be defined by the thing they're most ashamed of,' said Carla.

Jerry saw that freeze-frame moment again. Pictured the man's face, saw his own fear reflected back in his anguished expression.

'You said she was unused to looking after herself, but. I mean, how long was she in for?'

Even as he spoke, he sussed both the answer and its implications. 'Long enough,' Vivian replied.

'So, when she said that about living with someone who might murder you, am I on the right track in sussing why you found it inappropriate?'

'Like I said, it's not regarded as polite to intrude.'

Carla sighed.

'Oh, come on, Viv. He'll google it as soon as he's alone.'

'I don't doubt it,' Vivian told him. 'But you won't find much. The news coverage predates digital media. Well, I suppose you might find some stuff on the campaign and you can follow the trail from there, but I would remind you at this point that it's still in your gift to respect Millicent's privacy.'

Jerry liked how she put that. Maybe it would be easier not to know. And maybe it would be easier for Millicent if she knew he didn't know. But how could she be sure? And wouldn't she assume he'd found out? Maybe not, if she wasn't familiar with standard Gen Z behaviour.

While his conscience wrestled with his future conduct, his mind took a moment to grasp the significance of something else Vivian had said.

'A campaign? Did she claim she didn't do it? Was there a miscarriage of justice?'

Vivian wore a pained expression, like she was regretful she couldn't answer differently.

'She maintained her innocence . . . until she didn't. Or, at least, maintained a different kind of innocence. From claiming she didn't do it to claiming self-defence. It was all a bit of a mess, and her story was damagingly inconsistent.'

'She was convicted of murdering her boyfriend,' said Carla. She gave Vivian a so-sue-me shrug. 'It happened down in London, back in the early Nineties. She continued to deny it, said she woke up and found him dead. She maintained that for years. But the boyfriend had been abusive, and the case was taken up much later by campaigners arguing it should be ruled self-defence. Because the guy had been killed while he slept, as opposed to in the heat of the moment, campaigners were trying to use the case to make the authorities see that sometimes that can be the only option for self-defence if you're a woman who feels trapped and afraid.'

'Except that Millicent wouldn't cooperate,' added Vivian. 'For a long time, she still claimed she wasn't the one who killed him. And then a few years ago she backtracked. She finally she admitted she did it, while maintaining her innocence now on the grounds of self-defence. Unfortunately, changing her story so late in the day wasn't a very convincing look. Years of saying she didn't remember anything, then suddenly, following pressure from campaigners, claiming her crime was a premeditated act of desperation. As I said, it was a mess. But maintaining her innocence was why she ended up serving such a long sentence.'

'I thought that admission of guilt wasn't a condition for parole,' Jerry said. 'I take it that's bollocks?'

Carla scoffed.

'If you look at the stats, it's funny how people who maintain their innocence tend to find it harder to get parole than those who admit guilt. But this is more Viv's area. She taught law.'

'It's built into the bureaucracy,' Vivian said. 'Part of parole eligibility requires the prisoner to have completed certain programmes, but these programmes require an initial analysis of offence as a condition of participation, which renders prisoners maintaining their innocence ineligible. An effect of this is that not only does it hinder parole, but prisoners sometimes end up serving many more years than the minimum tariff set by the judge. Which is what happened to Millicent.'

'Jesus,' he said. 'A difficult life right enough.'

'That's why we have to make certain allowances for her, and you'll have to be ready for that if you want to live here. She is still undergoing a period of adjustment and can be confused by certain elements of modern life that we deal with as second nature. She can be somewhat unto herself and a little prickly when she feels threatened. But it's important to stress that she's not dangerous.'

'That's okay,' Jerry said. 'I think I could take her.'

Vivian smiled.

'In that case, the room is yours if you want it. You can move in as soon as you like.'

'Fantastic. Seriously, this is a life-saver.'

'Delighted to hear it. Now, before we draw up an agreement, do you have any more questions?'

Jerry did, but it was one only Millicent could answer.

Why would anyone maintain their own innocence for so long if that was the price?

Better Days

Lucio glided around the decks, radiating with the energy of the occasion. He moved from group to group, greeting everyone with smiles and embraces, some of them even genuine. Lucio had reason to smile, and there were people here he wanted close, albeit for a divergence of reasons: in some cases because they were friends, and in others because it meant he wasn't showing the motherfuckers his back.

He had thought about standing at the stern as his guests arrived off the gangway, but decided it looked better to delegate that: willing girls who wanted to make an impression, offering drinks and whatever else people might desire. It was someone else's job to welcome people on board. It was Lucio's role to remind them why they had come.

Produzzioni Sabatini always had a visible presence at Cannes, but this year, 1993, everything was going up a level. This wasn't even an official party. Those would be bigger: loud and buzzy occasions for schmoozing and networking, for making the first moves that would ultimately reel in the deals. Tonight was an intimate gathering of those who had played a part in making things happen so far, and those who were about to join for the next phase.

The Eighties had been good to Lucio. Shelves had needed to be filled in a million video rental stores around the globe, and for a few glorious years, it seemed you could sell anything as long as it featured what Stacey Golding called the three Bs: bangs, blood and boobs. But now the game was changing, and you had to stay ahead of it.

For the first time, Lucio would be making movies with an eye on theatrical release, because having his titles debut in cinemas was not only a revenue stream, it was a marketing tactic. A theatrical release was a status symbol, a hallmark of quality that pushed up the price of all ancillary rights. You could still sell *Kickboxing Commando Three* to a video distributor, but they'd be paying peanuts for it. If you wanted your movie on Sky, Star and Canal Plus, it needed prestige, it needed a pedigree. That didn't come cheap, but Lucio's ambition, allied to his track record, had attracted major investment. Credit Populaire de Paris had come in at just the right time, backing his six-picture production slate to the tune of eighty million dollars.

Lucio was hailed with a wave by Alessandro Salerno, who was sitting at a banquette next to Millie Spark. Millie was necking champagne and nibbling smoked salmon, while Alessandro was contentedly sipping single malt Scotch and familiarly chewing on an unlit cigar.

Lucio kissed Millie's hand, then Alessandro stood up to greet him, pulling him into a hug. There was genuine warmth there, mutual affection and respect.

Alessandro had been an acclaimed *giallo* director throughout the Sixties, his classic *Black Gloves and White Lace* remaining one of the most iconic and influential works of the genre. His style was imitated to the point of parody, and by the mid-Seventies, with *gialli* falling out of fashion, he was yesterday's man, reduced to directing episodes of a cop show for RAI Uno.

Lucio had given him a new lease of life, directing straight-to-video thrillers for Produzzioni Sabatini. Alessandro knew how to churn out product and still make it look polished no matter how tight the budget or the shooting schedule.

To the critics, working for Lucio was regarded as an admission that Alessandro's days as a serious director were over. The phrase most often used was 'prostituting his talent', but fuck those guys. Those assholes knew nothing about talent, or even about prostitution. They thought that because an artist became a whore to pay the rent, they ceased to be an artist. Lucio saw it otherwise. Someone prepared to be a whore just so that he could keep practising his craft: that was the kind of artist he admired.

He never even understood why 'whore' was an insult. Everybody's selling something. If you're not selling, you're not contributing. That was why he could respect the lowest prostitute more than the highest priest, and definitely more than any fucking critic.

It was one of the best parts of the Credit Populaire deal, that he could reward Alessandro for his loyalty by showing him some in return. It excited him not just as a producer, but as a fan. The man could frame a shot, could generate tension and atmosphere no matter what material he was working with. Now Lucio was in the position to give him the budget and the scope that would truly showcase his talent.

'This looks cosily conspiratorial,' Lucio said. 'So what are you guys talking about?'

'Monsters,' said Millie.

'Spielberg has just shot a movie about dinosaurs, using computer effects,' said Alessandro. 'It's changing the game. Creature features are going to be the province of blockbusters from now on. You can't compete with that using scale effects and stop motion or a guy done up in latex and a rubber suit. I'm suggesting Millie stick with guys like me, so she can keep making a living from spurting knife wounds and bullet holes.'

'I'll reserve judgment until I've seen it,' Millie replied. 'But don't knock latex and rubber. For my money, to this day nobody has done anything more jaw-dropping than Rob Bottin in *The Thing*, and that was thirteen years ago.'

As she spoke, Lucio became aware of the approaching figure of Alfie Bertrand, his arm around the waist of a girl he vaguely recognised. Her name was Monique something, from Napoli. He had cast her in *Zombie Ferox 3* in a role that had more nude scenes than lines, which had ensured she played to her strengths.

As Alfie caught Lucio's eye, he released his arm from the girl so that he could hold his hands wide in greeting.

'Signor Sabatini, what a magnificent soiree. Thank you for the kind invitation.'

Alfie was smoothly spoken, his sharp eyes belied by boyish, playful features. He had an easy charm which Lucio enjoyed but was not seduced by. Watching him work a room was much like how he imagined Millie would feel watching someone else's special effects on-screen: appreciative of the craft, but once you know how it's done, you can't help seeing through the illusion.

Lucio pulled him into an embrace.

'I almost didn't recognise you without your security guys. Did you give them the night off?'

'No, but I did give them the slip. I don't recall seeing their names on the invitation and frankly one cannot enjoy Cannes to the full if one is to be chaperoned the whole time.'

'I'm glad you could make it.'

'I'm honoured, Lucio. And I'm excited by what I've been reading about your slate. If you want to shoot in England, we would be happy to offer whatever support we can. I've got a chap looking into what tax breaks we can organise.'

'That's a conversation for another time, my friend. Tonight is for celebration.'

Lucio turned to the two guests at the table.

'Alessandro and Millie, this is Alfie Bertrand, who is the English Culture minister.'

Lucio did not introduce Monique. She hung back when Alfie released his grip on her, obediently fading into the background. The girls knew not to be pushy, though she did give Lucio a look of irritation at the slight, suggesting she was worth more than this. She knew the deal, though. Monique would be making herself fully available to Alfie tonight. This was a business for whores. In many languages, the words for actress and for prostitute were the same, but it wasn't simply about selling yourself for sex. In Monique's case, sex was what she sold to get something else she wanted. Lucio was paying her more tonight than she got for a week's work on *Zombie Ferox 3*, but it was the prospect of being in another movie, rather than the money, that was motivating her to comply.

'Junior minister,' Alfie corrected, shaking hands. 'Our Culture Secretary is Peter Brooke. Anyway, it's an honour to meet you both.'

'Are you sure about that?' asked Millie, a combination of archness and mischief in her voice.

'Why wouldn't it be?' Alfie replied. He was smiling but puzzled, and a little wary. A good politician senses an ambush.

'Because your government banned one of Alessandro's films and two of mine. They were on the infamous 'video nasty' list. I thought we were purveyors of depraved filth, according to your colleague Graham Bright.'

Alessandro affected a look of offence, but Lucio recognised the sparkle in his eye, enjoying the sport.

'*We know no spectacle so ridiculous as the British public in one of its periodical fits of morality*,' Alfie replied, deploying his warm smile and easy charm to ease the tension. 'So said Lord Macaulay in 1830, and I imagine the same was true one hundred and fifty years later. However, Mr Bright was not my colleague. I was only elected last year. I was at Oxford at the time of the video nasty panic, and probably watching those very movies on pirate Betamax.'

'That's as may be, but I don't recall any change in policy since then. Our films are still banned.'

'And that's why I'm aware we have work to do in restoring trust. My job is to make it easier for films to get made in the UK. And I admit, there will still be MPs who make a name for themselves railing against 'depraved filth', but that's politics. It's not hypocrisy, it's just different people in the same party who are working to different agendas. It's a bit like the newspapers that were so vociferous on this issue. The front-page headlines might be condemning a movie as morally corrupt, but elsewhere in the same edition, the film critic is giving it five stars.'

'And would you give my movie five stars? The one your government banned?' Alessandro asked, that glint still in his eye.

'He can't answer that,' Millie added, relishing Alfie's discomfort. 'He hasn't seen it. He doesn't even know its name.'

'*Blood Ceremony*?' Alfie replied. 'I've seen it twice. And I'd give it four stars. It's good, but not Signor Salerno's best. *Black Gloves and White Lace*, now that's a five-star movie.'

Alessandro held up his whisky glass and chimed it against Alfie's champagne flute. Millie clinked hers too, gesturing touché.

Last Supper

'. . . and the chef has just added a special of scallops, chorizo and black pudding served with a whisky crème sauce and a selection of seasonal vegetables.'

The waitress said this with a level of surprise and delight that Millicent would have considered more appropriate to announcing that the chef had just concocted a cure for cancer and would presumably be serving it with a jus of world peace and a foam of nuclear fusion. The girl was fresh-faced and boisterously youthful, a natural glow about her skin to match the radiant enthusiasm of her manner. She was someone who had her whole life ahead of her, and though a part of Millicent wished her the best, to her tired ears these days optimistic good cheer just sounded like high-pitched shrieking.

She remembered the first time she had chorizo, back in the late 1980s, how exotic it had seemed. Tapas bars had begun springing up across London, all of them playing the Gypsy Kings on the stereo and selling people San Miguel for ten times what they'd pay for it on holiday in Benidorm.

Chorizo had been one of the things she pined for when she was inside. Now that it was available to her, it meant nothing. Just a substance, a flavour. She wouldn't be ordering it. It could be the finest chorizo on Earth, but it wouldn't taste like it did in 1994 before everything fell apart.

They were seated in the brasserie part of the Roman Fort Hotel, a big place on Great Western Road that had clearly had a lot of money spent on it very recently. There was still a faint smell of gloss paint in the lobby. She wondered what it had looked like twenty-five years ago, and how bad it had got before someone decided to revive its fortunes. You could do that with a building, even if you had to rip the guts out. You could erase all the wear and damage, restore the soul of the place, ready it for a whole new chapter.

The student was sitting to her right, dramatically bringing down the table's average age while paradoxically making them all feel older. He had moved in with unseemly haste, obviously in a hurry to get away from whoever he'd been living with before. There was bad blood there, and no mistake. You didn't bail that fast to throw your lot in with three old ladies just because there was a dripping tap or you didn't like the décor in your old place.

Vivian had been planning this dinner for a week or so, but she invited the student along to celebrate his joining the household. He had seemed a little apprehensive when she told him the venue, but more reassured once Vivian had made it clear it would be her treat.

This would be Millicent's last meal, so it seemed fitting there should be a sense of occasion about it, even if nobody else at the table realised its significance. She used to wonder whether giving a condemned prisoner a final meal was a grace or a cruelty, whether it was right to grant them such an essential reminder of the life they were losing. But as she perused the menu, her only consideration was whether one was supposed to consume these pills after eating or on an empty stomach. She didn't suppose it mattered as it wasn't as though she was taking them for their prescribed medicinal bene-fits. But equally, she didn't want to make herself vomit, having ingested only a partial dose. She could end up hospitalised, with a lot of awkward explaining to do. She wondered what the parole implications were if she was sectioned.

She decided she would order the veal, mainly because it was the item on the menu guaranteed to most offend Carla.

'And you're studying film and television, or did I misremember?' asked Vivian.

'No, you remembered fine.'

'And what kind of thing are you covering this term?'

He looked uncomfortable to be put on the spot.

'Eh, stuff like social responsibility versus freedom of expression, that kind of thing.'

Millicent endured a brief moment of concern that Vivian or Carla might bring her into the conversation, but it was purely instinctual. Neither of them ever gave any indication that they knew what she had done for a living. At most, Vivian had picked up that it was something to do with make-up, but clearly she and her brother Tom had never discussed it.

In a way it pleasantly surprised her, as it proved that neither of her housemates had gone rooting for contemporary coverage of her trial. Vivian had once said something about respecting her privacy, but Millicent always half-assumed it was mere lip service. And in Carla's case, she just assumed she wasn't interested.

'I always think it's exciting when I hear young people taking an interest in the arts,' said Carla. 'It's a relief to know they're not all just hypnotised by their phone screens. There's nothing more vital than free expression, uncensored and unrestrained.'

The student looked faintly uncomfortable at the gushiness of this. He was yet to learn that Carla's enthusiasm usually had a prescriptive agenda. If she was talking something up, it was usually a pretext for disapproving of something else.

Millicent had seen his full name written down on the tenancy agreement and been surprised to observe that it was Jerome, not Gerard. Listening to his accent, she wondered how that had gone down throughout his childhood. He didn't sound like there would have been a lot of other Jeromes in his class. No wonder he was calling himself Jerry. She liked it though, and began thinking of him thus.

He was dark-skinned but his ethnicity was difficult to determine, and certainly not something she would ask (though if she waited long enough, Carla would, making a thing of not making a thing of it). Millicent would have pegged it as being somewhere south of the Med, north of the Sahara, but couldn't say closer than that. Certainly his surname, Kelly, wasn't giving anything away. It was all by the by, because in every practical respect he was about as exotic as a Hovis loaf. He had lived his whole life in small-town Scotland and dressed exclusively in heavy metal T-shirts, in her experience the whitest form of music known to man. Happily, his consumption of it had been entirely via his earphones. Nobody had a hi-fi anymore, it seemed.

Vivian seemed delighted that she had finally found someone to partake in this inter-generational notion of hers. She said it would be good for all of them to be exposed to a more youthful perspective on things, but Millicent suspected it was as much about changing the chemistry of the household, diluting the corrosive effect of Millicent by adding another personality to the mix.

Vivian had not imposed this project upon them by fiat. She had made it clear that it would only go ahead if everyone was comfortable with it. However, she had prefaced this with a talk about how this was a household that had always been open to change. This was Viv's way of subtly reminding Millicent of her and Carla's generosity in taking her in. She suspected Vivian had pulled a similar guilt trip on Carla to make that happen too.

Millicent had thus consented but would admit she hadn't exactly rolled out the red carpet. Carla maintained that her rudeness scared off the first two applicants, but the way she saw it, she had done everybody a favour. If they bolted simply because she had been lippy, then they were never serious in the first place, and had no concept of what the reality of living here would entail.

Jerome, by contrast, seemed utterly unfazed. She had no intention of making things difficult for him, as he wasn't going to be her problem. She had already settled on her plan by the time he pitched up, and she thought it would help the household to move on if her departure was to coincide with the arrival of someone new. Cycle of life and all that.

As they ate, Vivian and Carla continued to quiz him politely, but Millicent was only half-listening to his answers. There seemed little point in getting to know him, and she had even less desire that he should try to get to know her, as there was only ever one aspect of her life that people were interested in. She resented how it defined her. No matter their intentions, it was always there as a background hum, an unspoken context of all discussion. Even for those who believed her story, it was still the only story they saw.

She had heard it said that no matter how troubled a child's

upbringing, if one person sees them for who they can be, that changes everything. Unfortunately, the corollary was that as an adult, when you are not seen for who you are, your sense of self begins to diminish, until you feel that you're fading out of existence.

Nobody had seen Millicent Spark for twenty-five years. She was barely here anymore, and once she was gone, she would not be missed.

'I'm intrigued by your T-shirt,' Vivian said. 'I'm assuming it's a rock band. Meshuggah is Yiddish for crazy, isn't it?'

The image was an arresting mixture of the futuristic and the gothic, showing a human figure enveloped in metallic serpentine coils. It made Millicent think of *Tetsuo*.

'Aye, but the band are from Sweden. I saw them at the Academy last year. Think my ears are still ringing. They put on some show.'

Carla gave a familiar strained smile, her signature means of looking friendly whilst launching a criticism.

'It's just a shame there's such an environmental cost to these bands travelling from country to country all the time, taking so many planes, and all the diesel-guzzling trucks they must use to transport their equipment. Of course, who wants to be thinking about that when you're at a show.'

'I'm certain someone of Jerry's generation doesn't need lectures on environmental awareness,' Vivian chided gently.

'Sure, sure,' Carla conceded. 'But while everybody is conscious of the big issues, it's the million things we don't think about that have the most impact. Did you know that the clothing industry is a bigger threat than the fossil fuel industry, for instance? Nobody thinks about how many thousands of gallons of water are required just to make that one T-shirt, for example.'

'It was probably raining when he bought it, if that helps,' Vivian replied.

She and Carla exchanged a look, one that had years of complexity to it. Carla bit back frustration at being managed, while there was a weariness behind Vivian's defusing humour.

When she first moved in, Millicent had wondered whether the two of them were an item, as they had something of an old married couple feel about them, but she had learned otherwise. Millicent thought Vivian might be seeing a man, though she couldn't be sure as she was fastidiously discreet about it. However, she knew for a fact that Vivian had never married.

It turned out Carla had come to live with Vivian after getting divorced. The pair of them were very old friends, going all the way back to university in the Sixties and renewing their companionship in retirement. It bothered Millicent that her presence must be an ongoing strain on their relationship. Another reason her plan was for the best, for everybody.

Vivian was one of life's truly good people, perhaps the kindest Millicent had ever known. It weighed heavily that she was about to make a further imposition upon her. She hoped that Vivian would understand. She was particularly concerned that Vivian might think there was more she could have done, which was why Millicent had addressed that explicitly in the letter she was leaving.

In the meantime, all she could do was minimise the practical inconveniences.

'I've left a box in the hall,' Millicent said, her only contribution to the conversation so far. 'It's for the dump, but I wasn't sure how to go about getting it there.'

In truth, she just wanted them to know everything in it could be binned when they came to deal with her belongings. It wasn't as though she could leave it to anybody, as it was all worthless.

'You can organise an uplift online,' Carla said. 'I'll show you.'

'What's in it?' asked Vivian.

'Just old videotapes. Stuff from Alastair's place. I don't even have a VCR, so there's no point keeping them.'

Jerome raised his head from his food.

'I've got an old VHS player in my room you could borrow. Or I could connect it to the laptop and convert the tapes to DVD or mp4 if you want. Keep the films but save the storage space.'

'That's very kind, but there's no need. I don't think I could bring myself to watch them.'

Even back at Alastair's place, she had never been tempted. She feared it would be like watching old footage of a friend who was dead, except in this case the friend was her younger self.

'It's mostly horror films,' she added, wondering why she was volunteering this detail. She could have just said 'old tapes' and left it at that. Something in her suspected Carla would disapprove, and she had a contrary urge to feed that.

She did not disappoint.

'I know what you mean. No offence to your late brother, but I don't know how anyone could bring themselves to watch that stuff. Worse than pornography, nothing but a celebration of violence against women. Back in the day, we used to call them video nasties. They ended up getting banned, and for once that was quite right. I don't hold with censorship when it comes to the arts, but nobody could claim that such trash was art.'

'To be fair, a lot of material written off as pulp ends up being valued in retrospect,' said Jerome. 'Film noir, for instance.'

He was being polite, making his point without responding head-on. Presumably he knew it was a fight he couldn't win, so why lose credit with Carla over it? And yet he had felt the need to take her on. Millicent's instincts told her he was a gore-hound.

'Yes, but film noir movies were about complex human emotions, designed as acceptable mainstream entertainment,' Carla countered. 'Video nasties were designed to appeal to . . . well, actually, you have to ask yourself what kind of sick mind derives gratification from seeing people being butchered.'

Carla was no longer worried about giving offence to Alastair's memory, while ploughing on with her wrong assumption about who the videos belonged to.

'And you also have to wonder what kind of individuals would make such irresponsible material, prostituting their craft with no thought to the effect it was going to have on the minds of the people who watched it.'

Millicent didn't have the will to tell Carla she was ignorant and full of shit. She didn't have the will to engage, full stop. There was so much she could get into on this, but it just hurt to go there. What did it matter anyway? Millicent had lost every battle she'd ever fought, so there was no value in being drawn into a skirmish over something she no longer cared about.

Nonetheless, once again she found that her impulses had other ideas.

'You'll have to forgive Carla's circumlocution,' she told Jerome. 'Let me cut through the fog and say that the real root of her disapproval of such films is that people derive pleasure from them.'

'I said no such thing. But if people are deriving pleasure from watching women being—'

'Are you familiar with the Sex Pistols?' Millicent interrupted, addressing Jerome. 'Never trust a hippy. John Lydon said that. Wise words.'

Carla stood up.

'I've had enough. I'm not going to be spoken to like that.'

'Take a seat, Carla,' said Vivian with a sigh, her tone more stern than ameliorative. 'Calm down. There's no need for anybody to take the huff, we're all just talking.'

Conscious that she was drawing eyes from around the room, not least the staff, Carla sat down again, but she wasn't done.

'Easy for you to say. You're not the one being impugned and insulted. You always take her side and you always make excuses for her. It's never her having to complain that I'm the one being rude.'

This was true. This was all true. Carla didn't deserve to be putting up with Millicent; Vivian even less.

'I apologise,' Millicent said, getting to her feet.

'Now where are *you* going?' Vivian asked in exasperation.

'I'm going to absent myself for a minute by way of penitence. Get myself some air.'

Vivian waved a hand as if to say 'whatever'.

Memento

Millicent strode into the hotel lobby driven by an unexpected rush of purpose. It hadn't been her intention, but she had created the perfect opportunity, a final exit with a sense of theatre. They would not follow her, would not look for her if she didn't return to the table. Someone on the staff would say they saw her leave the building. The others would finish their meal, assuming she had gone home, and they would be right. Perhaps when they got back to the house and there was no answer from her door, they would assume she had gone to bed early and was already asleep.

Her time was at hand.

'Hey, Millicent, wait.'

She turned around to see Jerome following her out of the brasserie. She was touched by the solicitude of the gesture, though maybe he had simply had enough of listening to Carla's bullshit as well.

'I'm just going to take the air,' she told him. 'Go back to the table.'

'Take the air?'

He gestured towards the glass double doors, through which she could see that the rain was now tipping down.

Damn. He wasn't going to believe everything was okay if she headed out in that.

'Vivian says you like to walk,' he said. 'There's a lot of corridors in this hotel. Maybe we could explore for five minutes.'

'You shouldn't be out here with me,' she replied, anxious to get him back in to the brasserie so that she could grab a taxi. Now that she had committed to her final course of action, she did not want a loss of momentum. 'You should be sitting in there with Viv and Carla. They're the people you're going to be living with, after all.'

'Why, are you going somewhere?'

Millicent realised what she had said.

'No. No. I just mean . . . I don't know what I mean.'

The window had closed, but only for now. It would still be tonight. Probably best that it didn't come after a grand exit anyway, and she wasn't sure she wanted her last words to be an apology.

She found herself walking alongside Jerome down a long corridor, though she wasn't aware of making the decision to do so. She had followed his lead, taking her cue from someone else like she'd been conditioned to do.

'I always feel like it's temporary, living with Viv and Carla,' she said, wanting to offer an explanation for her previous remark, as she had this irrational fear that her intentions were apparent. 'But then I thought it was temporary when they first put me in a jail cell. You know all about that, I take it?'

He looked instantly uncomfortable, which was a yes.

'Only a little. I didn't google you. Vivian told me it would be polite not to.'

'Oh, that's Vivian. But google away. It's easier if I know what you know, rather than simply *wondering* what you know.'

He gave her a bland but uncomfortable smile. He had totally googled her.

'I didn't do it by the way,' she added. 'But I don't care whether anyone believes me or not.'

This was not true. Millicent did care whether people believed her, but she knew that she couldn't change whether they believed her, and she had learned that it didn't matter. The last people whose beliefs had actually mattered were the jury.

Millicent began talking despite herself.

'It's the only way to get by. You have no idea what it's like, sharing a house as a convicted murderer. I mean, I've heard people say it's awkward when there's a Brexity relative round for Christmas dinner, but it's a little worse when you know your fellow diners are picturing you standing over a corpse. And even if they say they believe you, you know it's going through their minds: what if she really did it? What is she capable of?'

There was an awkward pause. She realised it wasn't an easy state-ment for him to respond to. He looked like he was desperately thinking of a way to fill the silence.

'That's kind of how I ended up staying with you guys,' he said. 'I always got the impression the folk at my halls of residence thought I might be about to rob them. Maybe just my own insecur-ity. I tend to feel that way about uni in general, like I don't belong and am about to get found out.'

'I used to be like that when I was first in work,' she recalled. 'It was full of people from far posher backgrounds than mine, most of whose fathers were somebody in the biz. They were all born into it, growing up with an expectation of working there that I simply didn't have. Honestly, if you shouted out certain surnames on a set, half the crew would look round.'

Jerome's eyes lit up. Once more she had said more than she intended.

'On a set? You were in film, TV? What did you do?'

His interest frightened her.

'It doesn't matter,' she said, dismissing his question with a wave of her hand. 'It was a long time ago.'

Nobody had seen the real Millicent for twenty-five years, but maybe the truth was that she didn't *want* to be seen. That she couldn't bear it, because the person who would be revealed beneath her protective carapace was the vulnerable woman who hadn't been ready for all of this to happen to her.

'Perhaps another time,' she added, knowing there would not be one.

She felt bad about lying, but equally, she didn't owe the boy anything. She was wary of opening up to him; wary of opening up to anyone.

There had been a time when she was alive to the possibility that someone who just walked through the door could change her life. She never knew who she might end up working with, whose project would push her in new directions or alter the way she looked at her craft.

She worked in what was often described as a glamorous business, full of exciting people. But even against that sparkling background, Markus still shone.

He had worked for British Screen, selling international rights, but he also had an acquisition remit for Blue Lantern, a third-party sales entity. He showed up on the scene knowing nobody, but within no time, everybody knew him, and everybody liked him.

He was a platinum-grade networker. He would always remember salient details about people, not merely their names and who they worked for, and he found ways to help them out however he could. If somebody was working a stall looking hung over, he'd pop by five minutes later with paracetamol and Lucozade. If somebody mentioned they loved a particular band, he'd slip them a copy of the new album before it was released, or tickets for a gig. He was the kind of guy everybody was happy to see. If he was in a room, you knew it was a good room to be in. And if he was at a party . . .

Which was why, when they seemed to be hitting it off, she thought this was just him being him; that he was simply this charming and solicitous to everybody. When she realised that there really was something between them, that there was an aspect of him that was only for her, it was a feeling like she'd never known.

He was a good ten years younger than her. Not classically good-looking, but indisputably handsome; something rugged and outdoorsy about him. He was physically in great shape, with boundless stamina and an insatiable appetite for all manner of hedonistic pleasures.

He had sandy hair and these little parallel scars on his right cheek which he got from a kayaking accident when he was a teenager, on holiday with his family. His kayak got flipped over and he managed to cut his face on either the lip of his boat or his own paddle. He was never quite sure as he was upside down under water at the time. The scar was so pronounced because the two cuts were at such a close distance that neither could be sutured properly.

He was not the type who was normally drawn to her at all: they had tended to be bookish introverts projecting their sensitivities, as well as the occasional narcissistic pretty-boy actor who was just looking for adoration and notches on his bedpost.

Markus was exciting, and that made her feel that she was exciting too. He seemed to see her in ways she never saw herself. Being the focus of his attention felt like standing in the sunlight on a beautiful morning. She believed he was the kind of man who could change her life for ever.

Unfortunately, she was right.

They turned a corner into another long hallway, this one's walls hung with a series of photographs, old images in new frames. They were of functions hosted in the hotel down the years, each captioned by date rather than occasion to accentuate the establishment's heritage. *January 1st, 1987. December 25th, 1975.* Someone must have found the prints in a cupboard during the refurbishment.

'Hey, it's like *The Shining*,' said Jerome. 'I'm just checking I'm not in one of these from 1921.'

Millicent looked at one marked *June 13th, 1990*, probably a graduation ball: a group of young people looking unaccustomed in their ballgown-and-black-tie finery.

That word 'glamorous' came back to mind. To appreciate its true meaning, you had to understand that it derived from mystical lore. A glamour was an enchantment, an illusion that beguiled the observer, making someone appear beautiful and thus concealing the darker truth of what they really were. Millicent knew it was a spell that didn't require magic: it drew its true power from our desire to see what we wanted to.

She looked at another group shot, her gaze initially drawn by the date: *January 25th, 1994.* She thought with a shudder about where she had been right then, the photo providing a snapshot of how the world was indifferently getting on with itself while hers was falling apart. It was an entirely male gathering, ruddy-cheeked and beery-faced as they grinned smugly at the camera in their kilts and dickie-bows.

Then she saw something that made her legs give beneath her, and fortunately Jerome was close enough to grab on to or she would have collapsed. Her vision blurred as she felt his arms support her.

January 25th, 1994.

'Whoa. Steady. Are you okay?'

'No,' she said.

With his help, she backed against the wall opposite and crouched with her head bowed, bringing the blood back to her brain. She wasn't sure if she had hallucinated because she felt faint, or if she had felt faint because of what she was hallucinating. But what she imagined she had seen in that photograph had so upset her because it briefly shattered her fragile understanding of the life she had lived, and momentarily derailed her resolution to end it.

'Do you want me to go and get help? Or maybe a glass of water or something?'

'I just need a moment and I'll be fine.'

She was starting to feel better. The dizziness was gone and her focus returning. When she looked at the photo again, she would see that it had been auto suggestion, nothing more. Her reflections on glamour together with Jerome mentioning *The Shining* had put an idea in her head and her subconscious had run with it.

Millicent climbed to her feet and took a step closer to the photograph. She stared for a few seconds, satisfying herself as to the veracity of what she was seeing and willing it to resolve itself into something else.

It didn't.

This time, her feet remained steady and her vision clear. Clearer than it had been in three decades.

'How you getting on?' Jerome asked.

'I'm feeling better.'

'So everything's okay?'

'No. Everything is quite definitely not okay.'

'What's up?'

She directed his attention to the photograph.

'Do you see the chap third from the right in the front row, with the parallel scars on his cheek?'

Jerome picked him out with a finger. 'This guy?'

'Yes. That's Markus Laird, the man I served twenty-four years for killing.'

He looked that bit harder, curiosity overriding decorum.

'Fuck. No wonder you got spooked. I take it you didn't know his picture was here.'

'No, but it's not his photograph that troubles me so much as the date it was taken.'

'*January 25th, 1994*,' Jerome read aloud. 'Burns Night? Why is that significant?'

'Because I found him stabbed to death on January 23rd.'

PART TWO

Collateral Damage

Lucio knew it was a good moment to move on, much as he would have liked to stay and hang out with Alessandro and Millie. It was a party for everyone else, but for him a night like this was about work, about circulating far and wide. And for every genuine embrace with an old friend, there was also a fake and shake with some piece of shit he had to stay the right side of. Top of this list was the asshole standing a few yards away on the prow.

Florio Pacitti dismissed his entourage with a subtle gesture as he caught sight of Lucio heading his way. They stepped away obediently, the girls heading for the bar and the two male associates taking position to quietly enforce a perimeter around their boss while he granted Lucio an audience.

Florio cut a distinctive figure: tall and muscular with a shaven scalp stretching from a neck so thick it gave new dimensions to the term 'bullet-headed'. Lucio actually thought the guy looked like a thumb with a face drawn on it, but there was no one on Earth he trusted enough to share that description with.

Florio put his arm around Lucio's neck, pulling him downwards so his head pressed into his chest, his other hand rubbing the top of Lucio's skull. This playful roughhousing was ostensibly a friendly gesture, but its true purpose was to emphasise Florio's greater size and strength, an unsubtle reminder of the power dynamic between them. It wasn't something he normally did, either. The big thumb was compensating, and not merely for the fact that this was Lucio's boat and Lucio's party.

Lucio endured the schoolyard subjugation with a smile and a laugh, acting like he enjoyed it. This was all part of the bullshit dance he had to do with Florio, and with the men Florio worked for. Lucio had to pretend he liked him, but without ever quite acting like he genuinely believed it. It was as though Florio needed both parties to know that it was a compulsory tribute, like a fucking villager paying a tithe to the local aristo.

'With these big new movies, you think there could be a cameo for me?' Florio asked. Fortunately, Lucio could tell he wasn't serious.

'Hey, my porno days are behind me,' he replied.

Florio laughed.

'Fair enough, but when you go off to Hollywood, you don't forget where you came from, okay?'

This was Florio's way of conveying that though Lucio no longer owed them any money, as far as these people were concerned, you could never pay off your debts. They believed they owned you for life.

In the Seventies, Lucio had done a dozen different jobs in and around the movies, from runner to electrician to focus-puller to assistant DoP, as well as occasionally being a stage-hand, a script editor and an extra. He could carry out just about every task there was on a set, which was how he came to be known as the man who makes it happen.

By the time he was twenty-five, he was ready to step up to producer. Too bad that graduation coincided with the golden age of Italian movie production coming to an end. The swords-and-sandals epics, the Spaghetti westerns, the *gialli*: they weren't entirely over, but all their heydays had come and gone. You could smell their imminent decline like over-ripe fruit. But while the veterans mourned the coming change, Lucio looked to the future and saw opportunity.

He cut deals to re-use sets and costumes from previous productions, using them to shoot a series of porn movies that had both a period feel and higher production values than anything else on the market. With *Deep Throat* having taken porn mainstream in the US, some of his flicks even played theatrical dates, albeit mostly grind-houses on New York's 42nd St.

It was both an apprenticeship and a guerrilla campaign, learning to make movies fast and cheap, but always ensuring the end product looked like it cost five times its budget. 'Cutting a deal' didn't always mean paying the people who actually owned those sets and costumes: sometimes he had simply bribed janitors and security staff at Cinecittà and shot there overnight with nobody's official permission. In this game, everything was a transaction, whether it was paying somebody to perform on-screen, paying somebody to perform in bed or just paying somebody to look the other way. And there was nothing you couldn't negotiate.

When the home video boom came along, it quickly became clear there was far more money to be made by swapping hardcore sex for hardcore action, and Lucio was well placed to supply it. But though he knew how to make them cheap and he knew how to make them polished, horror movies and thrillers cost a lot more than porn. For one thing, you needed people who could act. You needed to shoot on thirty-five-mill, on Arriflex or Panavision cameras. You also needed stuntmen, make-up effects artists, blood squibs and car crashes. In short, you needed investment.

Fortunately, he knew a guy. Florio dealt coke, speed, hash and heroin to people on set and on the social scene surrounding Rome-based film production. The men Florio worked for were looking for opportunities to turn their dirty money into legitimate returns. Lucio didn't relish being on the hook to such people, but when it came to production finance, you seldom got to choose your angels.

It worked out pretty good for everybody. Lucio got to make movies that kept delivering the three Bs, and Florio's bosses were very happy with their end. They were also partial to the ancillary benefits of hanging out with movie directors, big-name actors and nubile starlets; to say nothing of enjoying the special attention of those very obliging *wannabe* starlets.

These days Lucio was financing his ambitious new slate from more legitimate sources, but Credit Populaire de Paris wanted much the same from the arrangement as his original backers. In both cases, there were ways they could have guaranteed bigger returns for their money, but a little glamour could be spellbinding. That was why Cannes was full of bankers right now, throwing cash at movie slates so they could have some of the magic rub off on them.

'I'll never forget where I came from, Florio,' Lucio said. 'It's written right through me. We never know where life might take us, but we are neither of us the kind of men who truly change.'

Florio slapped him on the back, pleased with what Lucio was acknowledging.

'Maybe you can make some introductions, open a few doors. We see a lot of opportunity in Los Angeles.'

'I'm the man who makes it happen, Florio.'

Lucio didn't see how it could hurt. He knew that his future success would change nothing: he couldn't escape by outgrowing these guys, only by them outgrowing him. Florio's people could do well in Hollywood, especially via the independent production sector. In the movie business, nobody looked too closely at where the money was coming from as long as it kept the Panavision rolling. That was how a small-time wheeler-dealer like Giancarlo Parretti could end up owning MGM: paying the right people to look the wrong way and dazzling the right bankers with stardust and pussy.

It made Lucio laugh how filmmakers depicted the gangster's life as glamorous: something for the viewer to aspire towards, albeit only vicariously for the duration of the movie. In his experience, gangsters aspired towards respectability. Being the one who dangled the promise of glamour to bend others to your will was the sign of true power.

As he moved away from Florio, Lucio could see a chauffeur-driven Mercedes pull up on the quayside and drop off a single passenger. Tonight's was an informal party, but it was one that nonetheless had a guest of honour, and he had just arrived.

Lucio took up a position from where he could observe Jean-Marc Poupard proceed down the gangway. He would intercept him in a few moments but didn't want to be seen waiting. The terms had been agreed, but until the money was in his account, it was wise not to upset the power balance. It was crucial that the Credit Populaire exec continued to believe he was the one who was chasing Lucio's business.

He knew something was wrong as soon as Jean-Marc stepped

onto the boat. Lucio had a girl standing ready to greet the banker with a drink, and to make it clear that she would make herself available to him in every way. Everything was a transaction. She understood that this would secure her a role in a forthcoming production, though Lucio had not specified whether she would have any lines, or even if there would be film in the camera that day.

Jean-Marc shrugged her off, refusing the drink and looking urgently for his host.

Lucio strode forth, restraining himself from conspicuous hurry. He had long ago learned that behaving like nothing was wrong was a vital first stage of mitigation.

His guest's expression was at once serious and apologetic. Lucio approached with a wide smile and made a show of putting an arm around him, subtly turning them both to face the water.

'Jean-Marc, you don't look like a man who is ready for a party. What's wrong, did the Dow Jones crash?'

'We need to talk privately, Lucio.'

Lucio led him belowdecks, out of sight of the other guests, every step of the short journey another moment to ponder what challenge he might be about to face. Jean-Marc had once hinted that the bosses were nervous about it being a six-picture deal, saying their conservative instincts inclined them to be more comfortable with a round number of five, but he had made it clear that was a worst-case scenario.

Don't worry about it until you have to worry about it, Lucio counselled himself.

Lucio gestured to Jean-Marc to take a seat in the galley. He opened the fridge and reached for a bottle of champagne, then withdrew his hand. It was superstitious, but it felt like tempting fate. He grabbed two beers instead and opened them on the worktop. He thought Jean-Marc was going to refuse his, but after a moment's hesitation he grabbed what was offered and downed a large gulp. He looked like he needed it.

'So, what's up?' Lucio asked. 'We still all good?'

Jean-Marc stared for a second.

'I came as soon as I could get away. I've been on a conference call for about three hours. Spent the whole drive over here wondering how to break it to you.'

'Break what?'

'It's MGM. Paretti. Credit Lyonnais Bank Nederland. It's all collapsing. There's subpoenas being handed down, arrest warrants, and never mind the SEC, the FBI are involved.'

Lucio stared expectantly. Jean-Marc took another gulp of beer.

'Lucio, Credit Populaire are pulling the deal. The fallout from CLBN is going to be nuclear. We're talking about a billion-dollar fraud here. The guys upstairs are spooked.'

'They want to renegotiate? How spooked are they? What terms are they offering now?'

'You don't understand. The deal is dead. They don't want anything to do with the film business right now. The bribery stuff that's coming out about Credit Lyonnais is so toxic, they don't want anyone thinking they've got their hands in the same pie.'

Lucio felt like the ship had evaporated and he was treading water, trying not to drown.

'What do they think I am? I'm not trying to buy a studio. My costings have been fully ratified and I'm financing completion guarantees on every picture. Didn't you explain what I'm all about?'

'Of course I did. But they've been doing their due diligence, and certain things that they were prepared to turn a blind eye to are suddenly a lot more conspicuous in the light of what's going down with MGM.'

'What things?'

'Your relationship with Florio Pacitti and certain of his associates.'

Lucio was about to plead that this deal was precisely the thing that would distance him from Florio, but he only had to look at the man before him to know his words were useless. As soon as they met, Lucio had seen what Jean-Marc was: an ordinary, conservative pen-pusher with a wife and kids back home in Clichy or some other affluent Parisian suburb. The kind of guy who at best, if he was walking on the wild side, might get to fuck his secretary at the annual sales conference. It hadn't been hard to turn his head. He must have thought he had gone to heaven when he came to

Cannes last year and met Lucio, who showed him good times like he could never have imagined.

Lucio, for his part, thought he'd won the lottery. But the very attributes that made Jean-Marc easy to dazzle were also what told Lucio nothing could save this now. The moment things get dicey, a conservative pen-pusher goes to what he knows. His eighty-million-dollar production deal had just disappeared.

'I'm sorry, Lucio. I spent the whole day trying to save this, but these guys see scandal as contagious.'

Lucio could barely think of any words to respond. There was an anger building, but it was so large that he knew it would be a while in reaching the surface. He thought of the favours he had done this guy, the money he had spent. A petty part of him wished he had a receipt. Then he heard his poppa's voice, words that had served him well in times when his emotions threatened to boil. *Don't burn any bridges.*

'I'd better go,' Jean-Marc said, getting up.

Lucio gripped his shoulder, swallowing back bile and drawing on great fortitude to find the words.

'Stay. We're still friends, aren't we? Or are you distancing yourself from me too?'

Jean-Marc looked uncomfortable at the suggestion.

'Of course not. I just didn't think you'd want me around.'

'Oh, what the fuck, it's a party, after all. Maybe my last one for a while, given the news. Do me the courtesy of enjoying my hospitality. For appearances' sake, at least. I'm not ready to break this shit to everybody tonight.'

'Okay. If you're sure.'

'I'm sure,' Lucio assured him, even offering a smile. 'Besides, this will pass. There will be other deals.'

Jean-Marc's solemn expression argued otherwise.

Unanswered

Jerry looked at the time and observed that he had slept until almost ten o'clock, which came as a jolt until he remembered which day it was and that he didn't have any classes until the afternoon. Nonetheless, he was always uncomfortable when he overslept, hit by a fear of losing time and of control. As a kid he would often get up early enough on weekdays that he could watch a whole movie before going to school. That had changed a bit once he hit his mid-teens, but he was still an early riser.

He must have needed it. He hadn't been sleeping well in the halls. It was hard to get his brain to shut down after a late shift at work and a brisk walk home in the cold, but latterly he had been struggling to get to sleep and stay asleep even on the nights that he wasn't coming in from the takeaway.

His first night here hadn't been much better. He had been disoriented by his unfamiliar surroundings and the minute the lights went out, his mind started trying to process a whole slew of new uncertainties. But last night, after stuffing himself with everything that was put in front of him in that fancy restaurant, including finishing off everybody else's desserts, his body had obviously decided to shut down for running repairs.

It wasn't just that, though. Having had time to adjust, something instinctive decided he was comfortable here, in a way he hadn't felt since his gran died.

He grabbed his phone – Danby's phone – from the bedside table, snug inside the protective flip-case he had bought for it. It was designed to look like a VHS tape, with a reproduction of the original Palace Pictures label for *The Evil Dead* on the front, sprockets on the back. He wondered whether he had bought it to express something about himself, or to conceal the fact that he was a thief.

He saw that he had a WhatsApp message from someone called Pip Morgan. It took him a moment to suss that it was Philippa, from his seminar group. That was why she had him as a contact.

Hi. I heard you moved out. I'm really sorry about how things went. Feel we got off on the wrong foot. Maybe we could grab a coffee some time. P

He had an instinctive urge to respond, let her know he appreciated the gesture, but another part of him cautioned that a gesture was all it was. These posh types sometimes had a bee in their bonnet about propriety and decorum. She just wanted to be able to tell herself she had done the right thing, then she could forget about him.

Still, he had a lingering unease over the whole phone theft business. Like oversleeping, he was wary when he didn't feel he had full control of his own behaviour, and now that he was staying in this new place, he was freaked by how reckless he had been at the old one.

He could hear Rossco's voice warning him, *Do not shit where you eat*, but that was incidental compared to the far greater vow to himself that he had broken, which was to *stop fucking thieving stuff*.

Why had he done it? It wasn't just that Danby was a fud.

Self-sabotage again. Part of him wanted to get caught, turfed out of the halls, turfed out of uni, because it would confirm what he suspected: that he didn't belong here. But he could see now that he was the one who had decided that. Nobody else. He had spent so much time thinking about all the ways in which he didn't belong, that he had been overlooking the ways in which he did. He liked doing his courses. Liked the reading, the lectures, the classes, even if they were full of snobby wankers.

He thought about what Millicent said last night, how she had been in a job where she felt like she didn't fit in, full of posh folk, all connected, all seeming like they were born to it. He wondered just how posh and connected they must have been, because Millicent seemed pretty posh to him, but that was the point, wasn't it? You can't give in, otherwise these places become the exclusive preserve of snobby wankers.

He really wanted to make a go of this now. But with that thought, he remembered that his future here was hanging by a thread. Self-sabotage. He had been handing in shite coursework, telling himself he didn't care, but he did. He really fucking did. And now he needed to write some absolutely primo essay to stop him getting emptied. Well, that wasn't going to happen lying in his scratcher.

A sniff of his pits told him he was a bit ripe. He grabbed his towel and was about to head for the bathroom but stopped to pull on a T-shirt and jeans first. He had done the same to go for a piss in the middle of the night.

He'd never been self-conscious about being seen wrapped in just a towel or wandering around in his scants when he was living at the halls, but round here it felt wrong. Like Vivian said, it wasn't the same as living with his gran, with family.

He didn't know if this was ageist, but he didn't want to be seen like that by any of the old dears. Though truth be told, he was more afraid of seeing something he was not supposed to. Was that ageist too? He didn't know. But it felt like it would be important to them. How they wanted to be seen, how they chose to be perceived, was the essence of dignity.

He ventured into the hallway and was instantly vindicated for his decision, for there was Vivian standing outside Millicent's bedroom. She looked kind of concerned.

'Is everything okay?'

'I'm not sure. I've knocked on the door and there's no reply. Millicent is normally up by now, hours ago in fact. She's usually the first awake, but she hasn't roused.'

'It was a big meal last night. I slept way longer than usual. Maybe she did too.'

'Yes,' Vivian conceded. 'But it's just that she seemed in a weird frame of mind last night and I'm wondering if everything's okay. She's been through a lot, you know?'

Jerry nodded, conflicted about having to hold something back. Millicent hadn't told the others about the photo that had caused her to come over all faint, and had asked him to keep it to himself also. He didn't see why she wouldn't want to tell Vivian and Carla, who seemed to be the only two people she really had in her life, but he respected that it was her call.

'I don't want to disturb her if she's maybe had a rough night,' Viv went on. 'But I'm just . . . Oh, I don't know.'

Jerry knew what she was concerned about, and why she was reluctant to put a name to it. He knew from his gran that once you reached that age, when friends started dying, you must begin to see it as a real possibility. That was why Gran had been weirdly ready for it when she got her diagnosis. Readier for it than he had been, anyway.

'If you're worried, you should just stick your head around the door. I don't think she'd mind you looking out for her.'

'Oh, you don't know Millicent,' Vivian replied. 'But still.'

Vivian knocked again, quite hard this time. Millicent would need to be in quite a slumber not to be roused by that.

'Millicent, is everything okay?'

There was still no reply.

Vivian sighed with resignation. She turned the handle then leaned around the narrow gap.

Jerry heard her gasp. Something in him froze. An indelible image filled his mind. The old man clutching his arm, his chest, slumping to the floor. Blood bubbling from the corner of his mouth.

'She's not here,' Vivian said. 'She must have got up and headed out before any of us woke. She likes to go out walking, but she normally tells me where she's heading and when she'll be back.'

'I guess she didn't want to wake you,' Jerry suggested.

'Yes. But I wish I knew where she might have gone.'

Jerry looked at the carpet and shuffled past towards the bathroom, feeling shitty that he was withholding the reassurance Vivian was looking for.

He knew exactly where Millicent had gone.

Dates

Millicent only knew she must have slept at some point during the night because she had woken from a nightmare. It was one she had several times a week: that she was back inside.

It was strange. In prison, going to sleep felt like the only true refuge, the part of the day she most looked forward to. It was a place where she could retreat into comforting oblivion, or escape to wherever her imagination might take her. And yet, on the outside, sleep had become the enemy, her subconscious a traitor that dragged her back to the place she most feared.

She didn't need to open her eyes to know it had been a dream. Merely the silence was enough. She sometimes found it unsettling how quiet it could be here in Vivian's house, because there had been so much noise in prison. Inside, there was never that level of stillness or silence. There were always voices echoing from somewhere: angry, distressed, admonishing, authoritative. There was always the jangling of keys from belts, the buzz of cell call bells, the clatter of inspection hatches, the banging of doors.

There was no incident or narrative to the dream, only a return of the pervasive awareness she had lived with all that time, of being there and knowing she couldn't leave; knowing this was what her life had been reduced to. Of course, the kicker was that upon getting out, and every day when she awoke, she was confronted by the reality that her life hadn't got much bigger, and nor could it ever again. There were still walls hemming her in, even if they weren't physical. She was still the wretch they had decided she was, the creature they had turned her into. That was why she had sincerely intended to kill herself.

Then she saw that photograph, and something changed. She had found a tiny crack in the wall, and through it glimpsed a world different to the one they had convinced her was real.

She and Jerome had gone to Reception to ask if there was someone who could tell them more about the picture. They were informed that the manager who had overseen the refurbishment had gone home for the day and would not be back until the morning.

Millicent reached the Roman Fort Hotel just before eight o'clock. After waking from her bad dream, and knowing that further sleep was unlikely, she had decided to just get up and get on. She presented herself at the desk, where she gave the name of Derek Connelly, the man she was here to see. The receptionist asked for her name in return. Her badge identified her as Magda. She spoke with a slight accent.

Millicent complied, but it made her uneasy. She was always afraid that people could see what she was, that prison was still stamped all over her and that people would despise her for it. And in this era she had been released into, people could look at phones and computers and instantly find out all manner of things.

She was consoled, having googled herself, that the more lurid information was too far back. Those tabloid stories were lost to time. They were still in archives no doubt, but not instantly retrievable by anyone with a phone and the requisite curiosity.

Magda told her that Mr Connelly would not be in until ten. Millicent nodded with quiet satisfaction and took a seat in the lobby.

A few moments later, the receptionist approached, crouching down beside where she was seated on a low banquette.

'I'm not sure you picked me up right,' she told her. 'I said ten o'clock. It will be at least a couple of hours.'

'Do you wish me to leave?' Millicent replied. She stood up, preparing to obediently absent herself.

Magda recoiled as though appalled by the suggestion.

'No, it's just that it's a long time to wait.'

'We have very different perspectives on time,' she replied.

The receptionist looked puzzled by this, but understanding that it required no further action, she returned to her desk. She glanced across every so often, looking up from her computer. After about ten minutes, she approached again.

'Can I offer you a cup of tea or coffee?'

'I'm quite alright.'

'Are you sure? On the house.'

'No thank you, I'm quite fine.'

Millicent hadn't had breakfast and a cuppa sounded nice, but her conditioned response was to refuse any kind of favour, especially from strangers and from people who held a position. She had an instinctive aversion to being in anyone's debt, of being beholden to anybody.

In prison, personal independence had felt like a vital element of survival. It was about reassuring herself that she didn't need anybody else's help to get her through; knowing she was not reliant on anybody else's good wishes or mercy. That was why she found it so difficult to accept all of Vivian's kindness, and was actually more comfortable with Carla's passive-aggressive resentment. It was also why she didn't want either of them knowing about the photograph. Ideally nobody would know. Jerome only found out because he had been there to witness her reaction. She had to offer him an explanation for why she almost collapsed.

That was what she had told herself anyway. Being back here in the lobby, where he had followed her last night, she was starting to see it differently. She hadn't needed to tell him anything. She could have simply said she came over all faint. She had been robust enough in rebuffing his curiosity about working on film sets. Why had she chosen to volunteer something so shocking, so personal?

Perhaps she had reached out to Jerome like a drowning woman grasping at anything that might keep her afloat. He had come out to the lobby offering solidarity just when she set her plan in motion, when she had every intention of going home to end her life. Maybe some part of her hadn't been on board with it. Or perhaps after all these years she had identified someone who might finally see who she really was.

The two hours passed, and just on ten she watched a

106

confident-looking male in a smart suit stride into the lobby, trading greetings with the concierge and bell boy. He went up to the reception desk where Magda dropped her voice as she glanced discreetly towards where Millicent was sitting.

Millicent immediately felt sick, a solidity in her guts that she had to endure whenever she was about to confront someone wielding any level of authority. Most of the time it was merely a matter of obsequious compliance and keeping her head down. The hardest occasions were when she needed something from them. Like an answer to the riddle that had defined her entire life.

She had long ago stopped asking questions. She never had the slightest notion who might have killed Markus, other than herself. She had been totally out of it that night, and had little memory of even getting back to her flat, never mind what might have happened after that. She suspected she had been Mickey Finned, but had no proof of that. She and Markus had hit a lot of bars that night, and she had taken a few drugs of her own volition. Even when it's a dealer you know, you can never be sure of the strength of a batch. All she knew for sure was that she had woken up next to his blood-soaked body.

She had endured years having it drilled into her that she had done it. Having spent every day living the consequences of a crime, it was tempting to succumb to the idea that she really must have killed him, because at least that version helped her life make some kind of sense.

'It's Ms Spark, is that right?'

'Yes, that's me.'

'I'm Derek Connelly, the general manager. I gather you've a query concerning one of the photographs we have on display?'

'There is somebody in one of the photographs who was known to me. I was wondering what you might be able to tell me about it.'

He gave an apologetic wince.

'I'm not sure how much I can tell you about any individual picture, because of how we laid hands on them. As part of the refurbishment, we had the idea to decorate the route to our two function suites, the Forum and the Antonine Room, and we put out an appeal on social media for people who might have old photographs of occasions hosted here. We had a fantastic response, as you no doubt saw. The earliest image we received was from 1945, from a ball to celebrate VE Day. That has pride of place in the Forum. We've used the particularly prestigious images in the function suites themselves. Can you show me which picture you were interested in?'

Millicent got to her feet and retraced her steps of the night before. Mr Connelly strode alongside her, telling her more about the refurbishment and the appeal for old pictures.

'Some people sent digital images, scans or photos of photos, and some sent original prints. I've not got around to returning all of those. It's on my to-do list.'

He looked sheepish.

'It's not one of those, is it?' he asked.

'No.'

Millicent steeled herself as they turned the corner, and a few moments later she was once more standing before the photograph of Markus in Glasgow, apparently taken after his death.

She stared at the people around him, faces she didn't recognise, men who did not look like they worked in the movie business. All men. They looked like they could have been public schoolboys: beefy rugby-player types. Was this a class reunion? No, the age range was too diverse. Maybe it was a general get-together for former pupils. There was something unsettling about the way they carried themselves though, the cocksure certainty in their expressions, but she couldn't quite say why it troubled her.

'This one?' he prompted. 'What is it you want to know?'

'I have to be direct about this,' Millicent said, though this was primarily an instruction to herself. 'The caption here says *January 25th, 1994*, so when I saw this picture, it gave me something of a turn because I knew this gentleman third from the right, and I can assure you he died on January 23rd.'

Mr Connelly's eyes bulged. She thought for a moment he was going to demand that she leave for somehow offending or impugning him. Instead he became flushed with embarrassment.

'I am most terribly sorry if that disturbed you. It's very possible that it's down to me.'

'I don't understand.'

'We get, as you can probably imagine, a lot of bookings for popular occasions, Burns Night among them, and they can't all be accommodated on the actual day. I finessed a few of the captions in order to create more of a sense of history about the photos. This one is captioned as Burns Night, but it could have been a few days before. I'm not sure what day of the week the 25th would have been that year.'

'It was a Tuesday,' she said, her voice threatening to fail her.

Mr Connelly lifted the photo from the wall delicately.

'Why don't you come with me into my office and we'll have a wee look.'

Millicent followed him, drifting like a ghost. She should have anticipated this explanation, but hope had blinded her, as it had been a long time since she'd felt any.

Mr Connelly placed the photo on his desk and carefully slid the print from beneath the glass. There was a label at the bottom, previously concealed by the frame.

'Aye, there we are. I'm terribly sorry. It was January 21st. A Friday night.'

Millicent felt that crack in the wall closing.

He handed her the photo so she could see for herself. Her eyes fell upon the date, then at the names, checking if she recognised any. She read them back and forth, back and forth, counting the heads as her consternation mounted.

The crack was opening again.

The man whose face she could not mistake, even after twenty-five years, stared out from the photograph, same as it had stared up from that blood-soaked bed. But he was not listed as Markus Laird.

'Which one was it you knew?' asked Mr Connelly.

'Des Creasey.'

The words felt alien in her mouth, but she had to speak them convincingly. Having come here mistakenly thinking a man in this photo had died before the date it was taken, she couldn't tell Mr

Connelly that she had also known him by a completely different name. He would just assume she was a wandered, crazy old bat, wasting his time.

'Can you tell me who sent you this photo?'

'Certainly. I'll have the details here somewhere. And I can give you a photocopy of it, if you'd like. I can also scan it and send you a high-res image if you give me your email address.'

Though she did have an email address, set up by Vivian, Millicent's instinct was once again to refuse. He was already placing the picture face-down on the glass of the device, which looked much like a photocopier.

'Oh here, there's a wee label on the back,' he said. *'The Blue Lamp Burns Society.'*

She had never heard Markus mention it. As far as he told her, he had been in Paris on the night of January 21st. He never spoke of any plans to visit Glasgow, never mind being part of a Burns Society there. And yet he acquired rights on behalf of a company called Blue Lantern Films. There had to be a link.

'Does that name mean anything to you?' she asked. 'Do they still meet here for Burns Night?' she added hopefully.

Mr Connelly shook his head.

'Way before my time. I only know the name as a film reference. I heard it as a pub quiz answer. *The Blue Lamp* was an old black and white movie that first introduced Dixon of Dock Green. That would certainly track.'

'What do you mean?'

'These boys look like polis to me.'

Corruptors

Jerry was walking along Great Western Road, approaching the turn that would take him up towards Charing Cross. He had felt Baltic at first, but it was okay once he got up a head of steam. He would be able to feel his fingers again any time now. The air was clear, and he was hoping his brain might get there too.

There was a book he needed for his Politics seminar, and the copies at the university library and the Round Reading Room were so much in demand that the librarians kind of smirked if you asked about it. The system said there were a couple at the Mitchell, though you had to read them on site and couldn't take them out of the building. It was a bit of a hike, but taking Shanks's Pony saved on a bus fare, and he needed the time to mull some stuff over.

He knew he was onto a sweet deal moving into this place. He was determined to make it work, determined that they shouldn't decide they'd made a mistake letting him into their midst. Problem was, he'd been in the house two days and had already lied to Vivian. Okay, not lied per se, but definitely committed what his gran would have called a sin of omission. It wasn't even that big an omission, in terms of the information he was withholding. The problem was that he had been forced to choose.

It had felt different last night: simply not mentioning the incident in the corridor seemed merely a matter of respecting Millicent's privacy. But this morning Vivian had been worried, and he could have allayed that but chose not to, out of loyalty to Millicent. Where had that come from? Just because she had freaked out over a picture. She could be going doo-lally. Hardly a sound basis for an allegiance. And what really troubled him wasn't so much that he'd made a choice then and there, but that he realised he was bound by a choice he had made the night before.

The law of unintended consequences.

As he crossed Woodlands Road, he told himself it was no big deal. Millicent would be back soon anyway and that would be that. It was up to her whether she told Vivian where she had gone and why.

So how come his instincts were telling him he was getting into something he might not be able to handle? Millicent had hardly recruited him into a major conspiracy, but he had this fear of being drawn in, and essentially his unease came down to the fact that he didn't know if he could trust her.

Wasn't it possible she was full of shit? How could he be sure the guy in some random photo was in fact the man she'd been jailed for killing? He only had her word for that. She could be a pathological liar. Certainly, there had been others who had decided they didn't trust her, enough for her to be locked away for twenty-four years. If you were a convicted murderer, wouldn't you want the new guy in the house to think there was some great mystery around you, other than the question of whether you did it? Nonetheless, he felt for her shame at the thought of complete strangers knowing the worst thing about her, and understood why Vivian wanted to protect her from other people's prurient interest.

No, instinctively he didn't trust her, but equally instinctively he felt protective of her. It was something about the way she scurried around, fearful and apologetic, like she was always hoping to pass through unnoticed. There was that awkward leggy gait too. His gran used to take him to Culzean Country Park some Sunday mornings, before the video shop opened. If you got there early enough, you would see deer. Millicent reminded him of the foals: inelegantly skittish, vulnerable and afraid. He had always wanted to cuddle one.

He had googled her, of course. When he told her he hadn't, he was lying out of politeness.

There really wasn't much to find. Millicent had been jailed at a time when the internet consisted of fifty people playing MUDDs.

One of the most recent hits was a story following the release of a woman named Sally Challen, whose conviction for killing her husband had been reduced to one of manslaughter. The appeal judge had accepted her claim of diminished responsibility following years of physical and psychological abuse. Millicent's name appeared at the tail end of the story, in reference to cases in which they were anticipating appeals following this verdict. Vivian said Millicent hadn't won any appeals but she did mention that her parole had been suddenly expedited. Jerry figured this verdict had lit a fire under somebody.

Even without the adverse effect of her denials upon her parole, it seemed to Jerry that Millicent had been put away for a hell of a long time. Folk were always shouting the odds about how life should mean life, but serving that kind of term had to be pretty unusual, surely. What led the judge to sentence her to such a harsh minimum?

That, he realised, was precisely the kind of prurient interest Vivian wanted to protect Millicent from, and fortunately for her, there was no way of satisfying it.

Jerry took the long way around at the Mitchell, going in the revolving doors at the front so he could walk all the way through the building. He loved coming here. It made him feel part of something greater, connected to a wider history. He was just a student, but one walking the same floors and picking up the same books as eminent scholars who had come before him. Maybe they had felt like frauds and impostors too.

He signed out the book he needed, then sought out somewhere to work through it, away from the hubbub of the main public floor with its café bar. He found a quiet room upstairs and was striding towards a desk when he noticed that its only other occupant was sitting before some strange, hooded contraption. Jerry had a look over the woman's shoulder and saw she was looking at pages from the *Daily Record*, twisting a handle to scroll them. The masthead and fonts were different, the pictures a grainy black and white. He saw headlines about Margaret Thatcher, photographs of police on horseback, wielding batons as they charged into a crowd of protestors. These editions were from the Eighties. This place had a newspaper archive, pre-internet.

He chose a spot close to the machine and sat diligently taking notes for his seminar, all the while keeping an eye open for when the machine would be free. About an hour or so later, he eagerly made his move.

It was a microfilm reader, which was 1960s James Bond stuff, though his excitement at engaging in illicit archaeological research made him feel more like Indiana Jones.

The buzz wore off sharpish when he got to the appropriate desk and started speaking to the archivist. Turned out this wasn't a database: he couldn't simply feed in Millicent's name and get a list of articles. There was no indexing, just reels of whole editions ordered by date. He knew that the murder had been on January 23rd, 1994, but he didn't know when the trial took place. It was going to be a long afternoon.

He loaded the appropriate spool and zoomed to a definition that let him simultaneously view as many pages as he could while still being able to make out the headlines. It took him a while to get the hang of the scrolling, which was initially way too fast because of the scale, though he quickly pegged that only the first quarter or so of any given edition would be news. The rest comprised features, opinion, sports and a TV guide with only four channels.

Jerry wondered how likely it was that Millicent's name would appear in a headline. He saw the word SPARK once or twice, all caps, but always as a verb.

He stopped and zoomed in closer every time he found a headline that made reference to murder or killing. The first couple of such stories referred to incidents that had taken place in Glasgow, which made him concerned that a murder in London might not have made the press north of the border. Then he remembered about the harshness of Millicent's sentence. If she had been jailed for that length of time, the case had to have been pretty notorious.

Then a headline jumped out at him and he knew that he had found what he was looking for. He experienced only the briefest thrill before it was replaced by a sinking dread in the knowledge that this was going to be about someone he knew. Even before he zoomed to read the text, he felt creepy and shameful. The anxiety he felt about accidentally walking in on one of his new housemates naked, seeing them in a way they would not wish to be seen: this was exactly what he thought it would feel like.

BLOODBATH OF THE VIDEO NASTY KILLER

Horror movie addict stabbed boyfriend to death after booze and drug-fuelled sex session

Cops today talked of their shock at the scene in a Tooting bedroom where Millie Spark (45) stabbed boyfriend Markus Laird more than twenty times in a flat full of horror videos.

The Video Nasty Killer. Jesus God.

Jerry's first thought was of Carla the night before, talking about horror movies. She hadn't known. She couldn't have known. She was a bit judgy, but she wouldn't have been deliberately cruel like that. He imagined she would be mortified if she had any notion.

He scrolled down through subsequent days' editions, observing how the story grew and developed: the headline point size going up, the allocated space getting larger.

VIDEO NASTY KILLER 'COPIED SICK FLICKS'

Tecs say murder re-enacted scene from horror movie

Jerry wondered who these technicians were, before he sussed that this must have been the tabloid lingo of a bygone age. They meant cops, an anonymous one of whom was quoted as saying the murder 'had direct echoes of *Child's Play 3*'. The story was accompanied by a still of Chucky, gripping a pair of scissors.

With a chill, Jerry started to see where this was going. His class had been studying it in examining society's relationship with cinema, though Jerry already had a firm grounding because he had heard his gran talk about it, with a rare bitterness. Under Margaret Thatcher, with unemployment rocketing, riots on the streets and society seeming on the verge of fracture from the effects of her policies, the government had been urgently in need of two things: scapegoats and distractions. In whipping up a massively dishonest moral panic over 'video nasties', they got both.

And of course, the tabloids were all-too-willing confederates. There was nothing they liked better than doing their wee dance of feigned outrage, something Jerry didn't imagine had changed much in forty years. These days they would fill a page with condemnation over some celeb's coke habit, a wrap of gak sitting in their jacket while they typed. Back then the reporters were fluffing their readers' anger-boners about horror movies, before probably going home to watch a pirate copy of *Cannibal Holocaust* their mate lent them.

The frenzy led to the Director of Public Prosecutions drawing up a list of banned films, meaning the police could come in and confiscate them if the local video store was found to be stocking any of the forbidden titles. Down south some poor shopkeeper got sent to jail for renting someone a copy of *Tenebrae*. The Tories and the tabloids milked the outrage dry until the government passed the Video Recordings Act in 1984.

Then, ten years later, they were able to go to the tit a second time, after James Bulger was murdered.

Jerry couldn't think of anything in his lifetime that remotely compared, so he could barely imagine how much the killing must have shocked people. Two ten-year-olds murdering a toddler, for fuck's sake. How the hell did you make sense of that? But as the country searched its collective soul looking for where society had lost its way, the trial judge had offered up a familiar solution. Towards the end of his summing up, and with absolutely no evidence to support it, he said: 'I suspect that exposure to violent video films may in part be an explanation.'

Child's Play 3 was specifically blamed in the subsequent tabloid rage-wank. Karima had shown them a picture of the front page of the *Sun*, dominated by the order:

For the sake of all our kids: BURN YOUR VIDEO NASTY.

'If you own one yourself, burn it safely,' it advised. 'If you have rented one, take it back to the shop and ask the dealer to destroy it.'

Aye, because burning videos wasn't at all like burning books, and anyway, everybody knew that always ended well.

Jerry had watched *Child's Play 3* after his gran told him about all this. It was laughably tame, but more significantly, it featured no stabbing scenes. He didn't know the details of Markus Laird's murder, but he strongly suspected the claim that it was in any way inspired by the film was bullshit. The purpose was obviously to push the public's well-primed buttons and to connect this murder to the wider outrage.

Jerry noted that the police source was not named. Either the hack had made up the *Child's Play* angle to boost the story, or someone in the police chucked it in there to ensure there was a greater clamour against their suspect. Either way, he could well imagine the climate of public opinion in which Millicent must have faced her trial. But there was a far worse revelation to come.

VIDEO NASTY KILLER WAS
GORE-CRAZED SFX SICKO

Millie Spark (45), accused of stabbing boyfriend Markus Laird to death while he slept, was today revealed to be a special make-up effects artist on several sick and depraved movies.

'She specialised in realistic gory effects,' said a colleague. 'Millie was obsessed with blood, and with spurting blood in particular.'

So now he knew what she did in the movies. She had worked in make-up effects, in the horror genre, in the Eighties. If she had been a musician, this was like saying she had played Woodstock, but Jerry didn't think that had exactly been the response back then; hence 'sicko'.

In his experience, the tabloid term for someone who worked on special effects was a 'wizard', or at least a 'whizz', but he guessed that was reserved for those working on films they approved of. The title had been stripped in this instance, in the context of the war against depravity.

By this point in the cycle, the story was worth a double-page spread, including lurid stills from a couple of movies she had worked on: *Blood Ceremony* and *Lucifer's Charade*. Jerry was pretty sure they were Italian. He was also sure they were both on the infamous DPP list. He noted there was no further reference to *Child's Play 3*, and deduced it couldn't have been one of her titles, otherwise they would have led with that. Not that they were short of a condemnation angle. The story was padded out with quotes from pro-censorship campaigners, one of whom was happy to ladle on the innuendo.

'When someone takes pride in recreating these things so realistically, you have to ask whether she's done that from imagination or from first-hand experience.'

More significantly, the spread also included a sidebar editorial piece, emphasising how seriously the paper was taking the issue.

Members of a whole generation of children are growing up in a culture that is saturated by images of gratuitous cruelty and bestial violence.

David Alton, Lib Dem MP for Liverpool Mossley Hill, is campaigning to keep this filth out of our homes.

'Films which revel in violence and in harrowing scenes, that must undoubtedly have an impact on young people that watch them, should be removed from our television screens,' Alton says.

'It's not about censorship, it's about the protection of society. It is about creating an ordered and decent society.'

We share his concern about how corrupting and sick these videos are, but in the case of Millie Spark, we now have a tragic and disturbing insight into how corrupting and sick are the people who make them.

It is quite wrong that we don't pillory the purveyors of this pornography. The people producing this filth are masquerading as decent members of society.

It is time we turned our ire on the corruptors.

Right here was why Millicent got the sentence she did. And this was only the *Record*, so Jerry could barely imagine what the likes of the *Sun* and the *Daily Heil* were saying. Society needed a scapegoat, and Millicent hadn't merely been someone who demonstrated the evil effects of watching video nasties. She had been someone guilty of creating them.

He looked her up on the IMDb, and there she was, billed as Millie Spark. She had started off in British TV: soaps and mainstream drama, before evidently finding her niche on *Hammer House of Horror*. Beneath that there was a screed of movie credits that ran off the bottom of the page. They were mostly European productions, including the two cited in the news story.

Jerry scrolled down to see if there were any others he had heard of, or even seen. When he reached the end of the list, he almost dropped Danby's phone.

The last movie she worked on was *Mancipium*.

The Phoenix

Millie had never felt so nervous about the prospect of killing someone. She would have thought that given the body count she had racked up, the blood-drenched repertoire of stabbing, slashing and impaling she had wrought, she should not be so anxious about one more death, but the stakes seemed higher than before.

There were a lot more eyes on her than she was used to as she worked to prepare the effect. Lucio had invited a journalist from *Fangoria* magazine to visit the set, and had ensured that every significant figure involved in the production was around Cinecitta that day and available for interview. Every time she looked up from where she was crouched over her work, Millie caught the watchful eye of somebody who had a major stake riding on this, or in certain cases, the eyes of individuals whose prospective stake in the project might make everybody else sleep a little easier. For instance, not only was Lucio's co-production partner Julia Fleet observing proceedings, but her brother Freddy Wincott had shown up too, which potentially had far bigger implications. And if all that wasn't enough, the British junior minister for Culture was here too.

In short, it would be a very bad time to screw up.

The actor was lying patiently on the floor as she put the finishing touches to preparing his impending demise. His name was Dante, a chiselled and muscular young man she had worked with before. He was dressed as a legionary, though historians would probably take issue with his tunic being black. This was for Millie's purposes, to disguise the means by which she would be inflicting his mortal wound. She had pre-cut the tunic along where the blade would slice, then lightly taped it together again so that the tear was invisible.

Beneath this she was carefully attaching a specially prepared condom. Millie's kit bag was always full of them. Whenever she had to open it at customs, she took it as read that they would assume she was a hooker. But until someone invented something else that was both strong enough to hold blood and flexible enough to be easily concealed, she would have to live with that.

For this effect, she had fed a ruler inside to stretch the condom and used a scalpel to cut along the length of it. Next, she had placed a length of black fishing line along it before sealing the slice with plastic tape. Then she had filled it with fake blood and knotted the open end. She fixed the condom in place by taping the ends to Dante's skin, leaving the fishing line to trail out invisibly across the tunic, with the rest of it disguised by the black backdrop, this being a night-time exterior scene of a military camp.

The *Fangoria* journalist crouched nearby. She asked Millie if it was cool to take a few photos.

'As long as you stay that side of the lights,' Millie told her. 'They already took the white balance readings and they go nuts if you cast a shadow they weren't expecting.'

'I'll be careful.'

Her name was Ruby Damson, which Millie would have assumed to be a pseudonym if she didn't write under the by-line of Blood-Red Ruby. Millie had read her pieces before, not just for *Fangoria* but for *Empire* and *Starburst* too. Lucio had been smart in offering her this exclusive access. The film would get a lot of early play to help build up an advance profile: it wouldn't merely appear on the release schedules one day along with all the rest. People would be talking about it. People would be looking forward to it.

Ruby photographed the clapper-loader writing on the slate. It stated: MANCIPIUM, SCENE TWENTY-FOUR, TAKE ONE.

More pressure. This wasn't the kind of scene you could afford multiple takes on. At this level of budget, the cost of film stock alone meant the director couldn't get precious. But when it came to a make-up effects shot like this, if you didn't get it right, it took a long time to re-set, every minute of which a whole load of personnel were being paid to stand around doing nothing.

'A camera is a machine for burning money,' Lucio liked to remind everyone. 'Every second on set, it is incinerating our budget.'

With Millie happy with her set-up, she told Dante he could get to his feet. He stood up slowly and smoothly, conscious of how his movement might tug on the tapes and dislodge the apparatus.

'Okay, we're good here,' Millie reported.

'Still need a moment,' replied Alessandro, who was in consultation with Umberto, his director of photography.

'Don't move a muscle,' Millie told Dante.

They shared a smile, a mutual acknowledgment that he didn't need to be told.

With a reporter's instinct for opportunity, Ruby sensed a lull in the proceedings and took a step closer.

'Can you tell me a bit about what you're doing here?'

'Trade secrets, I'm afraid,' Millie replied, tapping her nose. 'Just kidding. I stole this from Tom Savini. He did it in *The Burning*. Actually, I think he probably stole it from Dick Smith.'

Millie talked her through the effect, leaving out a couple of crucial details, and more importantly omitting what was going to happen during the take. She knew it would make for better copy when she saw it live – as long as it bloody worked.

'What can you tell me about how this project came to be? Is it true that a bunch of you cooked up the whole thing at a party on Lucio's yacht?'

Millie wondered who fed her that line, or whether she had embellished it from an offhand remark and was fishing for someone to volunteer more information by way of confirmation or denial. She responded with a variation on the party line.

'They say success has many fathers, while failure is always an orphan. There was indeed a long conversation one night, and I'm sure a lot of those present would like to trace Stacey's ideas back to their drunken contribution to it, but like any great movie, it starts with a great script. Stacey wrote something with a vision we could all share, a truly unique concept that was a perfect platform for a director of Alessandro's pedigree and just a playground for the likes of me.'

'And is it true that this script made Credit Populaire change their mind about backing Lucio? It's widely accepted that his production slate was collateral damage in the fallout from the Credit Lyonnais-MGM scandal.'

Millie smiled. She knew for sure who had fed Ruby that angle. Lucio wanted her focusing on a script that had blown away financiers at a time when they were in retreat from the industry, rather than on the fact that they had pulled a far larger investment due to criminal associations.

'You'd have to ask Jean-Marc Poupard about that. He's here somewhere. I'm sure I saw him earlier.'

Millie recalled the news sweeping through the yacht like the place had come ablaze. Everyone was delightedly telling the stories they had heard about Giancarlo Paretti and about CLBN: tales of bribery, excess and gauche vulgarity that had entertained people for years, but which now looked like doomed hubris, a house of cards that was always bound to collapse. Then someone, she didn't remember who, had asked the question that changed the tone instantly.

'I wonder if this has any implications for Lucio's deal with Credit Populaire?'

Jean-Marc was seen coming aboard, hurriedly seeking Lucio. The party atmosphere evaporated and people seemed to drift away, here one minute then gone the next. In some cases they perhaps felt their presence was inappropriate, like intruding on grief. But for most, given this was the film business, they fled because their instinct was to disassociate themselves with failure as fast as possible.

Millie was among the last hold-outs, a group of them sitting around a table drinking as though at a wake: herself, Alessandro and Stacey. It was partly a gesture of solidarity with Lucio and partly a matter of there still being drinks available and having nowhere better to go. To his credit, Jean-Marc had hung around too, perhaps out of propriety, not wishing to be seen slinking away having delivered this terrible blow. Alternatively, it was possible he just stayed because it was one last chance to fuck some nubile wannabe half his age. Millie remembered seeing him necking beers while some pretty young thing stared up at him like he was God

Almighty. Maybe nobody had told her he had just padlocked the vault. She knew she shouldn't be too hard on him though, given what happened after that.

She remembered Lucio finally emerging, nobody having seen him for about two hours. He had embraced Jean-Marc, demonstrating that he wasn't holding a grudge. Millie had been impressed. Lucio must have been feeling raw, but he didn't lose his dignity; or maybe he didn't lose sight of the bigger picture. Either way, it paid off in the long term.

Lucio joined them at the table, while Jean-Marc slipped off somewhere in the company of the girl. He seemed to recognise that he would be the ghost at this particular feast, leaving Lucio in the consoling company of other people whose plans had just been shredded.

'I'm guessing you all heard, so I don't need to say nothing,' Lucio muttered. He looked a little beaten up. Millie had never seen him this way. Nobody had ever seen him this way. Alessandro poured him a large single malt and he simply stared at it while everyone sat in the growing silence, nobody knowing what to say to him.

Then he suddenly necked the dram and clapped his hands, like he was bringing a meeting to order.

'Fuck it. Let's make a movie.'

'With what?' Alessandro asked. 'You going back to Florio? You really want to do that again?'

'Forget about where the money might come from. We start with the pitch and worry about that shit later. Come on, right now: let's say we've got ten million. What would—'

Stacey laughed by way of cutting him off, her throaty voice rasping with decades of whisky and cigarettes. Stacey had been a stripper – Racy Stacey – at a time when her profession was being squeezed by the non-certified movies that were starting to play the same grindhouses. She told Millie how she got to know one of the producers, a guy who was literally driving his films city to city in the trunk of his car. She convinced him to cast her in his next picture, a soft porn women-in-prison flick, and as she put it, 'more people paid to see my tits in that shitty movie in two months than in five years on 42nd Street.' She went on to become a stalwart of the US exploitation industry throughout the Seventies: acting, writing and producing. Then just when its heyday was drawing to a close, she met Lucio.

Millie had never been quite sure about the nature of their relationship. She was certain it had been sexual at one time, and Stacey was notoriously indiscreet about her libido, but she had to be twenty years too old for Lucio's tastes these days. Nonetheless, there was a bond between them. She had moved to Europe in the early Eighties, and Lucio had consistently found a role for her on one or other side of the camera.

'With respect, nobody's giving you ten million bucks, Lucio baby,' Stacey told him, probably the only person who could get away with saying that.

'Okay, five million. Let's say we have five million dollars, and we can only make one film, and it has to go theatrical in the US ahead of home video. What are we gonna make?'

'Five million won't make anything that will go theatrical in the US,' Stacey replied. 'Sorry, but it is what it is. Unless we're talking arthouse, and looking at who's around this table, I know we ain't talking arthouse.'

'I can make a five-million-dollar picture look expensive,' Lucio said. 'Been doing it my whole career. That's the route to take, in fact. Shoot on other people's sets, borrow their costumes. Cinecitta have had their Roman and Renaissance stages mothballed for years, nobody paying them a lira. I could cut a deal to shoot there.'

'Can we come up with a horror flick set in ancient Rome?' asked Stacey brightly, energised by the notion. She was a writer with instincts honed by her years in the exploitation business: give her an interesting hook and she could rattle out a script in a week.

Lucio shook his head.

'Couldn't market it. People get confused. These days they see period costume and they think it has to be drama or maybe adventure. Never horror. Just the poster would be a problem.'

'How about a Renaissance erotic drama?' Stacey suggested. 'You did pretty good making period-costume porn back in the day.'

'Erotic thrillers are still reliable for international pre-sales,' Alessandro observed, though there was weary resignation in his tone. Ever since *Basic Instinct*, it had proven a bankable formula to garnish an unremarkable murder mystery with a few sex scenes. Millie could imagine how a master of *gialli* must have regarded the rise of this derivative subgenre; to say nothing of having had to make a crust by directing them.

'No,' said Lucio. 'Low-budget erotic thrillers only play on home video. I need something that will get a theatrical release. Something that will get people talking.'

'If we have just one shot, it has to be horror,' Stacey argued flatly. 'It's consistently the most profitable genre in the business, and it's something we're all experienced at making. Not ancient Rome horror, obviously, but you know what I'm saying: go to what you know, play to our strengths.'

Alessandro frowned.

'Hannibal Lecter killed the slasher,' he said, his voice a low grumble. 'It made audiences care about the psychology of the serial killer. Before *Silence of the Lambs*, you could get away with motivations that were crazy abstract. Your classmates didn't come to your birthday party? Splat: kebab skewer through the throat for all of them.'

'That is so true,' Millie agreed. 'Seriously, back in the Eighties, I heard the pitch for *Sixteen Candles* and I thought it was for a slasher flick. Audiences want something more plausible now. They want to be captivated by the complex workings of a twisted mind rather than watching *Ten Little Indians* over and over.'

'Jason still does business,' Stacey countered. 'There's a new *Friday the 13th* movie coming out this summer.'

'That's his superpower,' said Lucio with a wry smile. 'You can't kill Jason, not even at the box office.'

'He's an anomaly, though,' Millie said. 'Name me another hit slasher movie since *Silence of the Lambs*. Alessandro's right: it's all psychological thrillers now.'

'Psychological thrillers need marquee names or a shit-hot script to stand out,' said Stacey. 'Five mill buys us neither.'

'Good,' said Alessandro. 'Because I don't want to make one. *Silence* was great, but the kind of movies it ushered in have been fucking dull. I believe there is still a market for true horror. For the spectacle and the ritual, for creepy superstition and a sense of evil that gets inside your head.'

'Nobody worried about the motivation of the creature in *Alien*,' Millie offered. 'And yet the film itself was all about the psychology.'

'Can't make a creature feature,' said Lucio. 'Monsters are fucking expensive. And *Alien* was pre-Hannibal. But I take your point. We need to come up with a horror story where the villain's motivation doesn't matter, and yet the film itself is all about psychology. How do you square that circle?'

Lucio stared down at the table while Alessandro poured him another dram, almost as a gesture of acknowledging the intractability of this Gordian knot.

Then it hit Millie, and she laughed out loud.

'What?'

'You just described two of the best horror movies ever made. *The Exorcist* and *The Omen*.'

At that point, Stacey's eyes had lit up, her brain clearly whirring. She put her arms around Millie and kissed her on the cheek.

'You're right. And I think I'm on to something.'

'Great,' said Alessandro. 'Now we just need five million dollars.'

Millie remembered everybody looking to Lucio, almost pityingly. He had smiled.

'Something will turn up.'

Alessandro and Umberto finished their discussion and the director called places. Ruby hurriedly stepped clear of the scene while the actors got into position. Sergio Kamaras, who was playing the assailant, stood before Dante, hefting a Roman sword. Its surfaces glinted in the light, though at this distance Millie could see how the edges had been blunted by the prop master. It couldn't have cut butter. Millie checked once more with the DoP to make sure her fishing line was black on black and not catching any light.

'Okay, speed,' came the call from the sound recordist, and a few moments later Alessandro shouted, 'Action!'

Sergio swung his sword and at the same time Millie tugged on the fishing line. It tore open Dante's tunic and seemingly cut a wide gash across his chest, which instantly overflowed with blood from the condom. Dante dropped to his knees, letting the camera linger on the wound as it bled, then slumped forward, dead.

Alessandro shouted, 'Cut!' and the set broke into spontaneous applause.

Millie felt heat in her cheeks and the tips of her ears as relief and elation flooded through her. She glanced towards Alessandro, who was giving her the thumbs-up, then behind the lights where Lucio's gathering of VIPs were gathered. To a man they were all grinning and nodding approvingly.

Privacy

'I was given your number by Derek Connelly at the Roman Fort Hotel. It's regarding the photograph you sent them of the Blue Lamp Society's Burns Supper in 1994.'

Millicent's voice sounded strangely echoey. She had taken one of the wireless extension phones into her bedroom for privacy, not wanting Vivian or Carla earwigging and asking questions. It was the bareness of the walls that was doing it, she realised, looking around. She had more stuff on display in her various cells than she had permitted herself here. She had been reluctant to hang any images that would evoke painful memories, but maybe she should have picked up a few prints. Stick up a crucifix and it would look like a nun lived here.

She had seldom spoken on the phone since getting out. She had used it more in prison, as back then there was someone she wanted to speak to: her brother. Now the only people she really knew already lived with her.

Every so often Vivian would gently ask: 'Have you thought about getting in touch with people you used to know?' She would mention Facebook and email. 'It's quite easy to put out feelers these days. It doesn't have to be awkward.'

'They're all probably dead,' Millicent had replied. 'And they won't want reminding of me.'

The name Mr Connelly had given her was Angela Whiteford. She was softly spoken, with a Brummie accent, and sounded too young to be the wife of anyone in the photo. There was a reverberation to her tone, like she was in her kitchen, and Millicent could hear the laughter and squeal of children in the background.

'Oh, yes. The picture belonged to my late father. I found it when I was clearing out his things a couple of years ago. I had it hanging in our spare bedroom until someone sent me a link to the hotel's request.'

'I am trying to find out some more about one of the chaps in the picture. By the name of Des Creasey. Does that ring a bell?'

There was a brief pause.

'I'm afraid not.'

Millicent suppressed a sigh.

'Very few of the names would mean anything to me, to be honest. I had just started primary school when that picture was taken. That's why I was happy to part with it. The only names I recognised from the caption were my dad's and Bill Geddes, because I knew him growing up. He and Dad were big pals. I think he was the one who organised those gatherings. He's who you need to speak to. He knew everybody.'

'Do you still have his number?' Millicent asked, bracing herself for being told Angela had lost touch after her father passed. At least she had a name to go on.

'No offence, but I'm afraid I'm a bit wary of giving out his number without his permission. Bill was quite senior in the force during some difficult times, and not everybody forgives and forgets. But if you give me your number, I can tell him what it's about and he'll get back to you.'

Millicent did very well to keep her voice steady at the mention of the police. She had been arguing the possibilities with herself all the way back along Great Western Road, but this seemed to confirm that Connelly's guess had been right.

'I would very much appreciate that, yes. Thank you.'

Millicent dictated her name and Vivian's home number.

'And can I just ask you, Mrs Whiteford, was your father in the police too?'

'Oh, yes. Everybody in the Burns society was on the force.'

Millicent disconnected the call and sat clutching the handset. The bare little chamber was the same and yet the whole world was different. The man she had known as Markus Laird was known to others as Des Creasey, and had been a police officer.

She felt her stomach lurch and feared for a moment she was going to be sick, but it passed. Puzzlement and curiosity were very effective anti-emetics.

Why had this never come out in court? Even if he hadn't been on duty, if the prosecution could imply that his job was any kind of factor, it would have been reflected in the charges. At the very least it ought to have been mentioned.

Like a rock dislodged after decades by melting snows, something shook loose in her mind: an observation that had jarred with her at the time but made sense only now. Markus never had any family present at the trial. He had been murdered, but there were never any relatives in the public gallery. No friends and no colleagues from the film business either, for a man who seemed a champion networker. At the time she thought it was because they were all abroad, or that it was a reflection on the superficial nature of relationships in the industry. But now she understood that it was because there never was a Markus Laird. There was only Des Creasey, police officer; and not an ordinary police officer either. He had to have been deep undercover, and operating abroad too. That meant Special Branch. And part of his cover had been screwing her.

Millicent was shaken from her revelations by a knock at the door and Viv popping her head around.

'Were you on the phone?' she asked.

Millicent looked at the handset. Vivian must have noticed the line was busy, and her bid for privacy was likely to have only heightened her curiosity.

'Yes. Sorry, were you trying to use it?'

'It's no problem. Who were you calling?'

Millicent's mind went blank as she tried and failed to think of a plausible lie.

'Sorry, that's none of my business,' Vivian corrected herself. 'Anyway, I need to speak to you about a possible wee trip away. I found this Groupon deal for a hotel up in Pitlochry for two nights, starting tomorrow. There's a swimming pool and a spa. I thought we could all treat ourselves.'

Vivian gave her an optimistic smile, aware that this was not as easy a sell as it might sound to anyone else. A few weeks ago she had suggested they all go on a city break to Rome. Millicent refused, pointing out she didn't have a passport. Vivian offered to help with all that, but the passport was merely an excuse. The truth was, she couldn't face being back there, confronting the memories of all that she once had, who she had once been.

Carla was still sore about it because Vivian decided they couldn't go off and leave Millicent alone, so the trip never happened. She was aware that Vivian was likely to take the same protective view if she refused on this occasion too.

'It's not really my thing,' she said, guilty about the look of disappointment that was already forming on Vivian's face.

'Is everything all right?' she asked. 'I was worried when you were gone from your bed this morning without saying anything.'

'I didn't want to waken anybody,' she explained, offering a smile. She then feared this might actually pique Viv's unease all the more as it was such an unfamiliar sight.

A paranoid part of her had always feared Vivian could tell she was intending to take her own life, and it wasn't like she could say, 'It's okay, I'm not planning to kill myself anymore,' by way of reassurance.

She couldn't say for sure that it wasn't still her intention, but it had most definitely been put on hold. The meaning of the last quarter century had just been altered and she wasn't ready to shuffle off until she had some answers.

She would also like some privacy while she asked the questions, and she definitely didn't want to be away from the flat if this Bill Geddes bloke called back. No answer he could give her would restore what she had lost, but at least she might go to her end with some sense of resolution.

She might get her sweet release.

'I think you should give the hotel break a try. It'll be really laid back, no fuss.'

'I'll be fine here, honestly. I don't want you missing out again on account of me, so you two should just go yourselves.'

'We can't leave you here all alone.'

'You wouldn't be. I've got Jerome now.'

Vivian thought about it. This clearly hadn't occurred to her.

'I think he prefers Jerry,' she said, which Millicent took as assent.

'I like Jerome. It suits him better.'

'Are you sure about this?'

'I think you and Carla deserve a little break from me. I believe they call it respite care.'

Cursed

The light rain that greeted Jerry as he emerged from the Mitchell had turned into hailstones before he even reached Sauchiehall Street, so he hopped on a bus. Annoyingly, it went off again before he had travelled a couple of stops, but having a seat meant he could watch the video he had downloaded. It was the *Complete and Utter Cult* episode that featured a segment on *Mancipium*.

He hadn't been able to watch it before because the memory was still too raw. It still was, but given what he had just discovered, he needed to get over himself. In fact, perhaps knowing someone who worked on the film would mean that it developed an association with something other than the worst night of his life.

Rossco hadn't sold the framed poster he insisted on holding onto that night, because of course he hadn't. The prick had it hanging on his wall the last time Jerry went round his place, three feet from the shelf where that *Star Wars* VHS was sitting. For Rossco it had never been about its material worth to anyone else, only its value to Jerry. He had the poster up on display as an act of territorial pissing. It was probably for the best. It was one more reason not to see Rossco again; as if all the other reasons weren't enough.

Jerry skipped forward to the relevant section. *Complete and Utter Cult* comprised film historian Danny Stone and the critic and film festival director Mike Carslake. As always, they had garnered takes from the usual pool of directors, film buffs and horror geeks, including the likes of Kim Newman, Jake West, Neil Marshall and Jason Arnopp.

The talking heads started by rehearsing the familiar stories and legends, some of them laughing at the ludicrousness.

'The articles that started this whole thing were mostly written when the internet was still in its comparative infancy,' one of them said. 'People could therefore not immediately go off and look things up for verification or further research and discover that the writer's fevered speculation was absolute bollocks, founded on nothing more than hearsay, exaggeration and wishful thinking.'

'My favourite rumour,' said another, 'was that the film was reputed to have been financed by Italian gangsters, perhaps as a money-laundering exercise. This in itself wasn't particularly outlandish, but it led to the claim that they had used real human blood and body parts in certain special effects, because as well as money laundering, they were disposing of human remains in plain sight.'

One by one they debunked the various myths and offered more prosaic explanations for why the film had never been released.

'As I understand it, there is a seed of truth to the legend,' said Stone, author of *From Grindhouse to Gorehound: The History of Horror*. 'Which is that the film was genuinely shocking – unprecedentedly gory and unpleasant – and distributors all over the place were asking for drastic cuts. The UK especially, as it wasn't long after the James Bulger controversy and the tabloids were going crazy. The director, Alessandro Salerno, baulked at this, and the producers decided to mothball the film, planning to submit it again when the climate had changed. Unfortunately, the climate was never right, it remained in limbo for a while, and somewhere along the line, the negative got lost. One day someone will open an old box at Cinecitta and they'll rediscover it.'

Another claimed the film had suffered a similar fate, but as a result of more underhand machinations.

'It was rumoured the project had certain similarities to a bigger-budget horror movie in development at MGM, and someone connected to the studio – but not directly involved – bought out the rights so that they could quietly bury it in order to keep the field clear. Ironically, their own project went into turnaround, but *Mancipium* stayed on the shelf. It might yet turn up, but the old box will be at MGM, not Cinecitta.'

Mike Carslake was far more direct, and perhaps the most plausible.

'The way I heard it – and I say this as a Salerno fan – when the producers saw his assembly cut, it was so terrible, so unutterably shit, that they burned the negative and claimed the insurance. And if there was a priest present at the burning, it was to say a prayer for the death of Italian horror cinema.'

A melting hailstone dripped from Jerry's jacket onto his phone. He wiped it from the screen with his sleeve and looked up to check the bus's progress.

When he looked down again, the talking heads were turning their attention to the supposed curse. Carslake was leading the charge.

'Alright, let's start with the story that Hideo Nakata's *The Ring* was inspired by rumours that a cut of *Mancipium* was distributed on VHS, and that everyone who got one subsequently died. *The Ring* was based on a novel published in 1991. *Mancipium* didn't shoot until 1993, so unless Koji Suzuki had a time machine, we can dispense with that one easily enough.

'As for the claims of bad things happening to people involved in making the film, that's harder to dismiss, but correlation isn't causation. Much is made of the facts that Alessandro Salerno committed suicide shortly after production ended, and that Lucio Sabatini disappeared from his yacht and is believed to have drowned around the same time. But what needs to be acknowledged is that Salerno is known to have suffered from depression, and it was more than a rumour that Sabatini had mafia connections and had previously used drug money to finance his films. I don't think we need to look to any supernatural causes to work out what might have happened to him.'

'It's very much like *The Exorcist* again,' agreed Stone. 'Ellen Burstyn claimed that nine people died during the shoot. But she counted Max von Sydow's brother and the still birth of a baby to the wife of an assistant cameraman. If you open up the pool to relatives, you'll find a number of deaths connected to any shoot. And as Von Sydow himself pointed out, the production lasted a year. That's a long window for someone to snuff it.'

'In the case of *Mancipium*,' said Carslake, 'the supposed curse alluded to deaths that never even happened. One of the claims in the original *Starburst* article is that the film's lead actor disappeared and was never seen again. It was presumably written before we had the IMDb, because these days it would take ten seconds to check that Paulo Nietti is very much alive and is still working in Italian film and TV today.'

Jerry's phone screen filled up with images of Nietti, underlining the point by showing him in a plethora of different roles down the years, charting his transformation from a jet-haired young heart-throb to what Jerry's gran would have called a silver fox.

It then cut back to Carslake.

'It says a lot about how and when myths build up that in the brief rash of late Nineties articles, none of them mention the fact that someone on the film's crew was actually jailed for murder. I can't remember her name, but it was a big news story, a real red-top feeding frenzy. She killed her boyfriend around the time *Mancipium* was in post-production, but the myth of the film hadn't been born yet. By the time it was gaining traction, nobody joined that dot, presumably because she was just a second AD or whatever.'

Her name was Millie Spark and she was a make-up effects artist, Jerry wanted to correct him. But the fact that these details had been forgotten only served to underline Carslake's point.

'See, what's interesting to me is the question of why the myth of a curse first develops,' he went on. 'Because once it does, it can become a self-fulfilling prophecy. People get excited by any anecdote that supports the idea, discarding anything that doesn't. They start by ascribing significance to the death of the director and the disappearance of the producer, then they start adding stuff that never happened. But what was it that started this accretion process?'

'I think it's similar to *The Exorcist* again,' suggested Stone. 'In there being a perception of something evil about the film itself: in both cases, a misunderstanding deriving from the film being about evil, and consequently a fear that they had tapped into something evil while making it. Obviously neither of us has seen *Mancipium*, but I recall talking to a *Fangoria* journalist who had read the script, and she said it did genuinely have some profound things to say about the nature of evil, things that would make people uncomfortable.'

'That's the tragedy, isn't it?' said Carslake. 'We'll never know. You could even argue that the mythology around this movie *is* its curse. It is remembered only for an association with death, not for what it might have had to say. It never got released. Its director took his own life. Its producer was almost certainly murdered. So even if you don't give credence to curses, you have to say that this was an ill-starred project which attracted more than its fair share of bad luck.'

Jerry felt a threat of tears forming as these words resonated. He thought he had got away with it, but the memory had come at him sideways. He didn't believe in curses, but there was no escaping the fact that *Mancipium* was a common factor linking the worst thing that had happened to Millicent, the worst thing that had happened to him, and by far the worst thing that had happened to that old man whose face still haunted him.

Keansy had been halfway out the window when the bloke came through the door.

It was one of the old boys from the photographs. He and Jerry stood there, each rendered motionless as they regarded each other with mutual horror. That was the freeze-frame image that would remain etched in Jerry's mind for ever after. The thing he could never go back from. The last moment before innocence ended.

That came when Jerry realised the look on the old man's face was something else, something more. It was not mere shock, but pain and fear; and the fear was not of the young man before him.

He was clutching his arm. Then he collapsed.

He was having a heart attack.

Jerry could hear the departing footfalls of Rossco and Keansy running away. He knew he couldn't leave, though. He grabbed his mobile to call an ambulance then realised they would then have his number. You could dial 141 to hide that, but he had heard the cops could still identify you if you had called the emergency services. He grabbed the landline, dialled 999.

He knew they recorded these calls. He put on an English accent, generic and regionless, unless there was actually a region where all the BBC presenters came from. He asked for an ambulance and told the woman who answered what was happening. She said it would be at least fifteen minutes, but told him she'd give him instructions what to do in the meantime.

He put the phone on speaker and knelt down, felt for a pulse. There wasn't one. Not even a hint. It wasn't just a heart attack, it was a full-blown cardiac arrest.

He heard her relay this to someone. He wasn't clear whether the implication was that this would bump the case up the priority list, or relegate it as a lost cause.

Still she kept talking, telling him to stay calm, helping him through it. Giving an ETA on the ambulance. Encouraging him to keep going.

His own heart was pounding as he carried out CPR, guided by her instruction and by memory of doing it at school. Pumping the chest, beating out the rhythm: *Ha, ha, ha, ha, staying alive, staying alive. Ha, ha, ha, ha, staying alive, staying alive.*

He recalled the slivers of saliva flecked with blood at the corners of the old man's mouth, the glassiness of his eyes as he stared blankly, emptily upwards. Jerry knew he was dead, but he couldn't stop, because if he stopped, that was when he had to begin living in the world where he'd caused this.

Ha, ha, ha, ha, staying alive, staying alive.

He remembered the woman asking him to check various signs and responses. Everything was negative. Still he kept pumping, the sweat pouring from him: Eight minutes, ten minutes, twelve. Still the glassy stare. Blood trickling now, not just flecks amid the phlegm. Then he had heard the siren. Then he had run.

139

Identity

The call came less than an hour later. Millie was staring at the bare walls again, wondering how she would feel if she put up a picture. She hadn't done so before because she never felt like she belonged, but maybe she would feel more like she belonged if she made the place more her own.

It couldn't hurt to put up a lobby poster from one of Alessandro's old *gialli*. If it wasn't a film she had worked on, that ought not to bring back anything agonising, only pleasant remembrances of a great artist. It wouldn't be like putting up a poster for *Blood Ceremony* or *Mancipium*; not that it was an option in the case of the latter, all mementoes of which seemed to have been erased from history. Maybe that was life telling her something.

She used to have one, of sorts: a full-page ad ripped from *Screen International*. Markus had given it to her as an olive branch after a falling out. She remembered looking at it after she was released. It seemed like an artefact from someone else's life; someone she had lost touch with, a long time ago.

Millicent crouched down to flip through the stack of framed posters leaning against the wall. As she did so, she glimpsed the suitcase under the bed. She had stashed it away so that nobody would see it until they came to clear out the room.

She knew she ought to unpack her clothes. She wouldn't be going where she thought she was going. Not yet.

The box of tapes out in the hall still had to go. Despite Jerome's offer to lend her his VHS player, it was a repository of memories that she wanted to keep sealed. Not so much the movies themselves, but the places she associated with them: Alastair's house, and her flat in London. She certainly wasn't going to move the box back into her bedroom so that it could sit there. She should deal with it while she had the impetus and while it was stacked, packed and ready to go.

She pulled out a framed poster of *Black Gloves and White Lace*, Alessandro's masterpiece. She'd start by hanging that and see how it made her feel.

She needed some hooks to hang it, as well as a hammer. There had to be one somewhere in the house, though perhaps they kept it under lock and key in case the resident murderer went crazy with it. Terms of release, Ms Spark.

She had just stepped into the hall when she encountered Vivian coming her way again, clutching the handset. Millicent realised she hadn't even heard the phone ring. She was so used to tuning out the sound, as it was never for her.

'Someone's asking for you,' she said, intrigued. 'A man.'

Millicent took the handset and returned to her room, trembling a little as she sat down on the bed.

She swallowed to steady her voice.

'Hello?'

'Yes, hello, am I speaking to Millie Spark?'

It was a male voice, English. RP, with more than a hint of public school.

'Millicent.'

As she corrected this, she felt a chill. She hadn't gone by Millie in a very long time. It was a name used by people who only knew her from headlines. She had given Angela Whiteford her full name, so either this wasn't Bill Geddes, or he was telling her he knew all about who she was.

'I believe you were making inquiries regarding the Blue Lamp Burns Society.'

'Is this Bill Geddes?'

'No, my name is Jonathan Rook, but Bill did call me, for the same reason that it's me who is getting back to you rather than him. Anyone inquiring into certain matters raises a flag, so Bill was obliged to inform me.'

'I had assumed he was no longer serving.'

'Oh, he isn't, but the bad guys never retire, if you see what I mean. Now, I believe you were asking about Des Creasey. Can you explain what your relationship was to him?'

Millicent thought about how much he must already know. Maybe he was just making sure she was who she said she was.

'The whole thing is, I knew him under a different name,' she said. 'I was under the impression he worked in the film industry.'

'And what would that other name be?'

She swallowed. Better she be the one to acknowledge what was probably in a file in front of him.

'Mr Rook, I have no doubt you are aware that I went to prison for the murder of Markus Laird, and for what it's worth, I maintain my innocence to this day. When I saw the Burns society photograph, it was the first time I became aware of his real name, and I only this morning learned that he was a police officer, I'm assuming undercover.'

'Des Creasey was Special Branch, yes.'

Millicent swallowed. It was growing anger rather than nervousness that was causing her voice to waver now.

'I was in a sexual relationship with Mr Creasey, while he pretended to be someone else.'

There was a pause.

'Miss Spark, I understand that you have valid questions, but as you indicated, these matters are pertaining to undercover operations, and I am under severe restrictions regarding what I am permitted to reveal. It's for the ongoing protection of personnel whose identities need to remain confidential.'

'Surely you don't need to protect a man who died in 1994.'

'What Mr Creasey was involved in remains part of an open investigation. Not ongoing, I should stress, but not closed either.'

Something tiny inside Millicent ignited. It was just a pilot light, but it was burning.

'Now that you have come forward, it strikes me that we may have some questions for each other,' Mr Rook went on. 'It's possible you could assist in certain lines of inquiry with regard to particular events: things you might have witnessed without appreciating their significance.'

Millicent allowed a silence to grow, before responding:

'I'll show you mine if you show me yours.'

'I wish it were that simple,' he replied. 'I will look into what I am allowed to disclose, and I will stretch the rules as far as I can, but either way, I think it would be best if we spoke in person, and soon. You're in Glasgow, is that right?'

Soon, he said. Soon was good. Millicent gave him the address.

'And who do you live with? By that I mean, is there anyone else likely to be present? Due to the classified nature of these matters, I have to be assured of absolute confidentiality. In fact, I must insist that you do not discuss any aspect of this with anyone else.'

'I understand. The other two ladies who live here are going to be away for a couple of days, leaving tomorrow.'

She didn't feel the need to mention Jerome, as he was always out all day anyway, and worked some evenings too.

'I'll be in touch,' Rook said, then hung up.

Millicent clutched the handset and felt a tear form in one eye despite herself. She had long ago learned to be wary of hope, but she could not deny that she had been shown a glimmer of a possibility that this went further than just her and Markus. That there was a bigger story to be told: one in which she might be able to clear her name.

Ultimatum

Jerry allowed himself a wee smile as he approached the corner and saw the name of the street: his upmarket new address. Staying on the bus as it had passed his old halls felt like the lifting of a burden, a reminder that you could take action to change what was wrong in your life.

He had to acknowledge that as bitter as the memories of it were, that night had been the catalyst for him turning things around, setting in motion the course that had ultimately led him here. So many times he had lied to his gran about what he was involved in: making her promises he never kept, never intended to keep, even though she was dying. Maybe even because she was dying, and he couldn't handle it. But that night was when he had made a promise to himself. He had seen, too late, everything she had been trying to protect him from. After that, he had cleaned up his act. Stayed home. Hit the books like a bastard. Grasped the ticket out that his gran had spent her life holding out to him. Geographically it wasn't so far, but in so many other respects it had taken him a million miles from the world of Rossco.

As he thought this, he felt an unease when he remembered how close he had come to blowing it, and how his place on the course was still under threat. But maybe he had pulled out of the dive just in time. In fact, maybe *Mancipium* was not a curse to him, but a blessing. It had been there when he finally chose the right path. Now, if he could get Millicent to talk about it, what an essay that would make. More than an essay: it could be a piece he might even sell, to *Empire* or something.

Turning the corner, he looked towards Vivian's place and saw a familiar figure loitering at the garden gate.

He couldn't believe it. Fucking Rossco was standing there, outside the house. How the hell did he find him? Jerry felt that cold knife in the guts again. He had moved a million miles away in so many respects, except the one that mattered.

'Jai, ma man. Long time no see.'

That was what he always called him. Jai. Never Jerry.

'Alright, Rossco. How's it goin'?'

They both smiled, each pretending like they had just lost touch and that it was regrettable. Each pretending that it wasn't creepy as fuck for Rossco to have shown up here like this.

'Aye, I heard you were up here at the uni now. What are you studying?'

'Film & TV. Politics.'

'Ooh-ooh.' Rossco made a mocking gesture, one reserved for anyone who was getting ideas above their station. It was the subtext to this whole exchange.

'You always liked your films, right enough. And what about the whole student lifestyle? You got cool flatmates? Pure rides, I'll bet. Pure filth, these student lassies, I've heard. You shagged any of them yet?'

Rossco wore a smirk as he asked this. He knew. Jerry had no idea how, but the fucker knew. Rossco always did his research before they hit somewhere.

Rossco glanced back at the house he was blocking the path to.

'I asked for you at your old halls. They told me you'd moved in with a bunch of auld dears. Nice digs, if you don't mind the smell of pish.'

'It's not like that.'

'Naw, I'll bet it isnae. West End, intellectual types. Sure doesnae look like a nursing home. Looks like the kind of place where folk have got a few bob.'

'Don't even go there,' Jerry told him.

'Oh, I'm there, mate, how could I no' be? It's the perfect score. You're already on the inside.'

'Aye, that wouldn't be obvious. Stuff goes missing after the new guy moves in?'

'Then you just make sure some of your own gear disappears, maybe your phone and your laptop. Then you've got a wee thief-in-the-night scenario.'

'Like the polis wouldnae see through that,' Jerry countered. He was trying to make it sound like they were arguing practicalities. They both knew they weren't.

He had largely avoided Rossco since that night. Barely saw him, and when he did, like at Gran's funeral, he hadn't cracked a light about going off to uni. He had slunk away. That's what this was really about.

Jerry steeled himself. He had to tell him straight.

'I'm not into that anymore,' he said. 'And I'm deffo not stealing from the folk I live with. I'm not risking getting flung out of this place and flung out of uni.'

Rossco's expression hardened, the way it always did when there was even a hint of dissent.

'You think you're it, don't ye?'

There it was, when subtext became text.

You think you're it: according to his gran, the greatest transgression in the eyes of a certain kind of Scottish waster. The crime was not of conceit, but of having the will and belief to better yourself, and the accusation always came from someone who had neither of those things. It was the scorn of someone who was trying to drag you back down because he knew he could never climb any higher.

Rossco's face became a sneer. He shook his head pityingly.

'What does somebody like you think you're daein' up here anyway? You've come fae fuck-all, Jai. You don't even know who your da' was. You've come fae fuck-all and you'll end up fuck-all. Folk like these auld dears you're stickin' up for, they laugh at the likes of us. So you're a fuckin' mug if you don't help yourself when it's wide open to you.'

146

There had been a time when Jerry thought he wanted Rossco's approval, but now he saw that he was merely afraid of him. He despised Rossco, and everything he had drawn him into. Yes, he did think he was it, if it was something better than this fud.

Jerry swallowed. His heart was going like a speedbag.

'I am helping myself. Just not in a way you would understand.'

Rossco's eyes narrowed in anger and Jerry braced himself. He might get a doing here, but it would be because the guy knew it was finished between them.

The moment passed. Rossco looked away as though mulling this over.

'Naw, maybe I wouldnae,' he said softly.

Then he pivoted on his heel and drove a fist hard into Jerry's midriff.

Jerry was doubled over, winded and helpless against the next attack. It didn't come.

'Sorry about that, Jai, but you shouldnae forget your mates. We go way back, don't we? In fact, have a wee look at this, bring back a bit of nostalgia here.'

He produced his phone and held it in front of Jerry's face, which was down around Rossco's thighs. Jerry saw his own image staring back, in miniature. It was a video. He was standing in the old man's living room, the rows of videotapes on the shelves behind him.

He remembered Rossco fiddling with his phone that night. Remembered him playing with his phone lots of nights. Fucker had been recording him. Not just that time, every time.

'Do you remember that one? Aye, how could you forget it. Old boy died, you said, didn't he? Poor auld bastard. Aye, we hardly saw you after that. It's a shame, but you cannae always trust people to stick by you. That's why it's wise to grab a wee bit of insurance.'

Rossco slipped the phone back into his pocket. Jerry thought about grabbing for it, but he could barely breathe. Fucker would have it backed up anyway.

'I'll be round this way again in a couple a days. You better have somethin' for me by then. Otherwise this is gaun tae the polis. You get me?'

Jerry put his hands on his thighs and forced himself into a standing position, all the time wary of a second blow. He took a breath so that he could reply.

'What happened to "don't shit where you eat"?' he asked.

'It's no' me that's eatin' here, cunto.'

Justice

Millicent leapt from her chair at the sound of the phone, putting down her book and scurrying across the room as she had done whenever it rang. So far, it hadn't been for her. In fact, it hadn't even been for Vivian or Carla half the time.

'We believe there may be government grants available for home improvement projects in your area.'

'Our records show that you may be eligible for a tax rebate.'

She kept hearing about old people being lonely, but clearly, as long as you had a landline, you would seldom be short of someone to talk to.

As she reached for the handset, she looked at the display and noticed that it stated 'withheld'. Mr Rook's number had been withheld too. She had dialled 1471 after he called, pleasantly surprised to discover that this still worked. She had been less surprised that he was protecting his number, given who he was.

'Hello?' she answered eagerly.

'Oh, good afternoon. I'm calling because I believe you were recently involved in an accident.'

She wanted to scream, but Millicent had long ago learned to suppress displays of rage. She had also learned that they have to come out somewhere, so they are best sublimated into other energies.

'God, yes, the accident,' she replied, her voice faltering. 'It was my sister. She was emptying the dishwasher and she slipped. She landed on the carving knife. She bled out in front of me, all over the kitchen floor. Are you calling from the coroner's office?'

There was a satisfying silence.

'No, I . . .'

'Just kidding. It wasn't an accident. I killed her. I cut open her abdomen, pulled her guts out and strangled her with her own intestines. And I'll do the same to you if call this number again.'

As Millicent pressed to hang up, she was already feeling guilty. The woman was only doing her job. She was going crazy with frustration, though. She hadn't left the house in more than twenty-four hours, worried that she would be out when Mr Rook called back.

Vivian and Carla had left around eleven, heading for this hotel in Pitlochry, but not before Vivian had thrust a brand-new mobile phone into Millicent's hands.

'It's pay-as-you-go and I've put twenty pounds' credit onto it. I've pre-programmed my number so that you can get hold of me in an emergency, in case you were out somewhere maybe.'

So now she had two phones that nobody was trying to reach her on.

As she walked back to her chair, the landline rang again. Once more, it said 'withheld'. She calmed herself. She would hang up politely this time. Being cruel made her feel a release in the moment, but it never felt worth it once the moment had passed.

As she answered 'Hello' she could hear a hubbub in the background, someone calling from a busy place.

'Millicent? It's Jonathan Rook. I'm sorry I've not been in touch sooner. It's been chaos at my end. Been trying to find a window. I'm on my way to Glasgow now, though. I'm on the tarmac at Heathrow. Are you free to meet this evening?'

'Absolutely. You have the address still, yes?'

'Yes, but I'm juggling a couple of things. Can you come and meet me in town? Do you know the Blythswood Hotel?'

'I can find it.'

'I'll meet you in the bar upstairs at eight, and we'll take it from there. Do you have a mobile number? I don't seem to have it.'

'I just got one today,' she told him, reading off the number Vivian had written down for her.

'I'll call you if there's any delay.'

'How will I recognise you?'

'Don't worry, I'll recognise you. It's my job. And I'll be showing you credentials to that effect, which I will require you to examine and verify.'

Millicent was glad he said that. If someone had shown up claiming to be a senior policeman, she realised she would have just accepted it without asking for proof. You didn't have the agency to challenge officialdom in prison. You did as you were told, and you didn't answer back. Even before incarceration, Millicent had always done what she was told, and expected other people to abide by the rules too.

That was why she had thought the law would protect her.

Better late than never.

When she was first charged, everything had felt temporary, like it would only be a matter of time before it was all sorted out. She thought the police would very quickly see through to the truth of it. Back then, she believed in justice.

In prison, justice became the friend who stabbed her in the back, the lover who seduced then betrayed her. The hope that killed.

Sometimes it just came down to numbers. She remembered calculating how much of her sentence she had served, and estimating how far behind she was on her parole process: how much closer to release she might be had she just played along. But the longer she served, the more she felt like it would compound the injury if she was to admit guilt now. It would provide a route out, but it felt like it would be at the cost of giving up something irreplaceable: the right to define who she was, what she was and what she was not. The right to name herself.

Eventually desperation twisted her logic. At first she had rebuffed the campaigners claiming she had acted out of self-defence, mainly because it wasn't true. Markus never hit her. She had hit him, in fact, as was stated by witnesses in court. It wasn't the evidence of an unstable temper and violent streak like the prosecution made out, and nor was it indicative of a stormy relationship. But it was a matter of record, and therefore a straw to clutch.

She started telling herself that winning an appeal on these grounds would still represent a kind of victory. She would be officially not a cold-blooded murderer, but rather a wronged woman who had fought back. Unfortunately, her stake in this gamble was to give up her denial that she had killed him. So now that part was a matter of record too.

That was what her belief in justice had got her.

The supreme irony was that from the beginning, her confidence that the truth would become clear derived entirely from how the whole thing appeared from her own point of view. In her job, Millicent took care and pride in considering the angles and anticipating the optics. She should have realised that it was how it looked to everyone else that would put her in prison.

Now though, thanks to an old photograph, it appeared the wider picture might finally emerge.

Blood

Millie was carefully removing the damp mess of tape and latex from Dante's chest, placing the debris on a metal tray. A grip once commented that her before and after routines reminded him of surgery, 'but probably with more blood'.

Lucio came over with a glass of champagne for her. He had another of the crew handing them out all over the floor, having cleared with Alessandro that it was a wrap for today. He didn't do this every night: Lucio had organised a little soiree to round off what was effectively an on-set open day. That didn't change Millie's schedule, though. She had a major effect tomorrow, and she wasn't happy with how it was looking during the video test shots. She was anticipating an evening in her workshop while everyone else partied. Not that this was a hardship: she was in her element on this movie.

'Which one is Jean-Marc?' she heard Ruby ask. 'Is he here now?'

Lucio waved to beckon the French financier, who had reappeared and was standing with Alfie Bertrand, Julia Fleet and her brother, Freddy Wincott. Money gravitates towards money, Millie mused. Freddy and Julia's father was the media baron Roger Wincott, owner of four national newspapers as well as – more significantly for everyone gathered here at Cinecitta – a UK cinema chain and home video label. As Roger's anointed, Freddy was in charge of both of these, though that was only part of the reason his interest in *Mancipium* had everyone on tenterhooks. Wincott International Media had been on the look-out for routes into the US, and having bought up a handful of regional television stations, the company was currently in negotiations to buy MGM, which was up for grabs following the late unpleasantness.

Nobody was saying it out loud, but everybody was entertaining fantasies of what might happen if *Mancipium* could get US theatrical distribution under the MGM banner.

Jean-Marc looked reluctant to swap their company for Lucio's, and not merely because standing next to Freddy put him in proximity to considerably greater wealth and influence.

'Here he is, my white knight,' Lucio said. 'They say I'm the man who makes it happen, but on this movie, this man *really* made it happen.'

Millie was struck by the body language between these two men lately, a mutual wariness which seemed entirely at odds with the air of bonhomie Lucio was projecting. She wondered if she was the only one picking it up. They had seemed genuinely pally in the past, and yet now that they had a mutual commitment, there was a frost in the air whenever they came in contact.

She guessed that despite Jean-Marc pulling something from the fire, Lucio had never quite forgiven him. She also suspected that Jean-Marc was regretting not simply running from the wreckage when he had the chance. He had convinced Credit Populaire de Paris to back this one project, but he seemed a very different person from the guy who was partying his way to an eighty-million-dollar investment. He was on set almost every day, micromanaging every line item and insisting on seeing all the dailies. He seemed to trust Lucio less with five million dollars than he had been prepared to with eighty. She guessed the difference wasn't in the numbers, but that this time Jean-Marc had skin in the game. He must have had to go some to convince his bosses, effectively staked his professional reputation to make this happen. But why would you go out on a limb for someone you didn't trust?

Ruby was asking that very question, after a fashion.

'I guess the thing everybody wants to know is why, following the Paretti scandal, with banks running screaming from the movie business, are Credit Populaire still investing in European film right now?'

Jean-Marc's eyes widened briefly, like he just had a vison of his bosses looking at *Mancipium*'s future box-office receipts and handing

154

him his coat. He took a large gulp of champagne, which seemed to help him regroup.

'You can't be so cautious that you write off a whole industry. Just because someone gets their fingers burned, okay, you learn from their mistake, but you still need to use the oven.

'Essentially it comes down to Lucio and his vision for a great movie with excellent commercial prospects. I don't want to comment on the criminal allegations regarding CLBN, but simply from a business perspective, they were over-exposed by backing too many projects. We are prepared to see how it goes with *Mancipium*, and then proceed on a film-by-film basis.'

Millie put down her champagne flute against a wall where she hoped it wouldn't get knocked over, then lifted one of her trays to take it to her workshop.

'Let me grab this other one for you,' said a female voice. To her surprise, and not a little discomfort, she saw that it belonged to Julia Fleet. Before Millie could tell her she would manage on her own, Julia had lifted the tray: one bearing a syringe and a length of tubing feeding into the end of a plastic arrow. It was from an effect she had used that morning, the arrow protruding from the actor's neck and spurting as though it had punctured the carotid artery.

'Thanks,' she said, basic politeness kicking in despite her instinctive reservations.

Julia followed her along the corridor to where she had set up her workshop. Millie wondered what kind of first impression it would make on a civilian. Half the floor was overlaid with trays of fake wounds, ragged and bloody stumps of limbs arranged on worktops next to pots of liquid latex. She found space for the tray she was carrying, and indicated a spot for Julia to put down her burden also.

Julia looked at her hand and found it spattered with fake blood. Millie handed her some paper towels.

'Thank you,' she said, dabbing her fingers clean. She then extended it for Millie to shake. 'I'm Julia Fleet, of Candledance Films.'

'Yes, I know. We've been in the same meetings. Millie Spark,' she added, realising her response might have sounded like a rebuke, or at least a bit huffy. It was probably both of these.

Julia looked uncomfortable at what Millie had implied.

'I know your name. I wanted to introduce myself properly. We've met as in, been in a lot of the same rooms in recent weeks, but we've never really talked.'

This was largely because Millie had made no effort to do so. She didn't imagine she would be considered worthy of Julia's attention, and certainly hadn't wanted to be patronised by some spoiled rich-kid dilettante. Especially not one whose father owned *those* newspapers.

She knew there was a bit of envy in there too. Julia was only twenty-five or twenty-six but carried herself with a poise Millie could not even aspire towards at twenty years older. As Millie had come to understand it, confidence in any given situation was about knowing you belonged, and she guessed there was nowhere you didn't belong when you knew your father could buy it in two minutes with just a phone call.

Maybe that was unfair. The one thing everybody knew about Julia was that she was the black sheep of the Wincott family. She hadn't done things by halves, either. At the age of nineteen she got married to Vinnie Fleet, singer with notoriously hard-living hair-metal band Cold Steel. The marriage only lasted a matter of months, and there were rumours that Vinnie was abusive; still others that Roger Wincott had paid him two million dollars to fuck off. Julia's only statement on the matter was that 'it was too much, too young', and that she was keeping her new name 'as a sign that I won't be defined by whose daughter I am'.

After being a tabloid fixture throughout her short marriage, she had disappeared from public view, and Millie had frankly forgotten about her until Lucio announced that she would be his co-production partner on *Mancipium*. He had been asking around at Cinecitta and discovered that her indie production company was prepping to shoot a Renaissance-set biopic about Michelangelo. Lucio had made an approach to see if the two shoots might share some costs and resources, but Julia had decided to come in a bit deeper.

Millie had heard nothing of Julia's venture into film, and would have assumed it was a vanity pursuit, trading on her father's connections for a few executive producer credits. To her surprise, it turned out Julia was operating at the low-budget arthouse end of things, where margins were even tighter than Millie was used to.

'That was just amazing,' Julia said, putting down the tray. 'I mean, to see it happening in real life.'

'Well, hopefully you won't ever get to see that in real life,' Millie told her.

'Sure, but you know what I mean: live, right in front of my eyes. Horrible, obviously, but in a good way. It was so exciting. All the projects I've been involved with so far have tended to be light on the throats being ripped out.'

This was the kind of patronising comment an arthouse film snob made about Millie's work, thinking they had disguised a slight as a compliment.

'Yes, it can be quite thrilling sometimes,' Millie replied. 'Down here in the gutter.'

Julia seemed to bite her lip. She wore a strange smile, like a private joke with herself.

'Among the purveyors of sick filth, you mean,' Julia said.

Millie had to look away. Julia was acknowledging Millie's point by invoking her father's newspapers. Touché.

'Believe me, you don't know where the gutter really is. I've been developing cross-border co-productions for two years. They say begging is good for the soul, but I think the primary benefit is that you just feel extra grateful whenever anything actually comes off.'

'What have you been involved in?'

'*Traces in the Sand*, *Our Better Angels*, and now this Michelangelo thing. Oh, and a Mary Wollstonecraft biopic which had the plug pulled four days into principal photography.'

Millie must have looked blank at the mention of the titles.

'Don't worry if you never heard of *Traces* or *Better Angels*. Nobody saw them, because they were crap. Well, not crap, just dull. But simply getting them made felt like such an achievement. That's why I jumped when I saw Stacey's script. I don't think I realised before how much I wanted a hit.'

'Everybody dreams of being a starving artist until dinnertime,' Millie said.

Julia laughed, and not politely either. It was the deep, rolling laughter of recognition.

'God, that's so true. I think part of what I fell for, what I wanted to be part of, was the ethos. This movie is truly scary and poses intriguing philosophical questions, so it has its artistic credentials, but at the same time it's a fuck-you to certain tastes and sensibilities.'

'A bloody fuck-you,' Millie agreed.

Julia gazed around the workshop, taking in the assembled (and disassembled) horrors.

'What have you got lined up for tomorrow? It's the crucifixion scene, right?'

'No, the schedule got re-jigged to do with Sergio's availability. He's got re-shoots in LA and won't be back until Friday now. We're doing the decapitation of the centurion instead: the death of the demon's first incarnation.'

'But isn't Sergio playing the centurion?'

'We're using Dante as a body double.'

Julia looked dubious.

'Honestly, stick a wig on him and there's enough of a resemblance. The fact that Dante's got a fucking tattoo on his arm is more of an issue, but I'm getting practised at covering it up.'

'I was more thinking of the fact that Dante's taller. Is that not a problem?'

'Not once we've cut his head off.'

Julia laughed.

'Arguably the first ever special effect used on film was decapitation,' Millie told her. 'Thomas Edison's *The Execution of Mary, Queen of Scots* in 1895.'

'I'm assuming you've got something a little more advanced lined up.'

Millie couldn't help but make a face. This was the effect she wasn't happy with.

She pulled back a protective sheet and revealed her construction:

a fake neck protruding from a chest-plate of Roman armour, complete with a jutting stump of spinal cord which also housed the blood tube.

'It's set up so that Dante can put his arms through the sleeves of this thing while his head is tucked out of sight. This is where Dante being taller than Sergio comes in handy: Dante has much longer arms. Sergio's looked weirdly stumpy in this thing. We won't be seeing Dante's face. In fact, that's the whole point: after the blow, the camera is going to linger on the stump spurting blood before the centurion collapses.'

'That's really clever,' Julia said approvingly. 'And yet I'm getting the impression you're not thrilled yourself.'

Millie shrugged. No point pretending.

'I always feel an effect should tell a story in and of itself. Maybe it's just that it's a decapitation. There's something too clean and clinical about them.'

'Not for the real Mary, Queen of Scots there wasn't,' said Julia.

'What do you mean?'

'Her execution was notoriously messy. It supposedly took several blows and the axe got stuck. Couldn't you do something like that, or would that be a whole other level of complicated?'

Millie felt a thrill at the possibilities. She immediately thought of the rig she had built for a later shot, of a pike being thrust through a victim. It was a fake chest above which the actor's head could slot through a hole, make-up blending the join to a false neck. It could easily be adapted for this.

'The actor's expression is the thing we always lose. A partial decapitation would allow us to show his face throughout. That's a brilliant idea.'

Julia shook her head, her expression mixing excitement with incredulity.

'What?' Millie asked.

'I think you're the first person who has reacted like that to something I've suggested.'

'What, here?'

'I think on any film set ever.'

159

Millie failed to suppress her look of surprise. Julia noticed.

'When you're young and female, they tend not to clap their hands and say: "Let's make that happen." No matter who your father is.'

'I didn't mean . . .' Millie mumbled.

'It's okay, I know what people think. And it's true there have been people who have wanted to get involved with Candledance because they think opening doors for me will open doors for them. Sycophancy is nauseating enough, but sycophancy at one remove is pitiful. I turned them all down. That's how I ended up making low-budget Europuddings nobody went to see.'

Millie smiled at Julia's humility and felt a little guilty about her previous assumptions. It was quite disorienting when you had decided someone was going to be an arsehole and it turned out you were wrong.

That said, there was an outstanding flaw in the picture she was painting.

'What's the score with your brother being here?' Millie asked. 'Is he just visiting you, or is it true he's interested in picking up *Mancipium* for the UK?'

'He is interested, and I get why that would be great, but forgive me if I'm not thrilled about it personally.'

'Why not?'

'It's a power move. This is his way of making my thing into his thing. I'm the film's co-producer, but right now out there on set, he's the one people would jump for if he snapped his fingers. And though I set up my own company and spent years toiling to get things made, if he distributes *Mancipium*, everyone is going to think it was him or my father that really made it all happen.'

'Could you live with that if it means the film's a hit? It would make your next project a lot easier to fund.'

'Oh, I understand the benefits, and I know how it must sound, like I'm self-obsessed and thinking everything's all about me. But you don't understand my family. Did you meet Freddy, at all?'

'Briefly. He came over to introduce himself and asked a few questions about what I had worked on before. He had seen *Blood*

Ceremony and *Plague of the Flesh*. I have to be honest, he was very charming and polite.'

'Yeah, watch out for that. I've moved in these circles all my life, so I've learned to read the game. They seem super friendly and interested, right up until the moment they have what they want, at which point they would cheerfully tread on your corpse to get to the buffet.'

'But that being the case, wouldn't it be good to have your interests aligned?'

Julia picked up a plastic knife, one concealing a mechanism that fed fake blood along the edge of its blade. She ran it curiously across her thumb, wincing when it left a streak of red, then wearing a wry smile as she saw the deception.

'People assume my family must be pulling strings behind the scenes to help me succeed. Truth is they would more likely be pulling strings to make sure I fail, so that I come crawling back to home and hearth. That's what they want. No more black sheep, no more scandal. If acquiring this film so that they can bury it is what gets that done, Freddy won't lose a wink of sleep over it.'

Millie's eyes widened as this hit home.

'See the problem now?' Julia asked. 'It might well be all about me, and that's what everyone else should be afraid of.'

Hanging

Millicent noticed the waiter making his way towards her again. She was still nursing the glass of tap water she had asked for when she first sat down, having felt obliged to make an order. According to her watch, she had been there almost forty-five minutes, and remained alone. Mr Rook had said he was on the tarmac when he called. Presumably there had been a delay.

She indicated that her drink was still more than half-full, but the waiter continued towards her.

'Are you aware your phone is ringing, ma'am?' he asked.

Millicent was about to answer that she didn't have one when she realised. She had been blithely tuning it out, assuming it belonged to someone else.

'I'm terribly sorry,' she replied.

She took it from her bag and looked carefully at the screen, not instinctively sure how to answer. Fortunately, green still tended to mean go.

'Hello?'

'Millicent? It's Jonathan Rook. I'm so sorry. Something urgent has come up since I touched down and I don't know when I'll be able to get clear. I don't want to keep you.'

'It's all right. I can wait. I don't mind.'

'That's very understanding, but the thing is, you might literally be waiting all night, or at least until they chuck you out of the bar. You should head home. I'll be in touch tomorrow.'

It was late by the time Millicent made it back from town. She didn't mind walking in the dark. It was cold, but the night was clear, and as she had negotiated Sauchiehall Street, revellers spilling in and out of pubs, she realised that she had acquired a superpower over the course of her incarceration. As a woman in her seventies, she was practically invisible. Nobody bothered her, nobody even looked at her.

As she opened the front door and stepped into the downstairs hall, it struck her that this was the first time she had been in this house alone. Vivian and Carla were gone for two nights, and Jerome was out too, working at his kebab shop. It was probably the first time she had been alone in any building since 1994. There wasn't a long list of things she intended to do with this novel and unexpected freedom, though. Mr Rook was going to meet her tomorrow, and she wanted that to come around as soon as possible. She would make herself a bite of supper, read for a while, then go to sleep.

As she proceeded to the kitchen, she noticed that the box of tapes was gone from outside her room. Jerome must have taken it. He said he had a VCR, though she didn't imagine there was anything in there that he couldn't get hold of on a newer format. Perhaps he planned to sell them. She couldn't imagine they were worth much nowadays, but what did she know about these things? The shops were full of vinyl records again, for God's sake. If people were inexplicably fetishising one inferior past format, why not another?

Either way, she was grateful to him for taking them off her hands.

With this thought, she felt a twinge of guilt as she recalled her encounter with him yesterday. She had been in the kitchen having tea and toast. He had chosen his moment, when Vivian and Carla were watching some TV show they both liked, one of those dismal reality things. People had become awfully easily pleased in the time she was away. When she went inside, the high-water marks had been *ER* and *Cracker*. Now viewers were content to watch other people bake.

'Did you find out anything at the hotel?' he had asked, keeping his voice low. The others wouldn't hear from the living room, but it was a means of conveying that he understood it was all confidential.

'I did, but I am not at liberty to say precisely what.'

He thought she was joking.

'I'm serious. I can't even tell you why I can't tell you.'

She would admit it had felt good to have a secret, and to know things were in motion of which she was a part. But equally, she had a strong urge to share it with someone, and he was the one who had been there when she saw the photo. She didn't owe him anything, she kept reminding herself; and more importantly, Mr Rook had stressed the need for discretion.

Jerome didn't press the point, and it became clear that this wasn't the highest priority on his agenda anyway.

'I was wondering if we could talk a wee bit about your experiences in the film industry. I found out you were a make-up effects artist. I'd love to get the inside track on production during the golden age of slashers. I checked the IMDb and saw you worked on *Blood Ceremony* and *Kiss of the Blade* among others. Back when it was all mechanical effects, no CGI pish.'

Millicent felt her throat swelling as he spoke, her eyes beginning to fill.

It was hard to explain why there was this block. It wasn't like she could say it was too soon to talk about things she had done three decades ago, but strangely it still felt too painful.

'I'm sorry,' she said. 'I just can't. My mind is full of other things,' she added, hoping this would suffice as an explanation.

But now, as she sat in the kitchen with a day's distance, she had the perspective to see that this welling of emotion had not been driven by what she assumed. Recalling Jerome's eager face sitting opposite, she understood that it was actually a response to his solicitousness: to someone wanting to hear about her, someone who saw her for what she once was.

She went to her bedroom and got changed into her nightie. As she undressed, she glanced at the picture she had put up, the poster for *Black Gloves and White Lace*. It looked good there. Yes, it provoked pangs, but they were intermingled with something else, something warmer.

The hammer and the picture-hanging kit were still sitting on top of the chest of drawers. She would hang another one in the morning, for a film she actually worked on. *Blood Ceremony* maybe, or *Lucifer's Charade*.

She would talk to Jerome about her films tomorrow, she decided. It would be hard, but it would be good for her.

Home

'So I decided that I would just stick a really long skewer up your arse and out your mouth, bung you on the gyro and start selling Jerry kebabs from Friday onwards.'

Jerry looked across at Aldo with a start, which only seemed to increase the look of amusement on his boss's face.

'Oh, we're back, are we? Yeah, I figured you werenae listening.'

'Sorry, mate,' he replied. 'Miles away.'

My mind is full of other things, Millicent had said. Jerry thought of how she teared up when he asked about her career in the film business. You never knew what you were treading into when you asked about someone's past, especially someone who had been through what she had. He would clearly have a job on his hands getting her to talk about any of it, and estimated it would take a lot of levelling up before he could unlock *Mancipium*. He didn't see how that was going to happen before this essay was due, and nor was he sure he had any right to pry if that was how she tended to respond.

That wasn't the main thing on his mind, though. For the past day and a half he'd been able to concentrate on little other than the ultimatum he was facing. He had gone from thinking he had finally found somewhere he could fit in, to feeling utterly alienated again as he contemplated this great betrayal.

He kept trying to tell himself he couldn't go through with it, but he had caught himself looking around the flat, instinctively assessing what might satisfy Rossco.

Time was running out too. He would have to do it tonight, while Vivian and Carla were away. At least Millicent didn't have anything worth thieving. He would feel the worst stealing from her. She had lost so much already.

The shop was quiet tonight, which was why Aldo was jawing away. They would usually talk about movies and videogames. Aldo was at the cinema several mornings a week before coming in to open the shop, the kind of guy who just loved the spectacle and wasn't inclined to be over-analytical like Jerry. He would go to see every superhero movie four or five times: even the DC ones. He was more discerning when it came to games, his tastes running very much to the old school. He told Jerry how he would rent discs from the video shop back in the day, staying up all night to complete them before they were due back. Jerry's gran had kept a section of those, an attempt to open up a new revenue stream when the business was starting to falter.

Tonight though, Aldo was talking back at the telly, which was why Jerry had zoned him out.

He looked up at the screen. It was showing the tail end of a piece about the Home Secretary.

'*This comes hot on the heels of Mr Bertrand's controversial plans for an expansion of stop and search powers,*' the reporter was saying, '*and demonstrates that he is very keen to put his own stamp on the department. Opponents are saying that his proposals have grave implications not just for civil liberties, but for government oversight of the security services. However, a Home Office spokesman said that the ongoing threat from terrorism meant that . . .*'

'I don't know why they keep fannying about around the edges,' Aldo said, talking over the report. 'Let's be honest: what they really want is to bring in a new crime of being brown in a built-up area. And that would be the pair of us bang to rights.'

'*Sources to the right of the party are saying they are pleasantly surprised by the impact Mr Bertrand has made, as he had long been perceived to represent the Conservatives' more liberal instincts. His appointment to Home Secretary was not without its opponents, with many saying it was a sop to Remainers in an attempt to promote party unity.*'

'Bollocks,' said Aldo. 'If Alfonse Bertrand is meant to be a liberal, what's their idea of a hardliner?'

'Let's hope we never find out,' Jerry replied.

'He's got his eye on the top job, hasn't he?' Aldo mused. 'They always like to act the hard man when they get ambitious. Wee pricks that couldnae fight sleep.'

Aldo channel-surfed for a few seconds then turned to Jerry.

'Tell you what, mate. It's dead tonight. Why don't you knock off and head home?'

'Really?'

'Aye. I'm blaming your T-shirt, actually. Who's gaunny come in for a kebab if the guy serving it has got CANNIBAL CORPSE written on his chest. They'll think that's what's on the rotisserie.'

Jerry had mixed feelings about this unexpected bonus. He got to head off sooner to his nice new home, but in order to stay there and not end up in jail, he would have to steal from his hosts. Tonight.

He started listening to the latest Gore Whore podcast in an attempt to take his mind off other things, but he couldn't get into it. Her YouTube videos were better anyway: it was never the same without the film clips.

As he crossed Byres Road, heading back towards Hyndland, he pondered whether Rossco was bluffing. If he leaked the video, surely he knew Jerry would tell them who he had been there with. Wasn't that mutually assured destruction?

Not if only one side had proof. The video showed Jerry. They would probably also be able to do something with the audio recordings of him talking to the woman on the phone, when he was doing CPR.

He hated himself for getting sucked into this shit. For not listening to his gran, the person he trusted most, when she was warning him about who he ought to trust least.

When he moved up to secondary school, Jerry got into a lot of fights over folk having sly digs: about his colour, or about having no parents in the picture and being raised by his gran. Even folk making fun of his proper name after the teacher read it from the register. In first year, with everybody jostling for status, folk used any angle they could to get a rise, trying to see how far they could push you. Jerry tended to push back pretty hard. That was what made Rossco take an interest in him. He was dealing in a currency that he could respect.

Rossco made digs about all that same stuff, but Jerry acted like it was a joke. This meant he got accepted as someone who could take the banter. Truth was, it was cowardly, just the path of least resistance. Rossco wasn't someone you wanted to get on the wrong side of. There were wee fuds who tried it on until you burst their nose, and then there were bams who really knew how to fight; who fucking lived for it. You got less shit if you were one of Rossco's crew.

Like a million eejits before him, he went along with things he shouldn't have so that he stayed on the inside: better to put up with Rossco as a low-quality friend than have him as an industrial-grade enemy. Started off tanning stuff from the loading bays behind the shops, and before he knew it, he was breaking into houses.

He told himself it was for the money, given how little his gran had; the two of them living off her pension and what savings she had left after the video shop closed. But the pitiable truth was that he kept doing it because he was too much of a shitebag to tell Rossco he was out.

He'd thought he could melt away. Thought he had escaped. But if there was one thing he ought to have grasped, it was that not getting caught wasn't the same as getting away with something. For one thing, you could never really believe you had got away with it, because deep down you needed to believe that the world was just. He wondered how many people confessed to things so that they knew they weren't living in a world where anyone could get away with whatever they had done.

Jerry hadn't been caught over what happened to the old man, but he had never stopped paying for it. He knew he could get away with stealing from his housemates too, but he'd have to look them in the eye every day.

And once he gave Rossco this, what would he ask for next?

He glanced at his watch as he turned onto his street. He was going to be home earlier than planned. He hoped Millicent was still up and about. If she was around, he wouldn't be able to do anything, and that would put this off at least a little while longer. A coward is always happy to run a wee bit more.

The place looked dead. All the lights were already out. Sadness and shame descended upon him as he approached the building. After tonight, even if he still lived here, he would no longer be a member of this household. He would just be the prick who burgled it.

Jerry had learned the hard way what it felt like when you couldn't go back from something. And there would be no going back from what awaited him behind this door.

Gloves

She woke when she heard the front door open, Jerome coming in from his shift. She was a light sleeper, a legacy of prison. She never had been before that, and didn't care to dwell on the irony of what she had slept through on her last night of freedom.

She heard him go into the kitchen, then come back out again. His tread sounded heavier than normal, but maybe it was just because the night was so quiet. He was getting closer, so he hadn't gone into his own bedroom or the bathroom. He was still new here, so she really hoped he hadn't forgotten which room was his.

A moment later, her door opened.

It wasn't Jerome.

It was nobody she had ever seen before, nobody who had any right to be here.

It was a man. He looked about her age, maybe younger. His build instinctively made her think of the photograph, what she had thought of as rugby types. But the detail that really jumped out was that he was wearing blue latex gloves.

Millicent scrambled from her bed, propelled by flight reflex. He was on her in a twinkling, gripping her in some sort of judo hold. She felt the room tumble and spin about her, her feet swept from the floor before she was pinned to the bed.

She cried out, the sound immediately smothered by a pillow over her face. It was held in place like a piston. She screamed through it but the sound was muffled, and far more horrifying, once she was done, she couldn't breathe back in.

She could see nothing except the pillow, her mind filled with the image of those blue latex gloves. Even in her panic and desperation,

171

she knew this was not a random event. This was linked to what happened to Markus. She had disturbed something when she saw that photograph, when she made that phone call.

Her life was ending in a sick joke. Two days ago, she had planned to kill herself, but as the pillow pressed down and her mouth sucked in vain for air, she knew that more than anything, she wanted to live. She had spent years waiting for proof that she wasn't a murderer, and she had finally seen it in the man who was murdering her.

The last thing she would ever see.

The Body

Jerry crouched alongside Millicent's bed and checked again for a pulse. There was nothing. He tried the neck, tried the wrist, tried the neck again. There was no doubt, much as he wished to deny it. He recognised that unseeing, glassy-eyed stare, and he knew what it meant. There was no point in even trying CPR. This was a done deal, and this time it had been no heart attack, no incidental consequence of a passive act. This was murder.

Once again, he had witnessed how quickly the world as he understood it could change. It had been less than a minute since he opened the front door.

He had crept in quietly, keen not to disturb Millicent and listening out for any hint that she might still be awake. He had left the lights off, aware that even the glow around the doorframe might be enough if she wasn't quite asleep yet. He could smell the toast that she must have had for supper.

He decided he would give it half an hour to make sure she hadn't stirred, then he would need to make his move. He would have to disappear his laptop and phone for a while, hide them somewhere and tell the polis they had been taken. In the meantime, he'd have to go down to Fonezone and get some shitty cheap Chinese tablet so he could still get his work done, tapping out his essays on the touchscreen. All because of fucking Rossco.

He was walking in his stocking soles to stay silent, which was why he so clearly heard the thump.

He had flipped the nearest switch and pulled open the door to Millicent's bedroom, light from the hall spilling in to illuminate a scene that knocked the breath from him.

Someone was kneeling on top of Millicent, holding a pillow over her face while her legs thrashed beneath him. The assailant immediately reacted to the light and the intrusion. He was an older boy, maybe in his sixties, but lean and wiry, dressed in a black top and trousers, no jacket. Prick was wearing plastic gloves. He didn't want to leave prints, and not because he was tanning the place.

The old boy turned and let go of the pillow, Millicent gulping air convulsively as it was removed from her face. He stepped onto the floor, pulling a blade. Like himself, it was short and slim but solid-looking.

Their eyes met, each sizing up the other. Then the old boy decided he fancied it and charged.

One second before that, if Jerry had been asked to describe the room, he would have mentioned only its occupants and its furniture. It was amazing how much more your senses took in without telling you, until you absolutely had to know. Such as the fact that there was a hammer sitting on top of the chest of drawers, about six inches from Jerry's right hand.

He had grabbed it as the old boy covered the short distance between them, knowing instinctively there was no time to draw it back. He had swung upwards, really just to ward off the attack, give the fucker something to worry about, hoping he would run. But the guy launched himself as Jerry swung, and had been in mid-air, one hand out to grab him, the knife drawn back in the other.

Jerry felt the hammer connect with far more power and force than he had brought to bear himself, though what he brought to bear was plenty. It was a fucking hammer, after all. There had been a crunch, the reverberation running up his arm. It was at once bluntly dull and horribly soft.

Millicent leaned over the edge of the bed where she lay as Jerry squatted next to the figure on the floor.

'No pulse,' he said urgently, confused. 'How can there be no pulse? I only hit him once, about twenty seconds ago.'

Millicent answered, her breathing still laboured and her voice hoarse.

'It's okay. I'm sure he'll bounce back.'

'Really?' he asked, both optimistic and wary that this meant the man might attack again now Jerry's guard was down.

'Absolutely. A nice cup of tea and he'll be on his feet in no time. Are you kidding? You *Last Boy Scout*ed him.'

He got what she meant. Bruce Willis had killed a guy with one blow.

'But that was just a movie,' he argued.

She sat herself up, her voice still croaky.

'If you smash the nose with sufficient force, and at a particular upwards angle, you drive fragments of bone directly into the brain. Voila, instant death.'

Her tone was coolly detached, like she was explaining how he had buggered the toaster.

Jerry looked at the man's face, his blank and frankly stunned expression. There wasn't even much blood. It looked like he could give himself a wipe with a hanky then get up and walk away. Except this guy was never getting up again.

'I've killed him,' Jerry said. 'I've fuckin' . . .'

His voice failed, his throat choked and tears formed in his eyes.

He felt a hand on his shoulder.

'I wouldn't go weeping up a storm over it. I don't think we lost a great humanitarian here.'

Jerry looked again at the blank-eyed face of this person he had just killed. He knew nothing about him, had never even heard him speak.

'Who is he?' he asked.

'You mean who was he,' Millicent answered drily.

'Do you really have to stress that?'

'Yes. I very much care to stress that he is the one in the past tense and not me. And I forbid you to feel bad about it. You just saved my life, Jerome.'

'Why was he trying to kill you? Is this about that photograph? Who are you?'

'You know very well who I am. I'm sure you've looked up everything you possibly could about me by now.'

'None of it would explain this.'

'Wouldn't it? I've been maintaining for twenty-five years that someone came into my flat and murdered my boyfriend. I think these events might be related, don't you?'

'What aren't you telling me, Millicent?'

'Nothing. I said these events might be related. I didn't say I know what the hell they're all about.'

'When I asked you about the photograph yesterday, you said you weren't at liberty to say. I think it's time to share.'

Millicent swung her legs over the bed and put her head in her hands, elbows on her thighs. She took a couple of breaths then straightened up.

'I was trying to contact anyone else who was in the photo. Long story short, I received a call from a man named Jonathan Rook. He said it was highly sensitive, and it must have been, because he was coming up from London just to talk to me. We were supposed to meet in town this evening, but he got delayed and called it off.'

The burglar in Jerry doubted this.

'This could be him right here.'

'What? How?'

'He asked you to come into town so you wouldn't be home. That way he could case the joint, break in and lie in wait.'

'Oh, God. You're right. He kept saying we needed privacy, asking who I lived with, who else would be around. I told him everything.'

Millicent glanced down at the body.

'Check his wallet,' she said. 'See if he has ID.'

'I don't want to touch him,' Jerry replied, physically recoiling at the mere suggestion. He could hardly bear to look at the guy.

Millicent sighed, then hopped off the bed and began patting his pockets.

She seemed unsettlingly phlegmatic about dealing with a dead guy in her bedroom, which made Jerry remember that this wasn't a first for her. At least he could be sure she hadn't killed this one, though that was hardly a comfort.

'No wallet,' she reported. 'Just a phone.'

'See if he called your number. That would confirm it's the same guy.'

She pressed a few buttons then handed it to him.

'I can't get it to work.'

Jerry had a quick look.

'It's PIN-protected.'

'Is there a way to get around that?'

Jerry immediately thought of Dodgy Donald at Fonezone. Yes, was the answer. But . . .

'Not in the next ten minutes. Looks like a burner anyway.'

'A burner?'

He forgot he was dealing with a time traveller from 1994.

'Disposable. A cheap piece of shit that can be tossed or destroyed. It's so that no calls related to whatever he was up to were made to or from his proper phone.'

Millicent climbed to her feet, offering him a hand up.

'Are you okay?' she asked.

'A world of no.'

'Do you need a minute?'

'I need about a fortnight.'

'That we don't have.'

'Why, what's the rush? It's not like he's going anywhere.'

'That's where you're wrong, I'm afraid. We need to get rid of this body.'

Surprise

There was a knock at the door of the workshop: softly polite, tentative even. Millie was not surprised to see that it was one of the production runners, who then popped his head around the frame.

'Hi. Lucio is asking if you'll come and join us.'

Millie could hear music from elsewhere in the studio: the treble notes jangling along the corridor and the bass thumping the wall. Lucio's little soiree had inevitably turned into a full-scale party. It sounded like there were an awful lot more people here now than had been attending the set in any kind of professional capacity.

'I'm working on an effect,' she replied.

'Yes. Lucio told me you'd say that. He said he's insisting because he has a surprise for you.'

She glanced at her watch and saw that it was past midnight. She must have been in here for close to four hours. That was what happened when she got captivated by an idea. She would slip into a meditative state and time just melted away. Sometimes it was like being possessed. She faintly recalled Julia popping by around nine-thirty, trying to persuade her to join the party. When she refused, Julia had returned two minutes later, bringing her a bottle of champagne and a tray of canapés for sustenance. Millie didn't remember eating them, but they were all gone, and the bottle was empty.

She had worked out how to implement Julia's idea for a partial decapitation in a way that would make the scene at once more horrific and kinetic. They would start with the sword already embedded in Sergio's neck and shoot his assailant, played by Paulo Nietti, pulling it out at maximum speed, then run the film backwards.

She knew it wouldn't be enough to reprise what she had done

with Dante's chest, blood spilling out along the line of the apparent slash. She wanted spray and splatter, and a condom wasn't going to cut it. This would have to be something far more voluminous, and it needed to be incorporated into the latex construction she would be attaching to Sergio's neck.

This was where the rest of the time had gone. She had tried various mechanisms, and nothing looked quite how she wanted it. Sometimes a break and a change of scene helped shake an idea loose, or let her see the problem from a fresh perspective when she returned.

'I'll be right there,' she told the kid, who gave her a thumbs-up and retreated.

Millie tore open a black bin liner, turning it into a sheet to throw over her work in progress. Then she headed for the party.

The music got louder as she walked towards the soundstages. She smiled as she observed that she could gauge her proximity to the set from the quantity of blood on the walls and floor. She wondered what an outsider would think if they just walked in off the street. They would be alarmed for a moment, but would quickly see through the artifice.

It would certainly be easier to explain than what she glimpsed through a partially open door to the larger of the shared dressing rooms. Stacey had slipped back there in the company of Joao, a young Portuguese bodybuilder who had been cast primarily for his looks and ripped physique. He had no lines in the film, but he was snorting one right then, from the naked breasts from which Stacey proudly claimed she used to make her living. Fortunately, both of them were too preoccupied to notice Millie's brief gaze.

She went through a set of swing doors, upon which the music became louder. It was coming from soundstage three, which was not in use. That would explain why the bass was thumping against the wall of her workshop, which was directly adjacent to the far end of the production floor.

She walked through another pair of doors and was presented with a familiarly lively sight. There had to be fifty more people in the building now than when she left after the last shot of the day. So often when the sun went down around Produzzioni Sabatini, there mysteriously appeared men wearing expensive suits and young women wearing considerably less.

She scanned the party for Lucio, more out of a desire to demonstrate her compliance than out of any genuine curiosity regarding what this surprise might be. Probably a script update. Well, if that was the case, she had one for him too. She couldn't wait to tell Alessandro about her idea, but she hadn't seen him amidst the throng yet either.

One person she had spotted was Florio, his unmistakable silhouette picked out against a blue spotlight. She was instinctively wary of him now in a way she hadn't been prior to the collapse of the Credit Populaire deal, the French bankers bailing specifically because of Lucio's connections to him.

Millie had seen Florio around various sets over the years but hadn't given much thought to who he was. If someone had asked, she'd have guessed that he wasn't a production accountant or completion guarantor. She suspected he was dodgy, but hadn't regarded it as her business to find out any specifics. That was probably a common perspective on independent movie sets. You could never be sure what might be going on *behind* behind the scenes.

Millie came from a very ordinary suburban background and considered herself conservative with a small 'c'. She had a weird flashback, thinking about what her classmates in Kingston-Upon-Thames would think if they saw her in the midst of all this. Never mind them, what would their fearsome headmistress Mrs Birtwhistle have to say? She was obsessed with 'decency', rigidly enforcing rules such as never allowing skirts to rise within an inch of the knee, and was particularly forthright regarding 'the circles in which one ought to aspire to find oneself'. Here Millie was, making what the tabloids liked to call 'sick filth', and doing it surrounded by depravity, decadence and sin.

It was all around her, but Millie didn't feel particularly involved in it. She certainly didn't consider that it reflected on her or that she had a personal responsibility to deal with it. In any field of work, there would be things you might disapprove of. You suspected they were there, but you didn't go out of your way to verify it. That was why the presence of Florio and men like him had never troubled her before; and even now, what she knew was sufficiently vague as to grant her a form of plausible deniability. There were things she didn't have to turn a blind eye to because they were seldom in her line of sight. That said, she always felt a nagging unease about the young women who appeared as willing adornments at these parties.

Sometimes they got minor parts in Lucio's movies, but mostly they just came and went. She wondered where he was finding them, as there seemed to be an inexhaustible supply. It wasn't like he could hold casting calls and attach such duties as part of the gig. She wondered if he was still making porn on the side.

One thing that made it easier for her to ignore them was that they tended to ignore her. There was one circulating with a tray of drinks, but she looked right through Millie as she passed, discounting her as a valid recipient. However, Millie had spotted a table laden with bottles and was making her way towards it when she saw Lucio; and more significantly, saw who Lucio was with.

It was Markus. That was the surprise.

Leviathan

Jerome stared at her with a look of dazed incredulity.

'What are you talking about?' he asked. 'Are you fucking high?'

He was reeling at what he had just done, shaking from the enormity of it. Millicent tried to tell him that he had done nothing wrong, but he wasn't yet ready to accept that. He would be, in time, but time was against them.

Under the circumstances she decided not to mention that her only regret over the intruder's death was that it had been so quick.

She had endured an aeon of agony beneath that pillow, fighting for breath as her lungs threatened to implode inside her chest. When the light had filled the room from Jerome opening the bedroom door, she had actually thought it was the moment of her crossing over, that death had come.

Indeed, death *had* come, just not for her. There had been a late cancellation so he had moved this little bastard up the appointment list.

'What we need to do is call the polis,' Jerome said. 'We need to tell them everything.'

The poor boy. He wanted absolution. He needed someone to confess to, someone who would say, *it's okay, you did nothing wrong, we'll take it from here*. But he'd have to make do with Millicent for that.

'Involving the police is absolutely the last thing we should do. You just killed somebody with a hammer.'

'It was self-defence. He broke into the hoose, he was trying to smother you and then he came at me with a knife. We need them to look into this. He's got a burner. He's wearing latex gloves, for Christ's sake.'

Jerome pulled out his mobile.

'I'm calling them right now.'

'I phoned the police when I woke up next to the body of my boyfriend,' she stated. 'I had every faith that they would see the truth of the situation and find out what really happened.'

That was enough to stop him. There was more she could have told him, had she needed to: something he really ought to know, but he was clinging on by his fingernails as it was. She couldn't afford to have him freak out. They would both need their wits about them.

Millicent was experiencing an utterly incongruous sense of strength and energy, probably some kind of endorphin rush from having come so close to death. But that wasn't what was driving her to take charge of the situation. Twenty-five years ago, some unseen entity had taken her life away then disappeared, seemingly forever. Then tonight, the leviathan had broken the surface again, albeit briefly. She wanted to hunt it down, but her primary concern was the awareness that once again, it was hunting her.

This man had planned to kill her and make it look like she died in her sleep. If Jerome hadn't come home early and intervened, she would be dead, and nobody would ever know how – or why. It was unlikely that a post-mortem would have been carried out on a woman in her seventies who had apparently slipped away during the night.

If they wanted her dead, that meant she was still a danger to somebody, though she had no notion who or how. Why now, though? They could have killed her when they killed Markus, she reasoned, before deducing that they needed her to take the fall, so as to disguise the motive for his death. After that though, they could surely have got to her any time in prison. And if her being on the outside again was a concern, why wait a year to act?

The answer was that she hadn't been a threat until two days ago. Prior to that, she hadn't known who or what Markus Laird really was. What this information had changed, she didn't know, but evidently it had changed enough.

Not that this unseen entity had been completely idle until now. She recalled Janice Duncan, her lawyer, saying she had never known so many hurdles to be put in her way, at every stage of every process. Janice always claimed somebody was pulling strings, but they had both believed it was a legacy of the tabloid hysteria and her consequent notoriety.

She even remembered Janice one day mentioning how her office had been broken into. Millicent asked if she thought it was related to the case, but Janice had waved that away as paranoia. 'The office is above a chemist's,' she had said. 'They were probably looking for methadone.'

Millicent wasn't so sure now.

She stared at the body on the floor, racking her memory for any hint that she had seen him before. Had she encountered him back then, in the film business, or among the cops, at the trial? She tried to imagine what he might have looked like all those years ago.

Then she remembered. She stepped over the body and reached into her chest of drawers.

'What are you doing?' Jerome asked.

She produced the copy of the photograph Mr Connelly had given her, rolling it out on the bed.

'I want to see if he's in this picture.'

She took a long look. It didn't help that his nose had been flattened into his face, but she was pretty sure he was the guy directly on Markus's left. She checked the caption.

'His name was Bill Geddes,' she said.

'Does that mean anything to you?'

Bill was quite senior in the force . . .

Yes, she thought. It meant they definitely, definitely shouldn't be calling the police.

'We should put his phone back in his pocket,' she said. 'Wipe it down first. We don't want to leave any prints.'

'Don't you want to hang on to it? I could get it unlocked in the morning.'

Millicent had begun to formulate a plan, but she didn't yet want to tell Jerome that it would preclude visiting whoever he thought could carry this out.

'As you said, it's a burner. It's unlikely to tell us much. Besides, I'd prefer that when his body is found, it doesn't look like he's been robbed.'

'Aye, but if the polis unlock it, there's a chance it's gaunny show he dialled your number.'

'My phone isn't registered in my name. Vivian only bought it this morning. It's a pay-as-you-go. My own burner, if you will.'

Jerome pulled a paper tissue from his pocket and gripped the man's handset with it as he wiped it on his T-shirt. She tried not to think about the extent to which he was swapping fingerprints for DNA as he slipped the phone back into the dead man's trouser pocket.

'Okay,' he said. 'But why are you worried about it not looking like he was robbed?'

'Because that way his death will look less suspicious.'

Jerome spluttered.

'What do you think the polis are gaunny say? "Aye, the boy's pan breid with his face smashed in, but it's cool, his mobile's still in his troosers. Put it doon as natural causes." This couldnae look more suspicious.'

'There is more than one way a man might end up dead and looking like this. It's all about where he is ultimately found.'

'Why, are you planning to stick him on a bench in Kelvingrove Park and hope the polis reckon a jacked-up squirrel stuck the heid on him? Or maybe that he tripped and was so distracted by the sight of a rare bird that he completely forgot to put his hands out for protection and stoated his face off a kerbstone at just the right angle?'

She let him rant. It was burning up the energy from his adrenaline jolt. She remembered herself at the same stage in '94. By this point she was already talking to the police down the phone, gabbling manically, incriminating herself.

'If he fell from a height into the river, he might have smashed into a rock beneath the surface. It could appear to have been a suicide or an accident. But most importantly, his body would be taken downstream, found far from here. That's the main thing.'

'So what are you suggesting we do? Drop him off the Kingston bridge?'

'Too many witnesses.'

Jerome gaped.

'I was fucking *kidding*. Christ, you are serious. You are seriously talking about getting rid of this body.'

'The alternatives are far worse, believe me. I thought you understood that.'

Jerome was pacing the carpet at the end of the bed.

'I understood why I should take a minute to get my heid straight, and now that I have, I can tell you this is a whole new level of crazy. I can make a case for why I hit the guy with a hammer, but I cannae claim I yeeted his body into the river in self-defence. I'd rather take my chances with the law while I can still justify what happened. We need to call the polis.'

It was time. He wasn't ready but she had to tell him, and he deserved to know.

'This guy *was* police. So was Markus.'

The pacing ceased.

'That's what I found out when I went back to the Roman Fort Hotel. Everybody in that photograph was police. He was undercover: Special Branch or MI5 or something, and Markus wasn't even his real name, just an identity. His real name was Des Creasey. I phoned the number of the woman who supplied the picture. It belonged to her late father. She said she would get in touch with Bill Geddes, the man who organised the Burns Night do, ask him to ring back. Instead I got a call from this Jonathan Rook, saying he couldn't give me any more information because it was classified, still pertinent to open investigations.

'I don't know how much of that was true. I don't know if there even is a Jonathan Rook, or if like you suggested, it was just this guy getting me out of the house. But what I do know is that what happened to me in '94 and what happened here tonight, the police are neck deep in both, and we don't know how high it goes.'

Reconnaissance

Jerry had often wondered how folk got along before Google Maps. He had once used Street View for checking out if the place he was heading to buy a second-hand DVD box set looked like a dodgy area. A quick scan had suggested yes, but he estimated that the residents would have looked at his own street in Dreghorn and concluded the same.

This was the first time he had used it to recce where he might best get rid of a corpse.

'I cannot believe we're doing this,' he said.

'Well, at least we're not eating him,' Millicent replied.

'What?'

'CANNIBAL CORPSE. That's what it says on your T-shirt. A band, I take it. The name is oddly familiar, but I can't think why.'

'They appeared in *Ace Ventura: Pet Detective*.'

'That'll be it. I saw it a couple of times. What was the name of their song?'

Jerry thought about it. In the movie, they had played 'Hammer Smashed Face'.

'I'd rather not say.'

He had his laptop on the kitchen table, Millicent standing behind looking over his shoulder. She was wearing black slacks and a dark grey polo neck. He noted that she had got changed out of her nightie in the bathroom rather than do so in front of their visitor, not that he was going to see anything.

He zoomed in on Kirklee Road. The bridge was wide with stone balustrades and the river looked deep enough.

Millicent gaped. He wondered what was wrong until he realised she had never seen this before.

'This simply shows you places, anywhere you choose?'

'Yes.'

'Can you show me what else is around?'

He pivoted the view and immediately saw that it wouldn't do. There were flats overlooking both sides.

He zoomed back out and checked a few more locations where roads crossed the river and the canal. Each one had homes nearby or in some cases, high sides that would be difficult to get the body over.

Was this itself conspiracy to pervert the course of justice, he wondered? Or did it not become a crime until they actually moved the body? Could you be prosecuted for thinking about doing something illegal if in the end you decided not to?

Jerry was still looking for another way out, aware that every moment's delay in reporting what had happened sunk him deeper into a mire of actions he would not be able to convincingly explain away. It still felt like the logical, reasonable thing to do was to contact the authorities. He couldn't help but think that if the local plods turned up, they wouldn't be connected to some grand conspiracy. However, the local plods who had first responded at Millicent's flat in '94 probably weren't connected to it either. That was just where the process had begun. And all these years later she still wasn't free of it.

She was right. This was the lesser risk. If they dropped him in the river and the body washed up miles downstream, there was nothing to connect it to them. The guy had taken all sorts of steps to make sure there were no witnesses. That would work for them now.

He tugged the view up towards Maryhill and zoomed in to another crossing. The river looked deep, and it was a long drop. He saw the logic in Millicent's thinking. If it had been a suicide from a spot like that, it was plausible that he might sustain such an injury.

'There are houses further along at one end,' he pointed out, 'but if you're standing in the centre of the bridge, you'd be obscured by the trees.'

'Trees are our friends,' Millicent said approvingly. 'Where is this?'

'Cowal Road.'

'Cowal Road it is, then.'

'Okay. Now we just have the trickier question of how we're gaunny get him there. You don't happen to have a car, by any chance?'

'No.'

'What about the deid guy?' Jerry couldn't bring himself to use his name. 'Were there keys when you went through his pockets?'

'I think so, yes.'

'So we can use that.'

'Keys aren't a car,' she pointed out. 'We don't know where or what is his.'

'You're forgetting it's the twenty-first century. Here in the future, you can just walk along pressing the fob and look for whatever motor unlocks and flashes its lights.'

She glared.

'I've been in prison, not a coma. We had tellies, much as the tabloids would wish it other. But even if we were to locate his car, I don't think it's a good idea. Here in the twenty-first century, there is a proliferation of CCTV cameras linked to licence-plate recognition. We don't want to be seen driving a vehicle registered to the body we got rid of, to say nothing of clothing fibres or DNA.'

'So what does that leave?'

'There's a wheelchair in the hall. We can put him in that.'

'And walk past those same CCTV cameras, wheeling a deid guy with his face smashed in?'

'He won't look dead, and his face won't be smashed in.'

Jerry was about to ask how she planned to achieve this miracle, until he remembered what she had done for a living.

Plain Sight

They got him into the wheelchair first, as Millicent wanted to work on him sitting upright. Jerry was shocked by how heavy the guy was, and developed a belated understanding of the term 'dead weight'. He had looked lean and short as he stood there gripping the knife, but it felt like his body was entirely stuffed with powdered cement. Fortunately, Millicent was stronger than he had assumed. It was because of the way she carried herself, that bowed and apologetic scurry. It belied the fact that she was tall and wiry.

Jerry felt tears forming again. The sight was horrific, somehow worse seeing him sit there slumped in the wheelchair than lying on the carpet. He really looked like a dead person now, his face pale, eyes glazed and lifeless, nose pulped. He had done this. Jerry had taken his life away.

The man had come here to kill Millicent and would probably have killed him too, but that didn't seem to matter. But maybe his tears weren't really for this guy. Jerry had never properly wept for either of the people he'd seen die. In the case of the old man, there had only been shock and not a little fear. And when his gran died, he convinced himself he'd had time to prepare for it, and that he would make it on his own. A technique also known as deny and defer.

'Close his eyes,' he said. 'I cannae stand it.'

Millicent pulled the man's eyelids down.

'Do you have any Play Doh?' she asked.

'No, because I'm eighteen. I've got Blu-Tack, though.'

'I can work with that.'

It only took her about forty minutes. The result wouldn't have

191

been ideal for the guy's Tinder profile, but it would certainly do for anyone passing in the street. She sculpted a new nose with Blu-Tack, attaching it to his face with something from the flight case she had retrieved from her room. She rendered it skin-coloured, then covered the rest of his face with foundation so it wasn't so pale.

She used a scarf to secure him in place and prevent him slumping over, tied around him at the chest. It looked worryingly conspicuous, but she wasn't done. She covered it by wrapping him in a tartan travel blanket, which Jerry would have to admit was an authentic touch. Finally, she stuck a baseball cap on his head with the peak down, before carefully sliding a pair of sunglasses over his ears.

'Where did you get that stuff?'

'Do you need to ask?'

He looked again at the cap. He had only noticed a picture of a cow on it, but a closer inspection revealed that the caption said: NOT YOUR MUM. NOT YOUR MILK.

As Jerry pushed the wheelchair out of the front door, the air was sharply cold, but this was because the night was clear and dry. Jerry bumped the chair down the front steps and onto the gravel, the crunch of which sounded troublingly loud against the silence.

He stopped at the garden gate while Millicent stuck her head around to check nobody was coming. They knew they weren't going to make it all the way to Cowal Road without encountering anybody else, but it was important not to be seen emerging from the house.

The most direct route was along Hyndland Road and Cleveden Road, but that was the main thoroughfare from the West End to Maryhill, so they took a longer route through quieter, winding residential streets.

It helped that it was now after two. There was never going to be many people around, but it did also make them more conspicuous. People might well wonder what the hell anyone was doing pushing somebody around in a wheelchair in the middle of the night, so Jerry gave some thought to how he might answer.

The first potential witness they encountered was a taxi, cruising along Great Western Road as they waited to cross. Jerry willed the lights not to change, wanting it to pass them at speed.

The lights changed. The taxi was going to stop right in front of them. Jerry felt himself stiffen.

'Bend over,' Millicent said. 'Like this.'

She leaned as if listening to the man in the wheelchair, turning her head away from the road and nodding in seeming agreement with whatever he was saying. Jerry did likewise, then kept his face turned away as they crossed at the green man.

They skirted some playing fields, trundling quietly past rows and rows of houses, all of them in darkness. Then at a junction ahead, he saw a police car. He willed it to keep going straight.

It turned left, heading their way.

Millicent stopped dead. She had been ice cool throughout all this, but the sight of the polis had understandably broken the spell.

Jerry shoved her in the back.

'Keep going. Just keep walking. One foot in front of the other.'

He could see that she was trembling, but she did as she was urged.

'Don't lean in this time, don't do anything unusual. Just walk.'

The police car passed them on the other side. Jerry breathed out. Then it swung across the road, did a three-point turn, caught up to them again and pulled in alongside.

The passenger window slid down.

Jerry stopped pushing, coaching himself to stay normal, not do anything inadvertently suspicious. He was conscious of a strong urge to stand between the police car and the dead guy.

'Everything all right, folks?' asked the polis, a Chinese woman. There was a younger bloke alongside her at the wheel. 'Is he okay?'

Jerry dropped his voice, as though urging her to do likewise.

'He's sound. Dead to the world.'

Jerry glanced down to indicate their passenger. As he did so, he was alarmed to notice that there was actually a small spatter of blood on his T-shirt. Fortunately, it was almost indistinguishable from all of the printed blood on it.

'Bit late for a stroll,' the polis woman suggested.

'Aye. My uncle here was round for a visit and we lost track of the time. We're just dropping him off.'

As soon as he said it, Jerry feared he had screwed up and began calculating the family structure that would explain him being a different colour from his 'uncle'.

'Where does he live?'

Thrown by his previous anxiety, Jerry drew a blank. He remembered how they used to plan for someone answering when they rang a doorbell, learning a similarly named street. He hadn't done that, and he couldn't just blurt something out because polis tended to know their geography. It would be a big red flag if he mentioned an address that was in the wrong direction from where they were headed.

It felt like ages, conspicuously so, then Millicent bailed him out.

'Maryhill. Two minutes from the football ground. Albert's a big Jags fan.'

She sounded cheery, hamming up the English accent too. Nothing sounded less suspicious than a posh voice.

'Yous wanting a lift?' the polis woman asked.

'Don't want to waken him,' Jerry replied, again keeping his voice low. 'He's actually had a few and he might get aggro.'

The polis woman smiled knowingly.

'Bit of a handful, is he?'

'Oh, you've no idea.'

An Accident

As soon as the police car had driven out of sight, the grace Jerry's stomach had so generously granted him suddenly expired. He ran to the kerb and was sick into the gutter.

'We're fucked,' he said, wiping his mouth with a tissue. 'That's the polis seen us with him.'

'Oh, for God's sake, dial down the drama,' Millicent replied, which wasn't quite the comforting response he was used to from a woman her age. 'It's all about appearances. They saw us with an infirm elderly blind man, wrapped in a travel blanket and being pushed in a wheelchair. That is not what is going to be found in the river.'

It was just after two-thirty when they reached the bridge on Cowal Road. Jerry was relieved to see that nobody had built a block of flats since the Street View images were taken, and that the bridge was indeed obscured from the nearest houses. *Trees are our friends*, he thought. However, it was a long straight road either side of where they needed to act, which meant that they probably wouldn't hear a car coming before it rounded the bend and had line of sight.

Demonstrating this point, a vehicle turned silently into view, another taxi heading their way. They resumed walking, not wanting to be seen loitering at this spot, then stopped again once the taxi was away.

In their favour, there was a streetlight out just past halfway. They stopped beneath it. Jerry looked over the side. He couldn't even see the water, just blackness beneath the bridge. He could hear it though, a low susurrus. He got a deep sense of power and motion from it. For the first time, he could believe that this was going to work.

'Okay, let's do it,' he said.

'Not yet.'

Millicent pulled away the sunglasses and the sculpted nose. Then she produced a packet of wipes from her bag and removed the make-up, Jerry looking back and forth for further cars. If one came, they'd have to hope the driver didn't pull over asking for directions. Divested of his make-over and disguise, their unprecious cargo looked very, very dead.

Finally, Millicent removed the baseball cap and untied the scarf.

This was the riskiest bit. They would have to move quickly, and just hope to fuck nobody came around the bend either side.

Jerry looked back and forth one more time then braced himself, ready for the exertion.

'On three,' he said.

Millicent nodded.

'One, two, three.'

The man hadn't got any lighter. He still felt like he was stuffed with cement, except that now it had set. Fucking rigor mortis. He was stuck in a sitting position, which made him very awkward to lift.

'Okay, change of plan,' Millicent said.

She went behind the chair and tipped the body forward into Jerry's waiting grasp. Fucker looked like somebody had blast-frozen a yoga session. Downward-facing dead.

Then she came around and they both groaned with the strain as they hauled him onto his back on top of the concrete wall, his legs in the air, bent at the knee. They balanced him there for a moment, their eyes meeting briefly as though to acknowledge this was it, the point of no return. Then they tipped him over, into the blackness.

They both held their breaths as they listened.

They listened a little longer.

Then they looked at each other again, each thinking the same thing.

Jerry decided he would be the one who said it.

'Should we not have heard a splash by now?'

'I was thinking that too.'

He got out his phone, turned on the flashlight.

'Fuck.'

The dead guy hadn't hit the water because he was suspended about ten feet above it, impaled on a branch. The banks either side were thick with trees, many of them overhanging the river, and this one had a split trunk pointing up at about twenty degrees. The force of the drop had driven it clean through his stomach and out his back.

Trees are our friends.

'Can you get him down?' Millicent asked.

Jerry rapidly assessed the situation.

'Not without a cherry picker and a hacksaw,' was the answer. 'He's impaled almost right down to the trunk.'

Jerry turned off the flashlight and stepped back from the wall before he was minded to jump over it himself. What he had just done didn't merely mean he was guilty of conspiracy to pervert the course of justice and attempting to destroy evidence. It was going to cast massive doubt on his claim of self-defence too, because if you didn't believe you had done anything wrong, why would you go to such lengths to cover it up?

Everything his gran had feared for him was going to happen, but much worse. He wouldn't be going down with some jakey sentence for house-breaking: he would be spending the whole of his twenties behind bars.

'Fuck, man. It's over. It's over. I am utterly humped here.'

Millicent took a step towards him and he felt his lip tremble as he anticipated her giving him a hug. Instead she prodded him in the chest with a surprisingly stiff finger.

'Get your shit together and quit feeling sorry for yourself. I keep reading about your generation being a bunch of snowflakes. I was hoping you might prove the likes of the *Daily Mail* wrong and show a bit of resilience.'

Jerry couldn't believe what he was hearing. She was the one who had dragged him deeper and deeper into this, and now she was going full Boomer on him.

'I didn't cancel the guy, I fuckin' killed him. And now he's up on display like an advert. What part of that should I be more resilient about?'

Millicent sat down. He was about to ask if this was some kind of huff, then he clocked that it would be pretty suss for the two of them to be seen pushing an empty wheelchair. They would need to hope they didn't encounter the same two polis again.

'This changes less than you think,' she told him.

'What, because the polis saw an old blind man? Because there's nothing to connect him to us? We were seen wheeling somebody around at two in the morning, quarter of a mile from where this guy's going to be found in a few hours, once the sun comes up.'

'They were always going to find the body. The authorities ruling it as accidental death or a suicide was a hope, not the plan. This just means we have to get going sooner.'

Jerry was unaware that there was a plan, beyond the one they had just failed to execute.

'Get going where?'

'Out of the country.'

He didn't need to ask if she was serious.

'Won't that make me look even more guilty?'

She put out a hand and gripped his arm.

'Jerome, what you need to understand is that after what happened tonight, the real threat isn't ending up in jail. Essentially, the police are just an instrument. Our enemy is whoever is wielding it. The real threat is that they are going to kill us.'

Lost

Millicent felt uncomfortably conspicuous in the wheelchair, but after encountering their first car since sitting down, she deduced that this was less resultant of her fear of being seen than her self-consciousness about being perceived as infirm. Being perceived as an old lady.

A voice in her head reminded her she was seventy-two. Its tone was neutral however, so she couldn't say whether it meant *how do you expect to be perceived, you're ancient*; or, *how ridiculous, it's not like you're ninety*.

A line from a movie popped up, Pauline Collins reassuring her reflection.

'Shirley, you're only seventy-two.'

Except that it was forty-two. Shirley Valentine was forty-two.

She remembered when seventy-two sounded like the nadir of dotage and decrepitude. It was a good thing nobody could have told her at the start of her sentence what age she would be when she left prison. She would have killed herself within the first month.

She realised she had never stopped to contemplate the reality of what seventy-two actually felt like. Since her release, she had been so fixed upon what was behind her that she hadn't contemplated the physical condition she was in. And the truth was, she didn't feel like an old lady. She felt fitter than in her forties. Back then she had habitually abused and neglected herself by combining borderline alcoholism with full-blown workaholism. These days, she walked several miles every day, because she could. Even in prison, she had exercised a lot, because there was bugger-all else to do.

The bottom line was, she was a long way from needing a wheelchair.

'Can you look up flights on your phone?' she asked. 'Or do you need to get back to the house and use your computer?'

'No, I can do that. One-handed,' he added archly, emphasising the role he had been allotted, like it was a metaphor for a whole lot more besides. 'Do you just want non-extradition countries, because I don't think there's a sort filter for that.'

She ignored the snarky tone.

'Look up Rome.'

'On it. Any particular reason?'

'It's a big anonymous metropolis with masses of tourists. And it's somewhere I know, so it's a place I can get lost but not *feel* lost.'

'You mean somewhere you knew,' he replied disdainfully. 'Three decades ago.'

'It's not Milton Keynes. There's a reason they call it the Eternal City. Just tell me when we can get there.'

'Not today, if we're talking Glasgow or Edinburgh. Should be flights via London. Let me check.'

This sounded less than ideal but it might have to do. As Jerome had observed, the clock would start running as soon as the body was found. When the police asked if anyone saw anything unusual in the area, there would be two cops with an answer worth investigating. She had read about facial recognition and all that electronic surveillance. It sounded like Heathrow might be a very easy place to get caught. Ideally, she wanted to be wheels-up before dawn, preferably bound for the continent.

'Aye, there's a couple we could get. It willnae be cheap, though. Would you take it badly if I reminded you that the main reason I moved in with three old women is I'm boracic?'

'Don't worry about the money,' she told him. Alastair had taken care of that. 'I can afford a couple of flights.'

'And once we get to Rome, what then? Are we going to live there? It's just, I've got an essay due.'

'I'm assuming sarcasm is a coping mechanism, and so under the circumstances I'm tolerating it, but I'd say you've got about three passes left.'

'I was serious with the first bit.'

They had reached the lights at Great Western Road again. They each scanned the passing cars, neither of them speaking but both looking out for the same thing.

They crossed without seeing any more police.

'We need to talk to other people who knew Markus. Find out if they knew or suspected anything about him other than what he presented to the world.'

'Who was he?' Jerome asked. 'What did he do back then? I'm assuming you're at liberty to say.'

'That's you down to two.'

'That wasn't even sarcasm. Just pointing out I'm in the dark here.'

'He was supposedly working as a sales agent for British Screen and a rights buyer for a company called Blue Lantern Films. The guys in the photo were called the Blue Lamp Burns Society.'

'As in Dixon of Dock Green.'

'How on earth do you know that?'

'I'm studying film and TV, remember? I'm assuming Blue Lantern was an in-joke name for his equivalent of Universal Exports.'

It was her turn to get the reference.

'Markus was no James Bond. But yes, safe to assume it never really existed. British Screen did, and still does, but it wouldn't have been hard for the police to organise some kind of cover. There would have been somebody redirecting the call if anyone rang up asking for Markus Laird.'

'So who else knew him? That's still alive, I mean?'

Millicent had to swallow back a lump rising in her throat. One of the first things she had done when Alastair got her on the internet was to look up some of the people she had worked with. She hadn't intended to reach out to anyone, but she was curious as to what they had done with their lives.

She had started with the most colourful, reckoning he would be the easiest to trace. She read that Lucio had been 'officially declared dead in 2001, having disappeared without trace in 1994'. It was suggested that he may have fallen from his yacht, but the reports hinted that his unsavoury connections might have caught up with him. She had thought immediately of that bullet-headed homunculus Florio, always hanging around, a token of all that Lucio had hoped to escape with the Credit Populaire deal.

Then she had looked up Alessandro, and learned that he had taken his own life after falling into a state of depression. She recalled how he tended to disappear following the creative frenzy of a shoot. She had always thought it was just exhaustion.

She hadn't looked up anyone else after that. She couldn't face the thought of what more she might discover. Learning about Lucio and Alessandro had just cemented the idea that the world she once lived in had gone forever. However, she had found some absolution in learning that they both died around the same time as her own life had fallen apart. When she was on remand, she wondered why neither of them had ever got in touch. All down the years she had assumed it was because they were angry with her, that they believed she had done it.

'A lot of the people we both knew back then are no longer with us,' she told Jerome. 'It might be a matter of talking to people who knew them, people who were in the biz. A lot of them were based in Rome.'

'People who knew people who knew a man who was faking his identity. Twenty-six years ago. This isnae me cashing in another sarcasm pass, I'm just stating how desperate that sounds. Is there naebody at less than two removes?'

'Well, yes, but as one of them is Alfie Bertrand, he's probably not the first person you ought to be calling when you're on the run from the authorities.'

Jerome was gratifyingly flabbergasted.

'You know the Home Secretary? Well, obviously, seeing as he's Alfie to you and Alfonse to the rest of us.'

'I knew him, yes. He was a junior minister at the time, though I'm sure he would have denied ever meeting me once I hit the headlines. Can't see him picking up the phone to "the video nasty killer" if I did choose to get in touch.'

'You said one of them. Who else?'

Millicent was reluctant to own up, but Jerome deserved to know there was a viable option, even if it was one she was reluctant to exercise.

'Julia Fleet.'

He spluttered.

'You know fucking Julia Fleet as well? Roger Wincott's daughter, who was at the Leveson Inquiry?'

Julia was one of the few people who had shown her some kindness, writing to her in prison with letters of support. Millicent had never written back. She had her reasons, but she felt slightly ashamed of that now. At best it had been impolite, at worst hurtful. That Julia would have understood perhaps only made it worse.

Millicent had never sought to make contact after her release, and not merely because it would have been almost as difficult as hitting up Alfie Bertrand. Far more than that, it had been because she was afraid of how it would feel to meet anyone from back then. But needs must when the devil drives, and the devil was driving bloody hard.

'Just out of interest, do you know anybody from back then who isnae an all-powerful evil bastard?'

'She and Alfie were both rather different people in those days. He was very active in finding ways for the government to support film production. And Julia was an independent producer, trying to operate away from the influence of her family.'

'But as the song says, he who fucks nuns will later join the church. Bertrand's a pure hawk now and Julia Fleet ended up helping run her father's right-wing shite-rags.'

'How do you know about the Leveson Inquiry anyway? You must have been about twelve. Ten, even.'

'We study this stuff in Politics. How do you know about it? Did you get *Parliament Live* in Cornton Vale?'

'I could still read the papers.'

'Old Roger made a fucking miraculous recovery though, didn't he? Looked like a decrepit old codger in front of that committee. He's looking much healthier and younger now, nearly ten years on. Sneaky bastard. Still running the show too, in his eighties. Why is it that evil bastards live forever?'

'Depressingly, I read that people who are bullies and exploiters tend to live longer, while those who are on the receiving end tend to die younger.'

Jerome didn't respond. She glanced back and saw that he was busy on his phone.

'Just looking her up. She took a back seat after the Leveson Inquiry and the phone-hacking scandal. Her brother got the nod, as he was less of a tainted brand. These days she's got a more low-key role with Wincott Media's European TV holdings. She's in charge of launching a new streaming service, based in Paris.'

Paris was also a big anonymous metropolis with masses of tourists.

'What are the flight options for there?'

'There's a flight out of Edinburgh at seven-forty-five.'

She looked at her watch. It was just gone three o'clock. They could be touching down on French soil before the police had even got the body down from the tree.

'Paris it is, then.'

'Fair enough,' said Jerome. 'I'll look oot my passport. I havenae actually needed it for travel since I went to Berlin with the school when I was sixteen. I look like a wean in the photo, which is ironic because these days I mostly use it for ID so I can get served.'

Millicent heard this but didn't take in any of it. Her escape plan had just fallen apart, mere moments after their destination had come into focus. It was only when Jerome started talking about his passport that she remembered she no longer had one.

Faces

Jerome froze, his hand hovering above the keyboard. His expression was one of confused disbelief mixed with reproach at her only confessing this now. The look of a bright young man encumbered by a mad old bat.

In her defence, Millicent had withheld this information as a mercy. Her reasoning was that there was no need for both of them to be nervous and apprehensive all the way to the airport and right up until the moment of truth. However, when he was keying in their details for buying the flight tickets, she had no option but to come clean.

'Are you down on your passport just as Millicent Spark, or are there any initials or middle names I need to know about.'

'You're going to have to put "Carla Louise Mooney".'

'What?'

'My passport expired back when Steven Seagal was still getting work. I never got a new one. Carla isn't using hers.'

'Fuck's sake, you cannae just use somebody else's. I know things were simpler back then and we live in a surveillance state now, but you're no' telling me they never had photos in passports back in the Nineties. You look nothing like Carla.'

'You don't look like your passport photo either. You said you look like a kid.'

'Aye, but *me* as a kid.'

'I don't need to look like Carla. I just need to look vaguely like her passport photo.'

'How are you going to manage that?'

'With make-up. It used to be my party trick when I was a

teenager. I would go to the loo and come back looking like someone else who was in the room. I needed a Polaroid in those days, for reference.'

'Is Vivian's passport not there? You're closer to her facially.'

'Yes, it's in her bedside drawer, but I can make a face look fatter, thinner, darker, lighter, a nose wider, flatter. It's all about shades, contrasts, lines.'

'Regardless, what I'm really asking is why would you choose the one that's got a fucking birthmark? Did you need an added element of challenge?'

'That's another sarcasm pass crossed off. And just for that, I'm going to leave you to work out the answer for yourself.'

It was still dark, the first rays of the sun not yet beginning to illuminate Edinburgh Airport as they got out of the taxi.

'Enjoy Belek,' the driver said as Millicent handed him the fare and told him to keep the change. He had been happily chatting about being there with his grandchildren after she mentioned that was where they were headed.

'Why did you say we were going to Turkey?' Jerome asked.

'In case he ends up talking to the police about taking us to the airport. I'm trying to leave a false trail.'

He gave her that look again. The mad old bat look.

'You'll be leaving an electronic one and you cannae falsify that.'

'So they'll know immediately where I've gone?'

'Actually, come to think of it, no. They'll know where Carla Mooney has gone.'

She strode through the sliding doors into the terminal building and was immediately assailed by an overwhelming sense of bustle. It was half past five in the morning, but the place was already a river of bodies. Millicent stopped on the spot, feeling like if she could just become a stone, it would all wash around her. She had to swim, though.

Jerome had overseen her packing like she was a child, showing her what she could and couldn't take in her hand luggage. She thought he was joking when he told her about the fluids.

'Well, what kind of diseased mind would ever imagine someone constructing a bomb made of liquid explosives?' she had protested. 'Is that even a thing?'

Jerome had said he didn't know, but warned her not to ask any such questions once they got to airport security.

He was guiding her towards that now, dozens of people being funnelled into an intimidatingly crowded holding area on the other side of a series of glass barriers. Nobody was manning these barriers, nobody was checking passports, but Jerome had told her this would be the case. The test would come when they reached the departure gate, he said.

The look on his face when she emerged from the bathroom as Carla had filled her with confidence, but it was draining fast the closer they got to the moment of truth.

Jerome had the tickets, holding them out as they approached the electronic barriers. Millicent watched them swish open and closed for other passengers and felt instinctively untrusting of the procedure.

'I'll scan your ticket,' Jerome said, gesturing her forward.

She shook her head.

'On you go,' he told her, his tone impatient.

'I don't think I can.'

Jerome glanced upwards in exasperation, perhaps wondering what he had done to deserve this. The answer was save her life, but no good deed ever goes unpunished.

'Millicent,' he warned sternly. 'There's a queue.'

Invoking Britishness was the last resort of the scoundrel, but it worked.

'Okay,' she said, swallowing.

He held her ticket against the scanner to open the gate.

She proceeded tentatively, slowly.

'Before they fuckin' close again,' he urged.

She took the crucial step, feeling that combination of anxiety and relief she got whenever she stepped off the bottom of an escalator.

Jerome scanned his own ticket and followed her through. He looked like he had barely suppressed a scream.

'Sorry,' she told him. 'These things scare the living daylights out of me.'

Jerome said nothing, still simmering. Then a few moments later his expression softened.

'*Living Daylights*. Capital L, capital D,' he said, demonstrating that he knew what she was getting at. Someone was murdered by a booby-trapped sliding glass door in Timothy Dalton's Bond debut.

'I think we should trade sarcasm passes for movie references,' he went on. 'I get one of yours, I get another pass. You get one of mine, I lose a pass.'

'Very foolish words, man,' she replied.

'*Withnail & I*, Bruce Robinson, 1987. Point to me.'

They shuffled forward and joined one of the queues, Jerome staying close by her side. The security area was even more crowded than the concourse downstairs, so many people corralled into one area.

'You okay?' he asked.

She nodded. Her anxiety levels were responding to the throng and the sensory overload: so many people, so much noise, electronic signs, TV screens, conveyor belts, colours, movement. But working against all of this was the feeling of something dormant but familiar, an awareness of being somewhere associated with a sense of adventure, of possibility. An echo from a time when the world was opening up before her, rather than being closed off for ever.

'I'm fine. If there's one thing that's not going to faze me today, it's lining up and being searched.'

She followed the instructions, obedient and compliant as she had been conditioned to be. They made their way through the metal detector arch and retrieved their trays on the other side. Jerome made sure he found a spot at the booth beside her while she put her toiletries back in her bag. She had put the make-up kit itself in her hold luggage, but kept a few items to hand for a final touch-up before presenting herself at the gate.

They proceeded along a wide corridor, emerging into the departure area. The sun had come up, and through banks of floor-to-ceiling windows she could see aeroplanes on the tarmac. In the middle distance, one was taking off from the runway, its massive bulk climbing languidly into the sky with impossible slowness. She suddenly felt a profound sense of what her freedom meant, of options and possibilities she had failed to appreciate over the past year, having been so mired in contemplating what she had lost.

'I never thought I'd be doing this again,' she said. 'Flying abroad. I don't think I truly realised I *could* do this again. Vivian tried to tempt me, but I was too timid.'

'I guess we should be grateful to Deid Guy for supplying sufficient motivation.'

She noticed that Jerome still hadn't used Geddes' name. It reminded her of the burden he was carrying; carrying for *her*.

They stood before a bank of monitors, so many destinations listed on the screens.

'Paris CDG. That's us,' he said. 'They're boarding pretty sharp. Gate fifteen. Come on, Carla.'

The reminder sent a jolt through her, leaving her tremulous as they approached the waiting area. She could see the officials at the door, a line of passengers handing over tickets and passports for inspection.

'I need to go to the loo,' she announced.

'Don't be long.'

She felt sick, but the only remedy was to be found at the mirror, not in a bathroom stall. She glanced again at the passport photo for reference, adding a few more licks here and there. The more she studied her reflection, the less she was convinced it would work. It had been a long time, such a long time, since she had practised her craft, and she knew Jerome's initial surprise at her transformed appearance had been at how different she looked, not how much she looked like Carla.

It could all be about to fall apart. Travelling outside the UK without permission was a violation of her licence conditions on its own, never mind the added offence of attempting to travel on someone else's passport. If this went wrong, she would be back in prison before the day was out. And if someone had decided they wanted her dead, they could get to her a lot easier inside.

209

She rejoined Jerome in the queue, just behind a mother and her little girl. The little girl was looking up, staring. Millicent wanted to offer her a smile, but she couldn't summon one. She was just too scared.

Her hands were visibly shaking as they reached the front. Had to be noticeable, a give-away, she reckoned.

The woman on the gate took her ticket and Carla's passport. She gave them each a cursory glance and handed them back. It looked like all she did was check the names matched.

'Nervous flier?' the woman asked.

She meant the hands.

'It's been a long time.'

'You'll be grand.'

'I think I will,' she agreed.

Millicent breathed out again.

She and Jerome proceeded down the gangway. They met with another queue, once again finding themselves behind the woman and the little girl.

'What's that red thing on your face?' the girl asked.

'Alison, you mustn't ask people questions about their appearance,' her mother chastised. 'I'm so sorry,' she said to Millicent, looking mortified.

'Oh, don't worry about it. Happens all the time.'

Millicent bent over and spoke to the girl in a gentle tone.

'It's called a birthmark, dear.'

'How long have you had it?'

Her mother and Millicent shared a smile.

Oh, about two and a half hours, she thought to herself.

They took their seats, Millicent at the window and Jerome beside her with the aisle one still empty.

'I've worked it out,' he said. 'Why you took Carla's passport.'

'Go on.'

'It's 'cause when someone has a birthmark, it's the first thing anybody notices. So it's gaunny be the main thing anybody examining the passport will look at.'

'Very good.'

'Do I get a pass for that?'

'No.'

As Millicent fastened her seatbelt, her nerves were still jangling but she felt energised. An odd thought crossed her mind. Sometimes you run because you are being chased, but sometimes you run simply because you want to see how far your legs will take you. She had devised a plan purely on instinct, executing it without hesitation, and it left her wondering whether being chased had merely given her a pretext for a desire that was already there.

She was on a plane. She was getting out of the country, going on the run, travelling under someone else's name. The leviathan had surfaced, but it wasn't the only one who could disappear beneath the waves.

'Catch me if you can,' she muttered to herself, possessed by a quiet determination.

'Steven Spielberg, 2002,' said Jerome. 'That's another point to me.'

Blessed

His smile when he saw her was like a shaft of light from the heavens.

Millie felt a surge of delight accompanied by an impulse to rush across the few yards that separated them and haul him into an embrace. Caution restrained her, however. He looked happy to see her, but she didn't know where they stood.

She had hooked up with him in Milan last month, when she was attending the MIFED film market. A sales agent of Lucio's acquaintance had organised a press conference to help drum up pre-sales ahead of principal photography. Millie had assumed Markus was just looking for a no-strings shag and had spotted nobody better on the horizon as MIFED drew to a close. That was fine by her. She had been more than happy to have a quick and uncomplicated fling with an attractive and charismatic younger man, and hadn't expected to hear from him once the market was over. She thought that was mutually understood, in fact. She had moved on to Rome to start the shoot and he had gone back to London.

But now here he was. On business, presumably, but why would Lucio have said he had a surprise for her, meaning Markus? Lucio didn't know they had gotten together.

She was tying herself in knots with possibilities and permutations. Or did she mean hopes? Then Markus cut through it all by striding forward and sweeping her into a kiss. It wasn't a continental peck on both cheeks either. Someone nearby muttered, 'Ooh la la.'

She felt light-headed, and she knew where all the blood had gone. She was having thoughts that would have given Mrs Birtwhistle a stroke.

Markus let her go and she somehow managed to stay on her feet.

'What are you doing here?' she asked.

'I flattered myself into thinking he was interested in acquiring our movie,' said Lucio. 'But apparently the only thing he's really interested in is you.'

The cautious part of her was trying to calculate the implications and asking her how she ought to feel about this. However, her heart's response was unambiguous, as it had been thumping away at the mere sight of him. She then started worrying about her appearance, as dressing to look good was seldom a consideration on set. However, that was her inner thirteen-year-old talking. The forty-five-year-old knew that once someone has seen you naked, their impression of you isn't going to be altered by what you wear next.

'I had to be upfront,' Markus told Lucio. 'I didn't want to impose on your hospitality under false pretences.'

'Any friend of the miraculous Millie is welcome in my company. Besides, I was under no illusions. You're developing a rep as the rights buyer who never buys any rights.'

'Hey, in this business, you never get fired over what you say no to. In the case of *Mancipium*, you should take it as a compliment. From everything I've heard, this film is going to be too good for the likes of us.'

By 'us' she knew he meant Blue Lantern rather than British Screen. It bought up multiple rights across various international territories, then sold them on to local distributors, the type of firm that kept the low end of the business ticking over. Firms like that regarded a lot of the movies as essentially commodities, buying and selling rights the way other people traded shares.

'That said,' Markus told Lucio, 'we are looking for higher-profile pictures these days. It's 1993, not 1983. There's more money in sell-through video than rental these days, if it's the right title.'

Lucio gave him a pat on the shoulder by way of acknowledgment. Whether he had primarily come here to see her or not, she had just witnessed the first phase of a negotiation.

Lucio wandered off, glad-handing someone else and leaving the two of them in each other's company.

'Is it cool, me showing up like this?' Markus asked. 'You looked pretty gobsmacked back there, and I'm trying to work out if me being here feels like a nice surprise or an ambush.'

'It's a nice surprise,' she assured him. 'I thought Milan was just, you know, casual, but I'm not averse to a reprise.'

'To be perfectly honest, I felt the same, that it was just a one-night thing. But after I got back from MIFED, I couldn't stop thinking about you. I figured it would pass, given our paths were unlikely to cross again soon, but then Blue Lantern wanted me to look closer at a few projects. I saw *Mancipium* on the list of possibles and I felt the hand of fate. I made that a pretext for a trip to Rome.'

'So you lied to Lucio when you said you were only here for me.'

'Just a teensy little bit. You don't get courted if you don't play hard to get. But the honest truth is, if you weren't working on this picture, I'd be in New York right now, or possibly Malaysia.'

His hand slipped around hers and she felt something pulse through her.

'So, do you want a tour of the set?' she asked.

'That would be great.'

She led him back through the gathering, which took a while as Markus's networking instincts never slept. The girl with the tray crossed their path and this time she stopped to offer both of them a drink. Millie knew she was only being afforded this courtesy on the assumption that she was Markus's plus one. She tried not to dwell on the irony.

'Am I nuts, or did I see Alfie Bertrand in here?' he asked.

'Where?' she replied, looking around. She couldn't see him in the crowd, but nor could she see Lucio either, and she'd been talking to him a few minutes ago.

'Earlier, I mean. Pretty sure I saw him walking past on the arm of some girl.'

'That would have been him, yes. He's been here all afternoon. And he didn't stop to talk to you?'

Markus looked confused.

'Why would he?'

'Don't you know each other?'

'No.'

'Must have got the wrong end of the stick. I saw him at MIFED and I kind of assumed you were primarily there because he was.'

Markus seemed caught off-guard, strangely wary of the idea they might be associated.

'Why would you think that?' he asked.

'Isn't British Screen ultimately overseen by the Department of Culture?'

Markus wore an expression of amusement, tinged also with relief.

'Technically, but our connection is much the same as if he were a junior Armed Forces minister and I was a squaddie. Suffice it to say, he hasn't been round the office for a coffee and a chat about the latest Peter Greenaway project. Him being in Milan was nothing to do with British Screen, and neither has him being here now.'

'You're not a fan, I'm guessing.'

'Actually, I think he's quite cool, for a Tory cabinet minister. Which admittedly is the lowest bar for coolness anyone could possibly imagine, but give him points for at least clearing it.'

Alfie Bertrand was the scion of Lord William Bertrand, aristo landowner and Tory grandee. Millie got what Markus was saying. Alfie was considered a rising star of the Conservative Party because they regarded him as bright and charismatic, but following the carnival of the shuffling undead that had populated the cabinets of Thatcher and Major, that wasn't saying much.

He had been only thirty when he was elected in 1992, and it was an indication that he was being groomed for great things that he had already been given this position. It was assumed that once he had matured, he would be a big beast in the party, with one of the more serious portfolios, but for now, they regarded his youthfulness as an asset.

'What do you make of him?' Markus asked.

'I'll give him this much: he has two very rare qualities for a cabinet minister. One is that he actually does seem to know his brief. I tried to embarrass him in front of Alessandro a while back, but he was clued up on his movies.'

'What's the other?'

'That he seems to have an interest in his portfolio beyond that of working out how to help the party's backers make money from selling bits of it. He seems genuinely interested in helping Lucio shoot in the UK.'

'And what body would be facilitating that? Would it be through the Arts Council or the National Trust?'

'No, that's my point. There are implications if he involved himself in a ministerial capacity. Alfie is offering to do this off his own bat. He likes the project, but mostly I think he's hit it off with Lucio.'

'I assume that has raised a few eyebrows in certain circles,' Markus said. 'I mean, no disrespect to Lucio, but it's not like Alfie's hanging out with Bernardo Bertolucci.'

'I know what you mean. At best you could call him a trash Svengali. I dug Alfie up about his party's attitude to horror movies, but he says that's just posturing, all part of the game.'

'Yeah, but I'm not only talking about Lucio's movies. Credit Populaire bailed because of his connections. I would have thought a politician might be wary of such associations, even at a couple of removes.'

Millie thought about Florio, wondering if he and Alfie even knew each other's names. She had never seen them together, and Lucio was very skilled at ensuring certain circles never overlapped.

'They say politics is always local,' she replied. 'If you're connected at two removes to East End gangsters, it's not a good look. If you're connected at two removes to Italian ones, it seems sufficiently remote as to be almost exotic.'

She walked Markus out of the party and led him to sound-stage two. The music was still throbbingly audible even through here, but it was a lot easier to hear each other speak.

'This is the legionaries' camp,' she explained. 'Where we were shooting today.'

She stopped him before he could proceed on to the hot part of the set.

'Keep off the grass,' she said.

'Got you.'

'And don't touch anything.'

'Can I touch you?'

She let him kiss her, his hand running down her neck and stopping before she wanted it to.

'What's over there?' he asked. He was looking towards the large wooden frames adjacent to the camp, the nearest section partly masked off top to bottom with black cloth in case anything crept into shot.

His voice was quieter after the kiss. The music seemed further away, or maybe it was just that it felt special to be alone together.

'Interior sets for the centurion's villa. Let me show you.'

Millie walked on soft feet, always instinctively mindful of the delicateness of these constructions, and hoping Markus would pick up on her gentleness too. You had to convey it on this side of the plywood walls, because once they crossed over, people unused to sets could easily forget they were essentially inside a fragile illusion.

She enjoyed the look of amazement in Markus's eyes as they turned a corner and found themselves inside a courtyard, columns lining three sides of walkways around a fountain in the centre.

'The production designer based this on an excavated villa at Herculaneum.'

'Agnello?' Markus asked, meaning the production designer on *Mancipium*.

Millie laughed softly.

'No. I mean the production designer on some sword-and-sandals epic back in the late Sixties. These are all recycled sets. A lot of them have been in storage for decades. The fact that everything is a bit chipped and faded actually works for us. Back then they were trying to evoke opulence, but we want everything to seem like the end of days, like things are falling apart.'

'So it's a horror movie set against the fall of the Roman empire? I'm kind of vague on the concept.'

'No. That's only part of it. We had to come up with a way of using all these old sets and linking different historical periods.'

'But the title is Latin, right?'

'Yes. It's to do with slavery. The film is about this charm, this amulet, which contains a demon. You think that you possess it, but really the demon possesses you. The demon draws power from taking lives, and as its creature, the more sadistic and spectacular the killing, the greater a rush you get. But like addiction, you need more each time to replicate the high.

'The first person to find it is a Roman centurion, but we follow it down through the ages. Seventeenth-century Florence, hopefully Victorian London. There's also a kind of witchfinder dynasty, sworn to contain the evil wherever it arises.'

'And presumably the possessed guy gets slain in each time period,' Markus said. 'Won't that make it kind of episodic?'

Millie smiled at the chance to reveal the cleverness of Stacey's concept.

'The possessed are all different, but they each become the same demon. They start off as ordinary-looking, unremarkable individuals, but once they find the amulet, they transform into, well, Sergio. Fair to say, he's a bit of an Adonis. Or maybe a Narcissus would be more appropriate.'

'For the actor or the character?'

'Both, to be honest.'

'Have you got the Florence stuff on this stage?'

'Not yet. We're moving it in here as soon as we strike this lot. But this is just the courtyard. Come and see the villa interiors.'

She led him down a narrow channel, more plywood belying the other world and other time that lay on the far side. They stopped at the kitchen, where she would have a lot of work next week, Sergio hacking and slashing his way through several of the household slaves as they prepared a meal.

She was about to tell Markus how she planned to rig up an impalement effect using a roasting spit, when they both heard a moan.

It sounded out once more, low and breathy. Quite unmistakable. They shared a look.

'Where's it coming from?' asked Markus in a whisper.

'Through there is the centurion's bedroom, appropriately enough.' Millie explained how Lucio got his start.

'He used to shoot high-production-value porn on old historical sets out of hours. I've always wondered if he's still moonlighting.'

'Period porn,' Markus whispered. 'Oh, no, that sounds like a whole other thing, which I nonetheless have no doubt there's a market for.'

'Let's sneak a peek.'

They proceeded stealthily towards the source of the noise, beyond the next row of plywood flats. Millie pulled Markus back as he headed for the open doorway. She knew the sightlines, every angle. It was her job. She dragged him around the side, where there were velvet drapes they could spy through.

Balancing on silent feet and holding her breath, Millie tugged back a tiny gap through which they saw not a porn shoot in progress, but the junior minister lying on the centurion's bed, being straddled by one of Lucio's girls. Though she wasn't wearing much, Millie could tell she was done up to look like Cleopatra, complete with wig.

Millie had to bite her hand to stop herself from giggling. She let the drape fall closed and gestured Markus to back away. It was touch and go, but she managed to contain her mirth until she had reached what she hoped was a distance beyond earshot.

'Am I going crazy, or did I see Alfie Bertrand's nuts in there?' Markus asked, adapting his earlier question.

She spluttered with laughter.

'You did indeed. Having his Liz Taylor fantasy. Or maybe it was Amanda Barrie.'

Markus looked blank.

'*Carry on Cleo*,' she explained.

'I think I'm starting to see why he's so interested in being involved in Lucio's movies. And all of it far from the zoom lenses and prying eyes of British tabloids.'

'Now you can't tell your bosses you didn't see something remarkable when you visited the *Mancipium* set,' Millie told him.

'I saw something remarkable before I left the party.'

Their eyes met, no question what was going on in each other's mind.

'Let's get out of here,' Millie said.

They were already undressing one another as they stumbled into her workshop, tripping over their discarded clothes. She pressed herself into him and Markus bumped against a table, the legs creaking on the tiled floor. There was a clatter nearby and they both turned to see that the jolt had upended a tub of liquid latex. Fortunately, the bin bag she had ripped open did what it was there to do, protecting what was underneath.

Markus grinned.

'Oh, shit. I've spilt all this white sticky stuff.'

'Not yet you haven't, I hope.'

'Speaking of which, you don't happen to have a condom?'

'Over there,' she indicated.

Millie pulled down her knickers as he stepped across and opened her kit bag.

'Jesus Christ,' Markus said, pulling out two handfuls of condoms. 'Is there something I should know? What kind of a fuck-monster are you?'

'I use them in my work. And as far as I recall, you're not a minor graze but the full slashed throat.'

She couldn't find a place on the floor where they might lie down without possibly clattering another table or disturbing a tray of equipment. The sink was their only option. Millie bent over it and pulled him into her from behind.

In the urgency and excitement of it all, he didn't last long, but nor did she need him to. She came as fast as she'd ever done. Then they both broke down into giggling again.

Pulling her clothes back on later, she found herself looking at the latex spillage, which had already dried. No damage and no real mess. She could scoop the liner up and bin the lot. But as she tugged carefully at one end, she noticed a strange thing: the white lump hadn't stuck to the polythene. Even the edges that were still damp would not adhere to the black plastic.

It was a revelation. Suddenly she saw how she could create a reservoir that would leak and spurt blood from multiple places at once. And she had made this discovery whilst shagging the handsome younger man who had flown to Rome to be with her.

This film was charmed, that's what it was. It was never supposed to happen, wasn't even an idea in someone's head a few months ago, yet it had somehow willed itself into existence, and everything about it seemed to fall into place. This bloody film was charmed.

PART THREE

Diversion

Jerry's phone told him the hotel was just ahead on Rue des Bons Enfants, but he couldn't see any awnings or signage to indicate they were in the right place. Then as he got closer, he saw an archway cut into the terrace above a short passage. They stepped through into this courtyard, a tranquil enclave that seemed to exist in a completely different place from the noise and traffic that had greeted them upon their emergence from the Metro.

The hotel was here, forming the centre of a horseshoe. It immediately made him think of the Continental from the John Wick movies.

'If Lance Reddick is on Reception, we should bail,' he said.

Millicent just stared. No points.

He had booked it on the train from CDG to Gare du Nord, Millicent grabbing the handset off him and scrolling the list until she found a place she liked the look of. She could have got nicer digs for the same money further out, but location seemed important to her.

She had also got him to show her how to transfer some money, as she didn't want the booking on her credit card in case the police accessed her records.

'Wouldn't they need a warrant for that?' Jerry had asked.

'Only if they were abiding by the law. As they've already tried to kill me, it's fair to assume that's not the case. And even if they were, they'll be able to get a warrant *tout de suite* if I'm wanted in connection with a murder.'

'Once they start digging around, it won't be long before they have my name too.'

'They don't have it yet though, whereas they definitely know mine. Anything that throws a little dust on our trail is worth doing.'

She transferred a grand. His balance never looked so healthy. Jerry had screenshotted it for posterity.

As it was only half ten in the morning and too early to check in, Millicent suggested they leave their bags and head straight to the WinVision Europe offices in Montparnasse.

'Don't you want to try phoning or emailing first, see if you can get an appointment? Make sure she's even there?'

'Advance notice just gives people more time to come up with their excuses. If Julia knows I am physically in the building, I don't think she'd ignore me. Especially if I make it plain that I only need a few minutes.'

'And do you think that would work better if you weren't disguised as Carla?'

'Shit,' she replied, remembering. 'I'm off to the bathroom. I'll be two minutes.'

Jerry checked the Metro route while she was away, but when she returned Millicent said she would prefer to walk.

'It's a bit of a hike.'

'It's Paris,' she said.

Jerry didn't know what that was supposed to mean, other than that it was the end of the discussion.

He started to get the picture within about a quarter of a mile. He wasn't in Kansas anymore. The place even smelled different: the sweet, warm scents of baking interspersing the crisp morning air. They passed little shops full of just one thing, like wedding dresses or old coffee machines. Tiny restaurants with only three or four tables, and more of those hidden courtyards glimpsed through archways and alleys.

He recalled how he felt when he had gone to Berlin with the school, and when his gran took him to Majorca: the striking, energising sense of being somewhere quite different to all that he was used to. Here though, it was intensified by the awareness that though he wasn't unaccompanied, nobody was looking after him.

He had often heard people say that modern travel had made the world smaller. To him the effect was absolutely the opposite. His world had been small because he had hardly been anywhere. He suddenly felt shamefully ignorant and uncultured, assailed by a sense of inferiority. He guessed that a lot of other people had felt that way too, which was why they had voted to retreat into insularity; and to drag everybody else back down with them, like Rossco.

He thought of Felicity talking about the Godard retrospective she saw in London. He understood now that she wasn't being pretentious: he was just being insecure. That was why he hadn't replied to Philippa's texts, too.

Dickhead.

The WinVision Europe headquarters was in an eighteenth-century terrace facing three similar buildings on a tree-lined square. He had been expecting concrete modernity, but was starting to appreciate another facet of what Millicent meant when she said, 'It's Paris.' There were two ornate wooden structures in the centre of the square: one a tabac stand selling newspapers, magazines and cigarettes; the other offering crepes made on the spot. The smell was amazing.

They strode in through the glass doors where a security guard intercepted them and politely directed them towards Reception. Millicent began chatting away in French to the woman behind the desk. She had confessed she expected to be rusty after all this time, but she sounded pretty fluent to Jerry, not that his National Five made him much of a judge. He guessed she could speak Italian too, as she said she knew Rome and had worked on several Italian movies.

He was latching on to the few words he recognised. None of them sounded like 'come right in'. Lots of *pas possible* and *pas aujourd'hui*.

Millicent stepped away, next to a pair of leather-upholstered benches.

'What's the sitch?' he asked

'She's asking if we have an appointment, what company we're with. It's like dealing with a computer. I'm trying to explain that I'm an old friend who's in town briefly, just trying to get her to pass on to Julia the fact that I'm here. I get the impression she's not prepared to do even that much because basically I'm nobody.'

Jerry looked at the scale of what surrounded him in this expansive lobby, all glass and marble. There were electronic barriers and uniformed security staff monitoring everyone who came and went, and everyone who came and went looked sharply dressed and officially credentialled. Up above in the atrium, through floor-to-ceiling windows he could see massive TV screens, offices and meeting rooms. Money and power and influence. People like Julia Fleet had layers upon layers of personnel and protection to prevent requests such as Millicent's even getting near them. The receptionist was only the first level of resistance.

'On the plus side, nobody said she's not here,' Jerry said.

'Yes. I think our best chance is if we wait and maybe catch her as she is leaving. I just need her to see me.'

She had barely said this when one of the security guards approached and started speaking to Millicent, his tone polite but firm. Jerry didn't hear the word *fenêtre* but he knew they were being told to pick a window.

'He says if we don't have an appointment, we can't wait in the lobby,' Millicent relayed.

It didn't matter. Jerry already had an idea.

'Do you speak English?' he asked the guard.

He wore a thin smile.

'A little.'

Millicent glanced at Jerry, subtly questioning. He gave her a tiny nod as a prompt to go along with what he was saying.

'She needs to sit for five minutes. She's feeling tired. We've come a long way. Just five minutes. Is that cool?'

'Five minutes, yes.'

'Do you need a drink of something?' Jerry asked as she took a seat on one of the benches. 'I'll go and get some water.'

'That would be most welcome, thank you.'

The guard gave him a nod of acknowledgment as Jerry headed outside. He made a quick purchase at the tabac then jogged back across the square, bottle in hand. Having handed it to Millicent, he walked over to the same guard.

'Toilet?' he asked.

'*Toilette, c'est ca.*'

The guard pointed towards the far end. His purpose made clear, Jerry got moving. He had reckoned the Gents would be his only chance for pulling this off, but as he proceeded through the lobby, he saw a cleaner emerge, seemingly from the wall, pushing a trolley. The cleaner had come from a storeroom, its door cleverly concealed so that it merged into the marble tiles. Even better. With the cleaner's back to him, heading for the barriers, he tried the door and found it unlocked.

It took him a couple of minutes to get things underway. He found a metal bucket and a stack of paper towels that were ideal for the task. Then he watched through a gap in the door and chose his moment to step out.

He chose poorly. There was a bloke in a suit who must have been walking close to the wall, and Jerry almost hit him with the door.

Jerry slapped his own forehead.

'*Toilette?*' he asked.

The man rolled his eyes.

'*A droite.*'

'*Merci.*'

A few moments later he sat himself down next to Millicent.

'What on earth are you up to?' she asked.

'I figured if they willnae let us go up to see her, we make her come doon and see us.'

'And how are you hoping to do that?'

He was about to reply 'Patience, young Skywalker' but realised he'd be conceding an easy point – and sounding like a wanker.

Just then, fire alarms began to go off all around them, the sound reverberating throughout the lobby.

'The way Neil McCauley got to Waingro.'

Another blank.

'*Heat.* Michael Mann, 1995. But I guess you were still in the big house.'

Within minutes the building was being evacuated. He and Millicent were escorted through the glass doors into the square, while behind them people were exiting from emergency stairwells and out through the lobby.

They stood at the edge of the designated muster point and watched as dozens of staff streamed out. It was far more than he would have thought the building could hold, but Julia Fleet was not among them. Jerry wondered whether she had gone out some separate exit for top-level execs, but he didn't share this thought.

Through the doors, he could now see smoke belching from inside the storeroom, where he had started a fire using lighter fluid bought from the tabac. The security guards had noticed the source and were hurrying towards it with hand-held extinguishers.

He had done it in a metal bucket so that it would burn itself out and not spread. This was going to be over in no time. He assumed the fire brigade would still need to attend, but if everyone was satisfied that they had contained the threat at source, they would tell anyone not already downstairs to stay put. That was if Julia Fleet was even here today. Just because the receptionist refused to pass on a message didn't mean she even knew that much information.

Then suddenly Julia was there, striding between two suits, heading for the square.

He nudged Millicent.

'On you now.'

Millicent started walking off in the wrong direction, leaving Jerry wondering if she had bottled it. Then he got the play: she was changing her angle of entry so that it looked like she just happened to be walking through the square when who should she happen to see but:

'Julia?'

She turned around as Millicent approached.

Nobody intervened, not even the two suits she was with. Jerry was expecting a phalanx of security people to immediately surround her, though that didn't mean they weren't there. Julia must have subtly given the nod that it was okay.

'Millie? Millie Spark? Oh my God, it *is* you.'

Julia pulled Millicent to her, looking quite taken aback. There seemed real affection in her embrace. Millicent hadn't been exaggerating. She really did know Julia Fleet, though she hadn't given the impression they were quite so huggy-close. It was France, though.

'Julia, I realise you must be incredibly busy, but seeing as we're both here, there's something I'd really like to ask you about. It would only take five minutes.'

Julia glanced back towards the building, as though weighing something up. It was all in the balance now.

'It's true I'm up to my eyes in it. But we're in the middle of a fire alarm and it's going to be ten or twenty minutes before the pompiers give us the all-clear, so why don't I buy you a coffee?'

Cowboy Days

Julia led them away from the muster point, surprisingly unaccompanied. The suits she had been with seemed to melt away without a word, but Jerry reckoned someone would materialise again, seemingly unprompted, should she need them to.

They followed her into a café just around the corner, where they were ushered to a booth at the back without a word being exchanged with the waiter. Jerry guessed she came here a lot.

'I'm sorry, I should formally introduce myself,' she said to Jerry. 'I'm Julia.' She didn't add the surname. He wondered if she assumed that he would know that part, hence the 'formally'.

'Jerry.'

'And you're Millicent's . . . nephew?' she suggested.

'He's actually my housemate. Long story.'

Their order arrived with impressive rapidity. He guessed high-power media execs didn't have time to wait, and you'd better recognise that if you wanted their repeat custom. The coffees came with a plateful of pastries. Jerry didn't realise how starving he was until it was put in front of him. He tanned a *pain au chocolat* in about three bites.

Julia took a gulp of her coffee then sighed, shaking her head.

'My God, Millie. I can hardly believe it. How long has it been? Feels like a lifetime.'

'Or a life sentence.'

Julia lowered her eyes briefly at this, though Millicent didn't seem to have meant it as any kind of dig.

'I wrote to you, you know,' she said. Her voice was soft, her tone solicitous, even humble. It was a far cry from the hard-as-nails performance he had seen in his Politics lecture. 'I don't know if they passed on the letters, but I want you to know I sent them.'

Millicent gave her a sad smile.

'They passed them on. I'm sorry I didn't reply.'

'I sometimes wondered if you hadn't written back because I didn't say anything about the charges. About what I did or didn't believe. I just didn't know what to think, but I wanted you to know I was thinking of you.'

'No, it wasn't that. I wasn't in good shape. I had nothing I wanted to say to anybody. But your words meant a lot. A few people wrote to say they didn't believe I could have done it, but strangely it meant more to have someone say they still cared about me regardless of what I'd done, regardless of whether they believed it or not.'

'I thought that if a woman kills her boyfriend . . . there's probably a good reason. But like I said, I was in the dark, and I didn't want to judge either way.'

Jerry had to stop himself from commenting about how her family's newspapers tended to take a different view, and were altogether less reticent with regard to the judging bit.

'I didn't kill him,' Millicent said flatly. 'For the record.'

She didn't mention that somebody *did* try to kill her less than twelve hours ago, because she would have also had to explain why that hadn't worked out for the guy.

Julia said nothing, merely nodded. Smart response: it could be read as accepting what Millicent had said without necessarily agreeing.

'But I'm trying to find out who did. That's what I need to talk to you about. I know it was twenty-five years ago, but how well did you know Markus back then?'

Julia seemed surprised, like it wasn't where she expected this to go. Jerry didn't see how she could imagine Millicent wanting to talk about anything else, but maybe that was wrong of him: defining her entirely by this, and assuming everyone else did too.

'Only through you, initially. I remember he became interested in acquiring various international rights, particularly for Asia, but he was dealing with Lucio on all of that. I knew him to talk to, but then he seemed to know everyone. He had an impressive memory for little details about people.'

'So you weren't aware he was an undercover police officer?'

This floored her.

'What?' she asked, eyes narrowing. 'An un . . . who told you that?'

'It's complicated, but it's the truth. Markus Laird wasn't his real name. He was never buying any rights, because there was no Blue Lantern Films. I don't know what his actual agenda was. All I know is that he used me to pursue it. I'm trying to find out what he might have been investigating, because I believe that's what got him killed. I think we're both aware that Lucio knew some dodgy people back then. And I also know he disappeared around the same time.'

Julia took a long drink of her coffee, like she was considering her answer. Or buying time. Either way, it didn't look like a memory she relished revisiting.

'Everything seemed to be falling apart back then,' she said. 'With the movie, I mean. We were late in post when Lucio disappeared. I ran around for a few days trying to track him down, while at the same time trying to get people paid so that we could finish the film. But then it emerged that the negative had disappeared too. Some suggested it was taken as collateral, to make sure Lucio paid a debt. Others that Lucio himself took the negative, maybe for safe-keeping if he knew something was coming down the line.'

'I was oblivious to all this,' Millicent said. 'I only found out about his disappearance less than a year ago. It was the furthest thing from my thoughts back then, but I always assumed the film would have been completed and had a life without me. Just like all the people I used to know.'

'The only life it had was as a footnote, or a campfire tale,' Julia replied. 'It occasionally gets a mention when someone does a thing about lost, abandoned or supposedly cursed movies. Only a few horror geeks have even heard of it.'

She sounded surprisingly bitter and hurt. Jerry didn't see why, when she had gone on to rise so high and end up swimming in money, but clearly it meant a lot to her.

'I've heard of it,' he said. Jerry hadn't been sure when to broach this subject with Millicent, but he felt like it was something Julia ought to know. Weird how you could see someone on TV and utterly detest them for what they stood for, but when they were sat in front of you, if they were in pain, you wanted to soothe it if you could.

'Through Millie?'

'No. I read about it, years ago. The myths. The curse.'

Millicent looked askance. She clearly didn't know about this stuff.

'Misremembered details, hysterical speculation and Chinese whispers,' Julia explained. 'Largely deriving from the fact that, well . . .' She swallowed. 'The fact that Lucio disappeared and then . . . Alessandro.'

Julia wiped a tear from one eye.

'We did still have video of the rough cut,' she went on. 'It was feasible we could have edited and released a VHS version as a way of recouping *something*. Most of the revenue for horror comes from the small screen, after all. But after all our work, all our ambitions for it, it was a soul-destroying prospect. That's what Alessandro was working on when he became so depressed. It crushed him.'

Julia seemed to have aged in the past few minutes, as the woman beneath the mask of the polished exec was revealed.

'It crushed me too. It was like . . . you know *Little Women?*'

'Yes,' Millicent replied. Jerry hadn't read it, but he'd seen the Winona Ryder and Christian Bale movie.

'I loved that book growing up. I took such inspiration from it. But it turned out I'm not as strong as Jo. She bounced back from her sister burning her novel. I never could.'

'Aren't there any surviving copies of the rough cut?' Jerry asked.

She gave a sad smile.

'I know that there are always rumours, people claiming to have seen it, but no. You ever hear that story about a marketing exec being shown the rough cut of *Dirty Dancing?* He told the producers they should burn the negative and claim the insurance. That's kind of what we did. The negative was lost, so rather than try to salvage something from a VHS transfer, we accepted the project was dead and cut our losses.'

Julia glanced up, over their heads, which was when Jerry became aware that there was someone standing behind him. As he had predicted, the suits had re-materialised, seemingly unbidden, though he doubted the latter part was entirely true. They were on a clock or there had been an invisible signal. Either way, Millicent's time was up.

'I'm afraid I've got to get going,' Julia announced, getting to her feet. 'We're already behind because of the fire alarm. I wish there was more I could say to help you, but it was all so long ago.'

Millicent and Jerry stood up too.

'It's lovely to see you again, truly,' Julia said.

'You too. And doing so well. You've come a long way from putting indie movies together on shoelaces and chewing gum. It must seem crazy now to think of the lengths you had to go just to raise a few grand.'

Julia wore an odd expression, like she was more frustrated than flattered by this, though it was clearly meant as a compliment.

'Everyone assumes that if you're in a lucrative and powerful job, you've made it. But I hope you're one of the few people who can understand that despite all the stress and the indignities, the shoelace-and-chewing-gum days were the time of my life. We were making movies! What's better than that?'

'Nothing,' Millicent replied.

'And I'm sure I'm not the only one who feels that way. You remember Jean-Marc Poupard? He's one of the top-level execs at Credit Populaire these days, but I bet if you asked him when he was truly happiest, he'd give the same answer.'

'So he's still alive? I've learned not to assume.'

'Oh, yes. We run into each other now and again. Come to think of it, his bank is sponsoring a new exhibition at the Musée d'Art Moderne. They're having an opening reception tonight. If you like, I could pull a few strings, get you on the guest list. Maybe he knew something about Markus, or what he might have been delving into.'

'You'd do that?' Millicent asked.

'It's done,' Julia replied, giving a look to one of the suits, who acknowledged with a nod. 'I wish I could help more. Wish we could talk more. Maybe when things calm down after this launch. I'll text you so you have my number. What's yours?'

Millicent fumbled for her phone.

'I promise not to hack it,' Julia added, giving Jerry a look that conveyed she knew what had been going through his mind the entire time.

She swept out a few moments later, leaving Jerry and Millicent alone in an otherwise empty café.

'I just had a cup of hot chocolate in Paris with Julia Fleet,' he stated, having to say it out loud as though to be sure it was real. 'Julia Fleet just *bought* me a hot chocolate, in fact. On any other day, that might seem strange.'

Millicent twitched her brow.

'*Con Air*,' she said. 'Simon West, 1997. Just so you know that referencing movies released while I was inside is not risk-free.'

Wreckage

The interior lighting of the Musée d'Art Moderne made the place shimmer, accentuating the sense of a vaulted space. It was at once like a cathedral in its verticality, and yet the antithesis of such places in banishing gloom with such vivid brightness. Millicent estimated it must be equally luminous during the day, with so much glass inviting the natural light, and a view of the Seine across the steps and the courtyard.

The darkness outside had taken her by surprise. She'd forgotten how night fell earlier and faster in Europe than back in the UK, and in Scotland especially. But what was really weird was realising that she had acclimatised to Glasgow and started to think of it as home. She had seldom visited Scotland before she went to prison, but then Alastair had retired to Glasgow, allowing his husband Tom to move back to his native city. Millicent had applied for a transfer to a Scottish prison, as Alastair was her only living relative. Her only regular visitor. The powers that be had dragged their heels but they made it happen eventually. That had been seven years ago.

Julia – or her underling – had been as good as her word. When they showed up at the museum, they were greeted by a young woman with an earpiece and an iPad. She checked Millicent's name then waved them through into the wing where Credit Populaire de Paris was hosting its reception. It appeared that the bank annually sponsored a touring exhibition of on-loan pieces, gathered from galleries around the country.

The reception was busy, dozens of expensively attired people wandering among the paintings. In her trousers and polo neck

Millicent felt, if not scruffy, then certainly rather drab by comparison. At least Jerome was likely to turn a few heads, bedecked in a particularly gruesome T-shirt bearing the words CATTLE DECAPITATION.

She noticed him checking his phone.

'Did you get a message from someone?' she asked, wondering if she needed to warn him not to give away his location.

'Just an automated thing logging the fact that I missed classes today. Wee pass-agg bot bastard. I'm already on thin ice, to be honest. I fell behind in my coursework. Now I'm supposed to get a doctor's line, or some other kind of documentation to prove I had a legitimate absence.'

'I can help sort that out for you.'

'Do you know a doctor?' he asked, brightening.

'No, but I can write you a note saying: "*Please excuse Jerome from classes this week as he had to kill somebody and go on the run.*"'

'That's not funny. You're sick.'

'So the tabloids kept saying.'

Millicent thought about how she was supposed to ask permission from Anne, her social worker, before leaving the UK. It felt like the least of her worries, but hovering in the back of her mind was the awareness that even if she evaded her persecutors, that insipid bumbling marshmallow of a woman could still prove her nemesis. Because she was serving a life sentence, if she was ruled in serious breach of her conditions, she could be automatically recalled to prison, and unable to re-apply for parole for a year.

'Aye, they called you that,' acknowledged Jerome, 'and I notice Julia Fleet called you Millie. Yet I've only known you as Millicent, and you keep calling me Jerome when my name's Jerry. I saved your life. You could at least call me by my right name.'

'You'll always be Jerome to me. *Because* you saved my life.'

He thought about this and seemed to accept what she meant.

'Okay, but what would I need to do to get Millie privileges?'

'I indulged Julia because that's how she knew me. Millie is a young woman's name. That's not what I am anymore. Not who I am anymore.'

She wandered the gallery, casting an eye out for Poupard, wondering what he looked like these days and whether she would recognise him. Not wishing this quest to be conspicuous, she spent much of her time looking at the paintings. Again and again she found her eyes drawn to the dates on the information panels, calculating how long each of the painters had lived. Some had endured deprivation, the late nineteenth century and the First World War, and yet made it to their eighties.

She was looking for reasons to believe in her own potential longevity. She had not known hunger or war: did that mean she might live longer than those who had? But what had prison life, even prison diet done to her?

At least she had always been skinny, she thought, looking at a female nude. There had never been much for gravity to get a grip on.

Attractive young men and women in waistcoats were circulating the room with trays of champagne. She had declined so far. When she went to prison, she had sorely missed alcohol, especially at the start when she most needed the oblivion of getting drunk. In time, she had just stopped thinking about it. She hadn't had a drink since her release because it was, quite absurdly, in her parole conditions. But as she was acutely aware that the insipid marshmallow was a long way from here, she changed her mind and accepted a flute from a waistcoated beau.

It was Veuve too.

Another passing beauty offered canapés. She nibbled between sips and gazed at paintings in a cathedral of art on the banks of the Seine.

'It's good to be alive,' she heard someone say.

Less than a week ago, she would not have concurred. But less than a day ago, a man had changed her mind with a strong hand and a pillow.

It *was* good to be alive. She had forgotten that.

There had been a time when she enjoyed her life to the full, before someone came along and stole it from her. Now that someone was back, threatening to take it away again, permanently.

She took another sip, but anger mixed with fear was making the champagne lose its taste.

Stepping back from the nude, she turned her head to look again for Poupard. She still didn't see him, but in her peripheral vision she was sure she noticed someone looking her way. It was a grey-haired man on his own, something about whom immediately made her think of the intruder who had come to kill her. It wasn't just that he was around the same age, but in the way he carried himself. He seemed similarly sprightly; wiry of build and light on his feet.

She watched him accept a glass and begin talking to someone. They seemed to know each other. He had arrived on his own and had met some friends.

Christ, she was becoming paranoid. She had to rein it in, or she would be seeing assassins everywhere. Then just behind grey-hair, she finally saw a figure whom she just about recognised as Jean-Marc Poupard.

The years had been kind, if not complimentary, in that he had clearly lived well. He had rounded out from neck to belly, his complexion ruddy and his nose a bulbous mass of rhinophyma, testament to decades of rich food and plentiful wine.

As their eyes briefly met, he wore a look of uncomfortable curiosity before he resumed talking to the people he was with. He was asking himself who she was and from where he knew her.

It struck her with some relief that, if and when he worked it out, the answer would not relate to what she was primarily known for back home.

Who she was here in France was not that.

'I've clocked him,' she told Jerome. 'Over there, by the Max Ernst painting of a weird forest.'

Jerome glanced subtly.

'The suave one who looks like late-period Giancarlo Giannini?'

'No, behind him: the chubby one who looks like late-period Gérard Depardieu.'

Jerome sneaked another glimpse.

'He keeps glancing this way,' he said.

'Yes. He's trying to place me, though as a senior banking

executive, there will be other calculations in play too. Which company I'm with, and how high up. Or whose wife I might be. All of it feeding into the most important question: how much deference to show.'

'At a do like this, he maybe thinks you're an artist,' Jerome suggested.

Bless the boy.

'I could live with that.'

Jerome surveyed his own attire.

'And maybe I'm in a metal band?' he offered hopefully.

'If I'm an artist, maybe he'll think you're my toy boy. It's Paris, after all.'

'A world of no.'

Millicent smiled at his discomfort, at the same time searching her memory for why his words were familiar. She had heard him use the phrase before, but it had rung a bell then too. She could ask if it was from a film, but the new rule in their evolving game was that if you asked and it turned out to be a reference you hadn't got, you were a point down. She was sure her memory was of a real person saying it, but she wasn't taking the risk.

'No offence,' he added, though it hardly seemed necessary. 'I don't mean to be ageist or anything.'

She smiled. After reading all that bullshit about snowflakes, what she had found was that in practice young people were genuinely concerned about being insensitive and hurting others' feelings. The coming world would be a better place for that.

She used to be that way too. Then prison had taught her that cruelty of the tongue was an important defence mechanism. Your bark might be worse than your bite, but if your bark was frightening enough, sometimes people didn't want to put it to the test. If you were prepared to be merciless in going after them verbally, then you were unlikely to be restrained in other ways. Somewhere along the line she had forgotten how painful it was to be on the receiving end.

'None taken,' she replied. 'It would be fair to say I am post-sex.'

The group Poupard was talking to dispersed, drifting off to look at other paintings. His eyes lifted again, seeking the next guests he might engage with. Millicent decided it was time. She met his gaze, gave him a wave, then she and Jerome walked across.

Poupard smiled by way of greeting. There was an accustomed confidence in his posture, masking the uncertainty. She didn't doubt he would be good at faking familiarity.

'Monsieur Poupard. It's been a long time, so I will forgive you if you do not remember me.'

She spoke in English, partly for Jerome's benefit, and partly as a hint to the banker.

'I must confess, you still have me at an advantage, Madame . . . Mademoiselle . . .?'

'Spark. Millicent Spark.'

A bite of the lip conveyed his apology for remaining none the wiser.

'I was the special make-up effects artist on *Mancipium*.'

Yeah. He knew now.

There was a lot to unpack from his resulting expression. A smile of recognition for sure, but one in which there were wires pulling up the edges of his mouth as though stagehands were hauling pulleys behind the scenes. Where Julia had been full of regret when talking about the movie, in his eyes there was wariness and suspicion at the very mention.

He regrouped, giving a wry shake of the head.

'Ah yes, a great shame. Bad times. Sad times. And what have you been working on since? Did you go off to Hollywood?'

Millicent was struck by his eagerness to change the subject. He seemed about as keen to reminisce as she was to answer his question. She wondered why Julia had implied the opposite, and gone so far as to get them in the door here tonight.

'Your days in the film business are not among your fondest memories, then?' she asked.

Poupard sighed.

'Sometimes when I talk about investing in art, sponsoring exhibitions, people ask: *but aren't artists crazy and unreliable?* I tell them: *try dealing with the film business. Give me artists every time.*'

It sounded like his media answer. She needed to get him to open up.

'I remember you coming to the rescue when we thought we had lost it all. The film only happened because of you.'

He winced, though it was unclear whether he was feeling regret at the memory, or frustration that she wouldn't let it go.

'You could say, as the Americans do, that I bet the farm on it, and almost lost the lot. Almost lost my job. I had to climb back out of the wreckage.'

'Who do you blame for that? I mean, how much do you know about what happened at the end?'

Poupard glanced over her shoulder, searching for someone else to talk to, or maybe gesturing to invite intercession, certainly less subtly than Julia had done.

'I only have second- and third-hand accounts of what was going on at that time,' he replied. 'As you may remember, I didn't have any physical involvement after the production left Rome.'

'Do you recall a man named Markus Laird, with Blue Lantern Films? They were an international rights broker.'

He screwed up his face as though trying to remember. It was hard to read whether the effort was genuine. His answer was equally ambiguous.

'The name is vaguely familiar, but it was so long ago.'

'Did you know he was an undercover police officer? Working with British intelligence?'

Poupard responded with a warm grin, which was far from what she was expecting until she realised it was entirely performative. It was aimed at the person he was about to greet, though still very much for Millicent's consumption. He was reminding her that he was an important man with other people to talk to: people who wouldn't ask awkward questions.

'I'm sorry, there is someone I have to speak to. It's been nice to catch up.'

He walked away, glad-handing the man whose eye he had caught, then loudly announcing, 'There is a piece I simply must show you,' as a pretext for heading to a different part of the room.

Jerome frowned as he watched him leave.

'He couldnae get away quick enough. I never even got time to establish that I wasnae your toy boy.'

'Though what we did establish was that he didn't regard his dabble in movie-making as the glory days,' Millicent replied.

'Aye. I'm wondering if your old pal Julia did it as a wind-up. Though I couldnae say whether the joke was on us or him.'

'It's not the kind of thing I could imagine her being flippant about. She seemed quite sensitive with regard to the whole thing. Maybe she . . .'

Before Millicent could speculate further, they were confronted once again by the smart young woman with the earpiece and iPad. She looked altogether less welcoming this time.

'May I just check your names once more?' she asked.

'Millicent Spark, plus one.'

She gave the thinnest of thin smiles.

'I'm sorry. There has been a mistake. You have been added to this list in error. I must ask you to leave.'

'Try Abe Froman,' Jerome told her. 'That's me.'

Millicent struggled to keep her face straight.

'Sausage king of Chicago,' she added, securing her point.

'That name is not here either.'

The young woman glanced towards a security guard also wearing an earpiece. It was not a direct summons, merely a warning to them that he would be deployed should they offer any trouble.

'You have fifteen seconds to comply,' Millicent said under her breath.

Jerome didn't respond, but he was walking like Robocop as they proceeded to the exit.

Paris by Night

'Was it something we said?' Jerome asked.

They were walking through the museum's neo-classical forum, heading towards the river. A group of skateboarders were enjoying the flat surfaces of the courtyard, picking up speed before performing jumps down its short staircases. She remembered when skateboards first emerged in the Seventies, how quickly they were predicted to vanish again. A craze, they were called, which implied that their popularity was resultant of people temporarily taking leave of their senses and that a restoration of natural order would soon see them gone. It was always the same when there was a cultural phenomenon of which the British establishment disapproved. Like video nasties, for instance.

'That's money men for you,' Millicent said. 'People in the arts are naturally drawn to the underdog. People in business only want to be associated with success.'

'Pretty suss that he didn't want to talk about it at all. I could understand if *Mancipium* had been an infamous flop, or a turkey. The movie never even saw the light of day.'

'You need to understand: even more than failure they don't like anything with a whiff of scandal.'

'Aye, but everybody likes to make oot they've a wild side, even boring money men. If I'd had one crack at making movies and my film was reputedly so scary it had to be suppressed, I'd totally want that on my CV. But that's easy for me to say. I never had skin in the game. How do you feel aboot it?'

Over dinner Jerome had told her more about the myths surrounding the film as alluded to by Julia, and shown her a discussion programme

246

on YouTube via his phone. Before that they had checked in to their hotel and grabbed a couple of hours' sleep.

She contemplated his question as they came down the last of the steps and turned left, heading east on Avenue de New York.

'I will admit it gave me a perverse sense of pride to hear that a film I worked on was deemed so terrifying, so evil that it had to be destroyed. But my principal emotion is loss. I would rather the film had been released and there was no legend. I'd rather have something to show for it. Most of all, I'd like to see it.'

The thought prompted her to recall Julia's air of regret, and her reference to Jo's novel being burned in *Little Women*. Julia had shown real warmth when they embraced this morning: more than she remembered existing between them back then. The years could do that. You might recognise something in a person that hadn't previously been apparent, as much resultant of your own changes since as theirs.

It was only as she listened to Julia talk about the film, and about Lucio and Alessandro, that Millicent realised how dismissive she had always been of the woman. Even once they got to know each other a little, she had never lost her perception that running around Europe playing the indie producer was all just a trip to Julia. A spoiled rich kid dabbling in something that was both a thrill and would outrage her family, like dating bad-boy rock stars. Millicent had never fully appreciated how committed Julia was, and how much the project must have meant to her.

More than it had meant to herself, she realised. Perhaps even more than to Lucio. To Millicent, it had just been a gig: admittedly a memorable gig, one that became a platform for her best work, but still a gig. When her part was done, she had moved on to the next one, a TV show shooting back home at Shepperton. Julia, it appeared, had put her heart and soul into it in ways Millicent never appreciated.

'Still,' Jerome said. 'I get that Poupard maybe doesnae want to talk about *Mancipium* for perfectly innocent reasons. But that being the case, all he needs to do is walk away. He doesnae need to chuck us oot the party. And he just breenged over to the first person he saw the minute you mentioned undercover polis.'

247

As they crossed a junction abutting the main road, Millicent's attention was drawn to raised voices. She saw that a man in overalls had clamped a small Renault and was proceeding to raise it on a tow, while two angry women harangued him impotently to stop.

It was only because she had turned to look that she noticed who else was on the same side-street. The wiry grey-haired man she had noticed watching her at the reception was heading towards the junction, presumably having exited from the other side of the museum.

She said nothing but lengthened her stride and caught a change in the pedestrian lights to cross the Pont de l'Alma. Once they had reached the other side of the four-lane bridge, she took Jerome's arm as he made to continue north-east along the main road.

'Let's go down this way,' she said, indicating the long slope of the Port de la Conference, descending to the very edge of the water.

'The hotel is more that direction,' he said.

'Yes, but this detour takes us along the banks of the Seine after dark and I never thought I would get to do that again.'

'Fair enough.'

'Also, and don't look round, but I think somebody is tailing us. A man I saw at the museum. If he follows us down here, we'll know whether I'm just being paranoid.'

Jerome heeded the warning. He didn't look round, but he got out his phone and used its front-facing camera to turn it into a rear-view mirror.

'What does he look like?'

'Old but spry, like the tooth fairy who visited last night and put all my teeth under the pillow.'

'I don't see him.'

'He's around. Trust me. I tried not to read too much into it earlier when I saw him looking at the museum, but it seems quite the coincidence that he should have chosen to leave at the same time we did.'

A Batobus had just docked as they reached the bottom of the ramp where the road flattened out, people spilling out from the station onto the tarmac.

Millicent chanced a look back once she and Jerome had merged into the crowd. The man wasn't there. She glanced up towards the parallel path abutting the gardens above. She didn't see anyone looking back down, but the route was lined with trees, so there was no way to be sure.

There *was* a way to disappear, though.

She led Jerome into the station building, where they would not be visible from above. They joined the queue on the pontoon, paid for tickets and climbed aboard the waiting Batobus.

Millicent kept an eye on the gangway until it departed. They were not followed aboard.

'Where are we going?' Jerome asked as the boat began picking up speed.

'Nowhere in particular. There and back again.'

'A Hobbit's tale,' he replied.

'Doesn't count. I haven't seen the films. I was quoting the book.'

Jerome took out his phone and pointed it at a sign posted on a pillar next to their bench.

'What are you doing?'

'Scanning a QR code. It lets you download an app that gives routes and schedules.'

It was weird hearing people talk about apps all the time. It had a very different meaning where she had been. An app was an application form. If you wanted anything, even the most minor permission, you had to fill one out. Prisons would be the last places on Earth that went paper-free.

'Vivian told me you lived with your grandmother back home,' Millicent said. 'That you were raised by her. Did she cope with the digital age?'

Jerome glanced across the water, to the lights on the south bank, as if he might expect to see her there. Vivian had told her that the woman died in August. It must have been particularly hard to leave home and make a new start when he had been so reliant upon one person all his days.

'She coped fine. Built up her own business with video rentals in the Eighties. I guess I never really got the stereotype of the old person baffled by newfangled inventions because I didn't recognise it. Gran was always embracing of new technology.'

'You must miss her,' Millicent said, and as soon as she did, she realised it was a daft thing to say. Of course he missed her, especially now, when everything was falling apart. Not for the first time, she felt horribly guilty for all she had dragged him into.

Jerome said nothing. She watched him bite his lip and blink, look away again. He nodded, swallowing.

Young people were making a lot of progress, but she could see that some things hadn't changed. Males were still reluctant to let anyone see their emotions. Especially the tender ones.

The boat looped around the Île de la Cité and they got off close to the Pont de l'Archevêché. They were the only ones to disembark, the vessel mostly full of tourists wanting the full trip.

'We'll walk along the south bank and cross at the Pont Neuf,' she said. 'The hotel isn't far from there.'

The walkway was narrow, a wall rising up to the road above on their left, an unguarded drop into the river on their right. She was surprised that the health and safety regulations so many bores complained about had not seen a railing installed.

'That was a film, wasn't it?' Jerome asked. '*Les Amants du Pont Neuf*.'

'Yes. Leos Carax, early Nineties. I remember the industry was buzzing with stories at the time. It ran insanely over-budget. They weren't allowed to shoot on the actual Pont Neuf so they built a replica. The lead actor Denis Lavant injured himself tying his shoelace – seriously – and they had to suspend production until he recovered. While they were waiting, a storm demolished their exorbitantly expensive set. Now, that is a cursed movie.'

It was very quiet on the quay. They passed a couple arm in arm, walking in the opposite direction, back towards the east. Once they were gone, she and Jerome had the quayside to themselves.

Millicent gazed across at Notre Dame, picked out against the glow of streetlights, its shape incomplete and thus unfamiliar. It had lost its spire and was cocooned in scaffolding. She had forgotten about that. She remembered seeing the fire on TV while she was inside. It had thoroughly depressed her, an early sign that the world she once loved would not be waiting for her when she finally got out. Now that she was seeing it for real, the sight gave her hope. It reminded her that anything can be rebuilt if you love it enough. Even her.

They were almost at the Pont Neuf, the path still empty but for a solitary drunk in a raincoat, meandering in his cups.

'Beaucoup zig-zag,' Jerome said.

She laughed.

'My gran told me her dad served in North Africa in World War Two,' he explained. 'That was what the locals said if somebody was pished.'

The nearer they got to the drunk, the closer his staggering took him towards the edge, beyond which there was that unguarded drop into the black and fast-moving water. Then he tripped over his own feet and began veering faster towards the Seine, seemingly unable to stop himself.

She and Jerome reacted simultaneously, running to intercept him, but as they reached within a few feet, he halted on a sixpence and stood up straight: taller than she had perceived, and perfectly sober. He was also holding an automatic pistol, concealed within his coat.

'Hello, Millicent,' he said. 'Lovely evening for a stroll, don't you think?'

Interrogation

He spoke in an English accent. This could be Rook, she thought, but she hadn't heard enough of either to accurately compare. What she could be sure of was that it wasn't the man from the museum. They had been flanked.

Millicent glanced up, where she could see only the backs of the green canopies covering the book stalls that lined the left bank above. The quayside was invisible to passers-by on the main road.

'I need both of you to take a little walk with me.'

'We're already taking a walk,' she replied. 'I thought we had established that. Who are you? What is it you want?'

'Just to talk. So why don't we all go for a quiet chat and see what we can learn from each other.'

He was addressing her but his eyes, and the gun, were on Jerome. He knew which one of them was the threat. She guessed he knew about last night, which meant this was the end of the line. Best-case scenario was they'd both end up in prison, the evidence manipulated accordingly. Worst-case scenario was he was taking them somewhere he could kill them without attracting attention.

'Let's talk here,' she replied. She wasn't feeling brave. It was just that stalling seemed the only option available.

His tone was calm, though with a hint of growing impatience.

'I won't ask you again. Start walking towards those stairs, quietly and with no fuss. That way nobody ends up paralysed for life with a bullet in their spine, okay?'

Actually, he wasn't merely calm. He was disinterested. That was what really got her in the gut. It had taken her a year, but she had finally rediscovered what freedom felt like. Now this bastard was

252

going to take it away again, from her and from Jerome, and he was acting like it was the last job of the day before he could knock off. She was nothing to him, nothing to them. Just a counter on the board to be pushed around.

It was time she pushed back.

He was tall, he was powerfully built, and he was armed. But he was also standing right on the edge of the Seine.

So she shoved him in.

She had altered her stance a moment before, though not in a way that was easily perceptible. If he noticed, he would have interpreted it as a slump of resignation, defeat. She was actually dropping her centre of gravity just a little, using her knees as a suspension system to transfer her bodyweight so that when she pushed him, there was real momentum behind it.

For a professional killer, his face was a picture as he hit the water.

Jerome looked almost as surprised.

'What the fuck are you doing? He had a gun pointed right at me.'

'If he was going to shoot us, he already would have.'

'That's easy for you to say: you're not the one he was aiming at.'

They both looked at the man thrashing and gasping in the water. It was freezing, she realised. He was struggling.

'Help me,' he shouted. He was a considerable distance from any of the steps that would let him climb out, and the shock of the cold was crippling him.

There was a lifebelt strapped to the wall a few yards away. Jerome ran towards it.

'What are you doing?' she asked.

'I don't want another death on my conscience.'

'First you're complaining I was reckless, now you're worried about this guy? Make up your mind.'

'These are not contradictory positions,' he replied, grabbing it from the hook.

'Okay, but remember he's still armed.'

She addressed the man in the water.

'Throw us the gun.'

'I d-don't have the f-fucking gun,' he shouted. 'I l-lost it when you pushed m-me in.'

Jerome dropped the lifebelt onto the ground.

'We don't have the lifebelt either. We lost it too.'

The gun duly appeared. They both flinched. He chucked it a few feet away, into the drink.

'I said throw it to us.'

'I'm l-losing feeling.'

His breath was shortening.

'Who are you working for? What's this about?'

'I can hardly speak. I'll tell you . . . i-if you can . . . g-get me out.'

Jerome picked up the lifebelt again. Millicent took it from him.

'N-n-nope,' she said. 'Answers first. L-l-lifebelt later.'

'Fuck you,' he snarled.

Not so disinterested anymore.

'You're making it very difficult for me to do the right thing here.'

'*Midnight Run*,' Jerome muttered. 'Martin Brest, 1988.'

'Why are you trying to kill me?' she asked.

'I'm not t-trying to kill you. Just want to talk.'

'Then talk. What was Markus Laird working on back in the Nineties? AKA Des Creasey?'

'N-never heard of him.'

Millicent turned away, handed Jerome the lifebelt.

'Screw him. Put this back.'

'Alfie Bertrand,' the man shouted, panicking. 'Alfie Bertrand was being a naughty boy. That's all I know. He kept slipping his protection. Des . . . sent to keep an eye on him. Des . . . ended up . . . Oh, Jesus.'

With that, he disappeared beneath the black surface.

'Fuck,' Jerome gasped. He grabbed the lifebelt from her and threw it to where the man had slipped under.

It had no sooner hit the water than he bobbed up and grabbed it. Millicent wasn't sure if he had faked it, but either way it would still take him a while to swim to a place where he could climb out.

'Go,' she said.

They ran towards the stairs at the Pont Saint-Michel, Millicent hailing a passing cab as soon as they were on street level. She gave the driver the name of the place where they ate earlier.

'You want food after that?' Jerome asked, incredulous.

'I don't want to give him the name of our hotel, in case someone gets to ask him where he dropped us off.'

'If they found us once, they can find us again. How did they catch up to us so soon? We've only been here a matter of hours.'

'Unless Poupard is part of this,' she suggested.

'Or Julia,' Jerome replied. 'She was the one who sent us to that reception after bullshitting us about Poupard being up for a stroll doon memory lane. You saw a guy there who ended up following us. Maybe she was placing us somewhere we could be picked up.'

Millicent thought about Julia's embrace this morning. Had it been a Judas kiss?

'I don't believe she would do that,' she said, though she knew she only had her gut to go on. 'If that was the case, surely she could have had us followed after she left us at that café. But maybe she knew there was a reason Poupard wouldn't want to talk about *Mancipium*.'

Jerome stared out of the window as the taxi passed the pyramid at the Louvre.

'If this is linked to Alfie Bertrand,' he said, 'Julia Fleet and Jean-Marc Poupard will be the least of our worries. Had you seen the gunman before?'

'He wasn't familiar, no.'

'What about the other guy?'

'Him neither.'

Jerome got out his phone and displayed the photo he had taken of the Blue Lamp Society print. He zoomed in and they both pored over each of the faces as he moved them into frame. None of them looked like a match, though given the years that had elapsed, it was difficult to make a comparison. Last night had been easier because the man had been lying there, albeit missing his nose.

'He didn't seem to know your name,' she said. 'I suppose that's something. Whoever they are, they're not omniscient and all-powerful. We're booked under your card, remember.'

'Maybe he just didnae *say* my name,' Jerome cautioned. 'The hotel might not be safe.'

'Quite frankly I'm too tired to care. I got no sleep last night and I've already paid for our rooms. I'm going to get my money's worth.'

Whores (i)

Millie once heard someone say it's not a real party until an ambulance turns up. It had felt like a more innocent time when she still thought that was a joke.

Lucio's boat was docked in Sorrento. They hadn't finalised the schedule, but they would be shooting in the amphitheatre at Pompeii, and at a farm property nearby that was doubling for the Spahn Movie Ranch in California. It felt like an appropriately twisted meta-take on the Spaghetti Westerns, to be filming in Italy to re-create a Hollywood cowboy movie location. Their film was partly about the seductive nature of evil: how being wicked could make you feel powerful when endeavouring to be good seemed to offer scant reward. How if you were a complete nonentity, you could become at the very least notorious. The demon of the amulet had its way of seeking out the weak-minded, the mediocre and the unfulfilled. Their London-set scenes implied that it had possessed Jack the Ripper. As a coda, the film would finish with Charles Manson, a failed wannabe rock star, finding the amulet in the dust.

Another reason the production had moved down here was that Alessandro lived in Sorrento and had an editing suite at his house, and Lucio was happy enough to base himself locally as they moved into post-production.

Millie was a little drunk, and she'd done a couple of lines too. It wasn't her drug of choice; she was more used to speed when she was pulling an all-nighter in her workshop, but it was on offer and she'd taken it. That wasn't an excuse for what she would later do, but it did skew her physical judgment, which was undeniably a factor in what happened.

She was wandering the boat in search of Markus, who had flown in, apparently on a whim, coincidentally once again on the night of a party. He had surprised her by showing up unannounced at the door of her hotel room. This had led to what it usually led to, but afterwards he had seemed in a hurry to get to the boat, and she had hardly shared a word with him since they boarded.

She walked past Alfie Bertrand, once again accompanied by some shiny piece of arm candy. Millie accepted it was a sign of getting old that everybody south of twenty-five looked like a teenager, but this one struck her as particularly young. Millie would have said she was half his age, and Alfie's age was barely in the thirties.

He was another one who always seemed to be around whenever Lucio threw a party. Once again, he didn't appear to have any security detail with him. Maybe you didn't get that when you were a junior minister, or you only got it when you were on official business, though she didn't imagine the IRA would respect the distinction if they fancied him as a target.

She spotted Freddy Wincott on the upper deck. His family had some huge property on Capri apparently, so she knew she shouldn't read too much into his showing up, but everybody was taking it as a very good sign.

Stacey had appeared beside her, champagne glass in hand, noting where Millie was directing her gaze.

'I saw him arrive,' Stacey said. 'He took a limo from his own huge fuck-off yacht just to travel a quarter mile round the harbour to this jetty.'

'Margaret Thatcher once said that a man riding a bus past the age of thirty was a sign of his being a failure,' Millie replied. 'I guess this is the other end of the scale.'

'It's more than that. Guys like Freddy, and like your man Alfie, it's about controlling perception. They only want to be seen in affluent settings, powerful places, getting in and out of expensive and exclusive vehicles. They don't like being seen on the street because that makes you look ordinary.'

'I hear you. I'm trying to put the deposit together to buy a flat in London. Roger Wincott is trying to put a deal together to buy

MGM. Which would be good for us, to be fair. As would Freddy buying the movie for the UK.'

'Yeah, everybody's excited when he shows up, like it's moving the needle on a complex process. It's bullshit. Freddy buying *Mancipium* would be chickenfeed. He doesn't need to think about it.'

'Julia thinks it's family politics,' Millie told her. 'That he's one-upping her.'

Millie left it at that, choosing not to share Julia's fear that Freddy might buy the film just to bury it.

'Sounds like family to me,' Stacey agreed. 'I suspect she's trying to one-up him right now. I just saw her talking to Sergio and they were both looking very friendly.'

Millie didn't see what this had to do with Freddy, but she had also noticed Julia and Sergio flirting with each other when she passed them earlier.

'I wonder if she knows his real motive in turning on the charm,' Millie said.

The reason they hadn't finalised the shooting schedule was down to Sergio being a dick, something for which he had demonstrated a talent that far outstripped his acting ability. He was looking for more money due to the production overrunning. Sergio was attractive, charismatic and charming, but he was also colossally egotistical, manipulative and selfish; one of those pretty boys whose beauty meant he hadn't been told 'no' anything like enough times in his life. Or as Markus put it, he was 'insufficiently familiar with what it feels like to be punched in the face'.

'It's not just about the money,' Stacey said. 'It's that Sergio thought he was cut out to be an A-lister one day, but everybody knows that if it was gonna happen for him, it would have happened already. So he needs to keep reminding everybody that he's special, that he's better than them. I've seen it a thousand times.'

She took a sip from her glass, a scornful smile playing across her lips.

'He keeps talking about how his last shoot was a Joel Silver picture, but you're not on the track to being an A-lister if you're playing one of the unnamed European bad guys whose only vocal contribution could comfortably be substituted by a Wilhelm scream. Lucio knows this.'

Sergio's demand had presumably gone down like a cup of warm diarrhoea with Lucio, but he was playing it canny. Lucio reacted calmly – externally at least – so as to keep him onside, telling him he would understand if Sergio had somewhere else to be, but there was no money in the budget to pay him more for the extra days. He of course knew that Sergio had nowhere else he needed to be.

Lucio also made sure Sergio heard he and Alessandro discussing how they could shoot the outstanding coverage without him, going with Dante as a double and using first-person point-of-view shots. They had talked with excitement about how it would put the viewer in the moment more, make them complicit in the demon's deeds. Whether they believed this or not was immaterial: the purpose was to make Sergio think they believed it, figuring his ego would over-rule his wallet and he would want maximum face time on-screen.

Sergio evidently hadn't given up.

'I'm guessing he figured the film's co-producer might take a different view over pillow talk,' Stacey said. 'Guy's a fuckin' whore.'

'Are you really a whore if both parties can pretend the payment was for something else?'

'If you're in this business, you're already a whore. You're always a whore. But she sees what he's playing at, right?'

'You'd think so, wouldn't you?' said Millie. 'But she might have her own agenda. She's got previous for dating glamorous bad boys.'

'Oh, the rock star dude she married.'

'Among others.'

Millie had since learned that Julia had gone out with a Premiership footballer with a reputation for on- and off-field thuggery.

'I think it's about pissing off her father.'

'Though in this instance it would be a twofer,' said Stacey.

'How?'

'Like I said, one-upping her brother.'

Millie's blank stare conveyed that she didn't follow.

'Oh, girl, you never noticed how Freddy looks at him? And you know Sergio's AC/DC, right?'

She'd heard rumours, but that wasn't the headline here.

'Freddy Wincott is gay?'

'No! Of course the anointed son of homophobic right-wing media tycoon Roger Wincott isn't gay. I wouldn't dare suggest that. Nor would I infer anything from the time I saw him with a strapping and shirtless extra at the party backstage at Cinecitta. I'm sure Freddy had suffered a spider bite in a sensitive place and that brave young man was selflessly drawing the venom out.'

Millie thought of how she had seen Stacey at the same party, also shirtless, also enjoying the company of a strapping young man. She reckoned the scriptwriter knew of which she spoke.

'You ask me, that's the real reason Freddy is drawing out his interest in this movie. He can get his rocks off far from the prying eyes of the same reporters and paparazzi his daddy would be training on anyone else.'

It was hard to deny. As Stacey said, Freddy could have snapped up the rights to *Mancipium* weeks ago for a sum that meant nothing to him. He didn't need to take this close an interest in one little film, and his sister's involvement now looked like a convenient cover. He only showed up when there was a party. As did Alfie Bertrand.

As did Markus.

Millie underwent a horrible reckoning, all the fears that had been bubbling under suddenly rising to the surface. She found herself wondering if he had just been using her to get close to Lucio; then beyond that, wondering who in turn he was using Lucio to get close to.

In retrospect, it probably wasn't fortuitous timing that right then she saw him emerge from the galley, Lucio departing in the other direction.

She intercepted him on the prow.

'Hey, remember me? I thought I was the reason you were here.'

Markus looked startled. Guilty even, though maybe he just wasn't ready for her aggressive tone. The booze and the coke had to be affecting her manner as well as her judgment.

'I told you I needed to talk to Lucio,' Markus replied. 'We're moving close to a deal for Blue Lantern to pick up the movie for seven territories in south-east Asia. It's kind of important,' he added, his impatient tone just the wrong side of passive-aggressive.

'Yeah, and I'm wondering if that's the real reason you're here, if that's always been the real reason, and I'm just a fringe benefit. You fly in, you fuck me, you do a little business and then you fuck off.'

'That's totally unfair, Millie. We're both very busy people trying to maintain a long-distance relationship. Think of the hours you've been working lately.'

His voice was calm, gradually getting quieter, the way men did when they wanted to control the tone and to avoid attracting attention. Consequently, it had the opposite effect.

'It's not a relationship, though, is it?' Millie replied, louder. 'I'm just your way into this scene. Don't think I haven't noticed you ogling all the half-dressed girls at these parties. Or am I meant to be grateful for getting the odd pity-fuck from a younger guy?'

Millie could hear herself speak as though she was a third person. She knew that what was spilling out of her mouth was an incontinent eruption of her insecurities, but it felt imperative, probably because she needed to admit her fears to herself.

'What else have you got going on? Girl wise? You keep showing up but you see more of Lucio than you see of me. Hell, you must see more of Alfie Bertrand than you see of me. Whenever he appears, that's a reliable harbinger that you will too. Surprised I don't start to get wet when I see him, as it means I'm in for a shag.'

Markus looked rattled, his practised calm failing him. Something she said had hit home, or maybe it was just that he was worried they would attract an audience.

'You're acting like a crazy woman. Have you been doing charlie? It makes some people paranoid.'

He grabbed her wrist and made to lead her away.

'Come on, let's—'

She didn't get to hear what he was going to say next, because she wheeled around and lashed out. She was enraged at being told she was paranoid and crazy, and she hated being grabbed like that, like she was a silly little girl.

She didn't mean to hit him that hard. She wouldn't have thought she was even capable of hitting him that hard. When she was a kid, she used to thump her brother Alastair on the arm when she lost her temper. She knew she could hit him because he was bigger and stronger, because he wouldn't hit back, and because she didn't believe she could hurt him, stick insect that she was.

She had been trying to thump Markus on the shoulder in retaliation for grabbing her. He just moved the wrong way at the wrong time, and the booze probably didn't do much for her coordination. She caught him in the mouth instead. There was an irony, given what she did for a living, that it was the only time her actions had thus far drawn real blood from another human being.

Millie felt time stop as she watched him put his hand to his lips and examine the trickle of blood, shocked and incredulous. She heard someone gasp, someone else laugh. A voice somewhere above said, 'Jesus Christ.'

Millie glanced up and saw Freddy, Alessandro and Florio, among others, gazing down from the deck overlooking the prow.

Absence

Millicent bought them both a nightcap 'to settle our nerves' when they got back to the hotel. She had invited Jerry to join her in a large brandy, but he wasn't much of a drinker, so he had hot chocolate instead. It was lush.

They discussed who else they might try to talk to, but after being incommunicado for a quarter of a century, Millicent didn't have much of a contacts book. Obviously there was one person who was deffo still around and who would be able to shed some light, but it wasn't like Alfie Bertrand was going to pick up the phone, any more than it was wise to let him know they were curious.

'The guy in the river said he'd been a naughty boy,' Jerry said as he all but chewed his way through his hot chocolate. 'Any idea what he might have been up to? Because it sounds a lot like Markus discovered something that meant he had to be silenced.'

'All I remember is that he was acting the playboy. It's true he was ditching his protection, I assumed so that he could avail himself of these wannabe starlets that seemed to be in orbit around Lucio. But he was unattached and not one of the Conservative Party's loathsome moralisers, so it was entirely his prerogative. I can't think of anything he might have done back then that would pose a threat to him today, or what proof could still exist other than hearsay.'

'I suppose it was the days before smartphone cameras, so there's not gaunny be any dick pics or a sex tape.'

Millicent stopped mid-sip.

'But there could be another form of proof. What if he's got an illegitimate child from back then? It would be a truly damaging time for that to emerge, with him on the front benches and tipped as a future PM.'

Jerry tried not to laugh too hard, lest she think he considered her stupid rather than merely out of touch.

'You really need to catch up with modern politics, Millicent. Our current PM won't actually own up to how many weans he has, and neither the media nor the voters seem to think him being a serial liar and a cheat is any reason not to trust him in future. I think proof that he was flinging his dick about when he was younger would actually help Alfie Bertrand these days.'

'No, you're right, of course,' she admitted. 'And now that I think of it, I can't see how it would have been the issue in 1994 when Markus was involved.'

Jerry got out his phone and called up the IMDb listing for *Mancipium*, running names past Millicent, asking her which members of the cast and crew had the closest dealings with Lucio and Alessandro, and which ones were likely to respond positively if she reached out.

'Top priority on both counts would be Stacey Golding. She wrote the screenplay, but she had a professional relationship with Lucio going back years.'

Jerry tried to find her online while they finished their drinks, just to establish whether she was still alive. None of the search results fitted the bill.

Millicent nodded, thin-lipped.

'Stacey is the person I would have least expected to still be with us. She was probably the hardest living woman I knew. And I knew her *after* her wild years.'

'How close were you? Did she write to you inside?'

'We were colleagues more than friends, you could say. But no, she didn't write. I never heard from her after *Mancipium* wrapped. Why?'

'I'm just wondering whether she also dropped off the grid around the same time as Lucio, Markus and Alessandro all died.'

Jerry looked at her IMDb listing, which stated otherwise.

'She still has a few writing and producer credits up until 1998,' he reported. 'Then nothing. No Facebook page, no Twitter account, no Instagram.'

'Is this the way we learn of our acquaintances' deaths now?' Millicent reflected wistfully, cradling her brandy. 'When we have drifted apart and lost touch, we don't learn someone is gone via a telegram from overseas or reading an obit in *The Times*. But by an absence of content.'

Family

Despite being utterly knackered, Jerry found himself unable to sleep because his whole body was still jangling from what had happened at the river. The hot chocolate had been the best he ever tasted, but now he was starting to think he should have opted for the brandy, followed by a couple more to zonk him out.

He was lying back, staring at the decorative cornicing until he began to see faces in the patterns: three in particular.

Rossco had said he would be back, and Jerry didn't believe he was bluffing. In fact, the more he had thought about it, the more he reckoned Rossco was going to burn him either way. Stopping him from getting above himself was the real motivation: dragging Jerry back down by the ankles so he was stuck in the pit with pricks like him.

If Rossco went to the cops, he wouldn't just anonymously submit his video either. He would supply details of who Jerry was, where he lived, what he'd done and when it happened. His face, name and current address would be flashing up on the same systems being monitored by the cops who had seen him and Millicent pushing that wheelchair. They would probably pull CCTV images from last night and cross refer.

The second face he kept seeing was one missing a nose. Jerry could still feel the reverberation up his arm as the hammer crunched into tissue, cartilage and bone.

And the third, of course, was his gran.

You must miss her.

And how. Hers was the voice he most needed to hear right now, the reassurance that could most soothe and the wisdom most likely to help. But there was the rub. He couldn't help but feel this was due him. This was his punishment for not listening to that voice, that wisdom, when it was available. For lying to her.

He heard a ping from his phone and saw that there was another WhatsApp message from Pip Morgan. Posh Philippa.

Is everything okay with you? You weren't in classes today.

Jerry would have to concede that this was more than just middle-class politeness, satisfying herself that she had acted appropriately. He reacted before he could paralyse himself with debating about it. Instead of replying, he hit the call button. He wanted to hear someone else's voice. Somebody who wasn't Millicent.

She picked up after two rings.

'Em, hey,' she said. She sounded surprised that he had gone to a voice call rather than just a message.

'Hey. Is this cool?'

'Yes. Totally. *Is* everything okay, though?'

He liked her voice. Liked her accent, loath as he might have been to admit it.

'Not entirely,' he replied.

'God, what's wrong?'

'Nothing I can really talk about.'

He winced as he said this. He really wanted to talk about it, and he really wanted to have something to tell her. She cared. He could see that now, hopefully not too late.

'Is it family stuff?'

'No. We had a break-in at the hoose where I'm staying.'

'That's awful. I'm so sorry.'

'Hey, don't worry about it.'

'No, now that you've been the victim of a real crime, I feel even worse about, you know . . .'

He was glad she couldn't see him. He felt such a prick about this.

'Please, honestly, forget aboot it. It's fine.'

'Fine never means fine.'

'Sometimes things arenae as they appear. Let's just say I've no reason to be mad at you.'

This was as honest as he could afford to be right now.

'I'm sorry I patched you,' he told her. 'It meant a lot that you reached out, but I was feeling huffy. Very mature, I know.'

'We're talking now. That's what counts, I think.'

'Aye. In the middle of the night. Why are you still awake?'

'Struggling with my paper for next week. I think I'm just feeling this pressure because my mum and dad have had to dig so deep to pay the tuition fees and I can't afford to let them down. My dad had a hard year with his business, so they were relying on my mum's salary for a while.'

'What do they do?'

'Dad runs a joinery firm. Well, it's just him really, and sometimes an apprentice. Mum's a teacher. The trust fund will kick in any day now, though.'

Jerry knew he had that coming.

'I'm sorry,' he said.

'No, I shouldn't have said that. It was a low blow. Especially if I'm wanting your help. I could do with some pointers.'

'What, on getting by on no money?'

'No, on this bloody paper. If you'd asked me back in the summer about cinema and society, I'd have had plenty of opinions. Different story when you have to write it all down and an academic is going to tell you how facile it all is.'

'So why would you want tips from me?'

'Oh, come on. I've heard you talk. You just totally get this, while I feel like a complete fraud. I'm always waiting for someone to tap me on the shoulder and say, *Hey, what do you think you're doing taking up someone else's place on this course?*'

They talked a bit longer, about movies and then music. She was big into pop punk, which he had to remind himself wasn't a crime. After a while she decided she needed to get to bed. He was sorry to let her go.

'Will I see you in class?' she asked.

269

'Maybe not for a few days.'

'Call me, then?'

'If that's cool with you.'

'It's Green Day's drummer.'

'Tré Cool,' he replied. 'You know, I've known the guy's name for years, but I only got that now, because . . .'

He couldn't tell her.

'Because what?'

Because he was in Paris.

'Never mind.'

He ended the call, his predicament flooding back into his mind. He could reassure Millicent she was getting her money's worth, as it looked like he wasn't going to waste a minute's worth of his night's accommodation on anything as frivolous as sleep.

He got out his laptop and sat it before him on the bed. Surrounded by more pillows and cushions than he had ever known, he began to work his way through the other names Millicent had picked out from the cast and crew. It proved a hard shift, performing searches for what turned out to be surprisingly common Italian names, then looking for clues that the person might be someone who hadn't quite made it in the movie business the best part of a decade before Jerry was born.

Having come up with nothing useful, he did a general Google search on *Mancipium*, just to see whether the little he had learned today helped focus the picture; if some detail might help connect one of these names to the people they were now. Having keyed in the word and hit return, he noticed that the results were slightly different from before, most likely because he was searching from a Parisian IP address.

It asked if he wanted to see results in other languages, so he decided to give that a shot, for what it was worth. Most of them, unsurprisingly, appeared to be Italian. He didn't speak it, but even without clicking the translate option he could tell that several of the results were about Lucio and his disappearance. However, considerably more of the hits were about Alessandro Salerno, so he decided to search that name specifically.

There were a lot of Italian newspapers, magazines and websites doing retrospectives on the *acclamato regista di gialli* to mark the twentieth anniversary of his death. Many were illustrated by the poster of *Black Gloves and White Lace* that Jerry had seen on Millicent's bedroom wall. The image was difficult to look at now without picturing the dead guy. Incredible to believe that it could overtake the *Mancipium* one-sheet for troubling associations.

They say nobody looks on the second page of Google, but Jerry clicked a couple more just to get that image out of his head. It was similar content, except that the twentieth-anniversary pieces gave way to tenth-anniversary articles. He also noticed a few references to the Italian metal band Blood Ceremony, coming up because they were named after one of Alessandro's films.

Then his eyes were drawn to something unexpected: the video for 'Heretic' by Crucifiction, who were rising stars of the Scandinavian black-metal scene. The video was familiar to Jerry but jarring here for being in the wrong context. He wondered what data-tracking algorithm had thrown it up as a result, figuring his own search history might be a factor: like when some 'anti-woke' crusader complained that advertisers were pushing a diversity agenda, but it turned out the ads were influenced by them repeatedly searching for 'Asian teens'.

The video was embedded on an English-language metal website. Jerry opened it in a tab to keep the song playing while he continued his search, and a scan of the text told him it was directed by Gabriela Pieroni, lead vocalist of Blood Ceremony. So that was the link.

Or so he thought, until he glimpsed the words 'daughter of legendary Italian horror director Alessandro Salerno'.

Millicent never mentioned that he had a daughter, though why would she? From the look of her, she must have been about ten when her father died.

He read on and learned that Gabriela had become much in demand to direct videos for bigger metal bands after her promos for Blood Ceremony caught the eye, and now it was her primary career.

Jerry did a separate search for her name, and quickly found an interview on the twenty-year anniversary of her father's death. He had to run it through Google translate, but just the headline was enough: TWENTY YEARS OF SEARCHING FOR ANSWERS.

She was all over social media, lots of photographs from shoots around Europe, but always coming back to the same place. It turned out all roads led to Rome after all.

Whores (ii)

Markus didn't look angry, so much as disgusted. That was what really wounded her. His face seemed to say, *what the hell was I even thinking, being with you?*

'I'm so sorry,' she told him.

'You need to get your head straight,' he said in a low register. 'And I need to be somewhere else.'

'Markus, we need to talk,' she offered feebly, but he was already walking away. She was about to go after him when she felt a gentle hand on her shoulder and heard Stacey's voice.

'Let him go. Now really isn't the time. Come on. Chill out and think of the make-up sex.'

'I don't think there's going to be any of that.'

'Oh, trust me, there will be. I've seen this picture. There will be more fighting too. And more make-up sex after that.'

'More sex before he fucks off again. That's the problem.'

'You're focusing on the wrong thing. What's important is that he keeps coming back.'

'Yeah, but I'm left wondering if it's me he's coming back to, or if he's coming back anyway and I just happen to be there.'

'Let's work it out over some more champagne.'

'I think I've had enough.'

'You haven't had nearly enough.'

Stacey led her to a banquette on the seaward side, which was quieter due to the breeze coming off the water. It was a little far from the nearest overhead heater, but Millie reckoned she could use some cooling down.

Stacey signalled to one of the crew, who brought over a fresh bottle and two glasses. Stacey poured regardless of Millie's objections, and with the glass in her hand, she decided just to go with it. She could anticipate how miserable and embarrassed she was likely to feel once she sobered up, so there was a strong incentive to postpone that.

She watched a girl go past, recognising her as Lula, who had played one of the demon's victims in seventeenth-century Florence, and now had a further small part as one of the Manson Family. She would be made up and costumed so that the audience didn't recognise her as the same actress. Millie had already seen her in a third get-up: she had been the one screwing Alfie, dressed as Cleopatra.

'Markus called me paranoid, but is it any wonder?' she asked Stacey. 'I mean, look around. I think I'm starting to see the true nature of Alfie Bertrand's sudden interest in European horror cinema. He was shagging Lula at Cinecitta and I saw him earlier with some new thing who looked barely post-pubescent. You said yourself, Freddy is only here to party. Why wouldn't Markus be too?'

Stacey shook her head firmly.

'Not Markus. Trust me, I have my ear to the ground on this stuff, and honestly, he's not partaking. As you said, he flies in and out, and true he has an interest in Lucio, but it is what it looks like: just business.'

She seemed earnest about this, though Millie was still feeling too raw to be truly consoled. And it wasn't the only thing that troubled her.

'Don't you ever wonder about these girls? Who they are, where they come from?'

Stacey fixed her with a stony look.

'The world is full of wannabes. They're looking for their shot.'

'As actresses. That's not what's being asked of them here, though.'

'Isn't it? They know we're not making Oscar material. Most of these girls, they can't act, they don't have any real talent. They're just pretty young things who will probably end up fucking somebody for money one way or another. This way they might get a part in a movie, something to be proud of, a story to tell the grandchildren.

274

Go ask them: nobody's being forced into anything. Lucio's not that kind of guy.'

'You say that, but do you honestly think they're doing something they want to? Making themselves playthings and adornments to sleazy older men because they've been promised a shot at fame?'

Stacey took a drink of champagne.

'We're in the exploitation business, Milquetoast.'

That was what Stacey called her when she was being prudish. Which by Stacey's reckoning was a lot.

'Don't you understand what this movie we're making is really saying?' Stacey asked. 'It's about willingly making yourself a vessel for ugly or awful things because it beats being a fucking nobody. You think I was just a stripper back in the day? Do you know where the term grindhouse comes from?'

Millie felt her cheeks burn. She did know, but she had never dwelt on the implications for Stacey's past.

'Everybody in this business is a whore. Probably best that you get the actual whoring out of the way first so that you're not precious about anything later on.'

Millie wanted to protest, but realised she was in no position to take the high ground. The presence of these girls had bothered her for ages, but she only finally said something to anyone when she thought it might affect her. Not because some girl might be being exploited, but because some exploited girl might be screwing her boyfriend.

She had told herself that she was powerless to object, that it wasn't like Lucio was going to change anything just because she was uncomfortable. The only option then would have been to walk away, and that wasn't an option she had been prepared to exercise.

Stacey was right: everyone in this business was a whore. Swallowing principles or swallowing cum, either way they were doing it to stay in the game.

'You want a refill?' Stacey asked. 'You look like you need it.'

Millie was holding out her glass when she became aware of movement on the dock. There was an ambulance arriving at speed, heading for their pier. For a moment, she honestly thought it might be for Markus, that the injury she inflicted had turned out to be serious.

It parked as close as it could get. Two paramedics in green uniforms emerged, pulling a collapsible gurney from the back and hurrying along the jetty.

'I think it's a strippergram,' she heard someone say.

They raced up the gangplank and headed inside with urgent purpose. They seemed to know exactly where they were going.

Millie would have liked to say that an air of quiet decorum and sincere concern descended, but with the music thumping, she wasn't sure how many people even really noticed; and of those who did, how many seemed to care. Maybe most of them really did think it was some kind of stunt.

The paramedics emerged a few minutes later. Someone was strapped to the gurney under a heavy blanket. It was Sergio. They had an oxygen mask over his face, one of them ventilating him with a self-inflating ambubag. The vain bastard still had his Ray-Bans on.

Freddy emerged behind them from the bulkhead stairs, looking grim-faced, just as Lucio hastened across the deck. Word was clearly spreading that it was no stunt.

'What's happened?' Lucio asked.

Freddy looked like he didn't want to answer, then seemed to accept that this wasn't going to be possible.

'It's Sergio. He collapsed.'

'How?'

Freddy sighed, wearing a regretful look. He made a subtle gesture with his finger under his nose.

'I think he found his limit. I carry a cellular. I called the paramedics. They said he's conscious, but they need to get him to the hospital to run checks. I'm going with them.'

'I'll come too,' Lucio said.

'It's a private ambulance. There's only room for one passenger. And I'm the one who has to sign off on the bill.'

'I'll pay you back.'

'Don't worry about it.'

As she watched him accompany the gurney down the boardwalk, Millie was thinking that maybe Freddy wasn't such an arsehole after all, though another part of her was wondering why he was so keen to take charge. Was he in containment mode because he had been the one with Sergio when it happened?

Confirming the answer to that question, Julia now appeared, cocktail glass in hand, inquiring as to what was going on. She hadn't quite managed that one-upping after all.

Perspectives

In the harsh light of day, and the harsher light of Millicent's expression, Jerry wasn't sure what he just told her represented quite the breakthrough it felt like last night. She didn't seem optimistic that they could arrange a meeting with Gabriela, or excited by the prospect of what it might yield even if they did.

Maybe he had just become so excited by his discovery because it was unexpected, and it was also possible that he had overestimated its significance because it had connected two of his favourite things: horror movies and metal.

'I remember her visiting sets a few times, but she won't remember me,' Millicent said. 'Like any little girl she was excited to see a few well-known actors in real life and wasn't paying much attention to anything else.'

She had Jerry's laptop in front of her at breakfast and was reading the Gabriela Pieroni interview he had found, without recourse to Google's translation.

'If she's some hot young rock star and video director these days, she's not going to drop everything to talk to an old woman who knew her father twenty-odd years ago.'

'She's hardly a rock star,' he argued. 'Blood Ceremony are small fry. That's why she's making her money directing promos for bigger acts.'

'In this piece, she is resentful of grave-robbers, as she calls them. "People digging up the past and spreading innuendo, looking for some great mystery that isn't there." She says she hates the myths surrounding her father's last film. Does that sound like someone who is going to want to talk to us?'

'We're not tripping over alternative options.'

'Can't you look again and see if you can find what happened to Stacey? I thought about it again this morning, and it struck me that you're looking at it from a young person's perspective. Just because someone isn't on social media doesn't mean they're dead.'

'Aye, but it does mean that she might as well be, as there's no way of getting in touch with her.'

'What about the other names I gave you, from the cast and crew?'

Jerry hadn't bothered looking. Once he found out about Gabriela, he had finally started to feel sleepy.

'Let's just see whether this door is definitely closed before I go chapping on any others. I'm gaunny message her on Twitter. Her DMs are open.'

'Her what?'

'It means she accepts unsolicited approaches. As does anybody whose income relies on getting gigs.'

Millicent watched him edit his Twitter profile on the laptop before firing off a message. It now stated that he was a freelance contributor to *Kerrang* and *Metal Hammer*.

'What did you tell her?' she asked.

'That I'm gaunny be in Rome and would like to interview her about her band and the visual aesthetics of metal.'

'Won't she be able to check and see that you aren't what you say?'

'If she asks me to send links to my work, I'm gubbed, but I'm hoping she's flattered enough by the interest. She's not that high-profile. It's not like she's got journalists banging on the door.'

'Except to talk about the one thing we want to talk about, and which she explicitly doesn't,' Millicent pointed out.

Jerry laughed with exasperation.

'Fuck's sake, are you always this pessimistic?'

'You've been in my world for two days, Pollyanna. I'd love to see how optimistic you are after a couple of decades of everything going wrong.'

Christ. He was trying his best to help her and she was acting like a wean. She needed tell't.

'Get your shit together and quit feeling sorry for yourself,' he replied, quoting her own words. 'If everything has gone wrong for that long, doesn't the law of averages dictate that it's more likely the next thing will go right?'

'That's known as the gambler's fallacy. Just because you lost ninety-nine times betting on a three-legged horse doesn't mean there's a greater chance of your luck changing if you back it again.'

'Aye, but I think your luck is already changing. It's just a matter of perspective.'

'Perspective? How rose-tinted would my glasses need to be? In the last couple of days I've had two people try to kill me.'

'And neither of them succeeded. Doesn't that count as a win? You've also successfully circumvented border security to travel on somebody else's passport, had coffee with an old friend, taken a moonlit boat trip doon the Seine, spent a night in a Parisian hotel, and noo I've unearthed a lead we didnae know aboot.'

That gave her something to chew over. She frowned, and he could tell she was struggling for a comeback. He had little doubt she'd find one, though. It was her signature move.

'A lead that we will only be able to follow if—'

Whatever she was about to say was stymied by simultaneous chimes from his laptop and his phone.

'Gabriela's replied.'

He turned the laptop around and let her read it.

That would be rad. I am shooting the new Crucifiction video over the next two days. Come visit the set. I'll send you the address.

'So are we riding that three-legged horse to Rome?'

Jerome looked so pleased with himself that Millicent had to suppress a desire to pick up the laptop two-handed and smack him with it. Just because he had received a positive reply, he was acting like this proved him right and her wrong about everything they had just discussed.

The force of her anger gave her pause, sufficient to ask herself where it had come from. She had felt her rage begin to well up when he told her to pull herself together, compounded by the fact that he was turning her own words back upon her. How dare he, this, this *child* who had done nothing, seen nothing; whose naivety betrayed how little he understood of what this cruelly capricious world could do to you.

But as he sat there, his expression hopeful and enthusiastic, despite the world of danger she had dragged him into, she saw things differently. He had been given a crash course in how wrong life could go, and he was just getting on with it. If he was naïve, would she wish her wisdom upon him? Would she take his optimism and replace it with her bitterness?

She felt terrible about having called him Pollyanna. He was putting a brave face on everything, but nobody should be having to deal with all this. Certainly not a young man who ought to be in his classes right now, preparing for a better life.

What she was really angry at was his youth. He had so much life in front of him, when so much of hers had been taken away. But she didn't have to view it that way.

She thought of last night, standing in a gallery by the Seine, sipping champagne.

Life is good.

Jerome was right. It was all about perspective. Not what was behind, but what was still in front of her.

'Rome it is,' she said. 'But not by three-legged horse, and not by air either.'

'Why not?'

'I don't want our movements to be traceable. Even though I travelled on Carla's passport, I booked the flights on my credit card, so maybe that's how they knew where we were headed. We're going to hire a car; or rather, you are.'

'Won't they know my name by now?'

'It's still possible they don't,' she said. 'But either way, the point is they won't know where we're headed.'

'They might if they trace us from CCTV number-plate

recognition. We can reduce the risk if we hire from some wee independent outfit. The big chains will be more easily searchable.'

Jerome worked the keyboard intently, and a few minutes later turned the laptop to face her again. It showed the website of a small rental firm in the Ninth Arrondissement.

'What are we going for?' he asked. The screen showed a list of vehicles alongside daily rates. 'As we're headed to Rome, how about a Mini?'

She passed up the chance of an easy point as her eye was drawn to something further down the page. It was a notion she was about to dismiss as not for the likes of her when she decided to shake off this conditioning.

'Book us that one.'

She turned the laptop around so that they could both see it. She was pointing towards a Jaguar F-Type convertible.

'Are you kidding? It's two hunner Euros a day.'

'If I run out of money before they catch me, I'll have done well.'

'Aye, but you could skew the ratio in your favour. You're gaunny run oot pronto if you're this extravagant.'

She put a hand on his arm.

'You were right about changing my perspective. Something I've learned over the past couple of days is that I have money in the bank. And by that, I mean life is money in the bank. Just because I was in the huff with the world didn't change the fact that it's been sitting there, waiting to be spent if I decided to.'

Descent

Jerry had never driven on the right, so it helped that it was an automatic, with integrated sat-nav. Less helpful was the fact that it was about five times more powerful than the only two cars he had ever driven: his gran's Jazz and the instructor's Corsa. He was shitting himself about pranging it, taking it so slow and cautious through Paris that eventually Millicent told him he was 'driving like a pensioner'. Once he got onto the Autoroute, he tried opening it up. That was even scarier. Millicent seemed to be happy, though. She had the top down and the seat heating on.

According to the computer, the trip was going to take at least fourteen hours, so he reckoned they could make it as far as Bologna or even Florence in time to check in somewhere for the night. It gave them plenty of time to talk, and talk Millicent did. He had never imagined her being so expansive, even allowing for the fact that when you had killed a guy and disposed of his body together, then lobbed another hitman into the Seine, it really broke the ice. Jerry's gran said grumpy old men tend to have been grumpy young men. He had wondered if Millicent was cantankerous and unapproachable when she was younger, so now he was starting to see that once upon a time, she may have been someone very different.

She told him everything she could remember about the shoot, starting with how Lucio's grand plans had burned down and *Mancipium* had been the phoenix that rose from the ashes.

'You never saw your finished work on *Mancipium*?' he asked as they approached Chamonix.

'I did see dailies. But if you're hoping I've got a VHS of the rough cut tucked away somewhere, then no, I'm afraid not. I did have one, but the police took all my videos away. It was among the ones that never came back: that and a handful from the DPP list. It was so that they could feed the tabloids a line about me owning "banned video nasties" and "sick filth".'

'So there could still be a tape of the rough cut lying in some vault at Scotland Yard?' he asked.

'No. It would have been destroyed. They made great play of how they were destroying the video nasties. They actually burned them.'

Jerry remembered this from a documentary. It didn't look totalitarian or dystopian at all.

'Fascist pricks.'

'My brother replaced some of them years later: tracked them down on eBay.'

'Original VHS?'

'Yes. He maintained they never looked the same all cleaned up on DVD. He looked after all my stuff while I was inside. Well, when I say looked after, it wasn't entirely altruistic. He had his own reasons for wanting a shedload of old horror movies. But as for *Mancipium*, all I had was a poster Markus made for me. We had a falling out and he surprised me with a visit when I was back in London after the film wrapped, gave me it as a peace offering. There was an ad that had run in the trades, which he cut out and had professionally framed.'

Jerry suddenly felt like he was driving in a tunnel, the sky and mountains around him disappearing and the walls closing in.

'I don't even have that anymore,' she added.

He knew what was coming. Saw it approaching as fast and sure as the lines on the road.

'My brother's flat was broken into. That's how he died: the police think he caught the burglar in the act. They said they didn't think he was assaulted, but just the shock of it gave him a heart attack.'

The tunnel was descending into the ground, deeper and deeper.

'I'm so sorry,' Jerry said, because he had to say something. His voice faltered, and he prayed she didn't notice.

'You would have liked him. He was a massive horror fan too, though that didn't sit well with his condition. He hadn't actually seen a new horror film since 2005. He had his first heart attack in the cinema watching a film called *The Descent*. He was warned by the doctor to avoid doing anything that would unnecessarily jack up his cardiac rate, so he rationed himself to films he had already seen, hence him re-watching all my old videos. No suspense, you see. Have you seen *The Descent*?'

'Yes,' Jerry answered, though it felt like he wasn't really present. The car was in a tunnel plunging into the earth, and he was outside it, watching an avatar of himself at the wheel. This was his own descent, into the darkness. This was his punishment, for a sin from which he could not ask forgiveness, because in order to forgive she would have to know.

And she could never know.

PART FOUR

Silence

Lucio was pacing, then sitting down, then getting up and pacing some more, like he had too much nervous energy and literally didn't know what to do with himself. He was also necking shots, as though that would calm his growing anxiety. It was like trying to put out a forest fire with a Soda Stream. Millie appreciated now just how good a bluffer he was in having given Sergio the impression he was quite sanguine about shooting the rest of the scenes without him. It was also clear that his affected ambivalence was purely a negotiating tactic. He genuinely cared about the guy.

Weirdly, when he was seated, Millie noticed that the very group who had been present at the conception of this project were reconvening at the same table: her, Lucio, Alessandro and Stacey. She just hoped that this bookending wouldn't prove significant.

Markus had not joined them. He was still on board, but there was little question he was avoiding her.

In the centre of the table sat the boat's phone, connected by a lengthy extension cable. Three times Lucio had picked it up, only to be reminded that they forgot to ask the paramedics which hospital they were taking Sergio to. For all they knew, they could have gone all the way to Naples.

After about two hours of it not ringing, they were finally delivered as they saw the ambulance pull up again. Worryingly, only Freddy and one of the paramedics got out. Millie hadn't imagined this would be Sergio coming back to the party, but it seemed surprising that an ambulance should return Freddy. She was forgetting who Freddy was, and that it was a private ambulance. He who paid the piper called the tune.

Freddy noticed the reception committee and waved, giving them a thumb-up gesture.

'Sergio's okay,' Stacey said.

The paramedic accompanied Freddy on board, and Freddy let him do the talking. Surprisingly, he was English. As she did anytime she encountered an ex-pat, Millie wondered what his story was, how he had ended up here. He was vaguely familiar too, making her wonder if their paths had once crossed back home.

'He had lost consciousness and as we were given to understand that cocaine overuse may have been a factor, we had to ascertain whether this was possibly due to stroke or heart attack. Initial tests have indicated negative on stroke, but he has exhibited mild cardiac symptoms. We believe alcohol and possibly other drugs may have contributed. We're keeping him in for observation and recommending he has complete rest for a few days. When we told him this, he said he was planning to go to Greece to convalesce.'

'He hangs out on Kos a lot,' Stacey told them.

'Surely he shouldn't travel,' Lucio suggested.

Millie wondered if he was still primarily concerned about Sergio's health or about him leaving the production with the shoot incomplete.

'We told him that. The doctor said he should wait a few days before flying, but we can't force him.'

'No,' observed Lucio wryly. 'Nobody can force him to do anything.'

'And whether he goes to Greece or not, he shouldn't be working for a few days yet,' the paramedic added, addressing this to Lucio. Millie wondered how much Freddy had told him on the way back here.

She watched Freddy accompany the paramedic to the ambulance, shaking his hand to thank him before he drove off. She was impressed if a little chilled by the glimpse she had been given into how people at his level operated. Millie knew nobody would be taking a backhander from any reporters for tipping them off about a movie-star OD scandal. The paramedics would be getting paid far more by Freddy to say nothing. He had moved rapidly to contain the situation. It was not Freddy's movie, it was his sister's movie, but by extension the family was associated with it.

She wondered if Freddy had paid Sergio for his silence too, and if it was more than he'd been asking for the overrun, hence expressing his desire to convalesce somewhere else. Either way, Lucio wouldn't be coughing up for those extra shooting days.

Shame

The sky was still gloriously clear, though Millicent noticed that the colours were darkening, the sun starting to go down. It had been a good day, she decided: one of the best she could remember in a very long time. That was something she wouldn't have predicted when she woke up this morning.

A part of her was expecting the carabinieri to pull them over at any moment, so she was savouring every second that it continued not to happen. She was learning to savour many things: not merely the simple pleasures she had forgotten, but the simpler fact that she was still here when others weren't.

She was used to these dissociated bereavements: being cut off from people for so long that learning of their death was merely a matter of confirmation. That was how it had been with Lucio and Alessandro. And yet it troubled her how Stacey had slipped away unnoticed, not only by her, but seemingly by everyone. That had hurt deep, despite she and Stacey never being that close. Perhaps it was her own ultimate fate that she was concerned about. After all, in someone's script, she was supposed to have died in her sleep two nights ago.

She had looked Stacey up on her phone, and found that posterity had no place for someone who made the wrong kind of art. There had been no obituary in the newspapers or in *Variety*, no retrospective at a festival or even an arthouse cinema. Had anyone even mourned her? Did she die alone? And if so, did whoever found her, whoever buried her, realise what a life she had lived, the contribution she had made?

Stacey's was a life that deserved to be celebrated, though many people would not have seen it that way. Uncomfortably, Millicent herself had to acknowledge that she had always disapproved of Stacey. Liberal-minded arts types didn't like to admit to moral censoriousness, but now that Stacey was gone, she was confronted by the truth of it. She felt disappointed in her own prudishness, but more disappointed to learn that Stacey was not still conducting herself shamelessly somewhere.

Jerome was quiet at the wheel. He hadn't said anything at all for several miles. Maybe she shouldn't have burdened him by talking about losing her brother. God knows she had already burdened him enough.

She was about to ask if he wanted to stop for another break at the next services when she was interrupted by her phone ringing. It sent a pulse right through her as she remembered that the last person to call had been Rook. Why should she be afraid, though? It wasn't like he could threaten her with anything she wasn't already facing.

When she lifted the device from inside her bag and saw the screen, she was reminded that there was one other person who had this number, and who had pre-programmed her own details into it.

'Oh, hi, Vivian.'

'Millicent? Is everything all right? I tried calling the house and there was no reply. I was worried because I rang last night too. It was quite late though, so I didn't want to try the mobile then in case you had gone to your bed. Where are you?'

She looked at the olive trees whizzing past, the mountains beckoning in the distance.

'Partick.'

'It sounds like you're in a car.'

'Yes, we're in a taxi.'

'We?'

'I'm with Jerome. We went to the cinema this afternoon, but it was bucketing when we came out and I decided to be a little extravagant.'

'And everything's been all right?'

'Yes, no dramas.'

She gave Jerome a mischievous grin, but his eyes were on the road.

'We'll see you tomorrow afternoon, then,' Vivian said.

This rattled her for a moment. She had been so preoccupied with everything else that she had forgotten Vivian and Carla were due back.

'Are you still there?' Vivian asked.

'Yes, but you won't see me tomorrow, as it happens. And Jerome won't be there either,' she remembered to add.

'Why, where will you be?'

She searched her mind for something that would explain their absence in a manner likely to put Vivian's mind at ease.

'We're going to visit Jerome's old stomping ground over the weekend. A little trip down to Ayrshire. We might even go to the seaside.'

'Well, that's lovely,' Vivian replied. She sounded a little surprised but also pleased. 'Good to hear you're getting out and about. It sounds like you're having quite the adventure.'

'Well, I'm not driving an open-topped sports car round the capital cities of Europe, but maybe I can work up to that.'

She said her goodbyes and hung up.

'What the hell did you tell her that for?' Jerome asked.

'What, about the capitals of Europe? It was a joke. She doesn't know where we are.'

'No. About us going to Ayrshire.'

'I needed to tell her something that would keep her from worrying. We don't want her reporting us missing, do we?'

He seemed unusually taciturn. Maybe he was just tired from all the driving.

She looked at a road sign listing distances: BOLOGNA 260 KM, PARMA 175 KM, MILANO 50 KM. It struck her that she hadn't given any thought to where their route would take them, only where they were headed and how far they might get before they had to break for the night.

'We should stop in Milan instead,' she said.

'If I get a ten-minute break and a coffee, I can push on through to Bologna.'

'I know, but it's just coming up for six. We could have a decent dinner and a good night's sleep, then an early start tomorrow. I know some places in Milan.'

As she said this, she remembered:

'Actually, I know some*body* in Milan. Or at least I did.'

Millicent lifted her phone and keyed in the name. The first search result was TRICOLORE FILM E TELEVISIONE. It remained a going concern, its logo updated but still incorporating the Italian flag on the left and the Irish on the right. She clicked on the contacts section and there he was, listed next to his office landline and even his mobile number.

'Ardal McGill,' she said. 'He's still there.'

'Who is he?'

'Sales agent. If anyone is going to take my call, it will be him. He could never pass up a potential lead. He and Lucio were made for each other.'

'And can we trust him?'

Ardal had known Lucio for a long time before Millicent met either of them, so she couldn't know where else their circles over-lapped. She wondered who else he might have been close to back then, and more importantly who he might get on the phone to as soon as they finished speaking.

'Let's proceed on the basis that we don't.'

The Impostor

There was no one of whom you could truly say they hadn't changed in a quarter of a century, but if Ardal McGill had been one of the men in the Blue Lamp Burns Society photograph, Millicent would have had no problem identifying the 2020 version of him. He had put on a few pounds, for sure, but he had always been a bear of a man.

Ardal had given her the address of a trattoria she remembered gathering in during MIFED in October '93, when he had organised a press launch for *Mancipium* ahead of the shoot. His sales company was based in Milan. To others, Cannes – the *Marché* – was always the biggest, but for MIFED, Ardal had homecourt advantage.

The trattoria had changed even less than him. It even seemed to be playing the same music: 'It's A Shame About Ray' by the Lemonheads wafting lazily from the speakers like it had been stuck on a loop for twenty-five years.

He gave her a tentative and slightly awkward air kiss, then shook Jerome's hand as she made introductions. They had never known each other that well, though they had known a lot of the same people. She was thus wary of how quickly he had agreed to the rendezvous. She remembered that he was indefatigably sociable, as reliably jovial as he was notoriously indiscreet, but what troubled her was that if there wasn't the promise of a deal to be had, what was in it for him?

He showed them to a table where, unbidden, the waiter brought a bottle of red wine and a couple of plates of cold meat and cheese.

'I'm in here so much, they even let me play my own Spotify,' he said. 'As long as I don't take the piss.'

'You're looking well, Ardal,' she said. 'To be honest, I thought you would have retired by now.'

'And do what?' he replied, his Dublin accent still undiminished by his decades in Italy. 'There's nothing better than this, Millie. It's not as exciting as the old cowboy days, though. No organising screenings with one reel missing and hoping the buyers are too pissed to notice.'

With that, he began pouring the wine. Jerome politely refused, at which point Ardal summoned the waiter and let him order an alternative. He seemed apologetic for his presumption.

'It's true then, what I'm hearing? That the younger generation aren't really drinkers?'

Jerome shrugged.

'I weep for the future. What the hell are you all going to blame when you fuck up?'

The waiter brought a bottle of lemonade. Ardal waited until Jerome had poured to lift his glass and say cheers.

'I note that you didn't ask what I've been doing with myself,' Millicent said.

Ardal's salesman smile faded.

'I know what you did, Millie, sure. And cards on the table, my own curiosity played a part in me agreeing to meet, because it was a story that never made sense.'

So maybe that was what was in it for him. Ardal always traded in gossip, because you never knew what doors the right piece of information might open. But that also meant he might have information that could open doors for her.

'It made no sense because I didn't do it. That's the simple truth. I woke up next to a dead body. I think I had been drugged. I was set up, and I'm trying to find out by whom. That's why I'm here.'

'Jesus. Well, in that case, I'm not sure there's much I can tell you.'

He looked both defensive and concerned for her.

'We might surprise each other, Ardal. How much do you remember about Markus Laird, the man I supposedly killed? Because let's just say I've come to learn that he wasn't quite all he appeared.'

Ardal took a sip of wine, a glint forming in his eye. He was a

297

dog who had caught a scent of something worth the pursuit. He didn't know what it might turn out to be, but he just loved to chase.

'I'm delving deep into the memory vaults here, but I always thought there was something about your man that I couldn't quite put my finger on. Markus appeared from nowhere, and suddenly he knew everybody, which isn't suspicious in itself, and maybe I was just jealous. I don't know.'

Millicent beckoned him to go on. Listening to this was like the set-up to something for which she already knew the punchline, but then all good jokes were in the telling.

'Do you recall Andrew Yates, God rest him?' Ardal asked. 'He was with Goldcrest back in the day, Working Title for a wee while. Died just a few years back. Andrew had a theory about Markus. Remember back in the early Nineties there was a couple of instances of guys pretending to be doctors? Somehow getting hired even though they were only paramedics or whatever? Andrew reckoned there was something like that going on: that Markus had acquired credentials to be at the markets, but was faking it. Markus was always there, but nobody ever sold anything to him. His firm, what were they called again?'

'Blue Lantern Films.'

'That's right. A name I'd never heard before and never heard again after he died. Blue Lantern never had a stall or an office at markets, and yet Markus was all over the place, talking to everybody.'

He emptied his glass then filled it again.

'Does that shed any light?'

Jerome was nodding but Millicent didn't want him hearing that punchline yet.

'It's consistent with what I have discovered,' she said.

'Which would be what?'

'I don't want to prejudice anything else you might have to tell me. Do go on.'

Ardal shrugged and took another gulp. He looked like he was enjoying himself.

'I had a pet theory of my own, but it might have been my dick talking. I thought maybe he and Alfie Bertrand were a secret thing. That was before I found out Markus was seeing you. See, my problem has always been that my gaydar tends to err on the side of optimism. I'm always hoping someone is on our team.'

'Why did you think they were a thing?'

'On the surface they appeared not to know each other, and yet they kept showing up in the same places, the same parties, but never quite in the same company. You learn to spot the signs, or at least you learn to try. It wasn't easy back then. And Milan was paradise compared to Ireland.'

'Was that why you moved here?' Millicent asked.

'No, I moved here because I had a job. But it was why I stayed here.'

He shook his head, a bittersweet expression on his face.

'I had some great times. Some great friends. But so many didn't make it.'

Jerome didn't appear to understand.

'AIDS,' Millicent said softly.

'I remember sitting here in this bar, during MIFED '92, drinking with Perry Byrne, who was production manager on *Screen International*. We used to run so many ads, and Perry always got them looking right no matter how late the artwork came in. Sitting in that booth over there was Oscar Moore, the editor. I used to argue the toss with him over sniffy reviews.'

He swallowed.

'Within a few years they were both lost. So many faces you'd see at MIFED and Cannes, then one year they wouldn't be there, and if they were gay, you feared they were never coming back.'

Ardal stared across the room for a moment, as though picturing the people who must once have stood there. The music changed, 'Sleeping Satellite' by Tasmin Archer giving way to 'Mr Jones' by Counting Crows.

'Anyway, I was wrong about Alfie Bertrand and it didn't take AIDS to kill Markus Laird. But that's all I can give you, I'm afraid.'

'You didn't have any personal dealings with Markus, then?'

'No, never. Sorry.'

He picked up a cube of cheese and was about to pop it in his mouth. His hand stopped.

'Well, not directly, but here's the thing. I was under the impression that Markus was buying a tranche of international rights, mostly in south-east Asia, for *Mancipium*. That, to me, popped Andrew's theory: finally, we knew of someone who was doing a deal with Markus. Except, it never happened. One day Lucio gets in touch and says all these rights are back on the table if I want to represent them. I normally only handle European sales, but he offered me extra points on the commission because he was coming to me late in the day.'

'Because Markus had died,' Millicent reminded him.

'No, this was while you guys were still shooting down in Sorrento.'

'That doesn't add up,' she said. 'At that point Markus and Lucio were seeing a lot of each other, and everyone was under the impression they were negotiating for Blue Lantern to license those rights. But you're saying Lucio had already authorised you to offer them around?'

'Maybe Lucio was using me as leverage to bump up the price: tell Markus he had to pay more because I had received an offer from Star TV in Malaysia or whoever.'

It was time for that punchline.

'No. It still doesn't add up because your friend Andrew was close to the truth. Markus was never going to buy any rights. He wasn't a sales agent. He was an undercover cop.'

Ardal gaped for a moment, then slammed both palms down on the table, causing all the glasses to shake.

'Fuck me, that explains so much.'

'And you weren't a million miles off either,' said Jerome. 'We think his job was to tail Alfie Bertrand. We just don't know why.'

Ardal gave a hollow laugh.

'It's all right there in front of you, isn't it? But you can't make sense of any of it until you can see the whole picture. I mean, how come he and Lucio were keeping up this pretence? What were they cooking up if it wasn't a film deal?'

'We don't know,' said Millicent. 'But we're pretty sure it got both of them killed.'

'Jesus.'

Ardal rubbed his eyes, seeing his history of the past three decades ripped up and rewritten in an instant. There was concern in his expression as he looked across at his guests.

'That being so, is it wise for you two to go poking this nest?'

'We've no choice. Someone came and poked ours. It's not safe back home.'

'They came for you back in England?'

'Scotland,' Jerome corrected.

'I always assumed Lucio got done in by his, ahem, connections. But it sounds too long a reach to be anybody from that shower.'

'I had wondered about Florio,' Millicent admitted. 'But everything we've unearthed so far says British. Whatever happened to him, by the way?'

Ardal rolled his eyes.

'Florio's in politics these days. I would say he's gone all respectable but he's fuckin' Lega Nord. Think I respected him more when he was a gangster. Anyway, who else are you talking to about this?'

Ardal ordered another bottle with a mere gesture, having polished off most of the first one himself. Millicent took solace from the thought that anyone harbouring a hidden agenda would be more abstemious, but she would still tread carefully.

'We're on our way to meet Alessandro's daughter,' she replied, judiciously avoiding mention of Julia Fleet and Jean-Marc Poupard. She had considered a vague non-answer about still trying to track down a few names via social media, but as they were meeting the woman under false pretences, she was hoping for one of those tiny titbits that opened doors.

'Oh yeah, Gabriela. I heard she's making pop videos now. I think she was veering off the rails for a wee while there, so I'm glad she's doing well these days.'

'You know her, then? Any pointers would be appreciated, especially as she's reputedly not keen on talking about *Mancipium*.'

He grimaced.

'Aye: for fuck's sake don't mention that you were talking to Ardal

McGill. She blames me personally for some of the more lurid myths surrounding the movie.'

'Why?'

'Because I am personally responsible for some of the more lurid myths surrounding the movie. I'm a fuckin' salesman, what can I say?'

'Which myths in particular?'

He took a big gulp of wine. It looked like he was steeling himself.

'Just before he went missing, Lucio sent out videos of the rough cut, trying to create a buzz. He thought it was going to be huge, convinced the market was ripe for an old-school slasher that had just the right supernatural hook. He was wrong, though. Nobody wanted to know. Around then I actually wondered whether Lucio had done a bunk because he had borrowed against pre-sales that now didn't look like materialising.'

Millicent was surprised to feel a twinge of hurt pride in learning that the film would have been a flop.

'Anyway, as you know, Lucio disappeared, and so did the negative. At that point it became a salvage operation. I had Julia Fleet and Jean-Marc Poupard and a whole load of other investors pressuring me to find buyers for a video-only cut. I was talking to a journalist about it, and I initially said it as a joke.'

He took another gulp of wine. He wore a regretful smile, one that said 'fuckin' eejit'.

'Said what?'

'That the reason . . . Actually, I missed a bit of context. I had followed up with Ricardo Rossini, an Italian home video distributor, but it turned out he had just died. So I'm talking to this reporter about how nobody was getting back to me, and I flippantly said maybe everybody who watched it fuckin' died.'

'That's what started the whole curse thing?' asked Jerome.

Ardal put up his hands.

Millicent suspected there was more to be told.

'It seems harsh that Gabriela would blame you just for that,' she said.

'Yeah, but that was just the start. Nobody was biting, so I came up with the idea to make the fact that nobody was biting part of the pitch. I put it about that people were rumoured to have died from fear after watching it.

'There had been similar stories around *The Exorcist*, about people dropping dead in cinemas. Utter shite. I was just trying to drum up some notoriety so I could flog home video rights. I knew the negative had gone missing, so I made up the story about it being burned in the presence of a priest. How do you sell a film that's been lost? You say it was so evil, so scary that it had to be destroyed. Didn't fuckin' work, though. In the end, they decided to cut their losses and write the whole thing off.'

'But the myth lived on,' said Jerome.

'Took on a life of its own, yeah. So when you speak to Gabriela, if my name does come up, please tell her I'm sorry.'

It was raining when they left the trattoria, so Jerome insisted on retrieving the car and bringing it round to pick her up. He was being particularly solicitous all evening, for some reason. Ardal had asked them to stay longer but Millicent told him they needed to get an early start in the morning.

The drops were pitter-pattering on the canvas roof as she pulled on her seatbelt.

'I've been fascinated by the *Mancipium* legend since I was aboot thirteen,' Jerome said. 'I never believed there was a curse, but I'm not sure how I feel learning it all came fae one guy trying to make a buck. It's amazing how quickly people will forget proven facts, and yet you can make up some weird bullshit and it lasts for decades.'

'The reason people don't value facts is because they belong to everyone,' she replied. 'Myths and rumours feel like secret knowledge, and so people prize them more.'

'I don't think he ever meant any harm. He seems a decent bloke. Very forthcoming.'

'Hmm,' Millicent averred.

'What?'

'I'm just a little suspicious of *why* he was so forthcoming. Why he was so glad to see me even though we barely knew each other back in the day.'

Jerome scoffed.

'Were you paying attention back there? Did you hear all that Nineties music? Sitting in this bar where he's drunk his whole life, talking about all the folk who are no longer around? He was pleased to see you because you're still alive.'

'I suppose,' she conceded.

Jerome stopped the car at traffic lights and turned to face her.

'I realise this is difficult to accept, Millicent, but the hard truth is, not everybody hates you.'

Guilt

Jerry heard the pings of various alerts as his phone reconnected to the hotel wi-fi. He would have to admit that it gave him a lift when he saw that one of them was from Philippa. He knew he didn't deserve a lift, but he needed one.

Pip, she called herself. It had annoyed him when he first saw it a few days ago. Now he found it kind of endearing, though he wasn't sure he could bring himself to say the name out loud. That was moot, as he wasn't sure he had Pip privileges. Did he want Pip privileges?

He called her. There were voices in the background when she answered: chatting and laughter.

'How's things?' she asked. 'Is your house all secure now?'

'I'm not there at the moment.'

'Where are you?'

He looked out the window, down onto Piazza Mercanti, where diners were braving the chill beneath outdoor heaters, strings of lights illuminating centuries-old buildings.

'You wouldn't believe me if I told you.'

'Try me.'

'Another time, maybe. What are you up to?'

'Not a lot. I was in the social space with some people. I'm just leaving, going up to my room.'

'It's Friday night.'

'Yeah, but I'm watching the pennies. Everybody is, this far into term, so Danby organised an improvised movie night down here.'

Jerry winced at the name but knew it would be conspicuous if he went all quiet.

'What was the film?'

'*The Disaster Artist.*'

'Good choice,' he had to concede. 'Was it Danby's?'

'Yes. Though we put it to a vote. My friend Chloe suggested *Suicide Squad*. She likes Margot Robbie.'

'Loath as I am to find myself on the same side as Danby, I have to say you made the right choice.'

'I know he's not your favourite person, but he got all this together. Saved a crap Friday night.'

'I guess we've found the one student at Glasgow Uni who knows what he's doing and doesn't feel like a fraud.'

'Actually, I think Danby is one of those people who comes across as confident because he thinks that's what is expected of him. I'm sure if you got to know him, you'd find he's just as insecure as everybody else.'

Jerry took her point, but nonetheless reckoned insecurities were the one thing he had more of than Danby. That was why they had got off on the wrong foot. He could see now that his instinctive dislike of the guy had been a displacement exercise in pure self-loathing. And Jerry had some nerve to be judgmental and disdainful towards him. Being an over-confident posh boy wasn't a crime. Not like breaking into houses and giving people heart attacks was a crime.

He had struggled to look Millicent in the eye tonight, having learned that the old man was her brother.

Alastair. The old man had a name now.

The silence ran on longer than he intended.

'Is everything okay?' Philippa asked.

Jerry swallowed.

'Can you imagine a situation where you've done something terrible to somebody, and you cannae tell them what you've done because you've grown to like them? But the only way you're gaunny live with yourself is if you tell the truth, knowing they're gaunny hate you for it?'

There was a long pause.

'Kind of,' she said. 'Is this about Danby's phone?'

'I really wish it was.'

Intruders

The address Gabriela had DM-ed him was in a light industrial area to the north of the city. The streets were flanked by near-identical low-rise units laid out in a grid, but it was easy to spot the one they were looking for. It had Crucifiction's tour bus parked outside, as well as trucks and trailers for lighting gear, catering, generators and toilets. There was also a burly security guard at the gate.

'Shite.'

'What?'

'It just struck me that I never mentioned to Gabriela that I would be bringing a plus one. Maybe we can say you're my photographer. You can take my phone and just keep snapping stuff. I guess if Soderberg can shoot a whole film on an iPhone, it won't look too suspicious that you don't have some big SLR.'

'Calm down,' she said. 'It's not about who I might pretend to be, but who I am. Your pretence was just to get our foot in the door. Let me establish my credentials and I'll take it from there.'

'Whatever you say.'

He was glad somebody knew what they were doing.

The security guard took his name, checked something on his phone and waved them through with a curt, wordless nod. If that was his manner greeting folk who were authorised to be here, Jerry really didn't want to see him in huckling mode.

They made their way between the parked vehicles. He glanced inside one of the trucks and saw rows of floods, profiles and followspots, hanging above a forest of stands. From inside he could hear the muted thrum of the music track, like if he was outside a gig.

When he turned around again, Millicent was veering off towards one of the trailers.

'You go on in,' she insisted. 'I'll catch you up.'

She was heading for the toilet. After a very early start, they had broken for brunch at roughly halfway, and she had drunk a lot of coffee. The stop had been tantalisingly close to Florence, a place his gran had often talked about visiting. He told himself he would come back one day, but he wasn't sure he believed it. It was hard thinking about the future, knowing your fate was in the balance between an unknown enemy and an old ex-con who didn't always inspire confidence that she knew how the modern world worked.

The further they had travelled, the less he thought about uni; and as for Rossco, whatever damage he might have done was so far out of Jerry's hands that it didn't seem to matter. To think he had been worried about having to steal from his housemates and then keep it secret. What he was keeping from Millicent made it seem trivial by comparison.

The building was a nondescript warehouse on the outside, but inside it had been transformed into a weird split world: three quarters of the floorspace done up to resemble the inside of a wooden barn, and the remainder looking like mission control. The centre of the space was filled with the band's gear; lights and cameras surrounded it.

The drummer and the bassist were in position, both made up with corpse paint. Jerry didn't see the singer or the guitarist, unless they were among the four figures in latex masks standing further back. He wondered if they were meant to be the audience. Facially they were done up like orcs, but they were all wearing black-metal T-shirts.

A girl with the inevitable iPad approached him as he stepped tentatively inside. She looked around Jerry's age and he couldn't decide whether that was reassuring. It might mean that someone so young wouldn't seem out of place here, or it could invite suspicion if this supposed freelance journalist appeared the same age as the junior production assistant.

Either way, he was grateful for his dreads, because at the very least he looked authentically metal.

'You are Jerry, right?' she asked in lightly accented English.

'Yeah.'

'Come right through. Gabriela is in the video village.'

He recognised Gabriela instantly from the Blood Ceremony videos, though her spiky silver hair was tamed under a black baseball cap. She was shorter than he assumed, maybe just over five feet, which accentuated the muscular look of her heavily tattooed arms in her cut-off T-shirt.

She was watching on a bank of monitors, a headset mic relaying her instructions to the floor. The production assistant held up a hand to Jerry, signalling him to remain still and quiet as Gabriela was calling action.

On the floor, the orcs began running from the back of the room. The bass player changed grip on his guitar, a headless model, grabbing it by the neck. On one screen the camera zoomed in for a close-up, showing bladed edges emerge from the body of the instrument, transforming it into an axe, which he then swung directly towards the lens before stopping.

'Okay, cut,' said Gabriela.

She muttered something to an older guy at the desk and the screens began replaying multiple angles of what they had just seen.

'Pasi, that swing looks kind of candy-ass,' she said, her words reverberating from the same monitors as the music playback. Jerry was surprised if grateful that she was addressing everyone in English, then he remembered that Crucifiction comprised two Finns, one Norwegian and a Swede. Her accent indicated that she had learned the language primarily from American movies. There was a hint of Italian but no more than that. Once again, Jerry felt insular and unaccomplished.

Gabriela walked out from the video village and onto the floor. There was a weird stillness about the place, everybody not directly involved holding position while she instructed the cameraman and demonstrated to the bass player how she wanted him to wield his guitar.

'I'll introduce you in a minute,' the assistant assured Jerry.

'No rush,' he said, and boy did he mean it. He glanced back towards the entrance, looking for Millicent, but she hadn't appeared yet.

They ran through several takes, then Gabriela came back across, checking them on the screens until she was happy.

Jerry felt increasingly awkward with every passing moment. Gabriela was in charge of a lot of moving parts, clearly had a packed schedule and he was here to distract her with lies.

She gave the word to begin setting up the next shot. Then she finally turned to acknowledge him.

'You must be Jerry.'

Gabriela extended a hand. He instinctively wiped his palm on his jeans then wished he hadn't. It just looked like he must have had something on his fingers.

'Yeah. Thanks so much for agreeing to talk to me.'

'My pleasure. Have you visited a set before?'

Best not to lie, he figured. He'd only dig himself a hole.

'No, truth be told. I mostly deal with live stuff.'

'I looked you up,' she said. 'I couldn't find any pieces with your name on them.'

Something in Jerry froze, though his rational side told him she'd allowed him to get this far, so it wasn't do-or-die.

'I publish under a lot of pseudonyms. Old habit from doing reviews. Some bands don't take criticism too well.'

'Did you trash Blood Ceremony, then?' she asked, a hint of mischief in her expression.

'Haven't had the pleasure. You guys have never played Scotland, to my knowledge. I'd have gone if you had.'

She smiled.

'Good answer.'

Jerry masked his relief. Weirdly, after months of impostor syndrome at uni, he was finding it easier being an actual impostor. He guessed it was the same energy as ringing those doorbells ahead of breaking into flats.

'This is Umberto,' she said, indicating the older bloke manning the controls. He turned around and shook Jerry's hand. Jerry immediately thought that if he actually made it to his sixties or seventies, he wanted to look old like this guy looked old. Umberto was somehow craggy but smooth, lived-in but youthful.

'He is my indispensable right-hand man. Director of photography, lighting consultant, electrical engineer, assistant editor and asshole wrangler. Also my uncle.'

Jerry looked again towards the door. It felt like introductions were being made, so now would have been a good time for Millicent to announce those credentials before he blew his cover and got chucked out of here.

'Are you a fan of black metal?' Gabriela asked.

'I'm pretty eclectic. I know everybody says that, but I like a bit of all the subgenres.'

'So how would you describe these guys?'

He wondered if, in the absence of providing any articles, this was some kind of test.

'Blackened symphonic progressive death metal,' he replied. 'With a hint of black-gaze and an occasional smattering of power-metal.'

He wasn't quite serious, just showing that he knew where the subgenre battle-lines lay.

She laughed.

'You really know your shit. You're gonna love this. Have a look.'

She muttered something in Italian to Umberto, who then called up some footage on one of the monitors. It showed the orcs, dressed in the same T-shirts, charging through a forest. Then the shot pulled back to reveal that they were converging on a clearing, at the centre of which was a barn.

'We shot this out in some woods near Perugia.'

'Wouldn't be black metal if you weren't out in the woods.'

'I know, right? The reveal is that they're storming the band's rehearsal space and the guys have to fight them off.'

Gabriela excused herself and went back to the floor to discuss something with her cameraman. Meanwhile Umberto called up the previous shot. The old man wore a grin of quiet satisfaction, like someone who has heard the same joke for the hundredth time but still appreciates its craft.

Jerry checked the IMDb on his phone. There was no listing for an Umberto Salerno. He tried Umberto Pieroni instead. Result. He had been DoP on several of Alessandro's pictures, including *Mancipium*.

As he watched Gabriela make her way back, he heard footsteps behind and turned to finally welcome Millicent. It wasn't her, though. Instead he was confronted by a tall figure in spiked leathers and corpse paint, carrying a black Gibson SG.

'Jan,' he introduced himself, in an unexpectedly soft voice. He was Crucifiction's guitarist.

'Jerry.'

'Where's Hulfi?' asked Gabriela, noticing the new arrival. 'Still playing videogames? We're going to need both of you for the set-up after next.'

'Last I saw him, he was in make-up.'

'Check this out,' Jan said, showing Jerry the guitar. He pressed what had appeared to be a volume knob but was actually some kind of trigger. A serrated blade emerged from the headstock, six inches long. It looked fearsome but was actually plastic.

'That's brutal,' Jerry approved.

'Don't play with it too much,' warned Gabriela. 'Building those guitars took half my budget and we don't have the coverage yet. You've still got some orcs to stab with that thing this afternoon.'

Jan performed a pike thrust with the SG.

'Umberto is going to CGI in some blood spray,' he said. 'It's going to be awesome.'

'Yeah,' said Gabriela. 'Wish you could convince Hulfi of that. He keeps complaining that CGI blood looks like a videogame. He would know, I guess.'

She called action on another take, the drummer hammering out blast beats while the bass player swung again with his axe, sending an orc sprawling.

Jerry checked his watch. It had been forty minutes and Millicent still hadn't appeared. Something was wrong. Maybe the security guard had encountered her returning from the toilets and there had been some miscommunication. She would have called him though, surely.

He started to wonder about her suspicions regarding Ardal, and how forthcoming he'd been, what secret agenda he might have. They had told him who they were heading to meet. Had he tipped someone off and she'd been taken?

'So, are you gonna interview us for *Kerrang*?' Jan asked, after Gabriela called cut again.

'I'm guessing you guys must have a tight schedule,' Jerry replied, by way of politely saying no, though he dearly wished it other. 'You're touring as of tomorrow, isn't that right?'

'We can make time today. There's a lot of waiting around. Can I see some of your stuff?'

'I don't have anything on me right now.'

'Just pull something up on your phone, or send me some links. I want to see what you're into, make sure you're not a hatchet man.'

Fuck, he thought. He tried to recall some metal writers' names, but chances were this guy would be familiar with the memorable ones.

Then there was a commotion on the floor. Another figure in corpse paint came charging onto the set, screaming as he ran. Hulfi, Jerry deduced, naked to the waist, his arms and chest also daubed in black and white paint. He was carrying a microphone that had a fearsome blade protracting from the shaft.

All eyes were on him as he drew the steel across his neck, opening a wound from which blood began to run down his chest.

Everyone froze except for Umberto, who got to his feet behind the console. He was the only one not looking at Hulfi.

The singer burst out laughing.

'I am . . . immortal!'

'Has Maria been taking night classes?' Gabriela asked, astonished. 'Who the hell did that?'

It was Umberto who answered, pleasure in his voice.

'She did. That's Millie Spark.'

Gabriela now noticed the woman who had walked in behind the more conspicuous figure of Hulfi.

'It's Millicent these days, Umberto,' she replied.

'She's fucking awesome,' Hulfi told everyone. 'I want wounds. I want to be bleeding during the final chorus.'

The security guard appeared at the entrance, belatedly reacting to the disturbance as Millicent strode towards the video village.

Umberto said something to Gabriela. Jerry caught the words *padre* and *artista*.

Gabriela looked accusingly at Jerry.

'You're not here to talk about black metal and videos, are you?'

He shook his head by way of confession.

'I know you don't like people dredging up the past,' said Millicent. 'But we really need to talk to you about the *Mancipium* shoot. I was there, so I know what's real and what's lies, and we've learned a few things you might want to know.'

Gabriela was looking edgy, defensive. The on-set security guard moved closer, waiting for a nod.

She looked instead to Millicent.

'This would have to be strictly quid pro quo,' she said.

'Absolutely. There will be no secrets. We'll tell you everything we've discovered.'

Gabriela scowled.

'You misunderstand. I want payment in blood.'

Jan looked freaked, even through the corpse paint.

'And wounds,' she added, smiling. 'From the legendary Millie Spark.'

The Fog

Umberto placed a large steaming bowl in the middle of Gabriela's kitchen table. It was a scaled-down *puttanesca*, a simple dish of spaghetti tossed in anchovies, garlic and chilli. Even before she tasted it, the smell took Millicent back to late-night suppers in apartments just like this at the end of a day's shooting. One of those apartments may well have been Umberto's, for all she knew. Back then, she didn't always pay attention: you all jumped in taxis and followed whoever seemed to know where they were going when you spilled out at the other end.

It was close to midnight when they had got to Gabriela's place. She said Millicent and Jerome could sleep there because by that time it was too late to check into a hotel. The shoot had massively overrun, Gabriela re-scripting and re-shooting on the hoof to make the most of Millicent's abilities while they were at her disposal. It was nothing too complex: mostly latex wounds on the band members to make it look like they had truly been in the wars.

Millicent must have worked nine hours straight but she didn't feel tired. It would hit her once she got some food and wine inside her, but for now, she was still riding the feeling. She had forgotten what it was to be useful. To be valued.

The band had been beside themselves. They were snapping pictures on their phones all day, when they weren't patiently sitting for her, having latex and foundation applied over blood reservoirs. She didn't have her old kit box to draw upon, but it turned out that sourcing condoms was not an issue when a rock band's tour bus was parked outside.

She watched Umberto expertly dish out the spaghetti with a pair of tongs. Gabriela had explained her uncle's multiplicity of professional roles. Millicent wondered if it also included minder.

'You never retired, then?' she asked him.

'Yes, I did. Back in 2013. But then I lost my wife a year and a half later.'

'They had been together thirty-eight years,' said Gabriela, with fondness.

'My son had already moved to California by then. He works for Microsoft. Gabriela saved my life. Gave me something to do, otherwise I would have stayed in the house with nothing but wine and memories. Too much of both.'

'He is not allowed to retire now,' said Gabriela, twirling pasta around a fork. 'He is indispensable. Also cheap.'

'And what about you, Millie?' Umberto asked. 'Are you retired?'

'As I told you, I go by Millicent these days.'

'You will always be Millie to me,' he told her, a warmth in his tone that made her tingle in places that hadn't tingled for a very long time.

The feeling didn't last, however. She knew there was no avoiding what had to be said.

'You could say I retired just after *Mancipium* wrapped.'

They both looked surprised and confused. Neither of them knew.

'Why?' asked Umberto. 'Did you get married? You were seeing that guy, weren't you? What was his name?'

'Markus.'

'That was it, yes.'

'No, we did not marry. But you could say our fates remained bound together ever after. That is why Jerome and I are here, and why we need to talk about Alessandro's last film.'

She told them about what had happened to her after *Mancipium*, giving them a moment to let it sink in.

'Last week I discovered that Markus had been an undercover cop. At the time of the *Mancipium* shoot, he was running surveillance on Alfie Bertrand. Do you remember him?'

'Yeah,' said Umberto. 'He was that politician. Kind of a playboy. Living it up away from your paparazzi. Whatever happened to him?'

316

'He is now the Home Secretary.'

'That's the guy in charge of the police,' Jerome clarified, which served to drive home the seriousness of their predicament. Obviously, explaining that there had been two attempts on her life would have done this more effectively, but they had agreed not to mention it.

'Shit.'

'We also know that while Markus and Lucio were supposedly negotiating a rights deal for *Mancipium*, they were actually conspiring on something else. We know you looked into this stuff, Gabriela. Jerome found an interview from a few years ago.'

Gabriela was nodding, but her expression was regretful, apologetic.

'Yes. I remember they headlined it something like "my twenty years looking for answers". The problem is none of that is true. I didn't spend twenty years, and all I found is that there *are* no answers.'

'Maybe it would help us if we even knew what your questions were.'

'They were the wrong questions,' she said. 'That is what it took me a long time to understand.'

Gabriela took a breath and sat up straight, shifting the seat backwards a little.

'I never really got to know my father. He had a romance with an actress half his age, and I was the result. I hardly knew him while he was alive. A few years ago, I got in a bit of a mess, ended up in rehab. When I came out, I became as obsessed as any horror geek with the mythology around this film and around his death. I think I became convinced that if I solved the mystery, I would somehow understand my father, and specifically understand why he killed himself.

'It was like I was searching in the fog, not because the answers lay there, but because the fog looked intriguing, mysterious. But fog is not just insubstantial, it is constantly changing. Every time I debunked some piece of bullshit, another mystery would swirl in to replace it. And there was a little bit of truth behind every myth. An actor did go missing. So did the negative. Somebody who saw a video of the film did die shortly afterwards. But none of it means anything.'

'What do you know about the negative?' Jerome asked.

'I know Lucio didn't take it. I remember my mama talking to Alessandro on the phone. She told me he was upset because someone had broken into his edit suite and stolen the film. But Lucio had a key. If he wanted the negative, he wouldn't have needed to break in.'

'Do you remember much about Lucio?' Millicent asked her, wanting to gauge how reliable the impressions of a ten-year-old might be.

'I remember he was always busy, always doing everything at a hundred miles per hour. I mostly saw him when I got taken to the set.'

'I remember you visiting your father when he was shooting *Lucifer's Charade*,' Millicent told her.

'Yes, but I mostly saw Lucio because of my mama. She was in some of Lucio's movies in the late 1980s, and I think they might have dated for a while. Not for long. I don't think Lucio ever dated anyone for long.'

Millicent worked it out now: Gabriela's mother was the actress Silvia Pieroni. Millicent recalled working with her but she never knew her and Alessandro had been a thing.

'You said an actor really did go missing,' said Jerome. 'But I was under the impression that had been debunked too. I mean, Paulo Nietti is working to this day.'

Gabriela raised her eyebrows, working hard to chew and swallow so that she could answer.

'Who said Paulo Nietti went missing?' she asked.

'I saw it on a YouTube discussion.'

'Yeah, that's what happens in the fog. Someone reads that the film's star went missing, and they know that Paulo Nietti was the biggest name in the movie, so they assume that's who it was. But Paulo Nietti wasn't a big name at the time. If anyone was the star, it was Sergio Kamaras. He played the demon.'

'Sergio,' said Millicent. 'He was tipped for big things at one point, had done some stuff in Hollywood. He went missing?'

'Another person who never worked again after *Mancipium*. I found out that there really was a mystery here. I tried to get in touch because I heard he had a dispute with my father and Lucio close to the end of the shoot. I thought there might be a clue there, but I couldn't track him down. It turned out nobody else ever could either.

'The newspapers had been interested in him because he was good copy. A half-Greek, half-Italian pin-up who was a bit of a bad boy: lots of booze, lots of drugs, lots of women. Rumours of men too.'

'He was an asshole,' said Umberto.

'He wanted more money,' said Millicent. 'That's what the dispute was about.'

'I searched through the newspaper archives,' said Gabriela. 'The photos, the stories, they all stopped after *Mancipium*. The paparazzi and reporters moved on to other targets. Then, years later, someone did a "where are they now" piece on Nineties actors, and that was when they seemed to notice that he had disappeared. It was rumoured that he had been diagnosed as HIV positive and had hidden himself away. There were crappy photos of people who vaguely looked like him, taken in Thailand or Goa or wherever. But the last known photograph of him was this.'

Gabriela got out her phone and called up a photo of a page from an old newspaper. The headline said something about him taking it easy after finishing his latest movie. He was sitting on a sun lounger in his familiar Ray-Bans and an Inter shirt, reading the *Corriere della Sera*.

The image dislodged a fragment of a memory, something to do with making him up for an effects shot, but Millicent couldn't quite bring it to the surface. Maybe it would come back to her.

'Can I have a copy of this?' she asked.

'Sure. I can email it right now.'

'Send it to me,' said Jerome, giving her the details.

'Okay, but you need to understand, it all turned out to be meaningless. I learned that this was taken by a paparazzo in Kos around the time my father was filming the final scenes back in

Sorrento. Whatever became of Sergio, it was nothing to do with my father, with Lucio or with anyone else on the shoot.'

Gabriela leaned forward in her seat, seeming to draw them all towards her. Her voice was lower, as though speaking from somewhere deep inside.

'In all this searching, what I came to realise was that I was looking in the wrong places. I was looking at the mystery associated with my father, rather than just looking at who he was. I thought if I could find out what happened to Lucio, why the negative disappeared, all those things, I might understand why he took his own life. It was only when I started talking to my mama, to Umberto and to other people who really knew my father, that I came to understand he took his own life because he had depression. I don't mean he was sad and low, I mean he had bipolar disorder.'

Millicent thought of Alessandro's work-rate, his furious bursts of creativity. Most people only got to see that side of him, she realised: the manic side. When he hit the other pole, he cloistered himself away.

'I have no doubt that the loss of the negative, along with Lucio going missing, was the trigger for this final episode. But my father was not "suicided" by bad men to cover up their crime.'

'Gabriela has been working with a mental health charity,' said Umberto. 'We both have. Making videos for social media to help raise money.'

'This is why I get angry with people who want to perpetuate the myths and the speculation.'

Millicent had little doubt what she was alluding to.

'Full disclosure. We spoke to Ardal McGill yesterday.'

Gabriela sucked her teeth.

'He asked us to tell you he is deeply sorry for the hurt he caused. He exaggerated a few things in order to try to sell the movie on video. I don't think he had any idea what it would lead to.'

'People like that never think beyond what they want. All lies have a cost. But if he has said he is sorry, I will accept that. We have all done things we are not proud of.'

'I think he has many regrets,' Millicent said. 'Mostly that so many people he once knew are no longer around. That was why we went to see him, really: we were looking for anyone still alive who may have known Markus. Lucio is gone, your father, Stacey Golding too.'

Gabriela and Umberto shared a look.

'What makes you think Stacey is dead?' Umberto asked.

'There is no trace of her online after the late Nineties.'

'Oh, there's more than a trace,' said Gabriela. 'Though I guess it is kind of niche. Stacey is very much alive.'

Millicent gaped, her heart soaring.

'She calls herself Violenta Divine these days.'

Jerome's ears pricked up.

'Violenta Divine? As in Gore Whore?'

'She has had a re-branding, you could say.'

'At the risk of sounding like a high court judge,' said Millicent, 'who or what is Gore Whore?'

'It's a podcast and YouTube channel focusing on exploitation cinema,' Jerome replied.

'She also runs the Crotch Deep Trash film festival,' said Gabriela. 'She still lives in Rome. I have her details right here.'

Unseen

It wasn't only Millicent who started to fade as soon as the food began to settle in her stomach. The day seemed to catch up with everybody at the same time. Umberto announced his intention to head home, while Gabriela asked Jerome to help her fetch some spare sheets and duvets.

Jerome thanked her for offering them a berth for the night. Millicent was once again impressed by his politeness. She wished she could have met this grandmother of his and passed on her compliments at what a good job she had done in raising him.

Gabriela told them it was nothing.

'It wouldn't be Saturday night if there wasn't some guy in a metal T-shirt who I only just met crashing on my sofa.'

As Jerome followed Gabriela out of the kitchen, Umberto lifted his jacket from the back of his chair. He glanced at Millicent, his expression unreadable but intent.

'Millie, can I have a word with you in private?'

'Certainly.'

Umberto beckoned her into the hall, conscious that Gabriela would return to the kitchen. He made his way to the front door and stopped there, where they were out of earshot and out of sight.

He addressed her in Italian, which added to her feeling oddly excited. She found him desirable, and it was an unsettling surprise to learn that she was still capable of harbouring such desires.

'There is something I need to tell you, away from Gabriela's ears.'

He glanced back down the hall, double-checking there was no one nearby. Millicent could hear Gabriela's voice in the living room, instructing Jerome in converting her sofa to a bed.

'Gabriela only knew Lucio as a little girl. She thought he was cool, exciting, you know? That is what a little girl sees. We both know he was . . . more complicated, and there is nothing to be gained by her learning this. But it is important that you know something. It is to do with Lucio and my sister Silvia, Gabriela's mother.'

Millicent felt her eyes bulge in response.

'No, no, it's nothing like that. Gabriela is most definitely Alessandro's daughter. Lucio and Silvia were much later, and they never slept together. That's what I need to talk to you about.'

A part of her was disappointed that Umberto merely wanted to tell her something, though there was an intimacy about his sharing a confidence which she was enjoying nonetheless.

'Go on.'

'They started dating when we were shooting *The Silken Trap*, one of those *Jagged Edge, Basic Instinct* knock-offs Lucio rattled out. It seemed to be going well, then Silvia suddenly broke it off. Lucio never knew why: he was convinced someone else was involved. He was right, but not in the way he assumed. Do you remember Bruno Canevari?'

'I recall the name, but it's been so long.'

'He was an electrician. He worked on Lucio's movies going all the way back from the porno days. I was drinking with him one night, sharing war stories about all the crazy shit Lucio had got us involved with.'

He dropped his voice even lower.

'Bruno told me that he had done some work for Lucio on his boat, installing a video camera behind a two-way mirror in his closet. It was so that Lucio could film himself having sex.'

Millicent closed her eyes for a moment. This was both horrifying and yet not entirely surprising.

'It was motion activated, so that Lucio could prep it in advance and the girls would never suspect.'

'Jesus,' she sighed. 'Lucio was always a sleaze, but I thought at least he was up-front about it.'

'As I understand it, he never shared these tapes. They were for his own gratification. But I could not let my sister go to that boat. I had to tell her.'

Millicent understood that part well enough, but it begged a bigger question.

'Why are you telling me?'

'I never knew about what happened to you until tonight. Now that you tell me Markus was an undercover cop, certain things start to make a new kind of sense.

'Remember how Credit Populaire pulled the plug and then suddenly Poupard managed to raise some funds after all? For years I wondered if Lucio had blackmailed him. Lucio supplied Poupard with women, at parties right there on the boat.'

Millicent saw the stark truth of it, this strange and unexplained behaviour now clear as day.

'They used to be so friendly,' she said. 'But then when Poupard helped finance *Mancipium*, there was always a tension. I thought it was because he was nervous over his investment.'

'When Lucio disappeared, I always assumed it was to do with Florio, a man with connections at the lowest depths of the Italian underworld. But what if he was blackmailing a man with connections at the highest levels of the British establishment?'

PART FIVE

Casting

There was an early morning chill in the breeze as Millicent and Jerome emerged onto the flagstones of the platform at the top of the tower. Such a bite in the air felt worth it for the clear skies it accompanied, a view of all Rome laid out before them.

She had never been here. She must have walked or been driven past it a hundred times, and it hadn't occurred to her to venture inside. That was how it went when you lived or merely worked in a city: you never did the touristy stuff. They were not tourists today, though.

Gabriela had woken them with the sound and smell of her espresso pot, explaining her early start with news of where they would find Stacey.

'I messaged her. She is going to be filming the intro for her new video at the Castel Sant'Angelo this morning before it gets too busy with tourists. If you want to talk to her, you need to get going.'

'She's happy to meet?' Millicent asked.

Gabriela looked coy.

'I wasn't sure what terms you guys were on. She thinks it's me who will be there.'

'Well played. And thank you.'

Jerome had briefly shown Millicent some videos over breakfast. Stacey's Gore Whore persona, under the name Violenta Divine, was a monstrous creation, and for that, kind of fabulous. She presented her discussions of exploitation cinema in costume appropriate to each subgenre, but definitely not appropriate in any other respect for a woman of her years. Sometimes she was got up as a witch or a vampire, though in each case, she looked like a witch or a vampire who supplemented her income as a hooker. She was obviously of the belief that there was nothing time had wrought upon those beloved breasts of hers for which modern underwiring could not compensate.

Gabriela told them Stacey was planning to film from the very top of the castle. They had bought their tickets and made the most direct ascent, ignoring all of the vaults and galleries. However, as they stepped out into daylight again and took in the view, the only figures interrupting it were a small group of Korean teenagers and a nun. They had got here too early, or perhaps Stacey had been chased out already.

A sudden gust caused the nun's habit to ripple, revealing a split that went all the way to the thigh, upon which Millicent caught a flash of suspender belt.

As she drew closer, she could see that there was a phone cradled in a miniature tripod resting on the nearby wall.

'Good morning, gore whores,' the nun addressed her camera. Millicent estimated that St Peter's Basilica would be framed in shot at her back.

'Today's selection is all about the nuns: nuns with bad habits. Killer nuns, Satanic nuns, vampire nuns, nympho nuns and nuns with guns. So don't forget to subscribe, and tell me in the comments: what can I get for you next, gore whores?'

She paused as though expecting an answer. Millicent gave her one.

'Nun of the above.'

Stacey turned around with a look of confused irritation, wondering who had the audacity to interrupt before being utterly thrown by the answer.

'Millie?' she asked, astonished.

'Hello, Stacey. Gabriela said you'd be here,' she added, letting her know this wasn't mere happenstance.

'So you served your time,' Stacey replied. 'Murder, wasn't it? Yeah, I read all about it. Never would have thought you had it in you. Then I remembered that night you cleaned your boyfriend's clock.'

328

She stopped the camera recording and pulled back her wimple, revealing peroxide locks that hadn't changed a Pantone in decades.

'Here you are, all these years later, back in Rome. Hitting up Alessandro's daughter. Tracking me down. What, are you looking up the old gang? Aw, shit, you don't got cancer, do you?'

'Ah, Stacey, sentimental as ever. How come I went to prison and you never did?'

'I didn't kill anybody.'

'I didn't either.'

Stacey seemed to weigh this for a moment, though she didn't reveal her judgment.

'Bullshit aside, it's good to see you, Millie. I'm glad you're still alive.'

'You too,' she said, and meant it.

'Who's your buddy? Family?'

'This is Jerome, my housemate.'

'Jerry,' he insisted. 'Big fan. Loved your special on cannibal movies last year.'

Stacey liked that.

'Dig your accent, kid. Hey, girl, long as you're here, you must come on the show. An exclusive interview with make-up effects legend Millie Spark.'

'If I can stay alive long enough, I'd be happy to.'

'What you talking about? You must be younger than me, and I'm not planning to drop dead any time soon.'

'You don't have anyone trying to kill you though, do you?'

There was a beat, long enough for Millicent to confirm that Stacey knew she was serious.

'What? Come on. Who the hell would want to kill you?'

She tried to smile as though dismissing it as ridiculous, but it was too late for that. Millicent could see it in her face that Stacey had answered her own question.

'There was something going on while we were making *Mancipium*. Something involving Lucio and Markus. I need to know what it was.'

Stacey gazed away across the city, then back at Millicent.

'You know all that *Mancipium* curse stuff is bullshit, right?'

She glanced at Jerome as though he might be the one filling her head with it.

'I've spoken to Gabriela, and I've spoken to Ardal. I know what's true and what isn't. But just because the curse stuff is nonsense doesn't mean there wasn't something shady going on.'

Stacey winced, a look of regret upon her face.

'I wish I could help, but I honestly don't know anything that Gabriela won't already have told you. She did a lot of digging, and—'

Millicent held up a hand to cut her off.

'I've seen your IMDb profile, Stacey. You didn't work for a couple of years after *Mancipium*. Was that because you needed a rest, or because you were lying low after Lucio disappeared?'

'It was because I couldn't get a fucking gig after Lucio disappeared,' she retorted. 'It's hard not to keep a low profile when nobody will hire you. I was back tending bar in a strip joint off Via Lombardia, and I would have been working the pole again if I was a few years younger. Then I got a job helping manage a little arthouse cinema. That would still have been my only income if it wasn't for YouTube and Patreon. Three hundred thousand subscribers, baby.'

'Markus was an undercover cop. Did you know that?'

That brought her back from her self-pity trip, though she didn't look as surprised as everybody else had.

'I didn't know that, no. Though there were times when I did think I smelled pork off of him. Problem was, there had been a period in my life when I thought every new person I met was an undercover cop. Once you've had so many false positives, you start to lose faith in your instincts. How sure are you?'

'Sure as we're standing here. I even know his real name. Des Creasey.'

'Doesn't ring a bell. How did you find out?'

'Dumb luck. Though now I've poked the nest, some people have become very agitated. But I suppose if you know nothing about what Lucio was up to, then you won't have to worry about them coming after you too.'

Millicent could see that her blow had landed.

'Why would I know what Lucio was up to?'

'That sounds like a rhetorical question, Stacey. You worked with him longer than anybody, before and after you were lovers. He trusted you.'

As Millicent said this, she saw something that had been right in front of her back then, so close up that she never recognised it for what it was.

'All those girls at the parties. I once asked you where Lucio found them. But he didn't find them, did he? You found them for him.'

Stacey met her eyes, making no attempt to deny it.

She pulled out a vape and took a pull, billowing smoke out into the sky.

'Fuckin' thing. I miss real cigarettes. I look like a fuckin' dragon.'

She took another pull, exhaled, then folded her arms.

'I had what you could call a kind of a casting operation,' she said. 'I still had plenty of contacts in strip joints and the porn scene. It's true, I found those girls. A lot of them got a break because of me. Some of them are still on fuckin' TV now because of me. But yeah, I prepared them, appraised them of a few realities.'

'I think the fashionable term now is "grooming".'

'Hey, Milquetoast, don't get all judgy if you want me to help you.'

'Did you know Lucio blackmailed Poupard?'

She took another drag.

'He never told me directly, but I worked it out. Wasn't hard: one day he's pulling the plug, next day he's putting his balls on the line for Lucio. I wonder if the French have a word for *volte face*.'

'And what about Alfie Bertrand?'

At that, there was a flash of fear in Stacey's eyes that she couldn't conceal. They both knew she wasn't a great actress.

She bit her lip, then answered. 'Lucio wanted a girl who was underage. There were plenty of them. They were lining up. You've no idea how I protected them, held them back, at least until they were older. Damaged little girls who would have done anything for a glimpse of a better life, or even just a break from what they had known.

'Lucio wanted a girl who would easily pass for eighteen, nineteen when she was all dolled up . . .'

Stacey hung her head. Her cheeks were flushed. For the first time, Millicent saw in her face something resembling shame.

'It was all about how young and innocent she was going to look on camera, naked, wasn't it?' Millicent asked.

Stacey swallowed. She glanced towards Jerome, clearly self-conscious about what she had to say. He was standing closest to the wall, looking out at the city, but she knew he was listening.

'In terms of a casting job, I excelled myself. Take off the make-up, take off the *clothes*, and this girl looked barely pubescent. She was post-pubescent, by the way. I'm not a fucking monster. She was fifteen, and she wasn't a virgin. None of them ever were.

'I thought Lucio was setting up Florio to get him off his back: get him sent down on a paedophilia beef. And then on the night of, I saw her on the arm of Alfie Bertrand. I thought it must have been a special request. The guy was offering to open a lot of doors back in the UK, so Lucio was meeting his desires. But in truth they must have been setting him up for blackmail, because everything went to shit soon after.'

'Lucio going missing, you mean?'

'That wasn't all. You guys spoke to Ardal, right? Did he tell you about Ricardo Rossini, the home video distributor?'

'Ardal told us he started the curse story as a joke after Rossini died, because nobody was getting back to him.'

'Well, here's what Ardal doesn't know. I was at the funeral. I knew Ricardo, through Lucio. They went way back. I spoke to his widow. Turned out he fell in front of a train. It was ruled an accident, but she was worried he had offed himself. She said he had been acting weird and paranoid after Lucio went missing. He told her Lucio had sent him a tape, said he wished he hadn't seen it.

'I'm sure I'm not the only one she said that to, so that shit probably fed into the myth about how scary the film was. I suspect the truth is that what really scared Ricardo was that Lucio had drawn him into some deep, dark shit.'

'Why did Lucio send him it?'

'It could have been an accident. He sent out screeners of the rough cut. I figure a copy of the blackmail tape wound up in the wrong sleeve and Ricardo saw something he knew he shouldn't have. The point is, I got scared after Lucio disappeared, because I knew he had fucked with the wrong people. Alfie Bertrand was in the British government. Those guys don't mess around.'

'Did you find out about Markus around that time too?'

She nodded, a note of apology in her expression.

'You know me, I read all the scandal sheets, Millie. I remembered you getting pissed at him and taking a swing that night on the boat. Wouldn't be the first time a broad got drunk and stabbed her asshole boyfriend. But let's just say an alternative explanation remained prominent in my thoughts. Lucio sets up Bertrand, then Lucio disappears and the one other British guy on the scene winds up dead?'

'*It might have been helpful if you had told the British police some of this,*' Millicent didn't say. '*Then perhaps they might have given less credence to the notion that someone with absolutely no record of criminal behaviour suddenly took it upon herself to murder her sleeping boyfriend,*' she didn't add.

She knew that back then the police would have dismissed Stacey's story as quickly as they had dismissed her own, but that was not what stayed her tongue. Something had changed. She had reined in her instinct to lash out. In the past, she had wanted to cause hurt because she was hurting. Now, the idea of hurting Stacey made her recoil. Did this mean she was hurting less? Did this mean she was getting better?

'I won't bullshit you. I was scared. I didn't know what was and wasn't connected. But time marched on, and eventually the dust settled. I'd like to say that I put it behind me, but when you get away with something . . .'

She took another puff, the vapour streaming between her botoxed lips.

'Truth is, you never really get away with anything. You're always living with the consequences. I lost Lucio. He was a friend. Maybe my oldest friend. Lost Alessandro too. Lost everybody, really, including you: that whole scene. But even though I paid a price, that don't mean there was an end to my sentence. All down the years, the fear never quite went away, that one day they were gonna come for me.'

She looked Millicent in the eyes, her own becoming bloodshot. 'How scared should I be?'

'Very,' said Jerome. 'They're coming for us right now.'

The Whip Hand

Jerry was looking down into the courtyard when he saw him, dressed in the same bespoke suit as before. He looked dapper and refined, not a grey hair out of place. The guy had been looking at his phone, then happened to glance up towards the viewing platform. Jerome ducked back, too late. There had been eye contact.

'It's the guy from Paris,' Jerry told Millicent.

'The one I threw in the river?'

'No, the one from the museum.'

They both looked down, but neither could see him, which felt worse.

'Fuck, where did he go? We need to get out of here.'

'How did he know we were in Rome?' Millicent asked.

Jerry was about to say he had no idea when the answer slapped him in the face.

'I think you being all over Crucifiction's Instagram and Twitter feeds might have had something to do with it.'

Millicent turned to Stacey.

'You mustn't be seen with us.'

'Don't worry. I don't only do ostentatious.'

Stacey pulled her wimple back down over her head and in a second she was effectively invisible. Nobody was going to look twice at a nun in her seventies, especially in Rome. Jerry wished they could disappear as effectively.

'He was in the western courtyard,' Millicent said. 'We need to exit via the east side.'

Jerry remembered how they had fled from this man before. He had not run in pursuit, but nor had he needed to.

'I'm just concerned that if we head for the main exit, we're gaunny run straight intae him. Or whoever else he has waiting for us. That guy you lobbed in the Seine isnae gaunny hold a grudge, is he?'

'Well, unless you know some other way out of here, I don't see what choice we have.'

As they descended the stairs and emerged into a curving stone-walled corridor, it struck Jerry that this place was weirdly familiar, even though they had come up through the other side.

'I do know another way out of here,' he realised. 'There's a passage that leads straight into the Vatican. The Passetto di Borgo. It's this way. Follow me.'

Millicent looked like she would take some convincing.

'You said you'd never been to Rome before.'

'No, but I've been in this building a hundred times. *Assassins Creed: Brotherhood.*'

She looked blank.

'It's a videogame set in Rome during the Renaissance. I played it a lot when I was twelve.'

'Lead on,' she said, gesturing him to proceed. 'Though I do wish you hadn't used the word assassin.'

He led her through a roped-off passage, then down a staircase and along another curving corridor. He was replicating a route he had taken dozens of times while fleeing and battling sword-wielding guards. There were none of those, nor any tourists and fortunately no staff either.

'It's just up here,' he announced.

They crested a sloping path and there it was dead ahead, behind a metal gate. Jerry ran towards it and gave it a pull.

It was locked.

'I'm guessing that electronic keypad was put there after the Renaissance,' Millicent said. 'Do you know any other routes?'

'Routes, aye. But any way you slice it, we're still goin' oot the same door.'

They retreated down the sloping path, stopping where he could look over a parapet. It was getting busier down below, dozens of tourists encircling the base of the tower.

'If we can get doon there, we're golden. There's got to be a hundred witnesses.'

'As opposed to the passages closed off to the public that you've taken us along so far?'

'I'm assuming sarcasm is a coping mechanism,' he told her, 'and so under the circumstances I'm tolerating it, but I'd say you've got about three passes left.'

'There's no way I'm only three up at this stage.'

Millicent had made a good point, though. Jerry led her as directly as possible back to the busiest route, taking the wide spiral ramp down through the tower.

He could see sunlight streaming in as they rounded the curve, the courtyard picked out more vividly beyond the comparative gloom of the spiral. There were plenty of tourists milling around out there, and no sign of any assassins, grey-haired or otherwise, though that wasn't necessarily a good thing. Knowing where their enemy *wasn't* offered little reassurance.

They proceeded around the base of the tower towards the exit, stealing glances left and right, trying not to be conspicuous in their haste. Then they passed through the archway and were out again, unavoidably picking up pace as they crossed the cobblestones and made for the footbridge over the Tiber.

They were a third of the way across it when Jerry heard a voice.

'Millicent. Jerry. We need to talk. I'm not the enemy.'

Reflex overcame caution and they both turned around. The grey-haired man was standing only a few yards behind them. His right hand was thrust rather awkwardly into his pocket. It could be his phone, but Jerry wondered why he would be concealing it from passers-by.

'You're sure as hell not our friend,' Millicent replied.

She turned again.

'Keep walking,' she told Jerry. 'He's not going to shoot us in front of all these tourists.'

'You're probably right. Though it's a bigger ask to chuck this one intae the river.'

They both resumed their progress, getting another few yards before he spoke again.

'Don't you want to know what this is all about?'

Millicent stopped and faced him once more. He had both his hands out in plain sight, a gesture of non-threat.

He stepped closer to the wall, out of the flow of pedestrians. Jerry and Millicent followed suit. There was a weird form of intimacy about it, a conclave in broad daylight, surrounded by dozens of oblivious passers-by.

'Okay, talk,' she said. 'Starting with who you are.'

'My name is not important.'

'So you won't mind if I call you Slartibartfast then, as a place-holder?'

'All right, for what it's worth, my name is Daniels. Hugo Daniels.'

Jerry reckoned it was worth fuck-all. That could easily be a place-holder too.

'Who are you working for?'

'That I am not at liberty to disclose.'

'Then what is there to talk about?' Millicent replied.

'It's who I used to work for that's important.'

'You were polis, weren't you?' Jerry suggested. 'Or more likely a spook.'

He gave a cold smile.

'One of the above, yes. There are certain individuals, late of my profession, engaged in a belated attempt to clean up after themselves. You could say that I am engaged in a clean-up operation of my own.'

His volume was perfectly measured, just audible enough, and his accent was posh-English. The type who seldom raised their voices because they were used to being listened to.

'Tell me about Markus.'

'Of course, yes. That is indeed the heart of the matter. But first we have to talk about Jean-Marc Poupard, whose reception you attended two nights ago.'

'As did you,' Jerry said, wanting the guy to know he had been clocked, though visibility had no doubt been his intention.

Daniels ignored this.

'Back in 1993, French intelligence shared with us the information that Lucio Sabatini had extorted financial backing from Credit Populaire via blackmail. He made a covert video recording of Poupard having sex with a young woman, an actress who had a minor part in one of Mr Sabatini's productions.'

'We had worked out that much for ourselves,' Millicent said. 'I'm guessing that was why Jean-Marc wasn't exactly delighted to meet up with somebody from the good old days. Is he who you work for now?'

'That, I told you, I am not at liberty to disclose. But what I can say, and what you don't know, is that when Sabatini made known his threat, Poupard immediately came clean to his bosses. He was a largely honourable man who briefly had his head turned by the glamour of the movies. In the light of what had recently happened with Credit Lyonnais, his employers were keen to avoid any scandal tainting their name, so they allowed Poupard to comply with Lucio's wishes by funding a single project.

'British intelligence was made aware of this because it had been noted that a junior minster, Alfie Bertrand, was beginning to move in the same circles. It was suspected he might be partaking of similar hospitality, and thus highly vulnerable. Des Creasey was despatched to operate undercover, to infiltrate Lucio's inner circle.'

'That part isn't news either,' Millicent said. 'I was his way in. He used me.'

'Indeed. And that is merely one of the matters that these individuals are keen should not come to light. There have recently emerged a number of scandals involving officers entering into relationships with innocent women unaware of their true identities, but it was claimed that these actions were as unprecedented as they were unconscionable. It would therefore be politically damaging to admit that a woman was being similarly used and deceived twenty years earlier. But this is the least of their concerns.'

'I don't follow,' Millicent said. 'You're saying Markus was pretending to conspire with Lucio but actually attempting to thwart him? Is that why he was killed? Are you saying Lucio killed Markus?'

Dapper Daniels was looking unaccustomedly awkward. Almost apologetic.

'Somebody high up decided it would be more valuable to let these events play out. That it would be advantageous to have leverage over a junior minister who was tipped for great things.'

He paused a moment, letting the implications sink in.

'Creasey . . . Markus's objective was updated accordingly. He was to come to an arrangement with Sabatini to obtain and control the blackmail material. Now, clearly events spiralled out of control at this time, and it was believed that the blackmail material was destroyed. The plot failed and all evidence of it was swiftly buried by those who hatched it.'

'And was my going to prison part of the burial process?'

'I can't say for sure. It was an episode all but forgotten, and certainly not a memory its perpetrators cared to dwell upon. Then last week you started asking questions and reminded everybody of your existence.'

'Inconsiderate old bat that I am.'

'Your discovery of Creasey's real identity raised the possibility that these men's historic misconduct might be revealed: a plot from inside the security services to blackmail a government minister with a view to making him their puppet thereafter. On top of that, they also conspired to allow the statutory rape of a minor. The shockwaves would be seismic.'

'The fact that the dude they sought to blackmail is now extremely well-placed to exact retribution will not have slipped their minds either,' Jerry suggested.

'Indeed. Which is why they are going to extreme lengths to protect themselves.'

'You mean trying to murder me,' said Millicent.

'Primarily they are interested in the possibility that a tape still exists, as this would grant them, at this precarious moment, the very leverage they sought back then. If they find the tape, it will be the Home Secretary who ought to fear them, not the other way around.'

Millicent stared at him thoughtfully. She had barely taken her eyes off him in fact, while Jerry continued scanning the bridge for his accomplices.

'All of which brings us back to the question I asked you right at the start, Mr Daniels: who do you work for?'

He paused.

'Let's just say I'm an interested party.'

'Clerks, Kevin Smith, 1994,' muttered Jerry.

'I beg your pardon?'

'It's Bertrand, isn't it,' Millicent stated. 'You work for Alfie Bertrand.'

'That is something I can neither confirm nor deny,' he replied. Which was as close to confirming as they were going to get.

'Who I work for is less important than what I want. I am interested in recovering the blackmail material, if indeed it still exists, in order to keep it out of certain hands. Because no matter what you might think of Mr Bertrand or his conduct back then, there is something very dangerous about unseen, unaccountable individuals having that kind of leverage – shall we call it *kompromat* – over senior politicians. Alfie Bertrand is tipped to be a future prime minister. I used to be in the business myself, which is why I know how frightening a prospect it is to have the intelligence services holding the whip hand over men at the highest levels of government.'

'So what do you want us to do?' Millicent asked.

'Come with me. I can protect you.'

He gestured west, towards the Vatican.

'I have a car parked two minutes away. We can help each other.'

Just then, a large group of tourists filed past, heading away from the castle. They were three or four deep, being led by a woman holding up a yellow umbrella. Millicent grabbed Jerry's shoulder and they stepped into the stream. They crossed the bridge under cover of the throng, then broke away and headed south into the labyrinth.

Cover-up

'Not an entirely tempting offer, was it?' Millicent asked. They were proceeding briskly along a narrow *via*, too tight for any cars to traverse. Consequently, she found herself walking down the centre of it, mindful of what might emerge from any doorway. She wondered if she would feel safer when they reached a busy main square, such as Piazza Navona, but she was aware that disappearing in a crowd could work both ways.

'I'd have found it more enticing if he said he had puppies to show me and there was a bottle of lube sticking oot his pocket,' Jerome replied. 'There was a massive elephant he was routing around. "*Events spiralled out of control*." Aye, the two people who conspired over the blackmail plot got murdered.'

'*Cui bono*,' Millicent said. 'Who benefits?'

'Alfie fucking Bertrand, that's who benefits. Daniels is his enforcer. He's the one who did Lucio and Markus. I think he's the one who took the negative as well, as a bargaining chip. Probably offed Rossini too. He was killed because he had seen the tape. Pushed under a train by the same fucker we've just been shooting the breeze with on the Ponte Sant'Angelo.'

Millicent wasn't so convinced by this aspect.

'How would he know Rossini had seen it? And how likely is it that an Italian home video distributor would recognise a British junior cabinet minister?'

'Likely enough that he and Bertrand weren't taking any chances. And nor should we. We see him, we run.'

They proceeded past a gelateria, where a family was sitting outside in the weak morning sunshine. A part of Millicent wished for their obliviousness, their biggest worry being how they would get the chocolate ice-cream stain out of their little girl's white dress. But she had endured half a lifetime's obliviousness. She felt sharply alive, and though much of that was fear, within it there was also a sense of awakening.

There was something just out of reach, just out of focus, that she sensed was tantalisingly close.

'Let's not give too much credence to what Daniels said either,' she cautioned. 'Most of what he told us, we already knew, or he might have assumed we already knew. If someone flat-out tells you their agenda, they're definitely not telling you their agenda.'

She was vaguely aware of an electronic chime nearby. Jerome's phone, most likely.

She turned to look at him and found him gazing back expectantly.

'What?' she asked.

'Sounded like a text,' he said.

'Yes, and?'

'From your phone.'

'Oh.'

She took out the handset from her bag. It was from Ardal. She showed Jerome the screen.

FYI - my apartment got turned over last night. Nothing taken but they hauled out all my old VHS videos. After your visit, I'm reckoning it wasn't a coincidence.

'Daniels wasn't lying about that part,' she said. 'They're looking for a tape.'

'And they're following us,' Jerry deduced. 'We need to warn Gabriela. They could be hitting her place next, and we know they don't play nice if they break in and you're still home.'

Jerome made the call.

'She's phoning Umberto and some metal roadies to come round in case she's next,' he reported.

343

Millicent felt relief that Gabriela had people she could call upon, but it didn't quite assuage her guilt that she was bringing danger and destruction to innocent people.

'Why would they think I have anything to do with this?' she asked in frustration. 'I didn't know who Markus really was, and they know that, so why would I know where this blasted videotape might be?'

Jerome wore an uncomfortable expression, as though what he was about to say was delicate.

'Didn't you say Markus came to see you in London? A surprise visit. When was that?'

She saw it now.

'It was the day he died. He turned up full of apologies, and we went out drinking. But you're saying . . .'

'What if he knew the heat was on and he was really there to stash a copy of the tape.'

Millicent felt her cheeks redden at the ache of another cherished memory turning out to be counterfeit. It was weird: she already knew everything about Markus was a lie, and yet it still hurt to have individual moments taken away.

However, there was still a problem with Jerome's theory.

'If he had stashed it in my flat, the police would have found it. They took a load of my tapes when I was arrested. I always assumed it was to tie the whole thing into the video nasty narrative, but now I can see that they were looking for something specific. They obviously never found it.'

'But didn't you say they took away the DPP banned titles and your copy of the *Mancipium* rough cut? What if Markus hid the tape inside the sleeve of something innocuous? A copy of *Pretty Woman* or something?'

'I had a whole shelf of French movies: *Jean de Florette*, *Manon des Sources*, *Delicatessen*, *Cyrano de Bergerac*. The police never touched those. Alastair told me he cleared them from my flat himself.'

'So they would still be in that big box of films back in the house?'

She felt elated. This had to be it: the thing that was just out of reach.

'Yes,' she said. 'They never found it back in '94, but they gave up the search because the whole affair had to be buried. Now it's worth finding because it's a game-changer. They want the tape so they can blackmail Alfie Bertrand. He in turn wants the tape so he can disappear it. But if we make the tape public, the house of cards collapses.'

'Lucky you never took that box to the dump after all,' Jerome said.

'Luckier still that you took it into your room, where they wouldn't have looked.'

Jerome stopped in his tracks.

'I never took it anywhere. I didnae touch it. I assumed you changed your mind and moved it back into . . . Fuck. It wasn't in your room, was it?'

It was so obvious now.

'*They* took it. That night, while I was out not meeting Rook.'

Millicent felt like a trap door had opened beneath her. She had to move towards the wall so that she had something to lean on.

'They didnae find it, though,' Jerome pointed out. 'Otherwise they wouldnae still be looking. They're following us, hoping you lead them to it.'

'The problem is that I can't lead them to anything. They're looking for something that doesn't exist, and as soon as they have satisfied themselves of that . . .'

She didn't finish the sentence; didn't need to.

'I need a seat and a drink,' she told him. 'A coffee anyway.'

There was a place just a few doors along. The waiter gestured them to a table outside, indicating the sunshine, but they continued indoors out of sight.

Millicent sipped her coffee and tried to gather herself. The taste and the smell of it were instantly revivifying, reconnecting her with who she had once been, here in this very city. She couldn't be the woman she was before prison, but nor did she have to remain the one it turned her into. Her years of drinking shitty instant coffee in cells and soulless canteens were behind her, and now she was drinking Italian espresso in Rome once again.

It also struck her that she now knew with absolute certainty that she was innocent. She had always been carrying around the possibility that she had killed Markus in a drug-fuelled haze and blocked out the memory. But what Daniels told her confirmed that she had been a scapegoat all along.

Jerome was sipping a hot chocolate like he had done in Paris. He had asked for marshmallows when the waiter offered. It was at such times that she could see the boy in him, revealing just how young he actually was. He was bright, though: informed, inquisitive, articulate and highly capable. He deserved to go far, and not to be shackled by self-doubt.

She had known so many successful mediocrities, untroubled by the impostor syndrome that made it so hard for a kid like Jerry to picture himself as belonging at the top. People who had gone so much further than their talents ought to have taken them, artificially buoyed by public-school confidence, an adamant sense of entitlement and plain old nepotism. Christ, she just had to look at the cabinet, where the mediocrity-in-chief reigned over a kind of reverse meritocracy.

Such thoughts brought her back to the issue of the Home Secretary. She wouldn't have described the Alfie she knew as a mediocrity. He was vain and privileged, spoiled even, and had been a playboy, but he had never struck her as scheming or callous or ruthless, which was saying something for a Tory. She was beset by the feeling that something didn't add up, and by the returning sense that the reason was just beyond her grasp, the true picture just out of focus.

She cast her thoughts back a few minutes, before she had convinced herself that finding the videotape would be her salvation. Jerome had been talking about how Alfie benefited from the death of Markus and the disappearance of Lucio.

Suddenly she saw that there was a whole piece of the puzzle they hadn't yet accounted for.

'We're forgetting something,' she said. 'Lucio wasn't the only

346

one who went missing. Sergio disappeared too. Where does he fit into this?'

'He doesnae,' Jerome replied. 'It was the myth bullshit, retrospectively linking him to the curse of *Mancipium*. He disappeared later. He was relaxing on holiday while all this was goin' doon.'

This was it. Something had troubled her about the picture Gabriela showed her, but she hadn't been able to work out what.

'Show me the clipping again, the one Gabriela emailed.'

He opened the file on his laptop so that she could see it on a large screen. Millicent pored over it longer than she had done at Gabriela's apartment, but there was nothing new in the image. All she saw was Sergio relaxing on a sun lounger, reading a newspaper, wearing shades and his familiar Inter jersey. If she could have seen the view from the back, she knew his name would be printed across the shoulders.

Jerome scooped up a marshmallow with his spoon and popped it into his mouth.

'Anything?' he asked hopefully.

'No,' she admitted.

Maybe it had just been the jolt of seeing Sergio's face after so long, and of learning that he was gone; that he was someone else from her old life whom she would never meet again. She thought of the hours she'd spent with him in her studio, putting demonic make-up on his face, affixing blood tubes and latex wounds to his sculpted, flawless body.

That was when she saw it.

Flawless.

Millicent pointed to Sergio's arm, where a curved black line poked out beneath the sleeve of his football shirt.

'What is it?' asked Jerome.

'A tattoo of a salamander. That thing was the bane of my existence. I had to cover it up so many times.'

'Why?'

'Because we used a body double for a lot of shots. He couldn't have a tattoo in one shot and not in the next.'

Jerome looked apologetic.

'I don't get the significance.'

Millicent smiled.

'It wasn't Sergio who had the tattoo.'

Archaeology

The late autumn sunshine felt warm on Millicent's shoulders, discernibly more so than in Rome though they had driven less than three hours south. She took a moment to appreciate it, another sensation she had believed lost. True, there had been a few pleasant days in Glasgow since her release, and she had been outdoors in the summer over the years, but it never felt like this. There was something about the Mediterranean sun, the quality of the light, the scent of the air that was both exotic and familiar: at once a sense of being somewhere far, and a sense of coming home.

The last time she had seen Dante Agielli was, coincidentally, right here at Pompeii, during those final days on the schedule after Sergio had left the picture. They had come here to film some amphitheatre scenes, as the seating terraces were better preserved than the Colosseum, which they were never getting permission to film in anyway.

Dante had been a spear carrier in the movie, dying three times as different minor characters. More significantly, he had also doubled for Sergio in several set-ups. Millicent had spent hours repeatedly covering his tattoo, which in accordance with Murphy's Law, had to be on his sword arm. He and Sergio didn't look super-alike, but with the same hair and the right make-up – or with a pair of Ray-Bans and the right football jersey . . .

They had found him very quickly on social media. There was no question but that it was the same guy despite how much his appearance had changed: the tattoo was an instant identifier.

Despite his public profile stating where Dante worked, Millicent had called Umberto anyway, for whatever assistance he might offer.

Or maybe just so that she had an excuse to hear his voice. He had been keen to help.

Jerome had teased her about how Umberto had taken her aside the night before, so that he could speak to her alone.

'I am post sex,' she had reiterated, by way of prefacing the more important matter of what Umberto had to say.

The queues were short as it was already late in the day. After purchasing their tickets, they proceeded to the education office, where someone told them where they were likely to find Dante, pointing it out on the map.

Jerome's expression was a picture a few minutes later when they crested the hill and he calculated the relative distance between how far they had already walked and where they were headed.

'Yes, that was my reaction the first time I came here,' she told him. 'Nothing really prepares you for the scale.'

As Jerome looked at the expanse spread out before them, Millicent's gaze was drawn to the volcano in the distance. She couldn't help thinking about how so much could be destroyed and eradicated so quickly and without warning. And yet, here they were, treading the same flagstones as Roman citizens once trod. What was long thought lost could yet be recovered. And things long buried could yet be revealed.

She was hauled back from her reverie by her phone. Once again Jerome had to prompt her to answer it because she failed to recognise the significance of the sound, unused to having such a device. And once again she felt fear at who might be calling her, before seeing that it was Vivian.

She remembered with a start that it had been two days since she last checked in. Vivian and Carla would have come home yesterday, but she had not. Would Viv believe that Ayrshire had proven more hospitable and alluring than anyone could have imagined?

'Vivian, hello,' she answered, as neutrally as she could manage.

'Millicent. Is everything all right?'

She sounded worried.

'Yes, fine.'

'Where are you?'

'We decided to take a trip on the ferry yesterday, from Ardrossan over to Arran. We checked in to a B&B.'

There was a long pause, long enough to unsettle Millicent, who was not an experienced liar.

'Vivian, is everything okay at your end?'

'Millicent, I know you aren't telling me the truth. I'm sorry, but when I bought you the phone, I registered it with my account, just in case. I was only looking out for you.'

'What are you saying?'

'My computer is telling me you're in Italy.'

'That's absurd. Maybe you registered the wrong number.'

'I registered it correctly. I was very careful, in case you needed my help. I know you're in Italy. Pompeii, to be precise. What are you doing there? I didn't know you even had a passport. Is Jerome with you?'

'Jerome is with me, yes. But I'm telling you, we're on Arran.'

'Millicent, I need you to be honest with me. There was a man here today, a policeman. He was asking where you were, if I'd heard from you.'

Millicent's heart was thumping. The idea of these people being at the house was disturbing. It reinforced the scale of their reach.

'What did you tell him?'

'I said you were in Ayrshire. That's where you said you had gone. I only checked the computer after he came calling. You're not in Ayrshire, are you. Or Arran.'

'No.'

'What's going on? Are you all right? Are you in some kind of trouble?'

'I can't explain right now. I'm sorry.'

She ended the call and turned to Jerome as they continued along the ancient street, scaffold shoring up two-storey ruins to their left.

'Vivian said a policeman came looking for me. Or someone saying he was a policeman.'

'Why would they be asking for you back home when they know we're here?'

'I don't know. Trying to find out what we might have told her, I suppose. Anyway, that's not the headline. Vivian also knows where we are. Some trick with the computer, apparently.'

'She registered your phone to her Google account,' he replied.

'Something like that.'

'Fuck. Of course.'

'What?'

'Now we know how they keep finding us. If Vivian can track your location via your phone, I cannae imagine it's beyond the resources of the intelligence services. That Rook guy has had your mobile number since the beginning.'

Millicent looked down at the handset like it was diseased.

'Should I throw it away, then? Or switch it off at least?'

'No. They already know we're here at Pompeii. Ditch it now and it makes no odds, other than letting them know we've sussed this. The advantage we have is that if we know they're tracking us, then we can think about where we want to lead them.'

Millicent felt considerably less sanguine about this development. She might as well be wearing an electronic tag. What if they were watching her right now? Once again, every passing tourist became a potential threat.

They found Dante at the Odeon, talking to a group of schoolkids seated at the front of the terraced steps. Things were just wrapping up, their teacher getting her pupils to politely thank him, then counting heads before shipping them out.

He was grey-haired and balding, roly-poly in his build, a teddy bear of a man with a demeanour particularly suited to addressing children. It struck her that he looked absolutely nothing like Sergio, though who could say what Sergio would look like now.

They waited for him in the seclusion of the tunnel leading to the Doric temple. Millicent knew that it might put him at risk if he was seen talking to them, and it would be important for him to grasp that.

'Dante,' she said.

He lifted his head, looked at her a moment and then smiled warmly in recognition.

'My God, Millie Spark. It really is you. Umberto said you were coming, but it still feels like such a surprise.'

He spoke in lightly accented English. It had been halting when she worked with him, as he had only just begun to learn. Now he was fluent.

'It's great to see you after all this time,' she said.

'And still here in Pompeii – you must think I never left.'

'We saw you talking to those schoolchildren. You're in the education department here, right? How did you get into this?'

He gave a modest shrug.

'I came into a bit of cash, just when I was starting to think acting wasn't going to work out. When you get killed three times in the same movie, you know you're never going to get cast in a leading role.'

'Serendipitous timing, then.'

'For sure. If my windfall had come a few years earlier, I would have burned it up on fast times. But I was just about old and wise enough to spend it on going to university. I studied Archaeology. Never looked back.'

'Congratulations,' she said. She was happy for him. He didn't look like he had mourned the end of his movie days.

'Thanks. And what about you? You know what, let's go get a coffee, catch up properly. There's a place up at the—'

'Dante, it's best we talk where nobody can see us. It's for your protection.'

He stiffened. At her request, Umberto hadn't mentioned why she was coming. She felt bad having to lay this on him, but she needed the truth, and fast.

Jerome produced the photograph on his phone.

'We need you to tell us what you know about this.'

Dante examined it, pretending to take his time. He shook his head, his expression regretful.

'Sergio. Poor guy. We worked together, as you know, but if you're looking for my take on what happened to him, it's no better informed than anybody else's. For what it's worth, I think it was drugs. I heard rumours about HIV, but even if they were true, drugs were still his biggest problem.'

'This is not Sergio, Dante. It's you.'

She pinched to zoom in on the arm, where the end of his salamander tattoo was visible. His hand went instinctively to his sleeve. He knew he couldn't deny it.

He swallowed, flashed his palms in surrender.

'Yeah, okay. This is me. I doubled for him off-set. Just once. It was no big deal.'

'Then there's no reason not to tell us about it.'

His eyes searched either side. He looked trapped but trying to disguise it.

'I think he was in rehab. He had overdosed and they asked me to go to Kos, pose for some photographs they would give to the press. It was to do with insurance, something about movie completion bonds. They had to cover up that he was having health issues, didn't want any drug scandal stories in the press.'

'They could have done that anywhere,' she pointed out. 'Why did they fly you to Kos?'

'They wanted to keep the paparazzi off his back while he was in rehab, put the press off his scent by sending them hunting in the wrong place.'

'Who is they?'

He hung his head.

'I signed an agreement. I'm liable if I talk about this.'

'They gave you a lot of money, didn't they? That's what paid for you to go to university.'

He said nothing.

'Was it Alfie Bertrand? A man called Daniels?'

'I'm really sorry. It was a long time ago, but the terms were pretty strict.'

'You travelled on Sergio's passport, didn't you?'

This had him spooked.

'How would you know that?'

She and Jerome shared a look. They had worked this out between them on the drive south.

'It was to create an official record of where Sergio was,' Millicent said.

'Like I said, they were trying to keep the media off the scent.'

'Dante, do you know why they got you to hold up a newspaper in this photo? It was to establish the date and frame the narrative. It was to make out Sergio was alive and well on Kos, when he was already dead back in Italy.'

She could see the anxiety in his eyes, the years of holding back a doubt he could not afford to entertain. His new life had derived from this one simple job. Sergio had not suddenly been posted missing. Rather, he had faded away unnoticed, but in time the questions had been asked, and Dante must not have wanted to admit to himself that he might know the answer.

'These people killed Lucio,' Millicent told him. 'They killed an undercover cop in England and framed me for it. I went to prison for twenty-four years. Then a few days ago they tried to kill me. They are cleaning up their mess, tying up loose ends that have come undone. You are one of those loose ends, Dante. You need to help us so that we can help you. Who paid for you to go to Kos?'

He looked both ways along the tunnel. For a moment she thought he might be about to run. When he spoke, they were not the words she was expecting to hear.

'It was Wincott. Freddy Wincott.'

Possession

They left the theatre via different exits, heading in opposite directions so that they weren't seen together. Dante had looked hollowed-out, the colour and energy that enraptured the schoolkids rapidly drained from his features. It was the face of a man whose secret fears had been confirmed. Millicent regretted that she might have put a target on his back, but the one on her own was bigger.

'So, where does Freddy Wincott fit into this?' Jerome asked.

When Dante had said his name, she asked herself the same question, and an answer had immediately presented itself.

'There was an incident on Lucio's boat in Sorrento, towards the end of the shoot. Sergio became ill: he had done way too much coke, booze and who knows what else. Freddy was all over it. He made some calls, got an ambulance organised. I assumed he took charge so he could pay off the paramedics to keep the story out of the news.'

She remembered Freddy accompanying Sergio to the hospital, insisting there was only room for him when Lucio offered to come too. She remembered how quickly the ambulance had turned up, how the paramedics had been martialled by Freddy. She assumed that this was simply the level of efficiency and control that great riches bought you, but now she saw that it was something else.

'I'm not sure they were real paramedics,' she said.

She pictured Sergio being carried out on the trolley, his face obscured by shades and an oxygen mask. Who leaves sunglasses on a patient when you're bagging them with oxygen?

'I think he was already dead.'

They were approaching the Forum. She stopped between two Doric columns, the green centaur statue straight ahead.

'He got rid of the body and organised a cover-up,' said Jerome.

Dante had told them he believed Freddy was protecting his sister's investment in a film he also planned to distribute, which made sense if Sergio had merely overdosed. But if he was already dead before Freddy called in fake paramedics, that painted a very different picture.

'If Sergio had died from an OD, they would have let it play out,' she said. 'It would have been a scandal, a tragedy, but not something Freddy needed to worry about.'

'If anything, it would have added to the movie's profile,' Jerome suggested. 'Like Brandon Lee in *The Crow* or Heath Ledger in *The Dark Knight*: the final film of a rising star cut off in his prime.'

'Freddy killed him,' she said. 'That's the only explanation for why he would need to spirit the body away and use Dante to create a false timeline.'

'Why would Freddy kill Sergio?'

Stacey's words echoed like a recovered memory from a past life.

Oh, girl, you never noticed how Freddy looks at him? And you know Sergio's AC/DC, right?

'Freddy is gay, but he wasn't out back then. I'm not sure he was even entirely out to himself. He was the son of a right-wing media tycoon, and the tabloids were even more openly homophobic in those days. He and Sergio, something was going on that night. Sergio was always very flirty, very narcissistic. Insatiably promiscuous, some said. I think something happened between them and Freddy couldn't handle it.'

'What do you mean?'

Jerome's face was so innocent, his curiosity guileless and unknowing. For the first time she wondered if he had any sexual experience at all, other than with himself.

'Kingsley Amis once said of the male libido that it was like being possessed by a madman.'

'Mancipium,' Jerome replied.

'Precisely. You are consumed by your desires, all judgment and reason abandoned. Then the spell is broken when you come, and you are left with the aftermath: deeds you can't undo, and a vision of yourself as something horrifying and shameful.'

Jerome nodded, his expression sincere.

'Let him who would deny it submit his browser history.'

'It must be hard enough for any young man, but when you are in a state of denial and secrecy about your true nature? I think Sergio seduced Freddy then Freddy killed him in a rage after they had sex. But what I still can't see is where Lucio and Markus fit into it.'

'I can,' said Jerome. 'If this all played oot in Lucio's bedroom, where the motion-activated video camera was set up.'

And with that, everything clicked into place. That was the night Stacey had supplied the underage girl. Millicent remembered seeing her with Alfie. It was supposed to happen at that party. But when Lucio and Markus checked the tape, they discovered they had captured something far more explosive.

'Lucio and Markus decided to blackmail Freddy instead,' she said. 'Or maybe even Roger Wincott himself. He was interested in acquiring MGM at the time. A scandal of this magnitude would have been catastrophic.'

'And Markus must have gone seriously off-script with this,' said Jerome. 'I can see his intelligence bosses being cool with complicity in covering up a murder: that kind of shit is priced in with what they do. But blackmailing one of the most powerful media players in the country, and one of the Conservative Party's staunchest allies? They wouldn't risk the blowback.'

'Freddy Wincott must be who these guys are really working for.'

'Or who Daniels is.'

As they stood amidst the Forum, there was a constant flow of people passing either side, which felt reassuring until Millicent remembered that any one of them could be watching. Then she noticed that one of them most definitely was. He was leaning against an empty plinth, staring at them and taking no care to hide it. He was dressed in a blue suit, distinctively smarter than all the tourists in their shorts and backpacks. He looked mid-sixties but good for it; a man long used to living well.

Then he waved. It was a subtle gesture, but quite unmistakable, and it functioned like a starter pistol.

She tugged Jerome to start walking.

'We need to go. Now.'

'What is it?'

'Blue suit. Directly behind. He just waved at me.'

There seemed little point in telling Jerome to disguise his interest. They both looked back. The man was now following them, proceeding at a leisurely pace. Something about that unnerved her more than had he been running. He knew he didn't need to. She noticed he had his phone in his hand.

'Would this be a good time to ditch my mobile?' she asked.

'Best wait until we're in the car, then just remove the battery.'

She saw the wisdom in it now. The man didn't know they had worked out how he was tracking them. That was why he was in no rush. But getting to the car quickly seemed an even greater imperative.

Directly ahead she could see the administrative buildings at the entrance to the site. Their experience in Paris told her that others could be waiting, ready to swoop, but they surely couldn't drag her and Jerome away in front of so many witnesses. If they made it to the Jag, the game would change.

'I'm thinking the Amalfi Coast would be a nice place to lie low,' she said.

Just then, she heard her phone chime twice in quick succession. She took the device from her bag and glanced at the screen. Both messages were from Jonathan Rook.

She opened the first and her screen was filled with an image: a dim and grainy photograph of a woman's face taken from above: eyes closed, pallid, lifeless.

Vivian.

Jerome grabbed the handset from her, thumbing the screen. The image was replaced by one of Carla, her face similarly colourless, similarly devastating.

Rook had killed them both.

Sorrento, January 22nd, 1994

There was a bite in the wind that reminded Rook that just because he was in southern Italy didn't change the fact that it was the middle of winter.

He hurried along the jetty on quiet feet, cushioning every footfall against the heft of the holdall slung over his shoulder. He had been here less than a fortnight ago, but there had been no need for silence then, only discretion. On that occasion he had been despatched to clean up a mess, but the problem had only got bigger since.

Sir Roger had always enjoyed close contact with the service, cultivating mutually beneficial arrangements: sensitive information quietly supplied or suppressed; propaganda lines and talking points faithfully reproduced; characters assassinated; messengers shot. Rook had been approaching forty when the offer came in to become his new head of security. The Cold War was over and it felt like the right time to get out. He had seen too many old lags put out to pasture with nothing to sustain them but crappy pensions, bad memories and paranoia.

He changed his grip on the bag. There was a weight to it deriving from more than its contents. The last time he had been here it was to carry out something highly illegal, but still the kind of thing he had accepted would come with the turf. However, what was in this bag represented the reality of what his new position truly entailed. He was working for Roger Wincott, after all. As he recently heard a guy say in a movie, *get in bed with the devil and sooner or later you have to fuck.*

Lucio Sabatini's boat was up ahead. It was part of the bullshit façade of success he was presenting to the world. In showbusiness, there was always a different story to be found if you looked behind the painted flats. This was where the fucker actually lived. He did have a place in Rome, but just some tiny apartment: one he rented, not owned.

There were no lights on. No wild parties tonight. The guy was keeping his head down because he knew he was in dangerous waters. He probably got a bit jumpy when he found out his negative had been stolen, and would be under no illusions that it was any kind of coincidence.

Rook climbed over the transom onto the stern and dropped the holdall. It hit the deck with more of a thud than he intended, but by this point the time for stealth had passed.

He headed down to the galley, passing the bedroom where he had been sent the last time he was aboard. He opened the fridge, grabbed himself a beer, took a seat on one of the banquettes and waited. A couple of minutes later, Sabatini emerged cautiously from his bedroom, clutching a knife. It was the same one that had been used to kill Sergio. He was barefoot, wearing only boxer shorts and a YSL T-shirt.

'You don't want to see the stats on who tends to get stabbed when someone with a knife challenges an intruder,' Rook told him, taking a swig.

'Who are you? What are you doing here?'

'Put the weapon down. I'm here to talk terms.'

Sabatini placed the blade next to the sink, the handle close for him to grab again if he needed to. His eyes went briefly to the ceiling.

'Did you damage something upstairs? I thought I heard a crash.'

'Just dumped my bag.'

'What the hell was in it?'

'Your negative.'

It wasn't, though. The negative had been destroyed on Freddy's instruction. The family were seizing the opportunity to get their errant daughter back into the fold by ending her ill-starred foray into the film biz.

'I think you know what we want in return,' Rook told him.

Sabatini scoffed.

'I reckon that videotape is worth a lot more to you than the negative is worth to me.'

Rook put down his bottle.

'Let me be clear that I'm offering the easy option right now. Easier for you, I mean. What's easier for me is simply to kill you and then kill your silent partner, Markus.'

Rook watched him flinch, the threat compounded by the revelation that they knew who he was working with. He regrouped though, putting on a pretty decent poker face.

'I don't only have a silent partner. I have an invisible one too. Anything happens to me, and that tape goes to the authorities.'

Rook had anticipated as much. That was partly why he was here. He picked up the bottle again and took another sip.

'So grab yourself a beer and let's negotiate.'

Sabatini shrugged.

'Okay.'

Rook waited for him to grip the handle of the fridge then shot him with a trank gun.

When Sabatini came to, he found himself lying on the transom deck next to the canvas holdall, his wrists and ankles bound with zip-ties.

He began shouting for help.

'Save your breath, Lucio,' Rook told him. 'You're all at sea.'

Sabatini struggled into a sitting position, from where he could see that it was true. All around was darkness, the lights of Sorrento left far behind. They were half a mile out from Capri, in a sheltered channel where the boat wouldn't drift too far.

Rook reached into the bag and produced a pair of secateurs, snapping them open and closed a couple of times in front of Sabatini's face.

'And now you're going to tell me who you sent that tape.'

The man made his living making horror movies. He had an all too vivid understanding of what happened when a spring-loaded fulcrum brought sharpened blades to bear upon flesh and bone. He gave up his insurance policy damn fast. Nonetheless, Rook had to cut a couple of digits just to satisfy himself that Sabatini was telling the truth when he said he hadn't sent a copy to anyone else.

He shot him with another trank dart after that. He didn't want him desperate and struggling during what was next.

Rook unscrewed a metal stool from the galley floor to use as a weight. He secured it to the unconscious Sabatini with more zip-ties, then chucked him into the sea. That done, he removed the holdall's main contents, which were a self-inflating dinghy and two retractable plastic paddles. It would get him back to Capri, where Wincott had a car waiting for him.

There would be a fog of confusion and uncertainty in the coming days. Whenever Sabatini was noticed missing, they'd find his yacht was gone and assume he was en route to somewhere. Even once the boat was discovered, it wouldn't be clear what had happened. That gave Rook plenty of time to complete the job.

His first destination would be Rome, to neutralise this Rossini character. Then on to London to deal with 'Markus'. That was less urgent because according to Rook's sources, Creasey was due in Glasgow first, staying there tomorrow night. Seemed he and a bunch of cops went up there every year for a Burns supper, an excuse to get shitfaced and catch up with ex-colleagues who had moved on to other things.

Rook knew he probably had time to intercept Creasey in Glasgow, but a Special Branch officer being found dead in a hotel room on a Scottish force's patch would bring unwanted interest and awkward questions. London offered him better cover.

According to Freddy, there were several witnesses to his girlfriend smacking Creasey in the face at that party on the boat. A tempestuous relationship would serve up the perfect scapegoat.

Checkmate

Jerry felt like the ground beneath him was buckling, giving him a gut-wrenching sense of how they must have felt down here when the mountain blew. The tectonic plates shifted and his world was consumed in fire the moment he saw Vivian's face: grey, pale and bloodless.

Millicent had to grab a railing as tears began to fall.

'They're both dead,' she said, her voice choking. 'Oh dear God, what have I done?'

Jerry looked again at the image of Carla on Millicent's phone, which was when he noticed the time stamp.

It wasn't what it looked like. It was still fucking awful, but nobody was dead. Yet.

'These were taken last night,' he pointed out. 'You spoke to Vivian about an hour ago. It's a threat. These were taken while they were asleep. He's telling us the game's up.'

As Jerry spoke these words, Millicent's phone rang in his hand, the screen identifying the caller as Jonathan Rook.

'Hello?' Jerry answered.

'Ah, you must be Jerome. Can I speak to Millicent?'

Jerry swallowed before responding, barely able to contain his anger.

'Millicent can't come to the phone right now. She's pegging your da' with a strap-on and he's loving it.'

'Sounds messy, considering he died in 1989. And I would caution you to watch your manners. You got the pictures, I take it?'

Jerry couldn't bring himself to reply.

'If you run, we kill them, and then we'll find you again anyway. We can do it tonight. It will look like carbon monoxide. They will find a fault with the boiler after the fact. And in case you're thinking you can warn them, we have them under surveillance. If you try, we'll know, and we'll kill them in a less gentle manner. So, I assume you understand that this is checkmate. What is it?'

Jerry said nothing.

'I didn't hear you. What is it?'

Jerry's mouth was dry, his voice a whisper.

'Checkmate.'

'I mean, it's been a trip and everything, but I think it's time we put an end to all this chasing around, don't you? Before someone else gets hurt. You're going to wait for me right where you are. Then we're going to walk together to my car for a drive and a chat: somewhere you can't throw anybody in a river. Or bludgeon them to death,' he added, reminding Jerry that these guys also wanted revenge.

Moments after Rook disconnected the call, they saw him ambling down the slope from the ruins, taking his time. A power move.

'This was why he was in no rush,' Millicent said, slumping defeated onto a nearby bench. 'Not just because he was tracking my phone.'

This was undeniable, but Jerry had worked out a more chilling implication. Rook could have sent these images whenever he wanted. His guys could have taken them the night before last, could have sent them yesterday. Doing so now indicated he had given up on finding the tape, which meant there was only one thing left for him to take care of.

'We're gubbed,' Jerry said. 'Unless you've got some amazing last-minute revelation about where that missing videotape might be?'

'A world of no.'

She offered a sad smile, acknowledging that it was an expression she had heard from him. She hadn't picked it up quite right, though. It was more suited to refusal than admission.

'Where's it from?' she asked.

'*Buffy the Vampire Slayer*. Arguably my first exposure to horror. Gran had the box set.'

She nodded to herself, evidently satisfied by something, though she didn't explain what.

'You don't happen to know a song with a lyric about finding my sweet release? My cellmate used to sing it.'

'That's *Buffy* too. Same episode, in fact. It's a dead guy who sings it.'

She glanced up the slope where Rook was approaching.

'That seems horribly apposite.'

He handed Millicent back her phone, taking his own from his pocket. The camera lens sat at the centre of one sprocket in the videotape image on the rear cover. He held it at an angle and began casually filming Rook as he descended the last few yards, then left it recording to grab the audio, for what it might be worth.

Millicent wiped away her tears and sat up straight, determined to look dignified as she confronted him.

'Millicent,' he said. 'Face to face at last. And I'm gratified that you both had the good sense to do as you're told. All that stuff about never knowing when you're beaten? Movie bullshit. People who don't know when they're beaten get other people killed.'

'What is it you want, Mr Rook?' she asked.

Rook wore an apologetic smile. He gazed across the ruins for a moment then back at the two of them, gently shaking his head.

'I really wish you hadn't come here. I had a notion it was where you were headed, so I had a long time on the drive south to think about why. But there could only be one reason, couldn't there? One person you wanted to speak to.'

'We're just taking in the sights,' Jerry said, as flatly as he could, trying to keep the fear from his voice.

'Nah. You were talking to Dante Agielli.'

'You thinking you should have killed him back in '94?'

Rook didn't respond. He glanced at Jerry's phone. Jerry wondered if he knew he was being recorded or was just habitually wary of it. He was curious as to why Rook was talking at all, why he hadn't marched them away yet. There was only one possible answer: he still wanted to know if there was a chance of finding the tape.

'I guess it's always a tough call,' Jerry went on. 'Having to balance tying up loose ends with leaving too many hats on the ground, too many dots for someone to join.'

'I don't need to ask if Dante spilled, do I?' said Rook.

'No comment. But it's not him breaching his NDA that you're worried about.'

Jerry looked him up and down: the designer suit, the Cartier watch; even the guy's haircut looked expensive. The bloke Millicent pushed into the river hadn't given off the same monied vibe, and nor had the dead guy back in Glasgow.

'You're not working for the intelligence services,' Jerry said. 'You're working for Freddy Wincott. And the others don't know your agenda, do they? They genuinely think there's a tape of Alfie Bertrand and some young girl. They don't know what really went down that night.'

Rook made a sarcastic clapping gesture, some Nancy Pelosi energy right there.

'Oh, it's more than that,' he said, turning to Millicent. 'They think the reason the Bertrand tape never materialised is that Markus went rogue and kept it for himself. Some of them even think you had a hand in it: that you and your lover were planning to blackmail Bertrand and live off the proceeds. Is that true, Millicent? Were you in on Markus and Lucio's plot before it all went south?'

'Markus used me to get close to Lucio. Everything else I know about this I've learned in the past week.'

'I believe you,' he said, shrugging. 'Geddes, the bloke who went to your house the other night, would have believed you too. He accepted the official version, that you were drunk and a bit of a psycho. He took it rather sore that you killed his mate. Des Creasey was the best man at his wedding, so he was a little over-eager, and consequently a bit premature. Made certain assumptions when he found a big box of tapes. Thought it was safe to proceed after stashing it in his car, but he was maybe in too much of a hurry to avenge his old friend.'

'Daniels is looking for the tape too,' Jerry said. 'Where does he fit in?'

Rook looked puzzled.

'Who's he?'

'Probably not his real name. He works for Alfie Bertrand. I wonder if he knows what that footage would really show.'

Rook glanced at Jerry's phone again, that videotape cover design drawing his eye. Jerry could see the cogs turning. In Daniels he had given Rook something to think about, something that wasn't in the script.

'If you know where the tape is,' Rook said, 'now would be a very good opportunity to cough up. As in, the final opportunity. Vivian would want you to. So would dear Carla. Come on. You're out of options and I'm out of patience.'

And yet still you wait, Jerry thought.

You're out of options. Know when you're beaten. Checkmate. The guy kept driving home that message. Maybe it was the conversation he and Millicent just had, but he thought of an episode of *Buffy*, in which people kept telling her how powerless she was. It was to keep her from realising that she was the one who held all the power over them.

Millicent had the goods on all of these bastards, whether they were working for Alfie Bertrand, Freddy Wincott, British intelligence or whoever. Jerry had been checking the news from home, and there was nothing about the police seeking them in connection with the dead guy up the tree. Rook's people hadn't reported Jerry and Millicent as suspects because they didn't want people pulling the threads, and they sure as shit didn't want Millicent talking to the authorities.

An ex-cop had been sent to break into her house and kill her. She knew all about Des Creasey, an undercover officer whose identity and rogue activities had been suppressed at her own trial for his murder. Millicent was the unstable element that connected all their hidden agendas. She was the one who could blow everything apart, and this videotape was the detonator. That was why Rook really wanted to believe she could help him acquire it.

'Out of patience?' Millicent said, her tone measured in a way that used politeness as a form of aggression. 'Mr Rook, I have been waiting a quarter of a century for answers, so don't talk to me about patience. It was you who put me in jail, wasn't it? You were the one behind the frame.'

Rook shrugged, a smug smile on his face.

'I don't know what you're talking about.'

Jerry couldn't help glancing down at his phone, the *Evil Dead* label visible above his fingers. Yeah, this guy definitely knew he was being recorded.

He was glad Rook's gaze was fixed on Millicent, as that meant he didn't notice Jerry's eyes when the tectonic plates shifted again.

Behind the frame.

Millicent's words echoed as he glimpsed his phone, the imposition of sound upon vision showing him what they had both missed.

Suddenly, he could see a way out of this.

'I can get you the tape,' Jerry said. 'I know where it is.'

Rook hit Jerry with a penetrating stare. He knew he was being scanned by a state-of-the-art bullshit detector. Fortunately, what would get him through this was all true: agonisingly, devastatingly true. It was going to cost him his relationship with Millicent, but that was the price he had to pay. The price he always deserved to pay.

'Amazing what the right bit of motivation can do,' Rook said. 'Like, force someone to make up any old shit just to buy themselves some time. You know nothing about this tape, son.'

'I know what's on it. A typical Lucio Sabatini production: lots of sex and violence. The murder of a rising Italian movie star and the steps taken to cover it up. Not something Freddy Wincott ever wanted to distribute.'

Rook's expression remained impassive, unmoved, but Jerry hadn't got to the money shot.

'More importantly I know where Markus hid it.'

That hit home. Rook's eyes narrowed, recalibrating the detector's sensitivity.

'The reason you guys never found it when you turned over Millicent's flat, the reason the police never came across it when they took away all her stuff, was that it didnae look like a tape. Markus gave her a present when he turned up for a surprise visit. It was an advert for *Mancipium*, a page torn out of a trade paper and framed under glass. The frame was just deep enough to hide the fact that there was a videotape lodged inside it.'

Millicent put a hand to her mouth, stifling a gasp.

Jerry understood that her shock existed on multiple levels. She knew instinctively that he was right about this, but it was the thing she didn't know that was giving her pause. Why would Jerry be offering something he didn't have?

She wasn't going to like the answer.

Rook relaxed his stare. Jerry could tell he wasn't buying it. But he would soon enough.

'Oh, well, if what you're saying is true, I can send someone around to pick up the picture right now, and that will be the end of the matter.'

'I wouldnae be telling you this if it was still in the hoose. I'm not a fuckin' idiot.'

'No. You're a fucking bullshitter. Millicent clearly knows nothing about this. You just pulled it out of your arse right now, didn't you?'

'No. I worked it out last night,' he lied.

'What, and you chose not to share this most crucial discovery with her?'

'I was hoping I wouldn't have to.'

This had him puzzled, and how Jerry wished he could leave him that way. But it was time to pay the ferryman.

'The reason I didn't want to tell her is the same reason it's not in the house. Millicent, I need you to tell him why that is.'

Millicent was looking at him with concern, no doubt confused as to why he was asking her to admit she didn't know what had become of the framed poster. It was all going to be clear very soon though, after which nothing would be the same between them. He was going to hurt her all over again, but it was the only way to convince Rook of the card they were holding. The only way to keep them both alive.

It took her a moment to find her voice.

'My brother . . . kept the poster for me, while I was in prison,' she said.

'Your brother's got it, then?'

She looked to Jerry for help, unsure how to answer.

'I need you to tell him everything.'

Her voice was faltering, her bottom lip unsteady.

'It was stolen. His flat was broken into. Alastair disturbed the burglar. He had a heart attack and . . . he died. The poster was the only thing they took.'

Rook looked at once compelled and confused. His mind was racing, trying to work out the angles.

'It was the only thing they . . . Are you telling me someone else knew? Was it this Daniels?'

'Millicent doesn't know who's got it,' Jerry said. 'But I do.'

He had to swallow, his voice starting to break up.

'I'm so sorry, Millicent. It was me. I was the burglar.'

She stared at him, uncomprehending. All the things that made it hard for her to understand this were also the things he was about to put a match to.

'I used to break into places, before I got my act together. I ran with some bad people. And I was probably the only person in Glasgow who would have known that poster was worth anything.'

His eyes filled, mercifully blurring his view of Millicent, who was gazing back, starting to grasp the truth of it.

'That night . . . It's the one thing in my life I wish every day I could undo. I stayed with him. I did CPR as long as I could. I don't know how long it was, but I couldnae save him. I ran before the ambulance got there.'

Rook cleared his throat, calling attention back to himself.

'This is all very touching, but where's the fucking tape? Tell me where I can get it and then we can all just go our separate ways.'

No, you're planning to kill us anyway, you prick, Jerry thought. Which was why he was formulating a plan to make that more difficult than Rook might assume.

'I'll give it to you once I know everybody's safe. A handover in a public place. Kelvingrove Art Gallery, this time tomorrow.'

'Or how about I just take you away from here and waterboard both of you until you tell me who's got it?'

'Because I've got a dead man's pedal, someone holding the tape. He's not seen it, but he knows what to do. I made the arrangements last night, as soon as I realised what I had. Anything happens to me or Millicent or Vivian or Carla, and you can kiss the tape bye-bye.'

Rook hit him with the stare again, but Jerry could have passed a polygraph on this one. Someone else really was holding the tape. He just didn't know it.

'Lucio had a dead man's pedal,' Rook said. 'And guess what: he and Lucio were both dead men very soon after.'

'Rossini wasn't Lucio's failsafe,' Jerry replied. 'He was sent the tape by accident. But at least now we know who killed him.'

'So what makes you think I won't find your guy too?'

'Rossini didn't have his tape parcelled up, stamped and primed to post to the *Guardian* inside two minutes. And that really would be checkmate, wouldn't it?'

Rook tried to hide it, but Jerry could tell he was rattled. There was a risk here that he couldn't afford to take. What Jerry just described was the whole ballgame, and they both knew it.

'How do I know you haven't already had your mate make copies of this tape? Once you hand one over, you could blackmail my client with another.'

'Aye, because threatening Freddy Wincott and bringing cunts like you down on our heads is totally what we want to be doing. We just want this to be over. Millicent deserves to live her life in peace, after everything you've done. That's all we're asking here.'

Rook thought for a moment.

'Okay,' he said. 'Kelvingrove Art Gallery, half five tomorrow. And if you try to fuck me on this, you know what will happen. Except, it won't be something anyone can blame on a faulty boiler, and I'll make you watch.'

Hate

As they walked back to the car, Jerry's heart was still pounding in the aftermath of facing down Rook. He kept glancing behind, afraid his bluff was being called and people were going to swoop in and bundle them into a van. He could hear his own pulse inside his ears, there being little else to drown the sound. Millicent hadn't spoken since he confessed. Not a single word. She remained in a trance-like state, eyes fixed ahead, expression blank.

He wanted to say sorry again, but he didn't believe he had the right to even speak to her yet. Begging forgiveness would feel like an intrusion, an act of needy self-indulgence: something *he* wanted, that took no cognisance of how she felt and what he had done to her. Forgiveness wasn't for him to ask; it was only for her to grant.

As he unlocked the Jag, he saw Rook a couple of rows away across the car park. The fucker was getting into an Aston Martin in a shade of blue that matched his suit. Wincott money.

Millicent climbed into the passenger side and put on her seatbelt. Still she stared ahead, never making eye contact, observing her omertà.

Jerry pulled out his phone and began looking up flights. There was nothing direct, but they could get back as far as Heathrow tonight, then fly up to Glasgow first thing tomorrow. They would have to discuss these things and a lot more besides, starting with the awkward issues of her paying for his air fares and the penalty for dumping this hire car in the south of Italy.

She watched him key 'Naples Airport' into the Jaguar's sat-nav, so that much was communicated at least.

Jerry drove in silence, trying to concentrate on plans: what they would need to do, who they could contact. It was impossible, though. He could only think about how close he and Millicent had become over these past few days. How his fortunes had become entwined with hers.

Bonding over killing a hitman and disposing of the body before fleeing the country. Hanging out with media bosses, driving around in a Jag convertible, helping out on a black-metal video, meeting the Gore Whore. It had been the time of his life, and all because of her.

She had made him feel that the world was full of possibilities he assumed were not available to the likes of him: that he could go where he liked, fit in where he chose. She was the second most remarkable person he had ever known. Which was why losing her felt like losing the first one all over again.

The trip took about half an hour. Millicent still hadn't said anything as he pulled into the rental returns area of the car park, but Jerry didn't have the option to remain silent any longer.

'I can't begin to imagine how much you hate me right now, Millicent, but there's some things we need to discuss.'

Finally, she looked at him.

'I've waited a long time to meet you, Jerry,' she said.

It was oddly wounding, confirmation of the unbridgeable distance between them now. She had never called him that. Not a single time. He instantly ached to hear her call him Jerome, but felt certain she would not address him that way again.

'And you're wrong about me hating you right now. I started hating you a long time ago. Long before I had any notion of who you were. Long before our paths crossed. I hated whoever you might turn out to be. My hate could have moved mountains.'

He forced himself not to flinch from her gaze, though he wanted to hang his head in shame. He swallowed.

'I'm so sorry. I—'

'Don't speak,' she commanded. Her tone was quiet but authoritative.

He sat there in another growing silence, throughout which he couldn't help calculating how long they had before the Heathrow flight left. He didn't even know if there were seats on it.

Then she spoke again.

'It was fourteen minutes.'

Jerry didn't follow, but he didn't want to disobey her last instruction. He let his expression ask for him.

'That was how long you did CPR. Fourteen minutes. The police were very nice. They put me in touch with the woman who took the emergency call. She said you stayed on the line with her all that time. The police deduced it must have been whoever broke in.

'I hated you until I learned that. Not just because you tried to save him, but because it had troubled me to think that Alastair was alone when he died. It helped to know someone was with him.'

She looked out beyond the car park, towards where Vesuvius loomed on the horizon.

'I often wondered about the fact that this burglar stayed for so long, rather than make good his escape. I used to think it was a courageous thing to have done. But what you did back at Pompeii was far more courageous.

'I've lost so much in life, these twenty-five years. But what I've learned this past week is that there is a lot of life still to be lived, so I can't let anger and bitterness about the past take away all that is good about my future. And I *am* going to have a future: because of you, Jerome.'

Extras

The great danger with any quest for answers is that you might find them. Millicent had always known this, but what she had not been ready for was that the answers could change so little.

For twenty-five years she had wanted to know who killed Markus, and for what motive. She had always imagined that when she was in possession of this information and finally found herself face to face with the man responsible, it would mean the tables had turned: that it would be her path to exoneration and justice. But seated on that bench in Pompeii, Jonathan Rook still held her fate in his hands. She remained at his mercy, powerless to prove what he had done and what she had not.

She had barely begun to process this when Jerome made his revelation. It was the answer that had the more profound impact, having fallen more precipitously. What she had learned about Rook she had learned by increments and degrees, piece by piece over days, while Jerome's confession had come fully formed out of nowhere.

All those months wondering who this burglar had been, this unknown figure who derailed her entire world for the second time in her life. It had felt like the most terrible betrayal, that it should turn out to be a person she had come to care for and to trust. But what was confusing her emotions was that it was the wrong way around. The act had come first, and then she had learned who he truly was over the past week. Therefore it could not be a betrayal, but nonetheless, there had been deceit, the withholding of an enormous truth.

She wondered when he had realised the connection. Her mind

went back to their conversation on the way to Milan, when she told him about the poster.

'*I'm so sorry*,' he said, and then he had gone quiet for a long time.

She had not been afforded any time to come to terms with all this, as she needed to focus on the immediate threat, and on Jerome's efforts to secure their escape. She had been both surprised and impressed, but as they proceeded away from Rook, she was not inclined to voice her gratitude. She was not inclined to voice anything. She felt unable to speak as she tried to make sense of her own feelings.

She had long wanted to meet this burglar, just to know who Alastair had been with at the end. What was so hard to come to terms with was that she instinctively felt glad to learn that it had been Jerome. That was sorely at odds with the enduring hurt of what he had done.

But what had he done? She remembered the doctor saying to her: 'In all honesty there is no way of saying for sure whether the intrusion precipitated Alastair's cardiac arrest. There is every chance that it was going to happen that evening anyway.'

And then Alastair really would have died alone.

She often wondered whether the doctor told her this so that she wouldn't consume herself with rancour and blame. She would have to concede that it helped. She knew that she would have been unable to deal with her loss properly if she was obsessed with questions of 'if only'. She had a deeper need than most to blame someone for all that had happened to her.

What she told Jerome was true. She had hated him, for a while. Then the woman from the emergency line had spoken to her. She said he sounded young, probably just a kid. After that, what she had come to realise was that she wanted to meet him, not to demand answers but to forgive him, because sometimes forgiveness was more important to the person who had been wronged.

What Jerome had done set in motion the chain of events without which she would never have learned the truth. Alastair would most probably have died anyway. She may well have ended up staying with Vivian and Carla. Perhaps she would have made good on her intention to kill herself. Or perhaps she would still have visited that hotel and seen that photograph. Then she would have made those phone calls, and she would have ended up smothered in her bed.

He had not merely saved her life: he had made her feel she had a life worth saving. Because of Jerome, she had re-learned the value of her life.

It was only fair that she granted him this absolution. In truth, she hadn't quite been ready to, but she knew she would need him at his strongest for what was to come.

'You've saved my life twice,' she told him.

'To be fair, I've only put a down payment on the second one. Rook is still planning to kill us.'

Jerome looked up the flights again on his phone. There were still seats on one that was leaving for Heathrow in ninety minutes.

'Were you lying about someone else holding the tape?' she asked, climbing out of the car. 'Because if it's back at the house, they'll find it. We know they were in there last night.'

'I wasn't lying. It isn't in the house.'

'So what about this dead man's pedal thing?'

'That part I was lying about. The guy who's holding it doesn't know he has it, which is crucial, because he's the last person on this planet I would trust. As soon as he knew it was worth something, he would probably try to flog it, end up . . .'

He didn't finish the thought. Another one railroaded it.

'What?'

'Nothing. Tell you later. But yes, we need to make it public. That's the thing I realised talking to Rook. They're not as powerful as they want you to think. As soon as all this comes out, they're fucked. All of them.'

Millicent found this difficult to believe.

'These are men with connections in very high places,' she reminded him. 'Not just Rook, but the people he is collaborating with. And Daniels is working for the Home Secretary, for God's sake. They can deploy considerable resources.'

'Can they, though?' he asked. 'I'm not being ageist here, but haven't you noticed anything about all the people that are after you? Rook, Daniels, the guy back in Glasgow, the one in Paris: they're none of them in the first flush of youth. I mean, it's possible they're working on the basis that it takes a pensioner to catch a pensioner, but I don't imagine that's the case.'

Millicent gave him a warning look. 'Where are you going with this?'

'Freddy Wincott couldnae despatch anyone new to deal with this without letting them in on why. Same with Alfie Bertrand. Daniels has to be somebody in the know from way back then. Same goes for the guys trying to cover up their own blackmail plot. They've probably still got a few contacts, but the point is they're not the authorities.'

She handed him her credit card as they entered the terminal.

'You book the flights,' she said. 'I need to go and do my make-up.'

She needed less time than on the way out. It was always easier to recreate a look than to construct it. Plus her hands were steadier because she hadn't just thrown a corpse off a bridge.

Jerome was waiting for her outside the ladies' toilets when she emerged.

'So, what's your plan?' she asked him. 'Are you going to copy this tape before you hand it over?'

'It's more about *their* plan. Rook doesnae intend for there to be any handover, at Kelvingrove or anywhere else.'

'No,' she agreed. 'He accepted your terms far too quickly.'

'We won't see them, but they'll be all over us, and as soon as I've got the tape, they'll move in and take it. After that, we'll just be another loose end they won't hesitate to tie up. So never mind mailing it to the *Guardian*: I'm ripping this thing and uploading it far and wide. But first we need to get them off our arses. Fortunately, we have an angle in that they don't know we've sussed how they're tracking us.'

Millicent was less sanguine about how simple that might be. These men might not be with the authorities after all, but they were ex-cops, trained in surveillance. They were of her generation, too: they wouldn't be placing all their trust in the electronic and the digital. If she really wanted to deceive them, she'd need old-school, practical effects that preyed upon people trusting what they saw with the naked eye.

'It won't be enough just to ditch my phone, or yours too for that matter,' she told him. 'We'll need to ditch their eyes-on surveillance at the same time.'

'Do you have any notion how we might do that?'

'Perhaps. What's the current tally in our little game?'

'I don't know, maybe I'm down one or two? What's that got to do with anything?'

'Because I've got a couple more references for you: *The Birdcage* and *The Thomas Crown Affair*.'

Jerome thought about it a moment.

'That's genius. We'd need some help, though.'

'Yes, sorry. Story of my life: ambitions too grand-scale for the budget. We'd need a lot of extras, and I don't have many friends. I don't even have Facebook friends.'

Jerome took out his phone.

'Millicent, you have more friends than you could possibly imagine.'

Corpses

'The . . . fourteen . . . thirty-five service from . . . Lanark . . . has been delayed by approximately . . . eight . . . minutes.'

The automated voice reverberated around the concourse as Rook checked his watch, the train he was waiting for due any second. He adjusted his earpiece and asked the others to acknowledge one more time. He had two more sets of eyes in play, which you needed in a place like this: a major railway station with a multiplicity of exits and any number of trains the subjects could be changing onto. He would have liked more bodies, but he was down to the bare bones. Geddes had gotten himself killed and Vaughn was in the hospital with a chest infection after the mad bitch threw him in the Seine.

He felt a vibration against his thigh. He knew it would be Wincott before he even took the phone from his pocket. He would be calling from the cabin of his Jetstream, in which he had flown Rook here from Italy that morning.

'Where are we?' Freddy asked, as always couching his terms in as much vagueness and deniability as possible.

Rook put up with it like he put up with a lot of other things, because he had been paid an awful lot of money to do so. Working for the Wincotts had proven the most astute decision of his life, a no-brainer in comparison to his previous career. It was phenomenally more lucrative, considerably less stressful, and it hadn't involved any mad Arab bastards trying to kill him. It had also come with generous share options on top of a very healthy pension for his retirement, which he had been two years into and thoroughly enjoying before he got the word that something dangerous had come loose from its moorings.

Frankly he had forgotten about Millie Spark, which was exactly the way it was supposed to have gone, for everybody. She had been a highly convenient patsy, the ideal means of allaying any suspicion over Creasey's death. Rook had broken into her flat in Battersea, taken her spare keys, copied them and put them back. Then he had followed her and Creasey around a few bars incognito, dropped a little something in their drinks.

When the court case came around, words were had in the right ears. Barristers and judges. Creasey had been working on sensitive matters: for his alias to come out would be highly dangerous to personnel still in the field, blah blah blah.

Her protestations ensured that she buggered her own chances of a timely parole, but even without that, certain mechanisms were in place: things with no documentation, no paper trail. Things that were never hard to procure when somebody had stabbed a copper to death while he slept, especially if it was a tart. It was as close as you got to throwing away the key.

They had to let her out some time, but nobody was worried about it. She had been incidental to the whole thing. If you had asked him a month ago, he'd have struggled to remember her name. Who would have thought some mad bitch in her seventies could turn out to be such a problem? Though it wasn't the mad bitch herself that was the danger, so much as what she might unearth if she started digging.

He and Freddy always knew they hadn't accounted for all the copies. He had found a third tape in Creasey's flat, but Creasey wasn't an idiot. Rook knew there would be another one stashed somewhere, and they had never found it. That tape was far more dangerous than the woman. Without it, she could scream from the rooftops about her theories, and about Des being Markus, but nobody would pay any attention.

It had been a hairy few days, he couldn't lie. On top of everything else, there was always the danger that one of these other clowns – who all thought it was Bertrand on the tape – might come up lucky. He hadn't just needed their cooperation to spread the workload: he had needed to keep them close, make sure he controlled what they found out. And he had a bone to throw them for when he finally got hold of the prize: a little switcheroo.

Freddy still had Lucio's tape, or at least an edited version of it. Rook had a copy on him right now: a VHS cassette that briefly showed Lucio's bedroom on the boat, then a bit of static, then three episodes of *Coronation Street* from 1995, like it had been accidentally taped over. It would be an appropriate punchline to the whole shaggy dog story of their failed blackmail plot.

'We're at Central Station,' he told Freddy. 'Everything is in hand.'

His other phone confirmed that his targets were on approach.

He'd had eyes on them since Pompeii, more or less. Toby Williams had watched them arrive at Heathrow, watched them check in to an airport hotel, watched them check out again in the morning. Williams had booked on to the same flight to Glasgow Airport, had followed their taxi to Paisley Gilmour Street, and was watching them from the same carriage on board the train that was pulling in any moment now.

Jay Morris had been through the house in Hyndland again this morning. The other two women had gone out, but Rook had no concerns that they had been tipped off, as Jay had already bugged the landline when he took those photos the night before. They had hacked Vivian Montgomerie's mobile days ago. Jay hadn't found anything, in accordance with what the kid had said. The bigger question was whether he was lying about the rest.

He heard Williams' voice in his earpiece.

'Okay, heads up, everybody. We have two targets emerging right now from platform eight. Male is dark haired, approx five-seven, wearing a light blue denim jacket with a lot of patches. Female is grey-haired, six feet, wearing a peach-coloured jacket.'

The descriptions were largely redundant, considering Williams had sent them all photos of both targets taken at GLA forty minutes ago, but it was both old habit and good practice.

Rook watched them make their way onto the concourse, where they stood for a few minutes, occasionally glancing up at the departure board. They must be changing trains here, maybe for the low-level platforms to Hyndland, or a mainline service to Ayrshire, where the kid was from.

Then the woman began to move, the kid following, but they weren't heading west towards the platforms. Rook watched them disappear down the stairs into the public toilets. He relaxed. He had already checked them as standard procedure, verifying that there was only one way in and out.

The station seemed to get busier all of a sudden, a particularly crowded train having come in. Weirdly, just about everyone coming off it looked the same: kids in dark hoodies all wearing this weird face paint, like the blokes in Kiss or something. There were more of them streaming in through all the entrances too, others coming out of the shops, the fast-food places, the toilets, everywhere. He glanced at the departure board and noted that one of the stations was Exhibition Centre. There must be a concert tonight.

Fucking teenagers. Always bleating about their individuality, and yet they were happy to be a bunch of clones, all looking the same. At least that would make his targets easier to track. They would be the only ones in the place not wearing hoodies and black-and-white make-up.

It hit him like a train. His target was a make-up artist.

'Anyone have eyes on?' he asked urgently.

'They still haven't come out of the toilets,' Morris replied.

'Yes, they fucking have.'

He looked around the concourse. There was movement every-where, dozens and dozens of people in hoodies and face paint.

'I've lost her phone signal,' said Williams.

Rook looked at his own mobile. It reported the same thing.

'Fuck.'

'No, wait, it's back on. It's moving. Fast.'

'Shit, they're on a fucking train.'

Rook scanned the departure board to see which service had just left, though it hardly mattered. They could get off anywhere and all his surveillance was parked back here.

They were gone.

Transformation

Philippa and her friend Chloe were waiting for them at the foot of the stairs outside the toilets, each holding out a black hoodie. Jerry traded his battle jacket for one, Millicent her peach coat.

It felt a rush to be in Philippa's presence. The last time he'd set eyes on her had been when he blanked her outside that tutorial, unable to walk away fast enough. Now he felt pangs that they both had to get moving.

'I owe you so much,' he said.

'Oh, I intend to collect.'

Philippa had been up early that morning at Vivian's place, posing as a leafleter. Following Jerry's instructions, she had printed off a load of flyers offering gardening work, posting them through all the doors on the street in case anybody was watching the house. When she got to their address, she had posted an envelope addressed to Vivian. It contained a burner phone Philippa had purchased, and a letter bearing the number of another burner, one Jerry had bought at Heathrow.

Vivian had rung immediately, and Millicent had talked her through the situation before passing her over to Jerry for some details.

Millicent handed Jerry what he needed, then went into the ladies', he the gents'. She had shown him how to do this last night, making him practise several times to improve his speed.

When they emerged a few minutes later, Millicent handed Chloe her suitcase and her mobile. Jerry had taken the phone out of his *Evil Dead* case, cracked the cover and removed the sim. He handed the device to Philippa, tapping the back where it said Samsung. An act of confession.

In the grand scheme, it was nothing compared to the one he'd made yesterday, and it must have come as considerably less of a surprise, but he still didn't enjoy admitting how much of a dick he'd been.

'I think you know what to do with this,' he said.

She rolled her eyes, but she was smiling.

'Good luck,' Philippa said, before she and Chloe headed up the stairs to catch their train.

As planned, he and Millicent left the toilets separately, she first. Jerry emerged about thirty seconds later and proceeded towards the Union Street exit. He kept his hood up and his eyes on the ground until he was down the stairs and out on the pavement.

Umberto was waiting on the near side of the street in a Mondeo, in the back of which Millicent was already seated. Umberto pulled away as soon as Jerry closed the door.

'And like that . . .' Millicent said.

'He's gone,' Jerry completed.

Umberto had flown to Heathrow from Rome last night, where he stayed at a separate hotel before taking an early flight to Glasgow. He had picked up a hire car then gone to a café on Byres Road, where Vivian handed over a holdall containing Jerry's VCR and all his cables. There were only a couple that he actually needed, but he hadn't fancied the chances of Vivian or Carla knowing a SCART from a Firewire.

Millicent handed him a stash of make-up wipes. The great thing about corpse paint was that it was a perfect means of disguising age, ethnicity and even gender. The downside, as he had discovered last night, was that it took as long to remove as it did to apply.

Millicent hadn't charged Gabriela for her work on the Crucifiction video, but there was no question that she was heavily in credit with the guys from the band. They had come through on a grand scale, putting the word out through their own and other bands' social channels. They had promised they would add Glasgow to their tour if the flash mob numbers hit a hundred. Jerry reckoned it had been close to twice that.

Jerry's burner began vibrating. Rook was calling, presumably first having spoken to Chloe, who had Millicent's phone.

He didn't sound in the best of humour; certainly wasn't coming over as smug and in control as he had at Pompeii yesterday.

'I warned you not to fuck with me, you little prick. You think you've been clever? Ask yourself how long it's going to take us to find you again. You'll be begging for the end before I'm finished with you.'

'Calm doon,' Jerry replied. 'I'm not fucking with you. You're still getting your tape: I'm just tweaking the handover arrangements. Call me paranoid, but I wasnae exactly confident you were gaunny stick to your end of things, so I've taken Millicent, myself and our house-mates out of the equation for a wee while, and I've set up a courier to get you the tape.

'My guy is gaunny meet you at Queen Street station in half an hour, outside Costa. He's got brown hair and will be wearing a dark blue jacket. He'll be carrying the tape in a Tesco bag. You identify yourself and he'll hand it over. Then you'll leave us the fuck alone.'

When they were planning it out, Jerry had thought about telling Rook an hour, but he decided it would be better to keep him on his toes, give him less time to think about taking alternative action.

He ended the call.

'And by the time you're at Queen Street, hanging about like a fanny, we'll be halfway down the M77 getting ready to tan Rossco's place.'

Umberto held up a hand, indicating he had a question.

'Remind me,' he said. 'Where will this Rossco gentleman be?'

The Courier

Fuckin' Jai, man. Boy was always a fuckin' snider. Rossco had never fuckin' trusted him. Thought his shite didnae smell. Thought he was better than the likes of him, more cultured or whatever. Smarter. Though to be fair, the boy knew a few things. Rossco had been pissed off Jai never got back to him when he was told, but give him his due, there was nobody else could have come up with a deal like this. Nobody else would have known that tape was worth anything.

He had called up, out of nowhere.

'Fuck have you been,' Rossco said. 'I hope you're callin' to tell me you've got somethin' tasty aff those auld dears. You're fuckin' lucky I've been busy. Went oot on the ran-dan for a few days, met a lassie, otherwise I'd have already sent that video tae the polis.'

None of this was true. He said this so's Jai didn't suss that he'd actually called Rossco's bluff. See, that was the problem with threatening to dob somebody in. If you actually pulled the pin and did it, you had nothing left.

'I tell't you, Rossco: that's not happening. But I've set you up something else. You still got that original VHS of *Star Wars*?'

'Aye. What aboot it?'

'I've got a buyer for it. He's offering two hunner.'

'Two hunner quid? You're at the madam.'

'Gen-up. Like I says to you, George Lucas kept messing with it, adding all his CGI pish, and now you cannae get the original, except on these auld tapes. There's a guy, a collector, who's trying to track one doon. He was aboot to pay three hunner quid for one on eBay. I told him I could get him a mint-condition copy for two, as long as it was cash-in-hand.'

'You just says he was willing to pay three.'

'Aye, but he can get it for that withoot leavin' the hoose. I had to go lower. He'll be at Queen Street station, four o'clock.'

'This better no' be a fuckin' wind-up.'

'It's legit. Older guy. Mair money than sense. But this means we're quits.'

'Aye, okay,' Rossco had said. Like fuck they were.

'What kind of bag will you have it in?' Jai asked.

'What's that to do with anythin'?'

'So he knows who to look for.'

So here he was, Tesco bag in hand. Fuckin' two ton for an old tape of something every cunt's seen a hundred times. No real. The versions with the CGI were better anyway. So were those ones with Ewan McGregor.

The boy would be in front of Costa's, Jai said.

Rossco had just come along the lane from West George Street when he noticed some guy sidling up. He was like Jai described: auld punter, well dressed, quite posh-looking.

'All right, I'm Rook. Now give me the fucking tape.'

'Give us the two-fifty.'

'What?'

'I know Jai says two hunner, but the way I see it, you've come this far anyway. Nae point in you goin' hame and spendin' fifty pound more on eBay.'

At this point, the boy sucker-punched him. Fucking went for the windpipe, but the cunt wasnae as fast as he thought he was. Caught Rossco a glancer then tried to grab the bag.

Rossco whipped it away and fucked it off his forehead, then booted him in the baws, at which point two more old boys jumped in. Rossco started laying into them as well. Then out of nowhere, all these polis appeared and hauled them off him. Huckled the three old boys, cuffs and everything.

'Are you all right, sir?' the polis said.

'Well, naw. I'm fuckin' two hunner quid lighter than I thought I was gaunny be.'

Snuff

It was about twenty past four when the Mondeo's sat-nav guided them into a rather drab housing estate, full of identical white-walled units. Jerome instructed Umberto to pull up outside the house at the end of the terrace.

'It will hopefully be all over at Queen Street by noo,' Jerome said. 'Rossco is probably gaun mental tryin' to ring me.'

Jerome had used his burner phone to call British Transport Police with a tip-off. He told them he had overheard some older blokes in a pub talking about how they were meeting a young guy in the station at four-thirty: they were meant to be buying something from him but were planning to mug him for it instead.

'It's bound to have ended up in a barney,' Jerome said. 'It never takes much to set Rossco off.'

All going well, Jonathan Rook would be in custody by now. But even if he wasn't, he was too far away to stop what was about to happen.

Jerome told Millicent and Umberto to walk up to the front door while he snuck around the back. Millicent guessed it was less obvious to the neighbours that somebody was breaking into a place if there were two people ringing the doorbell in broad daylight.

She heard the muted sound of breaking glass close by, and a matter of seconds later Jerome opened the front door. He already had the framed *Mancipium* poster in his hand.

'Moment of truth,' he said.

Millicent's heart was pounding as he pulled the backing off. And then there it was: an unlabelled black VHS cassette.

'He rewinds his tapes before he returns them,' Jerome said. 'My gran always liked to see that.'

Jerome plugged in his VCR then connected it simultaneously to his laptop and to Rossco's unnecessarily large television. Millicent wondered whether somebody was missing it, but that only reminded her of how the tape came to be in Jerome's possession right now, and there were greater things at hand.

'Better shut the blinds,' Jerome said. 'Don't want the neighbours catching a glimpse of what we're likely to see here. We're about to watch a snuff film, after all.'

As Millicent twisted the handle to close the slats, she noticed a large black Mercedes drive past. It was a high-end model with tinted windows, which seemed a little incongruous for the neighbourhood, but maybe that was a snobbish assumption. She had to silence her paranoia. Rook and his men didn't know where she was anymore, and right now they were far away, likely with their hands full.

Jerome was crouched on the floor between the VCR and his laptop. He ran a programme to start recording the playback, then stood up straight and began simultaneously filming the TV screen with his phone.

Millicent felt a weird mix of nostalgia and trepidation as the static on the screen gave way to the once familiar sight of a wobbly image stabilising as the tracking adjusted itself.

Jerome seemed to sense her unease.

'You want to duck this? Go through to the kitchen?'

'I need to see it,' she answered, talking as much to herself.

On the television she saw Sergio, standing by the side of Lucio's double bed. He looked so young; so much younger than the image of him in her memory.

She found herself responding to weird details, like how she remembered the shirt he was wearing that night. The sight of it made her think of how, at that moment, she was off-screen somewhere, not so far away, drinking with Stacey. About to argue with Markus. About to lose her temper and hit him.

Sergio cleared some space on the glass-topped nightstand, then laid out some coke, chopping it into lines with a dagger she

391

recognised as a prop from *Lucifer's Charade*. There had been two: a retractable plastic copy for stabbing scenes, and this forged steel original for those glinting blade close-ups.

How on-brand for Lucio to have kept it for this purpose.

Sergio snorted both lines and necked a glass of whisky before laying out and chopping some more. He glanced off-screen, beckoning the other person in the room. At which point Millicent heard the slam of a car door outside.

She opened the blinds and saw that the black Mercedes was parked in front of Rossco's house. Daniels had just got out of the driver's seat and was walking around to the pavement.

He opened the rear passenger door, out of which stepped Julia Fleet.

Props

Millicent looked back at Rossco's TV just as Julia appeared on there too: twenty-six years old, young and beautiful. A little drunk, a little high.

She and Daniels walked up the short, weed-strewn slabs of the garden path together, then rather needlessly rang the doorbell.

Jerome looked from Millicent to Umberto and back again, unsure what to do. They were cornered.

'Let them in,' she said.

Umberto opened the door.

'Signor Pieroni,' Julia said. 'How lovely to see you again. It's been too long.'

'Signora Fleet.'

She and Daniels stepped past him in the short hallway and proceeded into Rossco's living room.

Julia looked at herself on the screen, bent over, doing a line.

Daniels picked up the remote and switched off the TV.

Millicent's eyes strayed towards Jerome's laptop. He had turned it around with his foot, hiding the display, but Julia and Daniels both noticed it. There was still sound coming from it too.

'Are you ripping this?' she asked.

Jerome nodded, sighing.

He made to bend down and turn it off, but she stopped him.

'No,' she said. 'You *should* rip it. Then upload it somewhere secure. Make sure you each have a copy for your own protection. But you shouldn't watch it. Trust me on this. Never, ever watch it. Because you can't unwatch it.'

Julia crouched down and turned the laptop around so that she could see the screen.

'Spoilers. In about thirty seconds, Sergio is going to make a pass at me. I had been flirting with him, just a means of massaging his ego, keeping the talent happy. But there was no way I would sleep with someone I was working with, and definitely not someone so notoriously promiscuous. Not in those days.

'So I'm about to turn him down, and he's about to turn nasty.'

She clicked on something which hid the window and muted the sound, though Millicent could see the audio levels on Jerry's conversion programme, confirming it was still ripping from the tape. She really wasn't stopping this.

Julia stood up straight again.

'He raped me,' she said flatly. 'He knocked me around a bit, nothing that would leave a mark, but enough to make me understand how much stronger he was. Then he raped me.

'He held me face-down on the bed. That was when I saw the dagger. I stopped resisting. He seemed to think that meant I was into it, so he turned me around, and I grabbed the knife and stabbed him through the eye. I meant to stab him in the cheek, ruin his perfect looks. Make him always remember how he got the scar every time he looked in a mirror. But the blade bounced off his cheekbone and just went in so easily, so far.'

Millicent's eyes were drawn to the big screen, grateful for its blankness. She had been wrong: she didn't need to see this, only to know the truth.

'I didn't know what to do after that. In my head I was going to slash him and he was going to run away, but he was dead. I went to Freddy for help, and he took control.'

A tiny, bitter smile twitched her lips.

'Never was a truer word spoken. Freddy took control. Freddy owned me thereafter. My family owned me.

'Freddy has an edited copy of the tape. It shows everything up until the point when he enters the room, then it's cut off. There is no proof of his role. Nothing to connect him to the subsequent blackmail attempt and what happened as a result.

'Freddy and my father have held this over me all my life. You wonder why I gave up indie producing and came back into the fold? This is why. You wonder why I was the Wincott family scapegoat at the Leveson Inquiry? This is why.'

What happened as a result, Millicent thought. Lucio and Markus being murdered was what happened as a result. Her going to prison was what happened as a result.

Now she knew why Julia had sent the letters. Why there had been genuine warmth in her embrace back in Paris. Millicent had been her surrogate, serving a life sentence for stabbing a man to death. Millicent had gone to prison so that she could stay free.

Millicent glanced at Daniels, the last man standing among her pursuers, then back at Julia. All her questions had finally been answered, but there were new ones emerging.

'How did you find us?'

Daniels approached and took hold of Millicent's bag.

'If I may.'

He opened it and produced a small device.

'I had a tracker placed on you when you and Julia went for coffee in Paris.'

'Freddy had already been in touch,' Julia said. 'Telling me you were asking questions, warning me of the potential danger. Obviously he didn't tell me about the attempt on your life. He expected me to report back if I heard anything, help him track down the missing tape because of the threat it posed me. But I knew who it really threatened.'

Millicent recalled something Julia mentioned at their Paris reunion. Now she understood.

'*Little Women*,' she said. 'Jo was too forgiving when her sibling burned her novel.'

Julia nodded.

'Freddy burned my negative. And now I'm going to burn him.'

Millicent looked down at the VCR, still contentedly whirring as it unspooled its secrets into Jerome's laptop.

'What are you going to do?' she asked.

'I think, most likely, that I'm going to jail. Though probably not for very long; certainly not for as long as some. I will have very expensive lawyers. There will be plea bargaining. Mitigating circumstances, of which people will be far more understanding these days than they would have been in 1994.'

'I hope you're right,' Millicent told her. 'Speaking from experience, a single day in prison is a day too long.'

'I don't doubt it, but I've been the prisoner of what I did for twenty-five years. It's only when the truth comes out that I'm going to be free.'

EPILOGUE

Lockdown

Jerry looked out at the morning sunshine streaming into the hotel lobby as he made his way from his room in search of breakfast. The calendar stated that it was September, and even here in Rome autumn was on its way, yet weirdly it felt like spring because everything was coming to life again.

As the extent of the pandemic began to emerge, Jerry's thoughts had turned to those he'd met last year in Italy. He had worried particularly about Ardal, not just because he lived in Milan, but because he had already lost so many people. Indeed, it had seemed that the guy had hardly anybody left to lose, and knew too well the pain of seeing acquaintances struck down one after another. Happily, it turned out he was okay. Ardal had been in touch with Millicent throughout the summer months, partly for social and partly for business reasons.

Everybody had made it through at Jerry's end too. Theirs had been an effective little cell: Millicent, Vivian and Carla confined to the house and garden, with Jerry regularly dispatched to bring back supplies.

Vivian and Carla had needed a bit of reining in at first, but Millicent had handled lockdown like a champ. She hadn't been tolerant of anyone's complaints either. If anybody was inclined to whine about restricted freedoms, she had an unanswerable argument for putting things in perspective.

Everybody found their little projects to pass the time. One of Jerry's had been to educate Vivian and Carla, the latter in particular, in the fine art of horror cinema. Both of them had been willing to work on developing an appreciation of the genre after realising they had a star in their midst. They had stronger stomachs than Jerry might have assumed, but neither of them made it through *The Descent*.

They watched a lot of movies together, of all genres, though Millicent partook less than anyone else. She had a lot of advance work to get through: sketching, design, practice, testing and provisional constructions. Theirs was the only house in Scotland that had stockpiled liquid latex at the first suggestion of the shops closing.

Term was starting soon, and Jerry was impatient to commence his second year. He had redeemed himself with Karima after submitting a hell of an essay, having been able to draw on some very exclusive primary sources. However, before online classes started, there was just time enough for a holiday, or a city break at least. He had flown into Rome late last night and was looking forward to seeing some familiar faces this morning.

The first of these turned out unexpectedly to be Umberto's. Jerry encountered him exiting the dining room, prompting him to wonder what he was doing at the hotel, given that he only lived a few miles away.

He gave Jerry a warm smile, then shuffled past on delicate feet, saying he'd catch him at Cinecitta later. Jerry was getting a VIP tour followed by a live set visit.

He would have to say the guy wasn't looking his best, appearing altogether less suave and sprightly than Jerry recalled. Most likely he was just a bit hung over, but it was a remnant of the past nine months that any older person looking a bit peaky was an instant cause for concern.

Jerry proceeded into the dining room, where he saw Millicent seated at a table by the window. He hadn't seen her in three weeks, since she had flown out here to start work. She had a laptop and a folder of notes on the table beside her, an espresso in her hand.

'Well, good morning, Jerome. You got here all right, then. Are you well?'

'Grand, yeah. But I just saw Umberto. He looked knackered. Is he okay?'

'I think he had a rough night.'

'And how are you?'

She sipped her coffee and gazed out of the window, a smirk playing across her lips.

'I am post sex.'

Credits

Millicent gave the syringe a tiny squeeze to prime the feed and check the flow. She wiped away the excess blood that had leaked out, drying the area underneath with tissue paper before dabbing some more skin-coloured foundation over the slit. She had successfully reprised the binbag trick, but this time building the reservoir around a collar so that it could be placed on the actor's head when he was ready.

Fortunately, there had been plenty of time for trial and error. The spring and summer months had been a strange confinement, engendering in her an unaccustomed serenity largely at odds with everybody else. She might once have felt frustrated at her freedoms becoming restricted just when her liberty had been restored, but she had already learned that the real freedom was the permission she had given herself to enjoy life again.

For her, the weeks had passed quicker than any since the early Nineties, mainly because she had never had so much work to do. Real work. Things had moved surprisingly fast towards the end of last year, and she didn't just mean the court cases.

Julia had indeed got herself some expensive lawyers. Almost as expensive as Freddy's. He had near-infinite resources in that respect, ready to deconstruct the meaning of the tiniest fragment of evidence, obfuscate over each argument and dispute the testimony of every last witness. However, he was still up against a team of Italian prosecutors enjoying the cooperation of several retired gentlemen who had all cut deals to ensure they might get out of prison before they died of old age.

Rook rolled on him big-time, though he had little choice, as the others had all rolled on Rook. It turned out they didn't take it too well to learn that he had murdered their old mate Des.

Deals were done, pleas bargained. Nobody got what they really deserved, except maybe Julia, in that she deserved to be free of this. You don't deserve to be punished for killing a man who is raping you. A jury might not have seen it that way in 1994, but they did in 2020.

Freddy did get jail time. He wouldn't be away for as long as he ought, but he was finished: that was the main thing. And it had been fun watching his father pretend to know nothing about it. Nobody could prove anything, but then nobody believed the rancid old bastard either.

There was a knock at the door of Millicent's workshop. It wasn't the same one as she had used back in the Nineties: that was now part of the café in the Cinecitta visitor centre. She had soon got the new one looking just as messy though, invoking a sort of slaughterhouse feng shui.

It was her assistant Luna, a bright girl who she was training up. She had studied chemistry at university and did stage magic as a hobby: the perfect combination. She would go far.

'You've got to see this,' Luna announced. She was carrying a laptop. 'It's from Polaris Digital. It's an early render, but it still looks amazing.'

It was the title sequence, which was being produced out-of-house as one of the few computer-generated elements in the film. For the most part the effects were practical all the way.

Luna set it playing. It showed a point-of-view shot, the camera tracking the progress of a stream of blood down what appeared to be a maze. The lens remained just behind the head of the flow as it twisted and turned between golden walls, hard turns, curves and spirals.

The credits were superimposed in hammered steel. They flashed up one by one, staying on-screen for a few seconds each.

Sabatini Legacy and WinVision Europe presents
A Candledance Production
in association with Cerimonia del Sangue
Mario Trocci
Genevieve Zola
Andrea Carlotta
Director of photography . . . Umberto Pieroni
Music composed by Pasi Litmanen
Special make-up effects by Millicent Spark
Produced by Julia Fleet
Written by Stacey Golding
Directed by Gabriela Pieroni

Tears clouded her eyes. She wiped them away as the camera zoomed out to reveal that the blood had been running around not a maze, but the inscriptions upon an amulet. Then it pulled back further so that the amulet formed the dot in the 'i' as the film's title revealed itself.